Titles by Kathy Hurley

The Oantran Triad
ASPECTS OF ILLUSION

MORRIGAN'S EXILE

KATHY HURLEY

RavenSidhe Publishing
Meridian, Idaho

Published by RavenSidhe Publishing, LLC
Meridian, ID
www.ravensidhe.com

Publisher's Cataloging-in-Publication Data:
Names: Hurley, Katherine Ann., author.
Title: Morrigan's exile / Kathy A. Hurley.
Description: Meridian, ID: RavenSidhe Publishing, 2016.
Identifiers: ISBN 978-0-9912113-5-7 (pbk.) | 978-0-9912113-4-0 (ebook) | LCCN 2016959419
Subjects: LCSH Fairy tales—Ireland--Fiction | Magic--Fiction. | Witches--Fiction. | Ireland--Fiction. Fantasy fiction. | FICTION / Fantasy / Contemporary
Classification: LCC PS3608.U7693 M67 2016 | 813.6--dc23

First Printing December 2016
Printed in the United States of America   10 9 8 7 6 5 4 3 2 1
Copyright © 2016 Kathy A Hurley
Interior art by Kathy A Hurley
Cover art by AM Design Studios

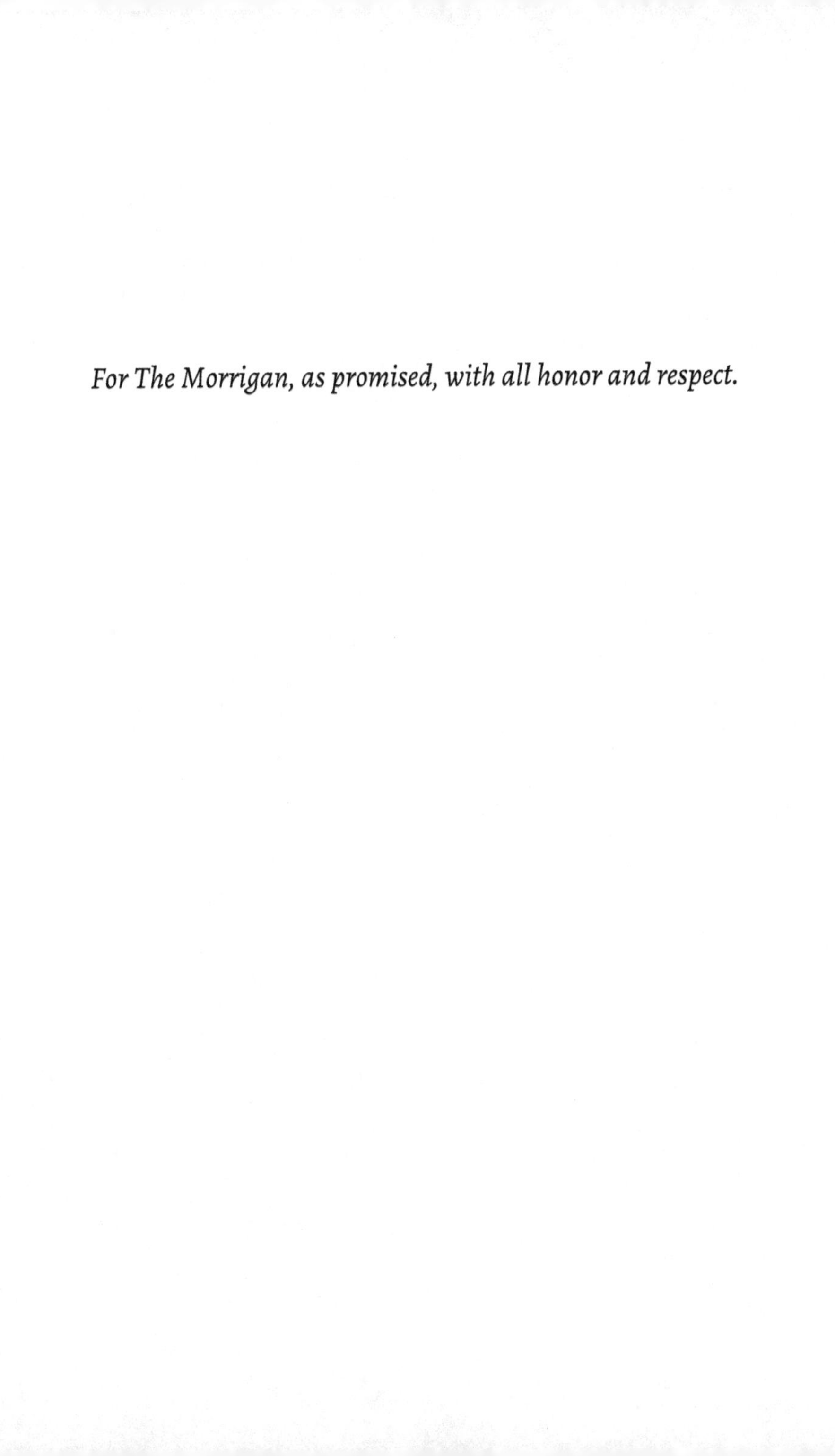

For The Morrigan, as promised, with all honor and respect.

ACKNOWLEDGMENTS

As always, thanks go to the Moxie Quartet, writing cadre extraordinaire. Among others who have long believed in and supported me through this process are my agent, Bob Mecoy, and my wonderful family. I also extend thanks to the very generous and helpful Irish Garda who was kind enough to answer the questions of this American writer, no matter how odd those questions might have seemed at the time. Thanks also go to Mhici and Colm, two Irish writers who were willing to help educate me on various details about life in Ireland. Their help was vital and deeply appreciated. Any mistakes herein, whether of translation or accuracy, are mine alone.

CHAPTER ONE

Brenna Callahan might be lost and tired right now, but she was lost and tired in Ireland. Somehow, that made all the difference. She'd never been to the Emerald Isle before, but it seemed as though she'd just come home after a long absence. Even the beginnings of exhaustion and jet lag hadn't put a dent in the sense of rightness she'd felt from the moment the plane touched wheels to tarmac at Shannon Airport.

It was just too bad that intuitive connection didn't include some kind of navigation system. She had to smile at the thought. Psychic GPS. Right.

Driving from Shannon to Strokestown, Connacht, soon after arrival shouldn't have been a problem. After all, her flight from the U.S. had only taken eight hours, and the drive up to her rental cottage near Strokestown should have taken less than three. The sooner she settled in, the sooner she could get to work on her travel article. However, several wrong turns due to confusing signs—not to mention several unplanned side trips down narrow roads blocked by cattle—had put the kibosh on that plan. If she never saw another cow's butt again, it would be too soon.

Now she was tooling along down the left side of another gravel road, and even the low beams didn't cut very far through the darkness and dense fog. At this rate, even if the correct turnoff was right around the bend, she'd be lucky if the light reached far enough off-road to show her the outline of the house she'd rented—no, *hired*. That's what they called it here. By the time she left, she'd be fluent in the local idioms if it killed her.

Brenna rolled the window down so she could stick her head out, but it didn't improve the visibility. In moments, a damp chill began to seep into the car. Now *that* was an experienced travel writer at work. She clicked her tongue, chiding herself. With all the research that led up to this trip, she should have expected this type of weather; after all, it was early October. But hindsight didn't make navigation any easier. Sighing, she reached down to close the window.

As she looked back at the road, she caught a glimpse of something small and bipedal, right in front of the car.

"Shit!" Instinct and adrenaline slammed her foot down on the brakes. Something thumped against the front bumper. The Fiesta lurched, sputtered, and died.

"No. Oh, please, no!" Had she hit a child? Trembling, sick with horror, she opened the door and stepped out. Immediately, her shoes sank into the mud on the roadway. She pulled one foot upward; it came free with a squelching sound. Her efforts fueled by adrenaline, she hurried to the front of the car. She stumbled against the bumper, looking for the small form she'd hit.

Nothing was there.

Frowning, she crouched to look under the bumper, but could see nothing underneath the car. She'd been sure she hit something; there'd been an impact. She reached, searching for a body, but her fingers touched only muddy ground. Had she imagined it all? A trick of the fog and shadows, maybe?

Weak with relief, Brenna stood and leaned against the bumper while her heartbeat returned to a normal rate. Just to be sure whatever it was hadn't been knocked off the road, she walked over to peer at the shoulder, but she found nothing there, either. The thump must have been the tires hitting a rut. She'd freaked herself out, and the jet lag probably wasn't helping.

Brenna sighed and turned to go back to the car. She hadn't taken two steps when the headlights flickered and died. Of course. They'd have to; it was the inevitable cascade of errors.

Luck o' the Irish to you, Brenna.

With the headlights out, she bumped into the car before she saw it. Rubbing her thigh, Brenna made her way to the driver's side door. She got in, turned the key in the ignition, and...nothing happened. She cranked it again; it did a lot of clicking, but that was all.

Brenna choked back a laugh. She'd started to shiver but hadn't noticed until now. Well, she could at least save herself from a chill if she could slog her way to the trunk—no, the boot—and get out her heavy jacket and the rain gear she'd bought at the airport. As soon as she left the car again a raindrop hit her in the face. *And cue the sprinklers....*

From somewhere off behind her, a dog howled. Or maybe a wolf. Did wolves still live in Ireland? Hand poised to unlock the trunk, Brenna hesitated, the hairs at the nape of her neck tingling. Beyond the hedge on the left side of the road, something screeched. Several somethings howled back, ululating. In chorus.

The *wrongness* hit Brenna like a gust of foul wind; it choked her breath short and brought the mental image of a host of dark forms hurtling through the night toward her, like the memory of a nightmare. Something was out there hunting—ancient, focused, and full of rage. Maybe it was instinct or maybe panic, but in that moment Brenna knew that even the inside of the car would not provide safety.

She sensed more than saw a shape loom up from behind the hedgerow on her left and position itself between her and the driver's side door. When she looked straight at it, she couldn't see it anymore, but the damage was done. Terror spurred her toward the bushes on the right side of the road.

Branches tore at her, but Brenna fought her way through them anyway, clawed her way through the hedge and scrambled over the wall into the field. She ran full-tilt through the mist but couldn't seem to go fast enough—childish nightmares come to life. Still, she kept on until she stumbled over a rock. Her left ankle twisted and she almost fell headfirst into the mud. She had to bite her lip against a cry of pain that might give away her position.

The howling had stopped and she couldn't see any dogs, but her ankle throbbed. She wouldn't be surprised if she'd broken it, but she couldn't just sit here in the middle of a field. With a stream of whispered curse words, Brenna levered herself upright. She meant to circle back toward the car, but after a few steps she stopped, her breathing ragged from the pain. It was no good; she'd never make it. As if on cue, pursuit noises started up again, closer this time. They must have caught her scent. She was about to become a statistic. The gardaí would be busy for weeks, trying to figure out why an American woman had been killed by a pack of wild dogs on Irish soil.

"May I assist you?" a man's voice asked from behind her.

With a cry, she whirled too quickly for the injured ankle. The man moved with impossible speed; somehow he caught her before she hit the ground and swept her up into his arms. For a moment, she thought about struggling, but he was already moving through the darkness, carrying her as if she weighed no more than a child.

A wave of exhaustion and the pain in her ankle made everything seem to blur around her. Only the man was solid. He smelled of earth, foliage, and some elusive spicy scent that she couldn't quite identify. Despite the fact that she probably should be panicking, she began to relax in his arms. It didn't make a bit of sense, but then, neither did anything that had happened since she'd thought she'd hit a child on the road.

"What about the dogs?" she asked, fighting to remain conscious.

"The hounds have gone," he said with certainty.

No more dogs. Good. "Who are you?" she asked, blinking up at him. The whole situation was surreal. Either she'd wandered into a dream, or the jet lag was getting to her.

He laughed, a low, musical sound that shivered along her nerve endings. "Would a name make me any more your rescuer or change any part of the situation in which you find yourself? Very well. If you must have a name, you may call me Ronan. It will do as well as any other."

"I'm Brenna," she said. "Brenna Callahan. I'm from the U.S. I swear I'm not usually this pathetic." At his chuckle, she blinked, trying to focus on his face while she tried not to think about the fact that she was muddy, she was drenched, and she no doubt seemed more than a little deranged.

She had no idea how far he carried her or in which direction, but after some time she began to feel numb, as though the chill had crept into her bones. Nevertheless, the beat of the man's heart under her ear was oddly comforting. She started to drift off, and jerked awake. She would not pass out. Absolutely not.

"Rest, Brenna Callahan. We've some distance to go, yet," he said in that amused tone. As if his words were a command, her head fell against his shoulder though she tried with all her strength to hold it up. The last thing she saw before pain and exhaustion claimed her was the blue of his eyes, which logic insisted should not have been visible in the moonless night.

Brenna jerked awake, panting. She'd dreamt that a pack of dogs was after her; for a moment she could still hear their howls. But there were no dogs here, wherever *here* was.

She lay on a double bed, pale sunlight streaming into the room through one small window. Someone had removed her clothes. She blushed at the thought that it might have been the man who'd rescued her—Ronan, he'd said his name was. Ronan...something. Oh, no. She hadn't even gotten his last name before she'd passed out in his arms.

Wide-awake, Brenna sat up, reached for the faded patchwork quilt that topped the other linens, and wrapped it around herself before she got out of bed. There was no sense in putting it off; she had to let her rescuer know that she was awake. Besides, she'd need her clothes, even if they were ruined; she couldn't lie around naked in a stranger's bed all day. Her boyfriend Brad's face came to mind, and she rejected the idea of telling him about last night's mishap. He tended to get jealous—only one of the reasons she needed to rethink their relationship.

Brenna tried her weight on the injured ankle. Strange—it didn't hurt at all. She must not have injured it as badly as she'd thought. There was one piece of good news.

The bedroom door led into a short hallway, which passed a bathroom and what looked like a linen closet. The hallway opened out into a living room on one side and a kitchen on the other, all neat, utilitarian, and obviously meant for one person to live in—two if they wanted to get cozy. Had Ronan given up his room for her? If so, where had he slept? Based on the furniture in the living room, it seemed the couch was the only other option, and it wasn't obvious whether it was a sleeper. She hoped she hadn't inconvenienced anyone, especially on her first night in Ireland.

"Ah, you're up. How do you feel this morning, dear?" a woman's voice asked. Brenna jumped. Ronan had a wife? But no, the woman who stood by the stove in the kitchen in front of a pan of sizzling bacon couldn't be his wife, could she? She had to be at least sixty, while Ronan had looked more like thirty, if that. His mother, maybe?

Brenna tried on a smile. "I don't seem to be much the worse for wear. Um...I'm sorry to impose on you. I didn't mean to cause trouble."

The woman smiled back. "It wasn't any trouble. I'm happy to do Ronan a favor. Now, won't you tell me your name? Most of the local people call me Old Annie, but I'd be just as happy were you to leave the 'old' out of it altogether." She had a soft brogue that was easy on the ears, but her voice also held genuine warmth that made Brenna relax despite herself. If Annie had any reservations about the stray she'd taken in, she hid them well.

"I'm Brenna Callahan; I flew in from the United States yesterday. I made the mistake of trying to drive straight to the cottage I hired without an Irish language map and a GPS system. Then next thing I knew, the car broke down." She grimaced. "Some travel writer I make."

Amusement sparkled in Annie's eyes. "Plenty of the signs are wrong, anyway. But never mind that. You're not far from the old Kildike place now—the only rental on this road. And as it happens, I'm the caretaker."

"You're A. Murrilly?" Brenna asked, remembering the name on the envelope she'd picked up at the rental agency in Shannon. This woman had been kind enough to forward the key there at her request; Brenna hadn't wanted to disturb the caretaker on a Sunday, no matter what time she got in. So much for *that* noble idea.

"Yes, that's me," Annie said. "Neighbor and stand-in for the landlord. You're actually not far from the cottage now. I'll show you how to get there from here across the fields. You can call a tow service to collect your car."

Brenna groaned. "The car. If you don't mind, I'd like to call someone immediately, before it causes a wreck."

"Of course, dear," Annie said, gesturing Brenna toward the phone. "There's a directory on the shelf just below the counter."

When she'd contacted a tow service and relayed Annie's directions to them so they could locate the car, Brenna hung up the phone and turned back to her hostess. "Thank you; that's a load off my mind. Now, were you telling me that I was almost to the cottage when the car broke down last night? If I'd known that, I'd have been settled in by now and you wouldn't have been stuck with a stray."

Annie chuckled. "Well, why don't you go take a shower? You can borrow the robe hanging on the inside of the bedroom door. By the time you've done that and had your breakfast, your clothes will be dry. I washed them out by hand last night. There were a few stains I couldn't get out, but they'll do well enough for now."

"You shouldn't have bothered, but thank you." Brenna turned to go back down the hall then paused. "Ah...where is Ronan, anyway? I wanted to thank him for his help."

Annie's smile slipped, and she turned to adjust the flame on one of the burners. A wonderful scent of cooking tomatoes wafted to Brenna; her stomach growled in response.

"Ronan doesn't live here, as I'm sure you must have guessed. He comes to see me sometimes, but I never know just when he'll turn up. Don't try to thank him; I know he wouldn't appreciate it at all. Best not to mention it, if you ever see him again."

Not thank him? Though Annie's back was turned, her tone had sounded as though she were serious. Brenna's forehead wrinkled in a frown which might have looked rude had Annie chosen to turn around just then, but she couldn't help it. If there really had been a pack of feral dogs after her last night, then Ronan had probably saved her life. In preparation for this first, all-important overseas assignment, she'd read volumes about Irish food, slang, general customs and attitudes—but she'd seen nothing about not thanking someone who'd done you a favor.

Still confused, Brenna retreated to the bedroom to find Annie's robe. She didn't want to risk flashing Ronan in case he chose to drop in during breakfast. For a moment, she had an image of Brad, of his dark, deliberately mussed bad-boy hair and steely grey eyes. She'd seen those eyes accusing, piercing, intent on bringing his opponents to their knees in the courtroom. Lawyer Brad, jealous Brad, impossible-to-live-with Brad. He definitely wouldn't appreciate the idea of her flashing a stranger. For a moment, anger heated her face when she thought of how hard he'd tried to talk her out of this trip in the first place, but sanity soon reasserted itself. This wasn't the time to deal with problems she'd left at home; not when she had plenty to deal with here and now.

In the bathroom a few moments later, she discovered that the rain had made an appalling wreck of her makeup. There was more expensive mascara smudged beneath her eyes than on her lashes, and though her face had largely escaped the mud that had wrecked her shoes and clothes, her normally light-brown hair was at least a shade darker then normal where she'd raked it with muddy hands, and her blue-green eyes looked wide and shocked. Some people would have assumed she'd been on one hell of a bender. She didn't even want to imagine what kind of impression she'd made on Ronan, let alone Annie.

The shower felt like heaven. Brenna scrubbed the grime out of her hair with some of Annie's herb-scented shampoo and rubbed at her face until she was sure the makeup wreckage must be gone.

She was tempted to just stand there in the comforting spray and pretend that last night hadn't happened, but finally hunger and the desire not to use up all of Annie's hot water drove her out of the shower.

In the kitchen, the older woman had set out plates piled with toast, steamed tomatoes, eggs, bacon and sausage; Brenna's stomach gave another loud rumble at her first whiff. Annie smiled in apparent amusement, the odd tension of a few minutes ago gone as though it had never been.

"I thought you might like a traditional Irish breakfast on your first morning here," she said, handing Brenna a fork. "You would have had this if you'd chosen to stay the night at a bed-and-breakfast, so it gives me an excuse to indulge myself a little as well."

Brenna eyed the huge plate of food. Would she commit a terrible faux pas if she failed to eat it all? "You mean people don't eat like this every day?" she asked, half-teasing.

"Goodness, no!" Annie said. "All those calories, all that fat.... But everyone deserves to indulge now and then. Eat your eggs and rashers, before they get cold. I don't have a microwave—never could seem to justify it."

Rashers—those were the bacon slices, weren't they? Brenna picked one up and bit into it, marveling at how much better it tasted here than it ever had back home. It was one odd little fact of travel she'd never been able to explain, even though up to now her primary experience had been in the United States and Canada. Nor could she explain how she managed to eat at least twice what she normally would have. Either midnight chases through rain-swamped fields with dogs on her heels agreed with her, or her enthusiasm for Ireland was reasserting itself now that she was no longer lost.

As Annie had promised, Brenna's clothes were dry by the time they'd finished breakfast. She offered to help with the dishes, but

Annie waved her away with another of those enigmatic smiles. Before long, Brenna was dressed and much better equipped to deal with the consequences of last night's misadventures. The sunny day outside had already given the lie to the rumor that it never did anything in Ireland but rain, and the beauty of the countryside made last night seem like a harmless bad dream.

Wearing a borrowed pair of long wool socks and rain boots, Brenna set out with Annie across the still-wet, sparkling fields. The older woman stopped briefly at a stile in the rock wall that surrounded her property. From an oversized pocket of her coat she retrieved a piece of the morning's bread, a very small glass bottle and a doll-sized bowl. She poured some white liquid—milk?—from the bottle into the bowl. Then she set bowl and bread under a thorn bush near the wall, recapped the bottle and slipped it back into her pocket.

"For the Good People," she explained in a matter-of-fact tone.

"The good people?" Brenna echoed, intrigued. Good People, as in faeries? Maybe this would work into her articles somehow.

Annie gave her a quizzical look. "Of course, girl. For whom else would you leave milk and bread outside? The cat?"

Brenna shot her hostess an apologetic smile. "I'm sorry. It's just that the documentaries I've seen and books I've read gave me the impression that most Irish people don't really believe in faeries anymore—even though no one badmouths them, just in case."

"Hst! Don't call them that, they don't much like that name. Call them the good people, the Sidhe, or the Gentry. There isn't a proper word for them in any language. Didn't your research tell you that much?" Not waiting for an answer, Annie climbed over the stile and started across the next field without so much as a glance back.

As Brenna looked at the faery offerings, a strange little shiver climbed up her back. It might have been due to her lack of a proper coat, for the day, while sunny, was not warm. She scrambled over the stile and hurried after Annie.

"I guess I read the wrong books," Brenna said, irritated with herself. How had she managed to miss the boat on this subject? She'd been thorough—or so she'd thought.

Annie gave her a mild look and a raised eyebrow.

"I think you'll find that more people believe than want to admit it. If you want to know more, I'll loan you one of my books on the gentry the next time you come to visit."

"That would be great, thanks," Brenna said, her mind already busy with ideas for the articles. Inadvertently, Annie had given her a great starting point. "I'll only be here until the end of the month, but in that time I'd be glad to hear whatever you want to tell me. I'm supposed to research a couple of articles on this area and some of the surrounding ones, and the slant I take is up to me. I'll have to run around a lot, but I'd love to take you out to tea at least once or twice before I go. It's the least I can do, after last night...." Brenna trailed off.

Annie was bending over something on the ground, and when Brenna came up beside her she had a frown on her face. Brenna followed Annie's gaze and saw that in this portion of the field, the grass had withered enough to expose quite a bit of mud. In that mud were some large animal tracks, like a dog's—or a pack of dogs.

"Be careful while you run around," Annie said, her voice gone very quiet. "Something was out here last night—something you won't want to put in your article."

A chill slid down Brenna's spine. "You mean, a pack of feral dogs are on the loose? No, that definitely wouldn't sit well with the tourists."

Annie was looking at her in some concern, but there was a sharpness in her gaze that hadn't been there before. "No," she said slowly. "I don't mean feral dogs."

Brenna swallowed. "Then, what was it?"

Annie kept staring at her. "You were out here last night. Why don't you tell me what you saw?"

"If it wasn't dogs, then I don't know what it could be," Brenna said. She described in detail what she'd experienced before Ronan's timely rescue. It was unsettling, though—the more she remembered about it, the more surreal it all seemed.

"Did you sense or feel anything strange before you heard the dogs?" Annie asked when Brenna had finished. Her voice had that intense, thoughtful tone again.

"I...I suppose I felt a little strange. Paranoid, like something was out in the dark, hunting me. But it was pretty spooky in the fog, and with a dead car and jetlag, I'm sure my imagination was working overtime." Of course it must have been that. Exhaustion could play all sorts of tricks on a person's mind.

"Imagination. Perhaps. Or perhaps there is a different explanation for it," Annie said.

Brenna shivered; the sun had chosen that moment to go behind a cloud. "I hate to say this, but this is starting to freak me out. Where I come from, people don't get chased through the fields at night by invisible creatures, and if they claim they have imaginary friends or talk to the dead, they have a decent chance of getting their own TV show. Or their own room in a mental institution. Take your pick."

Annie smiled, but she didn't look amused. "Plenty of people in the United States practice alternative religions, don't they? Wiccans, Druids, and others?"

"Well yes, but—"

"Then there are those who would have some idea of what I refer to. I know it's not in the mainstream, but I hope you haven't believed the misinformation commonly spread about it. The unseen world is everywhere around us—even in the United States.

I'm only talking to you about this now because I think you feel more than you want to admit. Am I right?"

"Well yes, but...I'm not a witch. I'm just a typical, everyday person. I don't have the Sight, or the gift, or anything."

"Don't you?" Now Annie was getting spooky again. "You sensed something last night. And who knows? You might have saved your own life. Or you might have nearly gotten yourself killed. Either way, you are lucky that Ronan showed up when he did, and even more so that he brought you to me. No doubt that was because my house was closest and he knew you'd be safe with me."

Brenna shot Annie a confused smile. "I'm sorry; I don't understand. I'd assumed...aren't you his mother?" It was more than a little strange, standing here in the middle of a muddy field, talking about faeries and the supernatural as though they were everyday occurrences. She shifted a bit, hoping Annie would take the hint to start walking again, but Annie continued to examine the prints on the ground as closely as might a woodland tracker.

"I'm not related to Ronan. And as I said, I don't see him often. What surprises me is that you saw him at all. He doesn't live here, so he easily might not have been here to save a damsel in distress. Even an attractive American girl who claims she doesn't believe in imaginary friends." Annie touched one finger to the middle of a paw print then snatched it away as if it burned her.

"Please tell me you don't mean to say that he's a figment of our mutual imagination," Brenna said. The light breeze had picked up; she started to shiver in earnest, and not just from the cold.

Annie laughed. "No, dear. He is as real as you or I. You should know that, after he carried you all that way."

Brenna remembered the scent of Ronan's skin, the warmth of his arms and the steady beat of his heart beneath her ear. No, if she had imagined him, she wouldn't have done nearly so good a job;

nor would she have felt the least bit disloyal to her boyfriend in having so vivid a memory of another guy. Still, it was a relief to know that he was real.

She took a deep breath. "All right. Let's say I did feel something before the dogs began to howl last night. The fact still remains that I panicked over something I couldn't even see. That's just not like me." Brenna wrapped her arms around herself, but it didn't help.

"Ah, but it is an understandable reaction, when you get between the Wild Hunt and its prey. Look." Annie pointed. Still shivering, Brenna moved closer.

A line of child-sized footprints veered off to the north, but gradually they began to change in length and indentation. Five steps later, they'd become the prints of a barefoot adult human—or at least, they'd be human if not for the claws...and the webbing between the toes.

CHAPTER TWO

Brenna frowned at Annie. "What do you mean, the Wild Hunt and its prey? And what could have made those footprints change like that—a kid in frogman boots playing out a monster hoax?" She tried to keep her voice casual, but her skin prickled with the same eerie energy she'd felt last night. The strangeness had a scent...almost.

Annie studied her for a moment, then shook her head. "This is not the best time or place in which to pursue this subject further. After you've settled into your house, stop round for tea and we'll have a talk."

Annie shot her a smile that was probably meant to reassure and started off in the direction that Brenna assumed led toward the road, but the woman's eyes held a measure of worry that hadn't been there before they'd found the footprints.

In Strokestown three hours later, Brenna stared at the garage receipt in her hand, still reeling from the price she'd just had to pay for the tow and initial assessment of her car. The rental agency had agreed to accept the mechanic's statement as to the condition of the car before repair; a snapshot of it mired in the muddy roadway was already on file with the garage. It could have been worse, even if this one blunder almost ruined her entire month's budget. Still, this wasn't exactly the Ireland experience she'd envisioned.

Brenna sighed and resolved to keep an eye out for a bank that would allow her to open an account for the duration of her stay. Her editor, Jay Marston, had already given her an advance on the articles he wanted her to write, so if she was careful, she should be able to manage—provided there were no more Wild Hunts or dead cars in her immediate future.

The mechanic nodded to Brenna as she made to leave the office. "Be ready on Tuesday, I'd say," he told her.

"Tomorrow? That's great news, thanks!" Brenna said, but the man shook his head.

"Tuesday, next week." He grinned. "There's a part I'll need to order in."

"Tuesday, next week, then," Brenna said, trying to smile at him. He was watching her so closely—what did he expect her reaction to be? Did he think she might insist that next Tuesday wasn't good enough? She wouldn't do that, even if it meant she'd have to take public transportation to some of the sites she wanted to investigate. Perhaps she could even work the public transport into her article, along with the price structure and schedules. Warming to the idea, she gave the mechanic a genuine smile before she stepped jauntily out of the office, aware of his curious gaze on her back.

She treated herself to lunch at a pub, then spent some time afterward getting a feel for the layout of Strokestown. In a small bookshop, she bought a guide to the nearby historical sites and a book of faery lore. Even though Annie had offered to loan her a book on the gentry, it might be handy to have one of her own. So many customs tended to grow out of myths that it would be a good idea to familiarize herself with local legends and superstitions as well. Maybe she could work them into her article, too....

Brenna stopped in the street outside the bookshop to scribble reminders in her pocket-sized spiral notebook. Jay had wanted a historic tie-in to whatever sites she chose, but otherwise left things up to her discretion, so her first article might as well be a self-guided tour of the ring-forts and faery haunts in the area. Annie would know where most of them were. Jay always said, "Local people *are* local color." The gentry—real or not—might just open a few doors for her. They certainly had with Annie.

Feeling much more cheerful than she had an hour ago, Brenna bought groceries, then stopped back at the garage to retrieve her laptop and rolling suitcase. Briefly, she considered taking a room in a bed-and-breakfast until the car was ready, but a cab ride to the cottage would be cheaper, if less convenient. Now, where did one find a cab here?

She was about to go back and ask the mechanic when someone called out from behind her. Startled, Brenna turned to see a man standing in the doorway of a pub across from the garage. He nodded to her and fired off what sounded like a question, but it was in *Gaeilge*. A friend from Chicago had once told her she had the Irish bone structure, but she hadn't guessed it was enough to get her mistaken for a native.

Still getting over her surprise, Brenna gave the man an apologetic smile as she walked across the street to him. She had to pull her suitcase behind her while she balanced the bag of groceries in her other arm, and the cobbles on the street didn't make it any easier. "I'm sorry, but I can't understand what you're saying," she said when she got closer.

"Ah. You're American. Even without the accent, I should have known. You look a bit lost. Can I help you?"

"I...I'm not sure. Are there any taxis here?"

The man smiled. He had the combination of black hair and blue eyes that she'd always found attractive—in fact, he looked like an even more ruggedly handsome version of Brad—and from what she could see of his body underneath his unfastened grey jacket, he was in good shape, too. He smiled as if to say, *caught you looking*. It was a damned good thing Brad wasn't here.

"A cab? Of course. Walk with me; I'll take you to one," the man said.

Brenna blinked. "I thought cabs picked people up, not the other way around."

He laughed. "In the United States, perhaps. Here, they park outside the larger hotels or at airports, or you can call the cab service and ask to have one pick you up. They don't normally drive around looking for stranded Americans."

When a woman in a dark blue coat walked up to the door of the pub and then stood waiting, Brenna realized she was blocking the way. She made to move aside to let the woman pass, and almost stepped into a puddle. She would have, in fact, if her new acquaintance hadn't taken her arm just in time.

"Thanks," she told him as she regained her composure. "I'm Brenna, by the way. What's your name?"

"I'm pleased to make your acquaintance. Call me Colm." Colm glanced at her luggage, frowning. "Is this all your baggage? Americans are usually festooned with bags and cameras."

Brenna glanced down at her laptop bag—all of six pounds between ultra-slim laptop and bag—neatly clipped to the top of her suitcase. The digital camera was small enough that it fit into her purse, out of sight. Efficiency must not be something Europeans expected in travelers from the U.S. She laughed. "This is it for me. Being a travel writer has taught me to pack light. Now, about that taxi...."

"We'll find one, sure enough." he said as they started walking.

"But there's public transport into town as well. The buses are frequent; I imagine you'll find that they go to most of the places you might want to visit. You said you are a travel writer?"

"Yes. I plan to do a series of articles on faery haunts. I thought I'd drive out to Tulsk to see the mounds after I get settled in."

"I know a number of sites, if you'd like a local escort. It'll be better than trying to find your way around the area on your own. Even with a good map, some of the roads can confuse people." Colm gave her a conspiratorial grin, as if he somehow knew what she'd been through last night.

"Thank you, but I don't know what my schedule will be. I thought I'd look around for a few days before I finalize my plans."

"Very wise," he said, though he still smiled at her as though she amused him. Which she probably did, in fact. Just look at the fresh entertainment come to town. *Thanks a lot, folks; I'll be here all month!*

Still, he *was* being very nice—solicitous, but without overt condescension. With his help, Brenna soon located a cab. As she strapped herself into the backseat, Colm took a business card out of his pocket and handed it to her though the window.

"In case you decide you'd like a native guide," he said. The card said he was an archeologist; that could come in handy, if she decided to take him up on his offer.

"Thank you," she said. "You've been a big help."

"Anytime," he said mildly, and stepped back from the side of the cab, which was parked half on, half off the sidewalk.

As the cab pulled away from the curb, Brenna looked back to see Colm still there, watching her with that same enigmatic smirk on his movie-star handsome face. Just what did he find so funny? Had he never met anyone from the U.S. before? Brenna checked to see whether her shirt was unbuttoned, then shrugged and sat back to enjoy the ride through the countryside.

The book she'd bought read like an encyclopedia of the fae; it listed every type of creature from folklore and legend in alphabetical order. Brenna sat in one of the cottage's two armchairs and flipped through the whole thing once, then started through it again from the beginning. The light had begun to fade by the time she reached the D's, but there was one thing she needed to know before she quit for the night. Trying to ignore the chill she felt, she flipped forward to the entry on the Wild Hunt.

Had she been putting it off? *Maybe*, she admitted as she scanned the pages. For some reason, her palms had begun to sweat. This was beyond silly; she couldn't be frightened of a myth, like a nine-year-old who'd just watched a scary movie. She might plan to include the paranormal in her article, but that didn't mean she had to obsess about one strange experience probably brought on by jetlag.

Annie believed in faeries and the Wild Hunt. Then again, some people believed in aliens and the Loch Ness monster, too. That didn't necessarily make them real.

Shaking her head as much at her own wild imagination as at anyone else's, Brenna went to the kitchen and made dinner, then spent some time planning how best to go about her research while she waited for the car to be fixed. At least with her suitcase locked in the cottage, she could carry a daypack and still be mostly self-sufficient on her ramblings. Maybe she'd even start her itinerary tomorrow from the bus station in town. This late in the year, the weather might prove unreliable; she'd do well to get started on the article as soon as possible, especially since she meant to include pictures.

When she'd finished her food, Brenna went out onto the front step to get some fresh air. It was early evening now, and very quiet. At her apartment in downtown Portland, Oregon, birdcalls mingled with traffic noise, and insect sounds were all but nonexistent unless she went out into the country. Here, the music of the night was all around her and streetlight glare didn't hide the stars.

As she stood there and breathed it all in, a strange feeling of connection swelled within her chest and brought a lump to her throat, just as it had when she'd first arrived. She'd never felt this way about a place before—not her parents' house when she was growing up, not the first city she'd lived in after she'd left home, and not even Portland, though there were things about that part of Oregon that had always drawn her. The rain, the crisp, cool air, the colors of the landscape...so similar to what she was experiencing right here, right now.

She drew a shaky breath as realization began to dawn. Could it be that she'd chosen to live in Portland because it made her think of Ireland? Had Oregon called to her subconscious as the next best thing to Ireland itself? Odd as that sounded, it was possible. Even likely, though she'd have been hard put to explain it to anyone, even the people closest to her.

The first time she'd watched a video of Ireland, she'd gone all teary-eyed. The reaction had shocked her; she'd had to hide it from her friends, who either would have called her a sap or assumed she'd had a fight with her mother earlier that day. But no matter how she'd seen it, in pictures, videos or news stories, Ireland had always called to her. It was why she'd fought so hard to get Jay to pick her for this assignment. She couldn't *not* come. And now that she was here, the dread of leaving hung in the back of her mind even though she had three weeks left.

Good heavens, what was *wrong* with her?

Blinking back the moisture that had gathered in her eyes, Brenna cleared her throat and gave herself a good mental shake. She was here now. That was what mattered. And she needed to plan her workload so she could make the most of the time she had.

Work was the key to any other insight she might gain while she was here, so work was what she had to focus on for now.

As to planning.... Jay might not be expecting the slant she intended to take with her first article, but with all the paranormal shows and books on the market now, he'd probably go along with it. She'd need to hit at least five or six of the ancient sites...maybe seven.

Something caught her eye, and she squinted into the dusk. Was it her imagination, or had one of the shadows moved, near the grove at the front of the property? She peered at it for a few moments longer, then clicked her tongue at her own foolishness.

Of course, nothing had moved, except maybe the gentle breeze she could feel on her cheek. She'd been thinking about the paranormal and managed to freak herself out—again. Sheesh. If her imagination was this strong, perhaps she should become a novelist. Spooked by shadows! Honestly. Come to that, Spooked by Shadows would make an okay book title, if she wanted to write a second-rate horror novel.

She glanced toward the grove again, and her heartbeat kicked into high gear. The shadow in question started toward her, and this time it had definitely moved—from the thicker darkness in the grove onto the front path. As it moved, it seemed to take on form.

Brenna backed up, a scream frozen somewhere in the back of her throat. Did they have 9-1-1 here? Did she have the number for the gardaí? Would they even reach her in time? When her body caught up with her brain, she whirled and took two running steps toward the house. Her hand touched the door handle just as a man's voice called after her.

"It is all right, Brenna Callahan, I mean you no harm. Do you remember me from the field last night?"

Slowly, Brenna turned to see Ronan striding up the path, dressed in jeans and a green wool jacket. So much for shadows. As she waited for him, she took a shaky breath and willed her heartbeat to slow down. In moments, he stood on the doorstep beside her, as tall and blond as she remembered, not to mention close enough to set all her nerve endings on edge. At least the heightened awareness was better than terror.

"You startled me; I wasn't expecting company. Won't you come in?" she heard herself ask, sounding breathless even to her own ears. "I wanted to tha...I mean, I hoped I'd get a chance to see you again and get to know you better."

She opened the door for him, watching to see whether he'd noticed her slip. Annie had said he wouldn't appreciate it if she thanked him, but the impulse was hard to resist. After all, he might have saved her life. Even if the footprints in the field turned out to have been a prank, it *felt* as though he'd saved her life.

"You offer your thanks too freely," Ronan said as he moved past Brenna into the living room and, ignoring the coat rack, took off his jacket and tossed it onto the back of a chair.

"I...I'm sorry," Brenna said. What else could she say? She hadn't thanked him for his help, had she? She'd caught herself in time.

"I might say the same about your apologies," Ronan said.

For a long, awkward moment, they stared at each other across the room while Brenna groped for a statement that wouldn't make her sound like an idiot. Then Ronan gave her such a gentle smile that Brenna's face flooded with warmth. Honestly, the man was a walking contradiction. Was it even possible to get to know someone this complex? And if it was, did she want to?

"I didn't come here to berate you. I came to warn you," he said, moving closer until Brenna could have reached out and touched him. She backed away—or at least, she thought she had. Flustered, she realized she'd taken a step forward instead, bringing her close enough to catch a whiff of the spice-and-foliage scent she remembered from last night's ride across the field in his arms.

For heaven's sake, even if he had rescued her last night, the man was still a stranger. He'd just walked up to her house after dark from who knew where and begun his visit by chiding her for her politeness, and here she was thinking about how good he smelled. Maybe *he* wasn't the one she should be worried about just now.

"Uh...I don't plan to take any more trips across the fields in the middle of the night. My car's been towed, so I think my troubles are behind me now." Oh, no, trouble was right here in front of her; there was no other description for him.

"Actually, I did not come here to speak to you about your accident, though the subject is related. What I have to say may sound strange to you, but I ask you to reserve judgment until you have heard it all," Ronan said. He reached out to tuck an errant strand of hair behind her ear, and she shivered at the intimacy. He seemed to have no concept of either personal space or the normal bounds of familiarity. Yet, she'd been the one to close that last distance between them, hadn't she?

"I doubt anything you can tell me now will be any stranger than what I've already heard and experienced since I got here," Brenna said on a nervous laugh. After a moment, she retreated to one of the armchairs that faced the fireplace. False refuge though it was, it made her feel more secure somehow. Ronan took the hint and sat in the other armchair across from her, though he perched toward the front edge as if he thought he might have to leave in a hurry.

He glanced at the books she'd laid on an end table: the faerie compendium and a well-read paperback romance novel. She thought she saw a flash of amusement in his eyes, though she might easily have imagined it. For an instant, she fought the urge to defend her choice in reading material, though he hadn't even offered a comment.

"When you stayed with Annie, she spoke to you about the Gentry, did she not?" Ronan asked now, his gaze intent on her face.

"She mentioned them, yes," Brenna said.

"When you left her house, did you not see a strange footprint in the field?"

"She told you about that, too?" Brenna asked. Of course. Ronan had been back to Annie's to see what had happened to his damsel in distress. Annie must have directed him here. Well, Annie seemed a sensible sort, apart from the babble about faeries. If she trusted Ronan, then he was probably safe. Probably. "Did she send you here to check on me?"

"No. Annie did not send me, though she told me where I might find you. But it appears that I am not the only one concerned as to your whereabouts. The Wild Hunt was after someone last night, and I fear he poses a danger to you. We are fortunate that I found you before he did."

"Annie mentioned the Wild Hunt, and we saw some footprints in the field," Brenna said, automatically reaching for the afghan that hung over the back of the chair and wrapping it around her shoulders. A frightened child with a blankie. When she realized what she'd done, she nearly laughed at herself, but she didn't let go of the blanket, either. "How do you know about the Wild Hunt, anyway? Do you practice magic, or something?"

"Yes, I dabble a little, as does Annie," Ronan said, smiling.

Dear God, he seemed perfectly serious. So he and Annie were both some flavor of pagan. It wasn't that unusual; as Annie had mentioned, there were plenty of pagans in the U.S. as well. Brenna studied Ronan for a long moment, fitting that information into what little she knew of him so far. At least it explained the odd things he was saying, and Annie's words and actions this morning. People who believed in magic were generally harmless, if they didn't take it to extremes.

She tried to smile. "I suppose now you'll tell me that whatever the hounds were after is horribly evil and depraved, and that—he, did you say?—turns into a monster during certain phases of the moon."

"Yes to the first part, no to the second. Wrong mythology. We're talking about the Gentry, here. The Sidhe—not werewolves."

The Sidhe. At the sound of the word, something colder than fear gripped Brenna's chest. "You can't be serious. The...Gentry...are just legends. Superstitions. They don't exist."

"If you believe that, then why have you already begun to change from referring to them as faeries to calling them the Gentry? I think a part of you knows that every legend bears at least some truth. The being I referred to is doubtless in disguise or has gone to ground; the Hunt was unable to capture him last night."

Brenna stared at him, trying to ignore the fine trembling that was trying to spread through her body. "So, let me get this straight. You came here to warn me that one of the Gentry is after me, the Wild Hunt is after him, and I should actually believe this? Do you know how crazy that sounds?"

"I know how it sounds to you. But nevertheless I had to warn you."

"Ronan, I barely know you. How do I know *you* aren't this fae creature in disguise?"

"So you do believe it is possible that the Sidhe exist." Ronan was still looking at her in that disturbingly intense way.

"I didn't say that! I...stop trying to confuse me. If you wanted to freak me out, you've done a great job so far." He had, too. Her heart seemed to be thudding against her ribs and she had way too tight a grip on the afghan.

His lips quirked into an almost-smile. "I do not mean to frighten you. But I do want you to be careful. Please, whatever opinions you may have formed of me, let my actions of last night guide your judgment as to my intentions toward you. There is more at stake here than you realize. I would not see you come to harm."

"What don't I realize? What's at stake? If you think there's something else I should know, just tell me. Don't give me the flowery Hiberno-speak, or whatever it is. Just use something close to plain English."

"There is much I could tell you, but I sense you are not ready to hear it just now, despite your words to the contrary. You are upset. I fear that I am the cause; that was not my intent. I will leave you now, but for your own safety and if you heed nothing else I have said, heed this. Do not go outside after dark, and pay attention to what your intuition tells you about people you meet."

Unable to utter a word, all she could do was stare at him while her mind tried to wrap itself around his words. Hadn't she heard this same dialog in a vampire movie at one time or another?

Ronan came to her, pausing before he reached the doorway to look down into her face. One of his hands came to rest on her shoulder, and with the contact, all her tense muscles began to relax. It wasn't a logical reaction, but for some reason it felt more natural than anything that had happened since she'd arrived in this country.

All too soon—and not soon enough—he dropped his hand and stepped back from her. "I am sorry if I have alarmed you, Brenna Callahan. I promise that I will speak to you in detail when the time is right. Until then, I will trust in your good judgment, whether or not you trust in mine."

He went out and started down the pathway without so much as a glance over his shoulder. Brenna watched him for a moment, then looked around at the yard and distant hedgerows. Don't go outside after dark, he'd said, yet he'd just walked off into the shadows.

She glanced back toward Ronan, but couldn't see him. He must walk fast, to be visible one moment, gone the next. Without him there, the night seemed even darker than it had been moments before.

Odd, how the man's presence could be so unsettling yet so reassuring, both at once. Despite his cryptic warnings, she'd had the sense that she was more secure with him there than she was without. He shouldn't make her feel that way, especially given the fact that he was probably delusional. Especially given the fact that he was too sexy by half.

Especially given the fact that you have a boyfriend, you idiot!

Brad. Damn. She hadn't called him since her "I've landed" phone message at the airport, but now it was the middle of his workday in Portland. How could she have forgotten? She should take the time to think about what that meant, but...not now. She didn't want to think about Brad now, when Ronan's words were still buzzing around in her brain and his enticing scent still filled her nostrils.

In defiance, she kept the front door open a few moments longer than necessary, but she couldn't relax until the deadbolt slid home, locking the night outside, where it belonged. Faery tales, unnamed dangers lurking in the dark, an old woman who believed in the Wild Hunt, and a man with weird protective impulses who went around rescuing women in the wee hours of the morning. If this was Connacht at its best, what tourist would want to come here?

Brenna gave herself a good mental shake, retrieved her laptop from its case and set it up on the kitchen table. She checked to make sure she had the internet connection touted in the rental ad, then spent half an hour on surfing and research.

On a whim, she looked up the university website cited on Colm

Lachlann's business card. No problems there, thank goodness. He was a respected archeologist with a body of published articles that would make anyone in the field jealous. She located his weblog, which was entertaining and witty, and portrayed an intelligent, sensitive man with a passion for conservation and Irish history. She would have searched for information on Ronan as well, but he hadn't mentioned his last name and she'd somehow failed to ask him. Annie probably knew, but she'd have to wait until a more sensible time of day to ask.

When she'd finally surfed her way into a calmer mood, she opened a file to begin the first travel article. At this point, she had little to start with, but a few paragraphs to slant the area as a possible haven for ghostbusters or myth-debunkers seemed the obvious way to begin.

CHAPTER THREE

From the vantage point of Rath Mor, the Great Fort, Brenna could see the low stone walls that crisscrossed the surrounding fields, and the fluffy white bodies of sheep like clouds in a green sky, unconcerned with what might lie under the mounds that dotted their pastures. She'd joined a tour from the Cruachan Ai Visitor Center in the village of Tulsk earlier that morning; by now her digital camera contained a wealth of photos and sound clips that she planned to use for her article.

Jay was going to be glad he'd sent her instead of buying a random Ireland story from a freelance writer; if these first couple of pieces went well, she might be able to kick off a whole series of articles on the folklore and legends of sacred places in Europe. The more she thought about it, the better she liked the idea.

Ronan's visit the night before had left her a little shaken, but in the light of day it seemed more like something she'd dreamt than something she needed to worry about. So far, today had been a blissfully normal Tuesday, though *normal* in Ireland didn't mean ordinary. Scattered rain showers fell under a sunny sky—a phenomenon that the tour guide called a soft day—and each new vista she encountered stirred her imagination. If magic existed, this was it.

The tour soon moved to another site, a smaller ring fort called Rath Beag, the Little Fort. Brenna climbed up its gentle slope to the top, then turned around to get her bearings. A much flatter, larger mound across the field drew her attention at once, and the more she stared at it, the more it intrigued her. Given its relative size, it had obviously been a place of great significance. Almost without volition, she took a step toward it.

"That's Rath Cruachan itself, seat of the ancient rulers of Connacht," the tour guide said, following her gaze. He looked as though he would have said more, but one of the other tourists asked him a question and he moved away to speak to him instead. Brenna barely noticed his departure; for some reason, she couldn't take her eyes off the great mound.

"*Táim ar ais*," she whispered. Then the strangeness of the words hit her. What had she just said, and in what language? It might have been gibberish, but somehow she knew it wasn't. It sounded familiar, as though she should have understood it, but couldn't quite remember what it meant.

Bemused, Brenna left the tour group and wandered across the field, closer to Rath Cruachan. If the smaller mounds had evoked a dim sense of long-extinguished fires and other echoes of a lost age, this large mound nearly overwhelmed her. She could see it teeming with life, with ancient roadways leading to it as a center of society and commerce. Even hidden under grass and sod, it somehow made her long for times and people long gone. If she could convey even a little of that feeling to her readers, she'd have done a fantastic job.

Obeying some inner prompting, she climbed to the top, where she could look out over the territory that had once been known as

Cruachan Ai. Beneath her feet, the ground seemed to breathe, almost as if it were a living thing that could sense her presence. Caught by an acute need to restore a lost connection, Brenna knelt to touch the grass. A sudden electric sensation shot up her spine and made her scalp tingle.

"Táim abhaile." Once again, words came to her lips, as smooth and sure as if she'd spoken them all her life. As if in response, a gust of wind brushed past her like the sigh of the land welcoming back a prodigal child. Tears prickled in the corners of her eyes; she blinked them away.

Well, if this isn't proof that I'm nuts, I don't know what is. Brenna swallowed over the tightness in her throat. Crying over a pile of dirt and stones, muttering aloud in some unknown language—she didn't know which was crazier. Shakily, she wiped her hands on her pantlegs and got to her feet.

A sense of homecoming wasn't unique to her, at least not according to almost every other American of Irish ancestry with an imagination and a blog. But did everyone who came here speak out in a strange language and feel the land breathe beneath their feet? That couldn't be part of the usual tourist experience.

It is good that you have returned. We have waited for you.

Brenna started, frozen in a crouch as she looked for the owners of the voices. If it was someone from the tour group catching up to her, she couldn't see them. Come to think of it, she didn't see the group on the other mound, where they'd been when she left them. She rose and turned in a circle, scanning the field, but they were nowhere in sight.

It was clear that not only was she spouting gibberish, now she was hearing voices as well. She couldn't stop to think about the implications yet, though. She'd consider them later when she was safe in her cottage with a cup of hot tea and a fire. Just now, she had more immediate concerns—like being stranded.

"Fantastic. I suppose now I'll have to walk." Brenna hurried down off the mound. She might have missed seeing the group; they must still be nearby, maybe at the side of the road where the bus had been parked, or at one of the other mounds in the area. Frustrated, she turned another slow circle, but aside from the sheep and a lone crow that scolded as it flew overhead, she saw no one, and the roadside space was empty except for a white Range Rover.

"Brenna Callahan, isn't it? I must say it's nice to see you again, but I think I just saw a tour bus leave. Were you supposed to be with them?"

Brenna jumped at the voice and turned to see Colm Lachlann striding toward her from around the side of the mound; he must have come up to the front side just as she'd run down the back. He smiled at her, and her heartbeat began to slow to a normal speed. At least she wasn't alone, and she'd met him before. That should have been comforting, though somehow it wasn't—not quite.

"Hi, Colm. They left me? You'd think the guide would have noticed I was missing," Brenna said at last, frowning as the oddity of the situation began to sink in. How had the tour group not noticed her atop Rath Cruachan, and how had she not seen them leave?

Colm laughed. "Some people are still superstitious about these places. Perhaps they left because they thought they saw a spirit of the mound, one of the Sidhe."

The Sidhe, again. Alarm skittered through her at the memory of Ronan's strange warning of last night. She looked at Colm sharply, but saw nothing but open friendliness on his face.

She tried to smile at him. "Well, if the tour group saw one of the Gentry and I didn't, then I want my money back, because I saw nothing of the kind."

Colm chuckled. "If they didn't advertise such an encounter, then I suppose that's just your lot."

"Too bad," she said, trying for light banter while she decided what to do. "If I had seen one of them, I might have asked for an interview; the magazine wanted me to get some local input."

"If you don't mind an all-too-human archeologist instead, I suppose I could provide some local input, if you like," he said, smiling. "May I offer you a ride back to town?"

"Well...." Brenna hesitated. "What are you doing out here, anyway? Do you live nearby? I don't want to interrupt your work or anything."

"Not to worry," he said. "As it happens, I'm just looking over some future dig sites. A half hour's difference and I would have missed you. Then you'd really have been stranded."

"Oh. Well, then I guess that's my good luck. I read about you on the Internet, but I didn't know you were working on anything in this area."

"Ah. You checked up on me," Colm said. Thank goodness, he didn't seem affronted. "Yes, I specialize in ancient sites like this one. Passage tombs, barrows, mounds...they all fascinate me. I could tell you stories you won't find in the guidebooks."

"I'll bet you can. But which dig sites are you investigating? I thought these mounds weren't supposed to be excavated."

Colm smiled. "I'll be doing a few of the smaller ones in this vicinity, though I have to keep it all very circumspect, wade through all the proper channels. You wouldn't believe the level of resistance to that sort of thing. It all must be done with the utmost care and respect for people's beliefs about the fair folk. And of course, there's the tourist trade to consider." He smiled as his gaze lit on the camera that hung on a cord around her neck. "As for tours...you never got to finish yours, did you? I walked my sites earlier, so I have the rest of the afternoon available, if you'd care to take a drive with me. I can show you some other mounds in this area, and then we could go to Carnfree."

Brenna glanced around again, but the tour group hadn't returned for her. "I appreciate that, but I should get back to the Heritage Center. I need to check my itinerary against their tour roster—see if I'm about to miss anything else I scheduled for myself today."

"*Did* you schedule anything else for today?"

"Well, I..." Brenna hesitated. On the surface, it was a no-brainer. She could hoof it down the road and try to find a farmer's house where she could call for a cab back to the heritage center, or ride in comfort in a bucket seat and learn all sorts of interesting lore from a man who'd made it his business to study the mounds in detail. It was a great opportunity, especially if he would provide a few quotes for the article.

Ronan, whose last name she still didn't know, wanted her to trust her intuition. Well, her intuition had prompted her to research Colm Lachlann, and he had something Ronan hadn't provided—legitimate credentials. In fact....

"Colm, this may sound strange, but would you mind showing me your drivers' license?" she asked. "A woman alone can't be too careful."

One corner of his mouth quirked up, but he reached for his wallet. "Worried I'm a sicko who drives around the countryside preying on stranded women? I guess I can't blame you, though I'm not sure how this will help."

"Humor me anyway?" she asked, smiling at him. Seeing the license would help, even if he didn't know why.

He handed her his open wallet, with his drivers' license displayed behind clear plastic. She took out the license and turned it over in her hand. It was exactly what she'd expected, of course, but the solid confirmation was good. From what she'd read about faeries, people were sometimes offered gold or other items in

Faeryland, but when they returned to the real world, the gold turned out to be leaves or some similar item. Well, this was the real world, and by the look and feel of it, Colm's driver's license was the genuine article.

Even if Ronan was right and the Sidhe actually existed, and even if one of them was running around in disguise, where would he get a web page, a verifiable university job, and a real driver's license? That'd have to be some amazing magic—or glamour, or whatever they called it—and surely it would be hard to maintain such detailed illusions for any length of time, especially with someone touching them. Plus, the license was plastic. Weren't all the illusions in the stories performed on natural objects like sticks, stones or leaves?

From all that she could tell, Colm Lachlann was just as human as she was.

She replaced the driver's license and handed the wallet back to him. "I would appreciate a lift, thanks."

Colm's smile widened. He seemed genuinely pleased at the idea of her company. "It's a happy coincidence that I ran into you here," he said. He extended his arm for Brenna to take—such a sweet gesture that she couldn't resist, despite the nagging voice in the back of her head that insisted Brad would not approve.

Brad. If he had his way, they'd be engaged before the end of the year. He was persuasive—as a lawyer, he had to be—but every time she thought about his inevitable proposal, a kind of panic rose in the back of her mind. She'd even had dreams in which she dashed out of the church while a confused Brad stood alone at the altar. That couldn't be a good sign. But again, this wasn't the time to deal with boyfriend issues, and even the thought of him felt like an intrusion.

Pushing away the mental image of Brad's disapproving scowl, Brenna smiled at Colm as they climbed over the stile at the side of the field. "I'm sorry to have been so paranoid."

"It's not a problem. You know, a man alone can't be too careful, either."

She glanced at him to see whether he was teasing, but they'd reached his Range Rover by now and his back was turned. He unlocked the front, retrieved several cardboard map tubes and a briefcase from the passenger seat and tossed them into the backseat, then waited for her to get in before closing the door for her. Apparently, chivalry hadn't died yet in Ireland.

"Cuchulain found that out the hard way, you know," he said as they buckled their seatbelts. He consulted a GPS unit on the dash, then pulled out onto the roadway.

"Found what out?" she asked.

"What I said a minute ago: that a man alone can't be too careful. He ran afoul of the Morrigan several times during his lifetime. In the end, the mistakes he made with her proved to be the death of him, according to the manuscript of the *Tain*."

"Morrigan. That name sounds familiar. I know I've heard it before, but I have no idea where." Brenna glanced at Colm, but his eyes were on the road. "I've tried to read several of the old heroic tales, but for some reason, whenever I start one, I never seem to finish it. I'm not sure why. I know I never got through the Tawn, or whatever you called it."

"The *Tain Bo Culigne*, or Cattle Raid of Cooley," he said. "But there are other stories of the Morrigan. Much older stories. She is one of the most powerful warrior queens of the Tuatha De Danann. Some consider her a goddess of battle, destruction and death. Only a fool would seek her out." His tone was serious, as though the Morrigan really existed and might be eavesdropping on their conversation.

Brenna tried to ignore the chill his words gave her. "I know this sounds odd, but when you refer to her in the present tense, it gives me the creeps."

"You aren't the only one," Colm said. Then he grinned, his smile sending a zing of awareness through Brenna. "I hope I didn't spook you too badly."

"You didn't." She forced her gaze away from that smile, though staring at the countryside didn't help as much as she'd hoped. Rather than providing a safe distraction, the view exerted its own pull on her senses.

On impulse, she pointed down a connecting road. "Turn down here, would you?"

Colm gave her a sidelong glance, but he pulled aside at the crossroads and stopped, letting the engine idle. "There are much more scenic routes to Carnfree."

Brenna peered in the direction she'd been contemplating. It didn't look much different from any of the other roads she'd seen, and Colm didn't seem thrilled at the prospect of deviating from their original destination. Carnfree would definitely be a good addition to the article, and besides, they were using Colm's petrol.

"Okay," she said, giving him a shrug and a smile. You're the native guide."

"Right, then; on we go." He smiled and put the Rover back in gear, continuing their progress down the original road.

"What's down there, anyway?" she asked. "I'm always curious about any roads and paths I see; I always want to know where they go, even when it's just a deer path in the woods." She smiled a little at the whimsy of it—but maybe that curiosity was part of what made her a good travel writer.

"We're just a bit to the southwest of Rath Cruachan, and down that road is the entrance to Oweynagat, the Morrigan's cave and place of power, as legend has it. In reality, it's a cramped little opening, and it can be pretty muddy and dark in there."

Oweynagat. She'd read something about it in the brochures

she'd picked up. Translated, it meant Cave of the Cats. Now according to Colm, it was also connected with the goddess of war and death, whose name for some reason filled Brenna with dread. Still, the cave might be worth a look and a write-up. Since Colm didn't want to go there now, she could always come back later when she had her car back. Being flexible was part of the job.

Even when they'd left the road to Oweynagat behind, though, she couldn't help but feel as if something beckoned her in that direction, much the way Rath Cruachan had earlier. As she stared out at the passing countryside, she could hear those same voices in her mind. Gradually they faded until one stern female tone stood out above the others.

You have returned from exile beyond the ninth wave, but you still have not chosen. You yet stand between the hosts, undecided, while time in your realm grows short. Will you become the warrior you were called to be, or will you flee the field? I offer you this one chance. Come to me, and seek atonement.

The words whispered through her mind as clearly as if someone had spoken them into her ear. Brenna glanced at Colm, but his eyes were on the road. Obviously, she'd heard it and he hadn't. She found herself gripping her notebook and pen, hard, and had to force herself to relax. What was wrong with her? It had been long enough since her flight that she couldn't blame it on fatigue.

Come to me, and take back that which you have forgotten. Come to me soon, before it is too late.

Even through the vibration of tires on pavement, Brenna imagined she felt a pulse from somewhere in the land beneath her, thrumming along her nerve endings like a giant heartbeat. Every hair on her arms seemed to want to stand on end, and that voice kept straying into her mind, beckoning.

None of the things she was hearing or feeling could possibly be real. These grass-covered bumps in the earth were just burial mounds and souterrains, places where people had lived and died centuries ago. They were stops on a tourist's roadmap, nothing more. She was here to do a job, not pick a very odd time to have an early midlife crisis and start believing in faeries.

She felt Colm's eyes on her and gave him a smile and nod in response to something he'd just said, but as the Range Rover ate away the distance between Tulsk and Carnfree, Brenna's body still hummed with the barely leashed energy she'd been sensing all day. In fact, if things didn't settle down soon, she might not get to sleep tonight. It felt as though she'd had a caffeine overdose.

By the time they'd finished their impromptu tour of Carnfree and returned to Tulsk, Brenna's head was pounding and all she wanted was tea, painkillers and a hot shower, not necessarily in that order.

CHAPTER FOUR

Back at the Cruachan Ai Visitor Center, Brenna popped a dose of acetaminophen, then sat beside Colm in the café while she waited for the last bus of the day to arrive.

"There's no need to call a cab or wait for the bus to take you back to Strokestown. I'll drive you," Colm insisted.

Brenna looked out the window at the rain, which had begun a drizzle without the benefit of sun to brighten it up. A bus ride might not require conversation, while a lift from Colm would, but his bucket seat was far more comfortable. She hesitated, then gave him a rueful smile. "I've already made you waste more of your petrol and your time than I should have."

"It's no trouble at all, I promise you. In fact, our immediate plans seem to mesh quite well. If you'd consent to accompany me again tomorrow, I'd be happy to drive you to some of the other destinations on your list."

So she had a willing native guide who didn't act as though her questions were idiotic. Add to that the fact that he was great-looking. There was nothing to hate about the situation other than the fact that it felt disloyal to Brad even if she kept it platonic. Things kept happening too fast; she needed to take it down a notch—at least until she'd had time to think and make a few hard decisions.

"Your tour-guide offer sounds great, but I think I'll have to take a...ah...rain check on that, no pun intended. I need to review my schedule, and I think I need a day's break. I gathered a lot of material today; I need to input it all and arrange the order of sites for the first article."

Colm smiled at her. "I don't envy you that job. I'd much rather dig around in piles of rubble than try to romanticize them to tourists."

"Romanticize? Is that what I do for a living? Hmm. I guess that's true."

According to the clock, it was closing time. Brenna finished her now-cold cup of tea, got up and refastened her mackintosh. Out in the parking lot, tourists began to form a line, huddling under umbrellas to keep their newly-purchased books and curios out of the rain while they waited for the bus that was due any minute now.

Brenna was just about to step from the entryway into the drizzle-turned downpour when Colm went still beside her.

"What is it?" she asked, puzzled at the expression on his face. A few tourists still waited for the bus, a couple of people in raincoats hurried toward the visitor center, and a janitor began to upend chairs on top of tables in the café. Nothing seemed wrong, but maybe she'd missed something.

"Unwelcome company," Colm said, tilting his head to indicate a man walking across the parking lot.

Brenna peered through the rain. The man was some distance away, but something about him seemed familiar. As if he sensed the scrutiny, he turned his head toward them. With a little jolt,

Brenna recognized Ronan. As he came closer, she could see the tension in his face, which hardened into anger as his gaze fell on Colm's hand on her arm.

"Brenna Callahan, may I speak with you alone for a moment?" Ronan asked.

Brenna squinted at him through the rain and the dull throbbing of her headache. "Ronan, what are you doing here? And what happened to hello and how are you?"

"Hello. How are you? May I speak to you alone, please?"

She sighed. "I suppose so. But as you can see, I was in the middle of something here."

"Yes, I see. But this should not take long," Ronan said. "If you will excuse us...." As he and Colm locked gazes, Brenna could have sworn she felt a palpable concussion in the air between them.

"Now, just a moment," Colm said. His hand on her arm tightened, along with his voice. "Brenna, if this...gentleman...is bothering you, you don't have to speak to him. We can leave now, or I can call the gardaí."

"No, don't do that. It's okay. I'll just be a moment," Brenna said hastily, and twisted just enough to pull her arm free without giving offense.

She grabbed Ronan's arm and steered him around the side of the building, out of earshot and out of some of the gusting wind as well. Colm let them go, but he didn't look happy. Worried might be a better description of his expression. He clearly didn't trust Ronan any further than Ronan trusted him, an observation borne out a moment later as Colm walked across the parking lot to a position where he could still see her.

Just great. Caught in a rainstorm and a pissing contest both at the same time. That took some kind of dumb luck.

"Ronan, what do you want?" she asked, keeping her voice low so it wouldn't carry. "That was very rude, I hope you know."

"I warned you the other night to be cautious of people you meet, and use your intuition. Did you not pay attention to anything I said?" he asked, deftly avoiding both her question and her accusation.

"I did pay attention. But I haven't had any trouble—well, except with the tour bus, but that's another story. Colm found me stranded when the tour deserted me, and offered me a ride. I've been with him for most of the day, and I really have no idea why I'm explaining myself to you, as if—" she broke off at Ronan's hiss.

"*Colm* is dangerous to you, Brenna." He actually reached out and took hold of her by the upper arms. Just like the night before, she relaxed the moment he touched her, though logic said she should have had the opposite reaction. She eyed him warily, but didn't pull away. She could always struggle when and if he did anything she didn't like, and Colm was still watching them. She saw him take two steps toward her, but she shook her head at him and he stopped. From his posture, he wanted to break something—like Ronan's head.

"Colm is dangerous to me, but you aren't?" she asked.

"Correct," Ronan said, sounding relieved. "Now, shall I escort you back to Strokestown?"

"No."

"But...did we not just establish—?"

"No. Look, I get that you don't like Colm. Apparently you two have some bad history, and that's unfortunate, but none of it involves me. Besides, I Googled him last night; he's legit."

"You...googled him?" Ronan looked puzzled.

Brenna lifted her chin. "That's right. The magic of the Internet. You can learn all sorts of things about a person that way. Now, I don't want you to think that I don't appreciate what you did for me the other night, but I'm fine now. And I'm capable of defending myself against a guy if he gets the wrong sort of ideas.

Any guy." She looked down at his hands on her arms, then met his gaze straight on.

"But Brenna, this is no ordinary *guy*. I believe he is the Sidhe I warned you about last night. I wasn't sure until I saw him just now, but—"

"Whoa—stop right there." Brenna held up a hand. "I'm telling you, Colm Lachlann is a legitimate, human archeologist with all the trimmings. I've seen and touched his drivers' license. I've spent more time with him than I have with you, and returned to tell the tale. He's been nothing but a gentleman to me, and from everything I can determine, he's as human as you or I. Yet here you are telling me he's a legendary being in disguise. Don't you think it's possible you've made a mistake?"

"It is possible, but not likely," Ronan said stiffly, still holding onto her.

She stared at him, trying to reconcile how crazy his words sounded with the way his very proximity made her feel safe, protected, just as he had the other night in the dark and fog, and again last night at her cottage. She was way too attracted to him, and it was playing havoc with her judgment. She'd even begun to feel a little breathless, like one of those women in a medieval bodice-ripper. Now *there* was an image she could do without.

"Well, I guess we're at an impasse, because as far as I can tell, all the credibility is on Colm's side right now," she said. "The only thing I know about you is that you're pagan, you saved me from some invisible and probably imaginary thing when I had my little panic attack in the fog that night, and Annie seems to like you, but...it's not much to go on, Ronan. If you want me to believe what you say, you need to give me more."

"I shouldn't have to," he said gently, and something in his eyes made her shiver deep inside. "You need to let yourself remember what you've forgotten."

Come to me, and take back that which you have forgotten. Come to me, before it is too late.

Fear surged, freezing her where she stood. Brenna stared at Ronan wide-eyed, unable to move. He seemed very aware of her distress, because he released one of her arms, while the hand that remained crept upward to her neck, and through it all, she just stood there gaping at him like an idiot. Shock. That's what it had to be.

Sanity reasserted itself a moment later. Ronan and Annie seemed to be friends, so it wasn't so odd that their beliefs were similar. Just because they both believed in the Wild Hunt and the Sidhe didn't mean she had to. Any of the strange things she'd heard or experienced could be the products of her vivid imagination and the stress of her first overseas assignment. It didn't mean she was going crazy, and it wasn't proof that magical beings were real.

That realization calmed her. It couldn't have anything to do with how good the warmth of Ronan's hand felt against her neck, or how her headache inexplicably eased under his touch.

"So you will go with him regardless of anything I say?" he asked quietly.

Across the parking lot, she could just make out Colm's expression. He looked angry. In fact, he started walking toward them as she watched. Brenna looked from one to the other, incredulous. Were they actually going to fight over her?

Unbelievable. Just who did they think they were? She might like to read about helpless medieval damsels, but neither of these men had the right to treat her like one! The rising indignation felt good; it helped replace the panic of a moment ago.

"I have no intention of going anywhere with either one of you. The two of you can work out your disagreement without me. Good evening." Chin held high, Brenna stepped out of his reach as though she hadn't just been standing there letting him touch her in such a familiar way.

She turned away from Ronan and started back toward the bus line. Halfway there, she couldn't help but look over her shoulder, just for a moment.

He was still there—for some reason, she'd had the oddest feeling he wouldn't be—staring at her with an expression of mixed concern and hunger that sent shivers down her spine. Anger at her own irrational reaction to him whipped her head back around and sent her hurrying to where the bus was pulling up and opening its doors.

"All right?" Colm asked, coming up to her.

"Fine, thanks," she said, and managed not to show him the anger she'd just unleashed on Ronan. Point for her.

"If you like, I could drive you home and help you write up details for the pictures you took. We could drink a cuppa while we work," Colm offered.

"Uh...."   Now *that* was a scintillating reply.   Confusion swamped her as she looked up at Colm's sexy, smiling face. For no reason she could define, she was suddenly tempted to take him up on his offer, but doing so would be as foolish as letting Ronan touch her the way he just had.

The fact that neither of these men seemed to trust the other didn't help matters. Besides, she was going home at the end of the month. Even if they were best friends and had nothing but praise for each other, she'd be crazy to get involved with either of them. If they wanted to have a pissing match, they could do it on their own time.

"I appreciate the offer, but it's been a long day and I'm tired," she told Colm. "But thanks for the tour; I had a great time. Once I figure out what my plans are for the next week or so, I might give you a call then, okay?" Or not.

Colm gave an exaggerated sigh and put one hand over his heart. "Rejected, and after such a delightful afternoon. I'm not sure I'll recover." Then he grinned. "I'll be expecting that call, Ms. Callahan. Don't disappoint me."

"Good evening," Brenna said, hurrying onto the bus, eager to put some distance between herself and both of the crazy Irishmen. A glance toward where Ronan had been standing confirmed that he'd gone. As the bus door closed, Brenna sighed in relief. Men complicated things. She'd probably be better off without any men in the picture at all. She was here to work, and she needed to remember that. If she focused on that, she'd be okay.

Darkness had fallen before she finally reached Strokestown and hired a cab to take her out to the cottage. As she looked out the cab window at the hedgerows, Brenna couldn't help thinking of her ill-fated adventure of two nights ago. Things looked just as they had then, even to the fog that crept across the fields and twisted its way through the scattered copses. It was creepy, but this time she wasn't alone. Or at least, she didn't have to *drive* alone.

At her cottage, she hurried to unlock her front door before the driver had gotten out of range. For some reason, now that she was all alone, she wasn't so sure renting a place outside of town had been such a great idea. She watched through the window until the cab drove out of sight, then gave herself a little shake and headed for the cold fireplace.

When the peat blaze she'd started had begun to take the chill off the cottage, she locked the doors, checked the windows, and changed into pajamas. That was when she realized she'd forgotten to call Brad. Again.

She glanced at the clock. It was later than she'd thought—almost eight-thirty. Back in Portland, Brad would be at some power lunch. Not a good time for her to call. By the time his workday was over and he'd fought his way through the quitting-time traffic, it would be the middle of the night here. Relief swept through Brenna. She wouldn't have to talk to him tonight. She could put off his inevitable grilling about her trip, itinerary, accommodations, everything, for another day.

Shock quickly followed the relief. She didn't want to talk to her boyfriend. Why didn't she? She'd been gone almost five days now. She should be starting to miss him at least a little, shouldn't she? And yet the idea of not speaking to him anytime soon just didn't bother her. If anything, it gave her an expansive, intoxicating sense of...freedom. She could breathe here, be herself here. Maybe for the first time in years. The first time in *two* years?

Oh, fantastic. Brenna closed her eyes, but that didn't forestall the sense of finality that made her breath catch in her throat. Eyes open or eyes closed, it made no difference. She and Brad were over—she knew that now. The relationship had been dying by degrees for months, but it was only here and now that she finally realized it. They weren't right for one another—never had been. But now it was as though the Irish rain had washed away the grime of romantic delusion, making everything clear.

Brenna took a deep breath and opened her eyes. Nothing looked different, though by rights it should. Hadn't she just taken a step into a different world—one with no Brad in it? Breakups and impending breakups were supposed to hurt more than this, weren't they? All she felt right now was relief.

She needed to let him know they were done, but a phone break-up was so crass; she couldn't take a cheap shot like that. She'd have to put off speaking to him, plead a hectic schedule, and tell him when she got home, face to face. It wasn't pretty, but it was the right decision.

For tonight, she'd go to bed early. The day had been long and unnerving enough to justify that. She had other issues besides

Brad to consider, but she just wasn't up to any more heavy revelations tonight.

She'd already doused most of the lights when she heard the sound of a motor out on the road. She waited for it to drive on by, but when it didn't she crept to the living room window and peeked out from the edge of the curtain. A car had stopped on the road near her house, idling. After a few moments, the headlights went out. Brenna tensed. Who would drive out here at this hour? It didn't look like Colm's vehicle, and Annie didn't seem to have one.

Should she call the gardaí? The last time someone had chosen to call on her during the night it had been Ronan, but odd as his sudden appearance on foot had been both times she'd seen him, she hadn't felt threatened by his presence. Had he returned in a car this time with another of his dire warnings, or was this someone else?

Someone else.

Adrenaline crashed through her veins. Brenna poised on the balls of her feet, ready to run to the telephone if anyone she didn't recognize came toward the house. But after a few minutes, the car drove away, a little too slowly for comfort, sans headlights.

Even after she was sure it was gone, Brenna stayed at the window, where she stared at shadows and listened for the sound of voices, or baying hounds, or even that strange non-sound that she'd sensed just before she'd let terror send her running through the fields like a lunatic.

Perhaps an hour later, all hope of sleep gone, she crept from the window and curled up in the chair closest to the fireplace. On a small table nearby lay the faery encyclopedia, the metallic letters on its cover glinting in the firelight. If she touched it and let it draw her into its world, would she find herself trapped? Maybe in a bad fantasy movie....

Cursing herself for a superstitious idiot, Brenna turned on the table lamp, opened the book to where she'd left off, and began to read.

CHAPTER FIVE

A noise halfway between a croak and a shriek cut through the fog of sleep. Brenna blinked, glancing around to see the clock on her bedside table, but instead her gaze fell on the embers in the fireplace and the stacks of travel books she'd left on the coffee table beside the armchair. It seemed she'd fallen asleep on the floor in front of the fireplace, like Cinderella. Why hadn't she had the sense to go to bed last night?

Last night. The car outside.

Fresh adrenaline coursed through her as she scrambled to her feet. She moved the curtains aside just a fraction of an inch so she could peer out the living room window. Thank goodness, the road was clear. The door remained locked and nothing in the yard looked out of place. She started to scan the bushes and nearby copse for movement or signs of disturbance, but at that moment, a crow launched itself into the air from the top of the tallest hawthorn tree. Brenna jumped backward and stumbled over the shoes she'd left on the floor beside the couch.

Damn, she was paranoid! She'd never be able to do her job if she jumped at every shadow. Nevertheless, she checked the door lock once more before she headed for the bathroom. Twenty minutes later, showered, dressed and ready for the day, she made a breakfast of milk and cornflakes and threw one of the travel books into her daypack. After another cautious glance into the yard, she headed out the door for the walk into Strokestown.

On the step, she had to dig her keys out from the bottom of her bag in order to lock the door behind her. When at last she had them, she reached for the latch then stopped, staring at the door. Where before it had been a weathered, blue-painted surface, now it bore a series of shiny, jagged lines. The lines crossed each other in places, curled in others; they bent her gaze to follow them like some kind of bizarre maze. Even as she looked at it, fear began to snake its way through her until it coiled itself into a lump in her middle.

Vandalism, or something worse? There was no way to be sure. But it seemed that whoever had been in the strange car last night had had an agenda, after all, and she hadn't even seen them come up to the door. The symbol seemed to flicker when the light hit it; or maybe that was a trick of the iridescent paint the vandal had used. Brenna reached out to touch it, but drew back at the last moment. It was odd, but she could have sworn the symbol had spines, like a cactus. That couldn't be the case; it was a flat surface. Nevertheless, when she reached toward it again, her fingertips gave such a sharp tingle that she gasped, jerked back and almost fell off the steps.

Well, if she hadn't been freaked before.... Adrenaline thudding through her veins with every heartbeat, Brenna wrenched the door open and headed straight for the telephone on the kitchen wall.

It didn't take the gardaí long to come in response to her call, but her relief when the blue-and-white squad car pulled up in front of the cottage was short-lived.

"You say you've had some vandalism, ma'am?" one of the

gardaí asked as he thumbed his way to a fresh page in his notebook. "Would you show us, please?"

"I'd be happy to, garda...?"

"Name's O'Shea, ma'am."

"Of course, Garda O'Shea. The mark is right there on the door, as I told you on the phone. Looks like some kind of cult symbol to me." Brenna turned toward the door. The other garda was frowning at the blue paint, peering at the hinges, handle and corners—everywhere but at the center, where the symbol glittered in the sun.

"I'm sorry, ma'am, but can you point the damage out to me?" he asked.

"What? It's right there, in the middle of the door. Can't you see the symbol?" Brenna asked. How could they not see it? Surely they weren't colorblind. And even if one was, what were the odds of both being that way?

Both gardaí squinted at the door as though that might help them focus better. Then one of them said, "Ah!"

"Do you see it now?" Brenna asked. Finally. Maybe the angle of the sun had been wrong before.

"If you mean this little scratch, I see it. But it doesn't look much like a symbol."

Brenna threw her hands in the air. "I'm not talking about a scratch. I mean the glittery symbol painted on the middle of the door."

The gardaí looked at each other, then back at Brenna. "Now see here, ma'am," one said. "I don't know what kinds of pranks people get up to in the U.S., but here we take things very seriously. I'll let this go with a warning since you're not local and you seem like a nice lady, but we can't respond to crank calls. Some would run you in for it. I'm inclined to be more lenient, so we're going to go back to town and forget this incident ever happened. I suggest you book yourself a tour or attend a *céilidh* or find some other way to spend your time while you're here."

Brenna stared at the door, where the symbol still glittered. "I don't understand why you can't see it, officer, but it's there, I promise you! I've never made a crank call in my life. I would never do that. I don't understand what's going on here."

"Well, ma'am, that makes three of us. If you get any more tangible vandalism, don't hesitate to ring. But for now, we can't see any damage here and we seem to have a little breakdown in communication, so...."

"You're leaving?" Brenna asked, though she needn't have stated the obvious. The second garda had already gone back to the squad car and Garda O'Shea had closed his notebook. Both shot her bemused looks that said they'd already labeled her a harmless nutcase. O'Shea took several steps down the walkway, hesitated, then turned back.

"Look ma'am, I think you believe you've seen something here. Sure, an' it wouldn't be the first time someone's run afoul of the good folk." His wink and exaggerated brogue made it obvious he didn't believe any such thing. "It never hurts to treat the gentry with respect. If you leave a wee bit of milk out tonight, maybe you'll have no more trouble."

He gave Brenna a nod, then retreated to the squad car. Both gardaí tipped their hats to her as they drove off; for a moment she just stared after them in disbelief. How humiliating! She couldn't be seeing things. She just couldn't. Yet, she had wondered whether she was hearing things, so perhaps the symbol was just in her mind.

Brenna went back to the doorstep, squeezed her eyes shut, and took a deep breath. If the door looked normal when she opened her eyes, she'd know the gardaí were right and she *was* losing it. But if the symbol was still there when she opened her eyes, then maybe she needed help of the kind you couldn't get from a psychiatrist. A part of her wanted to believe this was just her imagination in overdrive; no doubt, there were medications for that. But if she hadn't imagined it.... She opened her eyes.

It was still there. Oh, shit, it was still there.

She went back into the house, dropped her things on the kitchen table and gazed around the room. Everything in here looked normal, even the back of the door. But she was willing to bet that if she went outside again, the mark would still be there. Her college psych course hadn't prepared her for anything like this. This was either a symptom of a disorder she'd never read about, or there was a symbol on her door that only she could see. Either way, the prognosis didn't seem good, especially given that she'd been hearing voices.

Why was this happening? She hadn't spent the first thirty years of her life fighting to get things just the way she wanted them only to lose it all to some kind of mental breakdown the first time she left the U.S.!

Despite her revelation of last night, she felt an urge to call Brad. The urge left just as quickly as it had come. Brad would laugh and call her melodramatic. Or worse, if he did take her seriously, he'd urge her to take the next flight back home; hell, he'd even make her psychiatric appointment himself. No. She'd come too far to give up now.

There had to be a logical explanation for all of the strange incidents since her arrival. No one in her family had a history of personality disorders. She'd never had panic attacks or even mild phobias, which meant that either she'd just had an unprecedented psychotic episode, or this was a genuine paranormal experience. Given the resources available right now, there seemed only one way to find out. Brenna took a calming breath and reached for the telephone.

Annie answered on the third ring. Hoping she didn't sound like an idiot, Brenna forced herself to explain about the symbol she'd seen on the door. She half-expected Annie to dismiss her as the gardaí had done. Belief in faeries or no, Annie had come across as a woman who took no nonsense, so her request for further details about the night before and her immediate agreement to come over was something of a surprise. Sitting at the kitchen table, Brenna sipped a cup of tea to calm her nerves and waited for Annie to arrive.

"Brenna!" Annie's voice called from outside a short while later. "Are you there? Come out right now, and use the back door."

Brenna hurried through the back door and around the cottage to find Annie peering at the front door, her brow furrowed in concentration. Hope crept in, though the apprehension remained. "Annie, thank goodness! Does this mean you can see the mark, too? I'm not crazy after all?"

"What do you mean, can I see it? Of course I can see it. The question is who put it there, and why? You haven't been in Ireland long enough to have made any enemies, have you, girl?" Annie's tone was sharp, but her grip was gentle as she took Brenna's wrist to pull her away from the door.

Enemies? Brenna's mind seized on Ronan's warning and began to pick over the implications. He thought a fae creature was after her. Yesterday, she'd have been willing to bet that was impossible. Today, she wasn't so sure, especially since Annie could see the—what had she called it?—the sigil. Brenna realized she'd begun to twist the heck out of the hem of her sweater, and had to force herself to let go.

Annie rummaged in a tote bag she held and withdrew a black feather, a butane lighter, and what looked like a bundle of dried herbs bound with red thread.

"What will you do with that?" Brenna tried to sound calm and interested, but stress made her voice thin.

"We have to remove it, of course," Annie said, as if Brenna should have known.

"But what exactly is this thing we're removing in the first place?" Brenna asked. "I mean, other than an occult symbol that apparently no one but the two of us can see?"

"It's a sigil meant to draw negative energies to anyone who stays in the house," Annie explained. "If left alone, it would soon have begun to function much the way a poltergeist might. It's obvious that someone doesn't want you here."

"But—"

"Quiet; let me work. Then we'll discuss this further." Annie closed her eyes. After a few moments, Brenna felt a vibration in the ground beneath her feet, gone so quickly that she might have imagined it. When Annie opened her eyes, it was as if the harmless older woman was gone, replaced by a stern, commanding presence that made Brenna shiver in an instant of recognition.

Annie gave her a grim smile and used the lighter to ignite the tip of the herb bundle. It flared, then subsided into a steady curl of smoke. Annie muttered something in a language that Brenna could swear she'd never heard but that sounded somehow familiar and waved the feather across the smoke, which wafted toward the symbol on the door.

The instant the smoke struck it, the sigil flared with red light. As Brenna watched, the light pulled itself off the door to wind into a sinuous red vapor, which twined with the herbal smoke as though the two streams were a pair of grappling serpents.

"Don't breathe it," Annie warned. She muttered something again in that naggingly familiar language.

Brenna stepped back, holding her breath. After a while, the herbal smoke began to draw in and absorb the red vapor until none of the latter remained. At last, Annie reached over to give her a poke in the ribs. Brenna gasped and drew in a breath of juniper-scented air. Annie shot her another of the sardonic smiles that didn't seem to belong in that gentle face. Then she began to move around the house, waving more smoke toward each window as she passed. She smudged the back door as well, then proceeded to lead Brenna through the house, carrying the still-smoldering herb bundle into every room, closet and cupboard. Somehow, they managed to avoid setting off the smoke detector.

"That was some light show. Should we do the toilet, too?" Brenna asked when they'd finished, trying to dispel the tension.

Annie didn't seem amused. "This isn't a game, girl. Someone wants you gone, badly enough to work a spell against you. Just be glad you aren't in the hospital now." Annie tossed what was left of the bundle into the fireplace, where it hit one of the larger embers, blazed up and disappeared in moments.

Fear clutched at Brenna again. "A spell? First, you tell me I nearly ran into the Wild Hunt. Now you tell me that witches are after me?" This simply could not be happening. There was no guidebook to cover situations like this.

"Not witches, necessarily," Annie said. "But whoever did this isn't concerned about how you choose to label him—or her, whichever the case may be. You saw what happened with the guards. Few people will believe you if you tell them someone is using magic against you. I've cleansed and warded the house, so you should be all right for the moment. But someone with knowledge of *draíocht* has targeted you for some reason. We need to find out why."

"Dree-uckht? That's...what? Black magic?"

"No. *Draíocht* is Irish for magic, but magic isn't black or white. It just is." Annie's gaze was so intent that Brenna felt as though she should be taking notes.

She groaned. "Annie, part of me still can't even believe all these things are happening. I'm just a normal career woman, not a witch or a psychic. I can't have this weird stuff in my life. I need to finish researching my first article, get it written and email it off to my boss. I need to call my boyfriend later and be convincing enough that he won't know I'm about to break up with him. I need—"

"You *need* to know whether the attack was personal or just a dangerous prank. You need to know who did it and how to protect yourself in future. You mentioned a light show? That means you saw what happened in the astral dimension, the plane between the human world and the Otherworld. You are more than a psychic and so much more than a *bandraoí*. I should have realized at once; I'm surprised you haven't yet."

Brenna sighed. Evidently, *normal* was determined to exit, stage left. "Okay, I admit I saw the thing on the door, and I saw what happened when you removed it. Maybe that proves I have some sort of paranormal gift. But the gardaí already think I'm nuts, and so would most other people, as you've already pointed out. That leaves you and I seriously outnumbered on the psychology scale."

Annie nodded. Her eyes, so fierce just moments ago, were now thoughtful. "I understand, dear, but eventually, you'll just have to make a choice and go with it. You can try to pretend nothing's happened and all your paradigms haven't been ripped apart, or you can accept the fact that there's magic in the world and deal with it as necessary."

Since Annie had seen the symbol and removed it, either that meant both of them were hallucinating, or there really was something to this magic business. Brenna wasn't sure which was worse news. "I'll try. And thanks for your help with that...sigil thing," she said.

"You're welcome," Annie said. "Now I'm off home. You have a lot to think about, and I'm sure you want to get on with your work."

She turned to go.

"Annie," Brenna said, stopping her. "You mentioned the Wild Hunt before, and the Gentry. Ronan told me he thinks one of the Sidhe means me harm. And now there's this curse symbol. Do you think it's all related?"

Annie paused for a moment, considering. "Has anything else strange happened since your troubles on the first night? Have you had any visitors?"

Brenna frowned. "Other than Ronan, you mean? He stopped by once to warn me about the aforementioned Sidhe. And then last night a car pulled up and parked on the road outside the cottage for a while, then left. I didn't see anyone get out, but this morning, there was the symbol on the door. I guess they could have gone up the road out of sight and then doubled back on foot to get at the door without me noticing."

"Ah." Annie said. "That tells me what I needed to know. The Gentry wouldn't need cars to get around, and they certainly wouldn't drive up in one to study a potential victim. I think that gives us the strong indication that the sigil, at least, is of human origin. As to one of the Sidhe being after you, I'd tend to trust Ronan's judgment about that. He's very knowledgeable about *draíocht*. The Wild Hunt had to be chasing something—or someone. They were typically sent out after traitors or oathbreakers. A rogue Sidhe could be extremely dangerous, especially if he or she managed to elude the Hunt."

"Fantastic," Brenna said, trying to keep the apprehension at bay. It seemed the trouble wasn't behind her, after all. "If I go with the theory that magic and magical beings exist, then I have to believe that I've somehow attracted magic-using stalkers of two different varieties, who might or might not have anything to do with each other. But no matter who or what might be after me, I still need material for my articles, or I won't have a job to come home to. Any recommendations about that?"

"If I were you, I'd just keep an eye out for anything that doesn't seem right, and be extra careful while you're touring the area," Annie said. "Also, if you don't mind some more personal advice, I'd recommend trusting your deeper instincts. They can save you when logic can't."

Annie caught Brenna's gaze one last time. The stern taskmistress of moments before was gone, leaving only the kind neighbor who had offered her hospitality when she was stranded in the fog. Brenna managed a smile and a nod, but her smile slipped as Annie turned and headed down the walk. She had always prided herself on being competent, in control. This situation proved that control was just an illusion.

For a day that had such a poor start, this one had turned out quite well. In the back seat of the cab on the return to her cottage, Brenna checked her digital camera one more time, cycling though the images she'd captured that afternoon. All of her pictures looked clear and professional, and the information she'd gleaned from the tour guide had netted her quite a few anecdotes she hadn't found in any of the guidebooks.

Better still, she hadn't heard any echoes or voices at any of the places she'd visited, including the county museum that housed the Rahara Sheela-na-gig. Even the ancient Castlestrange La Téne stone, carved all over with sinuous whorls and lines, hadn't sparked the response she'd had at Cruachan. Thank goodness.

The cab rounded a corner then pulled up next to her cottage's walkway. Brenna gathered her things, paid the driver and got out. She'd picked up a cell phone and made service arrangements in town earlier, and she'd even been efficient enough to grab dinner at a café while it was convenient. Now all she needed was a bath, some hot tea, a little computer time and maybe an hour to curl up in an armchair in front of the fire before bed. As the cab drove off, she retrieved her keys from the pack and strode down the walk, sighing in satisfaction at a day's work well done.

Just as she stepped up to the door, she glimpsed movement at the corner of the house. She jumped, letting out a shriek before she realized who it was.

"Ronan! You scared me half to death! Why are you here? I wasn't expecting you, after our last conversation."

As he walked up to stand next to her, some tension deep inside her loosened its grip, but her breathing became shallower and quicker. He was having his usual effect on her—calming and exhilarating at the same time. How did he *do* that?

"Annie told me what happened, but I am here by my own counsel," Ronan said. "You may find yourself in more trouble than you realize, and I would like to help you in whatever way I can. I should stay here tonight, in case your attackers return."

"You're here by your own counsel? What are you, from the Middle Ages? No one talks that way anymore. In fact, chivalry is long dead in most places, and women today are self-sufficient. I've already had the gardaí out here; I'm sure they'd be happy to confirm that I don't need a watchdog." Despite the words that seemed to fly out of her mouth, the urge to touch him was so strong she had to step back to keep herself from moving closer.

He blinked at her. "From what I have seen, women like you are far more vulnerable than they should be. I've no doubt you could change that, but you can't do it in one night. Let me help you. It's no shame to you to allow a man's help when you need it. Or to have a...watchdog, as you call it."

"No. I've said no, and I mean no. It's a word modern women say a lot. Get used to it, Lancelot." Brenna raked a hand through her hair and her daypack fell down over her shoulder, making her drop her keys. Ronan picked them up and silently handed them to her.

"I am sorry you feel this way. I'll return when you are in a more reasonable mood. Good evening, Brenna." He turned and walked away down the road, and within minutes Brenna lost sight of him. It was as though one moment he was there, and the next, he wasn't. Creepy.

She went inside, muttering to herself. Men without a hero complex were hard enough to deal with. The last thing she needed was for Ronan to think that since he'd rescued her once, she couldn't get along without him. Sure, the sigil on the door was scary, but if she allowed it to get to her any more than it already had, she'd end up a basket case. Best to just do her job and get the hell out of Dodge.

After dinner, Brenna went to the sink to wash the dishes she'd used. Outside, the night was quiet, so she tuned the radio to an all-Irish station. A lively piece of fiddle music was playing, which somehow made the lack of a dishwasher seem less of an annoyance. Brenna found her foot tapping along with the beat. When it ended, the Deejay came on. He had a nice brogue.

Brenna listened for a few moments, then stiffened. It wasn't a brogue at all; he was speaking Irish, of course. Irish language station, Irish language. Really? No kidding. But the fact that she was an idiot wasn't the real problem. The problem was that she hadn't immediately registered the fact that he wasn't speaking English because on some level, she'd understood the words. In fact, some of the phrases that tripped off his tongue sounded a lot like the words she had said on top of Rath Cruachan. Could she somehow have been speaking in *Gaeilge*?

Brenna forced herself to go on with the dishes, but it wasn't easy. She couldn't explain running away from an invisible pack of hounds or babbling in a language she'd never studied any more than she could find a reason for some cult-driven vandal to put a curse symbol on her door, or for a perfect stranger to warn her that one of the Sidhe was after her. Not even insanity—hers, Annie's, or Ronan's—could possibly account for all of it. But all of it had happened. Obviously she had to accept that magic was real, and someone nasty was after her for reasons she didn't understand.

Magic was real. Under different circumstances, that discovery should have been wonderful, exciting. Given what she'd seen of it thus far, though, it didn't seem wonderful at all.

Outside the window, the sky had darkened. As she watched the shadows lengthen near the copse and the hedgerows across the road, Brenna's shoulders tightened. Would the vandal return? Should she have taken Ronan up on his offer to stay with her? He'd had her at his mercy when they'd first met; surely if he meant her harm he would have taken advantage then, or at any time since. Instead, he'd rescued her and taken her to safety, and still seemed to be trying to protect her, even though she'd brushed him off twice.

She'd been too harsh earlier. Harsh and rude. Even if being so strongly attracted to him had thrown her for a loop, and even if his unwarranted protectiveness was disconcerting, it didn't mean she had to push him away so violently. She'd have to apologize whenever she saw him next.

Movement near the copse caught her eye—a black shape that separated itself from the trees and began to move down the walk. Somewhere in Brenna's middle, fear coiled itself up and squeezed. What now? She couldn't look away from the thing even as it came closer. A moment later, she could see its eyes shine in the light from the kitchen window.

Every muscle tense, Brenna backed away from the sink, fumbled in one of the drawers and came up with a carving knife. It might not be as good as a gun, but it was better than nothing at all. Brenna gripped the weapon, crept into the living room and pulled the curtain aside just a crack. Damn, was this about to become a nightly routine?

The shape on the walk wasn't human; it was much too low to the ground for that. In fact, it looked like a...dog. Brenna blinked. Wait a minute; it *was* a dog—a large black dog whose breed she couldn't identify. It gave a soft *woof*, turned around three times and then lay down on the step as though it belonged there.

"Go home, doggie," Brenna called through the door. She knew it must have heard her, but it didn't move. Instead it laid its head on its paws and closed its eyes as if to indicate that it meant to stay right where it was. Brenna watched it for a few minutes more while she tried to get her breathing back under control, but the dog didn't move.

Hadn't she read something in the faerie encyclopedia about a black dog that was a harbinger of death? If that were the case, then what did it mean when the damned thing took up residence on your doorstep? Or was it one of the hounds from the Wild Hunt, assuming Annie was right and such a thing really existed?

No way. Get a grip, Brenna. It had to be just a dog: a real, flesh-and-blood animal. The most logical explanation was usually the correct one. Usually. Just because she'd had a few paranormal experiences since she'd arrived didn't mean they all would be. In any case, the dog's eyes didn't glow and it hadn't tried to tear its way through the door.

After her heart rate had returned to normal and her visitor had done nothing but fall asleep with its nose tucked under the tip of its tail, Brenna sighed and went back into the kitchen to put the knife away. If the dog was still there in the morning, she'd feed it her breakfast scraps and see whether it had a collar. But she was not going outside tonight, not even if a menagerie converged in front of the cottage.

She put more peat on the fire and spent some time reading the faerie encyclopedia, leaving off at the letter L. When weariness threatened to send her to sleep on the couch, she gave up and went to bed.

She woke some time later, sobbing without tears, screams forcing themselves from her throat. She would have sat up, but her body refused to move, as though part of her was still in the nightmare while the rest of her lay paralyzed in the bed. She flickered between the two like a strobe, and she couldn't do anything about it.

Her dream-self wore leather armor, dyed with madder and woad to the color of charcoal. Other warriors surrounded her, some of them monstrous in form, with misshapen limbs and scaly, almost fishlike skin. Others looked human, but their eyes were the shade of pale green that Brenna had only ever seen in a rare shark's eyes at an aquarium.

Their opponents were tall, golden people, with eyes that seemed to stare right into Brenna's soul. Her heart clenched at the sight of them, yet for reasons she couldn't begin to fathom, she was fighting them. Her spear drew their blood; harsh words spilled from her lips as she battled them with magic and metal. The monsters beside her waded forward, wielding huge bronze swords like scythes, cutting the fair-haired people down in front of them like wheat in a field. One of the fair folk called out to Brenna, but a monster cut him down in mid-shout. The man fell to the ground in front of her, his eyes already dimming. Brenna cried out at the sight, seared by pain so real that if felt as though she were the one who'd been sliced open.

As Brenna tried to blink tears from her eyes, something wet and red splatted her on the cheek. She raised a hand to wipe it away then realized it was blood—it was raining blood. The *boom* of thunder sounded overhead, and from out of the clouds came an unkindness of ravens, their bodies limned in lightning. Their harsh cries blended with the din of battle and Brenna's screams, while through it all her body lay in the bed, twitching, shaking as she struggled to bridge the gap between sleep and wakefulness.

One of the ravens plummeted to earth. It grew larger as it dove; by the time it landed atop a rise in the landscape it had become a tall, red-haired woman, who caught Brenna's gaze across the battlefield. The rage in those cobalt eyes seemed to pierce through Brenna's heart. *Remember who you are, fealltóir,* the eyes seemed to say. *Remember where your heart lies, where your trust is given, where your vows remain. Come back to us.*

CHAPTER SIX

*C*ome *back to us, fealltóir...come back...come back...Brenna....*

"Brenna! Come back, now; you're safe. Shh. I have you. You're safe." A pair of arms circled her, and a familiar woodsy-spicy scent met her nostrils as she took a shuddering breath. Her body felt strange—heavy, cumbersome. But lethargy and a sense of calm began to steal over her as a man's voice murmured to her in Irish. She had just enough strength to close her hands over his upper arms, lean her head against his shoulder and rest her forehead in the curve of his neck, but somehow that was enough. She slept.

The alarm clock woke her early the next morning. Still groggy, Brenna blinked and tried to focus on the numbers, none of which made sense for several moments. Then, memories of the nightmare began to filter through the haze. War cries, spears, blood everywhere. The beautiful golden man falling before a monster's sword, his eyes full of shock and disbelief. And worst of all, the woman whose name Brenna somehow knew was Anand, hair flying and eyes full of rage, staring into Brenna's soul across a battlefield full of men and monsters.

Why had she called out the name Fealltóir? It wasn't a proper name—Brenna was sure it wasn't—and the memory of how it had sounded on Anand's lips made her feel shaky and ill. But for that matter, who was Anand? Brenna had no answers.

Stiffly, she sat up and got out of bed. It had all been just a vivid nightmare, that's what. She'd probably slept in the same position all night, which would account for the kinks and stiffness. Nothing a hot shower and a cup of tea couldn't fix.

As she reached for her robe, her gaze fell on the pillow. For a moment, she stared at it, frozen. Then her heart started pounding again, all thought of caffeine drowned in the rush of adrenaline. The pillow was smeared with blood, far too much of it to have come from a nosebleed, dried into a stiff, reddish-brown mess that no amount of washing would remove.

"Oh, shit! This isn't happening. This just...isn't...happening!" Brenna ran down the hallway to the bathroom and looked into the mirror. Her hand shook as she touched her hair, which was matted with dried blood. It looked as though—

"I've been in a war zone," she finished the thought aloud. She could have sworn she'd only been dreaming, but this was blood—real blood. If something looked and smelled like blood, then ergo.... Somehow, she *had* been in a war zone, one where people—even now she couldn't quite call them humans—fought monsters, and showers of blood rained from the sky. She'd been here and she'd been there, both at once. If she reported this, the gardaí would think she was a kook they should lock up or ship back to the U.S. on the next available boat. They'd never trust her on an airplane at this rate—not unless they hogtied her and dumped her into the baggage compartment.

Somehow, her life had become the script for a horror movie.

That thought kept repeating itself as she washed the blood out of her hair and off her body. She scrubbed so hard that when she'd finished, her skin felt tingly and raw. Maybe it was foolish, but she couldn't resist the urge to peek around the shower curtain every few moments. It took a while before she felt clean enough to leave the water.

Returning to the bedroom, Brenna dressed hastily, then stripped all the linens off the bed. She bundled the pile into her arms, carried it to the living room and poked up the fire, adding peat to coax it back into a blaze. When it was ready, she cut the linens up with kitchen shears and then burned the strips one by one, until nothing remained but ash. She could buy the landlord more sheets, but she wouldn't have been able to explain why the old ones looked as though a person had been murdered on top of them. It was a good thing the mattress was covered in some kind of plastic wrapper, or there'd be hell to pay.

Hell. Oh, how apt. Still shaken, Brenna went into the kitchen to make herself some tea and toast. Maybe the normal morning routine would take away the horror that lingered in her mind. Maybe. One could hope.

Belatedly she remembered the black dog. She peered out through the kitchen window, craning her neck to see down the side of the house to the front steps, but the dog was gone. A little disappointed to find that her visitor had left early, Brenna began to clear up the remains of her breakfast. It would have been nice to have someone to share another piece of toast with, even if that someone couldn't hold up a conversation. The dog could have listened to her talk about the nightmare without passing judgment.

A phone call from the garage distracted her for a while, but soon her thoughts returned to blood and nightmares. Desperate, she pulled out her laptop and began to work on the article. *Blood.*

Nightmares. Bloody nightmares.

Normal. She needed normal. Doggedly, she filled in yesterday's details and rearranged picture files, but no matter how much she tried to focus on her work, the dream images kept crowding into her mind.

She pushed on for almost half an hour, but it was no use. She kept fingering her hair, half-afraid her hand would come away smeared with blood. When a loud croaking sound came from outside the kitchen window and she saw a large crow peeking in at her from the windowsill, she couldn't take it any longer. She glared at the crow, slammed the laptop closed, got up and grabbed her coat, keys and purse.

She opened the door so hard it banged against the side of the cottage, startling the crow into flight. It landed in the nearest hawthorn, and Brenna could feel its beady gaze on her back as she crossed the yard and headed across the connecting fields to Annie's.

"It was real blood, Annie! Even assuming magic is real, how do we explain that?"

Brenna realized she was gripping her tea mug hard enough to whiten her knuckles. She had to relax her fingers before she broke Annie's hand-thrown pottery. The steam from the herbal tea rose in a fragrant cloud that teased Brenna to inhale, relax and stop taking things so seriously. Unfortunately, she couldn't. Like it or not, it was time to deal with the problem before things got further out of hand, and apparently, that meant embracing her inner witch.

"Theoretically, it's possible to exist in two realities at once," Annie said. She looked calm, as if what Brenna had told her was commonplace. "If you were, as you describe, flipping back and forth between the physical state of your dream and the physical state of your waking life, then it might explain why some of what happened in the dream carried through."

Brenna shook her head. "But that's impossible, isn't it? There's only one reality. A dream is just...well, a dream."

"Not always," Annie said. "Sometimes a dream can be a memory, or a precognition of something to come."

"Well, given the gods-and-monsters motif, I doubt it was either of those. I mean, this was like a battle scene from an epic fantasy movie, but...different."

Annie studied her, frowning. "Nevertheless, my feeling is that your subconscious is trying to tell you something important."

"What, you mean like Freudian theory? What about the blood? You can't just combine psychology with quantum physics and go on like everything's normal."

"I'm not. I'm combining magic with quantum physics, with a dash of psychology thrown in."

Brenna found she was throttling the mug again, so she set it down. Her hands felt empty without it; the rest of her just felt cold. She managed a weak grin. "Well, thanks for clearing that up. I feel so much better now."

Annie held up a hand. "Humor me for a moment. You came for help, and it's help you'll get. I want you to recount every strange thing that's happened to you since you stepped off the plane, even the parts you've already told me. There has to be a pattern we're not seeing."

Brenna thought back to her arrival at Shannon Airport. Nothing had seemed weird until she'd encountered the Wild Hunt on the way to her cottage. Concentrating, she traced a verbal path forward from there. Partway through, Annie held up a hand.

"Wait. You said that when you were on top of Rath Cruachan, you spoke in a different language? Spontaneously?"

Brenna nodded. "Yes. The only other language I know at all is some college-required Spanish, but it wasn't that."

Annie studied her for a moment. Then she got up, walked to a bookcase and returned with a large green clothbound volume, which she held out to Brenna. "This might be of interest to you. Why don't you look at it for a moment while I stoke the fire. It's chilly in here."

Brenna took the book. It didn't look unusual, other than that it was coffee table sized and Annie didn't seem to have a coffee table. When Brenna opened it, though, her fingers tingled. She glanced at Annie, but the other woman's back was turned as she added peat to the fire.

"*Cath Maige Tuired*," Brenna read aloud. When Annie still didn't turn, she shrugged and read further. In moments, she was lost in a fascinating saga of tyranny and injustice.

"Can you tell me what that book is about?" Annie asked as she returned to sit in the chair across from Brenna.

Brenna looked up to find Annie watching her. "It's about a conflict between two ancient races—the Tuatha De Danann and the Fomoire. The Fomoire enslaved the Danann for a long time, but then the Danann rebelled, won a huge battle against the Fomoire and took control of Ireland. But why ask me? I assume you've already read it?"

"I have, yes," Annie said. "But you shouldn't be able to."

Brenna frowned. "Why not?"

Annie was looking at her as if she'd just sprouted wings. "Because, my dear, that book is written in Irish."

"What? No, it's...not..." Brenna looked back at the page in front of her. To her surprise, the words that had been so clear a moment ago had morphed into a series of complicated spellings that bore no resemblance to anything she'd ever tried to read before. And yet...if she slipped back into a partial trance and allowed them to tease at the edges of her mind, they almost made sense.

"Annie, how is this possible? I was reading this—but now I can't. When I first looked at it, it made sense to me."

"My guess is that some part of you knows how to read *Gaeilge*."

A shiver traveled from the base of Brenna's neck down her spine. It was just like the other night with the Irish radio station, only worse. "I've never lived in Ireland, Annie. I was born in Vermont, spent a few years in Washington State as a child, then later moved to Oregon. I've been to Canada a few times, Mexico twice, and Europe never before this."

"Oh, I don't mean in this lifetime. In fact, it needn't even have been in Ireland. You could have learned how to read *Gaeilge* anywhere Irish people tended to settle, in any century since the written language developed. You may have spoken it long before that. But that isn't what matters most. I suspect that whatever all these strange events relate to dates from more than a few decades back. Your current body might be in its thirties, but your soul is much older."

"Great. As if the Wild Hunt, faeries, and magical vandals weren't enough, now I've got past lives haunting me? When does it end?" Brenna threw up her hands then slapped them down on her thighs.

Annie gazed at her, unperturbed. "I think the real question is when did it begin? You mentioned that the voice at Oweynagat said you'd returned from exile beyond the ninth wave. Long ago in this land, traitors were exiled, taken out to sea well beyond the ninth wave, and set adrift in a coracle with no paddle. The fact that the voice mentioned the ninth wave to you suggests that a past life is deeply involved. I think you should do a hypnotic regression to find out which of your former lifetimes is connected to this one, and why."

Great. This whole thing had passed strange and gone straight to bizarre. Brenna took a deep breath and let it out. "Well, I still don't see how a monster nightmare and a disembodied voice could have anything to do with a past life, but I'm getting desperate here. Whatever you want to do, let's do it."

"Just like that? You seem to question esoteric things, so I wasn't sure you'd want to do this."

"Hell yes, I question everything. Usually, that's part of my job. But you're right about this; I need to know what's happening to me. If a regression can help me understand any of it, then I need to do it."

Annie gave her a half-smile. "You could always go back to the States."

"Well sure, that's probably my safest bet. But for as long as I can remember, I've wanted to come to Ireland, and most of this trip is on the magazine's dime. I'm permanent staff, not freelance, and that's rare for a travel writer. If I go back without even one article, I'll lose my job. I've worked for too long to get where I am to allow that to happen. Plus, I hate the idea of running home like a scared little girl, especially if part of what I'm running from is myself. I'll just have to deal with this as best I can until I have what I came for."

Trixie, Annie's cat, picked that moment to jump onto the chair arm. Purring, she butted her patchwork head against Brenna's hand before settling into sphinx position. Brenna stroked the cat; it was better than clutching a tea mug for comfort.

Annie nodded. "Well then, it appears we have some work to do. I suggest we get started right away."

"Great. What do I have to do?"

"Make yourself comfortable." Annie gestured toward the couch.

Minutes later, Brenna lay on her back under a quilt, shoes off, eyes closed, listening as Annie guided her through a meditation. The combination of warmth and quiet punctuated by an occasional pop from the fireplace and the drone of Annie's low voice lulled Brenna into a sense of relaxation she hadn't known in a long time.

"At the bottom of the stairs, you find a hallway lined with doors on both sides," Annie said. "Walk down the hallway until you come to the door you are most drawn to. Stop in front of it. This is the door to the past lifetime most related to the events of your current one. Behind it, you will find the answers you need. When you are ready, open the door."

Brenna visualized the hallway as Annie instructed. On the way down it, she glanced back and forth at the doors. They were different sizes, shapes and colors, but none stood out in any way she recognized as special. She went on for what seemed a great distance, but felt no pull toward any door in particular.

As the doors began to look increasingly dilapidated, her mental steps began to slow. The end of the hallway lay just a short distance ahead—she could see a portrait of herself on the wall there—but still none of the doors called to her. It looked as though she wouldn't find any answers here, despite what Annie thought.

Damn it! Why couldn't she have an easy answer, just once? Despite the freakiness, it would have been helpful to find a past life connection at work, to find that she had some ability or destiny that could explain what was happening. Apparently, though, that wasn't the case. She didn't know whether to be relieved or disappointed.

The last door on the right looked as though it belonged on the front of a thatched hut like the ones she'd seen on TV documentaries about ancient African societies. She hesitated. Should she go through it as a last-ditch effort, or turn around and start back up the corridor in the opposite direction? Maybe she'd missed the door she was supposed to have opened on the way down. That'd be just her luck. Brenna spun in a slow circle, scanning the hallway.

As she turned, she noticed something in the left corner, just to the side of her portrait. It wasn't a door, exactly, but looked more like the opening of a passage tomb like the ones she still needed to visit for her article research. She shivered, caught by the image. Most passage tombs were megalithic, weren't they? Something told her this one was even older. Spiral patterns marked each of the stone uprights, and groups of short lines crossing or perpendicular to another long line marched across the capstone—some kind of ancient script? When she inhaled, she caught the mingled scents of earth, lichen and lime.

This was the one. The answers were here, or nowhere. Brenna reached out to touch the stone, then snatched her hand away. All her instincts screamed at her not to go in, but at the same time, she felt a pull like nothing she'd yet experienced. Fear tempted her to hurry back up the hallway, open one of the other doors and perhaps observe the life of a farmer in Japan in 1700, or a British housewife in the 1920s. But this portal in the corner, slightly askew from the normal march of time, had to be the answer, like it or not.

Brenna took a breath, then ducked beneath the capstone before she could change her mind. Hunched over between the uprights, she moved inward, then downward. Almost immediately a grey light began to filter through a vertical crack at what must be the far end of the tomb. When she touched the crack, it widened. She passed through, emerging into the purplish light of near-dawn on the other side.

As though from the other end of a long tunnel, she heard Annie's voice, still trying to guide her. "Once you have stepped through the door, look around you. Notice where you are."

Brenna's perception split, as though she were both observing and participating in the memory. She saw herself in a clearing surrounded by oaks and hawthorns, and she wasn't alone. Even as that detail registered, a leaf-bladed knife whipped through the air toward her. She ducked just in time and the knife stuck fast in a tree trunk. Nearby, a woman in black leather armor circled her, mixed fear and loathing apparent on her face even in the darkness. In fact, the dark seemed not to impede her vision much at all. Brenna matched the woman's steps, anticipated her next move. From the depths of her mind, a black rage surfaced. One of them would not leave the clearing alive.

Brenna glanced down at herself and saw that she wore similar armor. The other woman, then, was a fellow warrior from the same group. That couldn't be good. In fact, the whole situation was wrong. This fight should not be happening, should never have begun.

The other woman—Clothra, that was her name—moved in as if for a blow, then feinted to the left and lashed out with a splayed hand. The spell shredded Brenna's armor as though it were cardboard. Pain lanced through her side and she felt the rush of warm blood. It was bad, but not fatal if she ended the fight quickly. Hounds bayed somewhere in the distance; she had to hurry.

The patterns of a last, desperate spell whirled through her thoughts. She formed it, powered it with some of her life energy, and hurled it at her opponent with all the force hate could muster. Like a ball of solid air, it struck Clothra in the face and snapped her head to the side. She crumpled, wheezing. Brenna was on her before she hit the ground. Brenna's knife hand whipped up and back.

"Please, Daireann, no!" Clothra rasped. Her eyes flashed with terror, but it was too late. Brenna's knife plunged toward Clothra's unarmored neck....

"No!" Brenna's eyes shot open. She bolted upright, startling Annie, who stifled a shriek. After a moment, Annie put a hand on Brenna's shoulder and pushed her back down onto the couch.

"What happened? What did you see?"

Brenna blinked, trying to focus on Annie's striped wallpaper rather than on the image that seemed stuck in front of her mind's eye. She was shaking, and for a moment, she thought she might pass out.

"I can't...."

"Goodness, you're a mess. Take a couple of deep breaths. In...out...in...out. Try to think objectively about what you saw, as though you were just watching a film. Did you see anything that might explain what's been happening to you?"

"I'm not sure. I saw myself kill someone, but I'm not sure how a murder I committed in my very first lifetime could possibly—"

"Wait. Did you say your *first* lifetime?" Annie drew back, her gaze sharp on Brenna's face. "Most people never see back that far. Ancient lives, yes, but...your *first*? How many would you say you'd had since then? About how many doors back was it? Twenty, thirty?"

Brenna thought back to the hallway. "Um...if I count this lifetime, one-thirty-nine is the number that pops into my head."

"One hundred and thirty-nine?" Annie repeated, sounding shocked. "Jesus, Mary and Joseph!"

"That's an unusual number?" Brenna asked, though by the expression on Annie's face she needn't have bothered.

"It's a little unusual, yes," Annie said at last. "To begin with, you'd have had to die young in a number of subsequent lifetimes in order to have had so many, even if your first lifetime happened early in the history of man. And then there's your specific total. In magical numerology, three is the number of binding and establishing, and nine is the number of wholeness and completion. If we were dealing with an Eastern belief system, I'd say you have some serious Karma coming due—right here and now. Can you tell me what you saw?"

"Well, the whole thing was...odd." Brenna sat up cross-legged on the end of the couch.

"Odd, how?"

"Odd as in the door looked like a megalithic tomb, but the society on the other side wasn't Stone Age. It was more like ancient Celtic, but that isn't right, either. I think my name was Daireann. I was a warrior in black armor, and so was the woman I was fighting." Brenna's hands tightened on the quilt, which she'd dragged up around her shoulders. She forced herself to recount the story as far as she'd seen it. "I think I killed Clothra, even though she pleaded with me not to," she finished after a few moments.

"What do you mean, you think you killed her?" Bless Annie; she looked more intrigued than shocked.

"Well, I had my knife ready to plunge into her throat, but I didn't stay to see the actual stab," Brenna went on. "I'm sure I did kill her, though. We were the only two in the clearing, and with all the hate I had for her, there couldn't be any other end to the fight."

"Hmm. No battlefields? No monsters?"

"No. No monsters. Unless you count me." That was true, and yet...was it possible the battlefield dream and this past-life memory were connected? What would be the consequences if they were?

Annie sighed. "Well, whether that was your first lifetime or not and whether it related to your dream or not, you need to go back and see the rest. In my opinion, you didn't see enough."

"I saw enough to know I was seriously messed up in that lifetime," Brenna said, shuddering. "I can't get those images out of my head. If I was a murderer, any number of spirits from my past could be after me for revenge, and I'm not sure I even blame them."

"But you didn't see what led to the...killing...and you didn't see what happened after. You barely know any details about the society and your people. You've left a lot of information behind. For that matter, how do you even know it was murder?"

"It had to be. I felt such...guilt. It was overpowering. Even right now, when I think about killing her, I feel as though everything's closing in on me, as if I've done something I can never make up for—not in a hundred lifetimes." Brenna swallowed over the tightness in her throat. "I know I should go back and try to find out more, but I just...can't. Not yet. Thank you for trying to help me, though."

"Don't thank me," Annie said. "I didn't do anything. We don't yet have the information we need, and I can't help feeling that the magical vandalism and your other experiences are connected to this somehow. The circumstances are too unusual to be mere coincidence. I think we need to bring you up to speed on some psychic protection techniques, at the least."

Brenna considered for a moment, then nodded. "I suppose you're right. In fact, I know you're right. I just need a day or so to process all this, and then I'll call you, okay?"

Annie regarded her soberly. "Don't wait too long."

"I won't. And thanks again."

Brenna stood up and folded the quilt, then reached for her coat. The movements helped to further normalize the situation. By the time she reached her rental cottage, the horror of the morning had faded to the numbness of shock.

She was a murderer. Or she had been, once. She'd have to come to terms with that idea, not to mention the notion that dreams could be more than just dreams. Add the Wild Hunt and magic-using vandals to that mix, and it made for one freaky kettle of soup. Annie was right about one thing; she didn't know anywhere near enough to handle this type of situation on her own. She'd go sightseeing tomorrow to clear her head, and then she'd go back and learn whatever her witchy neighbor wanted to teach.

CHAPTER SEVEN

The next morning, Brenna was surprised to see Ronan striding up the walk. The sight of him brought back a foggy sense of him holding and comforting her after her nightmare, but of course that couldn't be the case. He couldn't have been here the other night; it was just part of the dream. But it had also been the one good part. Vivid, too. Even now, she could remember how his arms had felt around her, the scent of his skin, the sigh of his breath against her ear as he'd murmured to her....

Stop it, Brenna! she admonished herself. *You haven't broken up with Brad yet; you don't have any right to let this guy comfort you, even in your dreams.* Nevertheless, she still owed him an apology.

"Good morning, Ronan," she said as she led the way into the kitchen. "Would you like some tea?"

"I appreciate the offer, but no," he said, smiling. "I came to see how you are. Did you have any trouble last night?"

"You mean, other than insomnia from having too many things on my mind?" Brenna stared at his face, but saw only warmth and concern in his eyes. The urge to trust him was stronger than ever.

Maybe the question wasn't so much whether to trust *him*, but whether to trust her intuition about him.

"I would be glad to listen, if you want to talk," Ronan said, which confirmed that he couldn't be just a harmless, normal guy. Most guys she knew didn't want to listen to women talk; they just endured it whenever they couldn't get out of it. That was what Brad did, anyway. Five minutes of attention, tops, and then his eyes would start to glaze over. Once or twice he'd even wandered away right in the middle of her sentence.

"That's nice of you, but I'm not sure you really want me to burden you with my problems."

"You are no burden," Ronan said, and Brenna's cheeks heated. "At least your vandals have not returned."

Brenna's pulse sped up at his words. "As far as I can tell, Annie's spell worked. No more curse sigils. But I did have a visitor last night and the night before. A stray dog showed up and went to sleep on the doorstep. He was gone both mornings, but he acted as though he was familiar with the place. I wonder whether he lives at one of the farmhouses in the area. Maybe someone who lived here used to feed him once in a while."

"Anything is possible," Ronan said. "And just so you know...that protection spell was not only Annie's. I added more wards to it, just in case."

"Uh...okay. More wards are good." There. She hadn't said thank-you. For whatever that was worth. Something about that particular quirk nagged at the back of her mind, but she couldn't quite pin it down.

He smiled at her. "I understand that much of what is going on seems strange to you. I cannot blame you for your wariness, but please know that I will do everything in my power to see that you take no harm."

She met his eyes, and they stared at each other for several

moments in silence. His gaze was so warm, so caring. And something...more. It made the breath catch in her throat.

"Ronan?" she managed finally.

"Yes, Brenna?"

"What are you trying to say? Are you going to try to scare me again? Because if you are, I don't want to hear it. I'm already way, way over my comfort level on the subject of magic and faeries and magic-wielding vandals, and I'm still not completely sure you're on the up and up."

Ronan's eyebrows rose. "On the...up and up? This is some odd American phrase? Since I'm not familiar with the term, I cannot assure you that I am any such thing. But I can assure you that my intention this morning is not to alarm you. I came to ask if you would consent to my accompanying you on your pilgrimage. I would like to make up for my rudeness the day I saw you in Tulsk."

Well. That wasn't what she'd expected, but he seemed so concerned for her that her rehearsed apology flew out of her mind altogether. Spending the day with him would give her a way to get to know him better, and, perhaps, they could both make up for past mistakes. He chose that moment to give her a smile that made her whole body tingle.

And fools rush in....

"Ah—I suppose that would be all right," she told him, hoping she didn't sound as breathless as she felt. "My pilgrimage, as you call it, will include a drive to Knocknarea, in Sligo; I want to see Queen Maeve's cairn. The garage called yesterday to say my car's ready early, so we won't have to take the bus."

Ronan cocked his head, considering. "Knocknarea. Yes, that is perfect. If we go on from there toward Galway, we will reach the caves of Keshcorran. If you desire to visit many of the Sidhe mounds and sacred sites in Ireland, you must see that one."

"Well, sure, that sounds great. Let's go, then. I have my

daypack ready. We'll have to walk into town to pick up my car, unless you already have transportation."

"No, I do not drive. But otherwise, I am at your disposal. Get your things and let us be gone."

"Okay. Just give me a moment." Brenna turned her back to make sure the fire would burn out on its own, which also hid her amusement at Ronan's old-world manner of speaking. It was charming, if a little quaint. But she'd take it and the old-world manners that seemed to go with it. There were worse ways to spend a day, and far worse company to spend it with.

At the garage, Brenna paid the final bill and made sure her rental papers and insurance were in order. It was a relief to have the car back; quite a few of the places she wanted to visit were off the beaten track and not all had tours available, especially now, well after summertime.

Standing beside it on the sidewalk, Ronan eyed the Fiesta but made no move to get in. "You mean to drive us to Sligo—in *this?*"

Brenna gave him a wicked grin. "Why not? I know it's not a limo, but I'm not that bad a driver. I promise to stay on the left side of the road." She opened her door and got in. In a moment, Ronan followed suit, and after a delay while he wrestled with his seat belt, they were off down the N5 freeway to Tulsk, where they turned onto the N61 north to Sligo.

At first, Ronan seemed tense, but gradually as they zoomed along through the gorgeous countryside, he appeared to relax and enjoy the ride. Brenna listened, fascinated, as he related details about various landmarks she'd never seen mentioned in any of the guidebooks. He and Colm were both fonts of information about historic Ireland. With Colm, it made sense because of his archeology career. But Ronan's knowledge went so deep that it almost seemed as though he'd stepped out of the pages of some historic novel.

At a lull in the conversation, Brenna gathered her courage and asked him the question that had been on the tip of her tongue all morning.   "Listen, Ronan, since you seem to know your history—can you tell me anything about a warrior woman called Anand? And about...someone called *Fealltóir?*"

Ronan looked at her sharply. "Where did you hear that name? Was it listed in one of your history books?"

"Well...no. It was in my nightmare, two nights ago. I know that sounds strange, but—"

"No. It does not sound strange at all. Tell me about Anand. What did she look like? Did she say anything to you?" He seemed interested, and it was a relief to give in to the temptation to confide in someone. Besides, even if she didn't know him all that well yet, dreams were a safe topic, weren't they? Everyone had them. As they neared the outskirts of Sligo, Brenna told Ronan the details of the dream as clearly as she could remember them. Some of it had been a bit fuzzy.

"That's all I remember," she said at last. "I think something woke me then, because the battlefield just faded away. I...I think I fell back into normal sleep after that." Her face tingled as she remembered the last part of the dream—the part where he had held her in his arms. He definitely didn't need to hear that juicy little detail.

Ronan's blue eyes searched hers. "Anand is the Morrigan's common use name. She is known by several other names and titles as well."

Brenna squirmed in her seat. The Morrigan, again. Why would she have nightmares about an ancient Irish battle goddess?

She realized she'd asked the last question aloud when Ronan spoke. "Technically, *an Mór Ríoghain* is not Irish, Brenna. She is of the Tuatha De Danann, a race far more ancient than even the earliest Irish."

The Tuatha De Danann. They'd been in Annie's book—the one written in *Gaeilge*. Realization tightened Brenna's hands on the steering wheel. If Anand was one of the Tuatha De Danann, then it was likely that she, Brenna, had once had something to do with the Danann as well. Could they have been the people she'd seen in the memory regression—Clothra's people? Surely not *her* people, since she was human. But she'd been fighting against Anand—the Morrigan—in the dream. Could it be that the battle in her nightmare and the battle in Annie's book were the same? She had a terrible suspicion that they were. Her stomach clenched, and she felt again that closed-in sensation she'd experienced after the regression.

"Brenna? Are you well?" Ronan was asking.

No. "Yes, I'm...fine. Tell me about *Fealltóir*."

Ronan frowned. "That isn't a name at all. It means betrayer. Was someone called *fealltóir* in your dream?"

"Ah.... Oh, look! We're here," Brenna said brightly, suddenly desperate to change the subject. They'd arrived in Sligo proper, and she'd spotted a café with convenient parking.

She'd also murdered one of the Tuatha De Danann and betrayed the Morrigan in her very first lifetime.

As she pulled the car over to the curb and parked, some part of her brain was gibbering in fear. "Are you hungry? I am. Come on; it's my treat," she managed to say. Normal. She needed something normal right now.

Ronan looked as though he'd have preferred to stay on their previous subject, but he got out of the car and accompanied her into the café.

All through the lunch she could barely taste, Brenna's thoughts were full of chaos. She kept seeing the Morrigan's beautiful, angry face in her mind's eye, hearing again that word that held all the weight of shame and devastation. *Fealltóir.* Betrayer. How could she have murdered someone and betrayed the Morrigan? She'd never betrayed anyone—well, in *this* life, she hadn't. Her friends knew she was loyal beyond the call of duty. Her co-workers knew she'd never stab them in the back. An image of her knife arcing down toward Clothra's throat rose in her mind, but she pushed it away.

Fealltóir. It felt as though something slimy was oozing all over her soul. No problem she'd ever encountered before had seemed this horrible; no disagreement or falling-out had ever hurt so much. Worse, she could no longer explain the feelings and memories away or dismiss the fact that what was happening was real. She felt like a small animal whose hiding place had been exposed.

If she was a murderer and an oathbreaker, at least it explained some things. The fae encyclopedia said the Wild Hunt was usually sent out to hunt down traitors, and the Sidhe Ronan said was after her could be some kind of enforcer. Maybe she'd escaped before, and this was the first lifetime in which she'd returned to Ireland and effectively put herself back into Sidhe jurisdiction. Maybe she hadn't gotten between the Wild Hunt and its prey that first night. Maybe she *was* its prey.

Staring down into the depths of her teacup, Brenna shivered. It seemed as if all the boundaries between myth and reality had begun to blur the moment she'd set foot on this island.

The view from the top of Knocknarea was amazing, as was the fact that a person could see five counties from the summit. No wonder so many people believed that the cairn here belonged to a Celtic ruler as fierce and proud as Queen Maeve.

By the time Brenna had taken several digital photos and hiked back down to the car park again, she felt better than she had in days. The fresh air—not to mention the idea of walking in places where legendary heroes once walked—filled her with energy and beat back the sense of foreboding she'd struggled with all morning. The professional, rational part of her brain had managed a reboot.

Or maybe her improved mood had more to do with her present company; she'd be lying to herself if she didn't admit that much. With Ronan as a tour guide, it was almost impossible to stay upset. The longer she was with him, the more she was able to relax. His courtly manner aside, he'd told her fascinating things about the landscape and history that no guidebook could match. Besides, she'd be a poor travel writer if she couldn't appreciate great scenery when she saw him—ah, *it*.

Back in the car park, Brenna gave Ronan a smile of pure exuberance, and nearly laughed aloud when he returned it. Odd, how such a little thing as two people flashing teeth at each other could make the worry recede further, but it did. So far, this one day had been worth the entire trip, and despite all the alarming things that had happened since she'd arrived, Ireland still pulled at her as much as ever.

Ronan remained silent as Brenna started the car and headed south toward Kesh, but often as she drove she caught him watching her, as if she were a puzzle he wanted to solve. Somehow, the notion didn't bother her as much as it had at first. Being with him here in the light of day, sightseeing and eating lunch together was so...normal. When he smiled at her from the passenger seat, she could almost believe that she hadn't met him in a field while on the run from a pack of mythical soul-eating hounds. Almost.

Not far south of Ballymote lay the caves of Keshcorran—seventeen caves located at the foot of a steep limestone cliff. Brenna parked the car just off the access road and she and Ronan headed toward the slope that led to the caves. He looked bemused as she madly snapped pictures, but she just grinned at him. Maybe Colm was right and Americans were—how had he put it?—festooned with cameras, but she meant to document all the sights and sounds of this experience that she could. Not all of it had to be for the article; some could be just hers, to look at later when she was back in the States feeling homesick for a country not her own. She was about to switch to video mode when Ronan laid a hand over hers, lowering the camera to her side.

"You have your images. Why don't you put that away for a time and just *be* here? Be here fully, experience the place with all of your senses, not those of a machine."

"Oh-kay. Sure. All of my senses. Why not?" She turned the camera off and stowed it in her daypack, but she knew she would just have to get it out again once they entered one of the caves. Jay and the editorial staff were nervous that they hadn't funded a trip for a photographer as well, but she'd show them they hadn't needed to. If she did this right, it was sure to lead to more international assignments, though she doubted she'd find any that appealed as much as this one did. Who knew? She might even be able to get Jay to send her back here again for some follow-up in a year or two.

Ronan took her hand to help her up the slope, and by the time they reached the top, she was hanging on with both hands, out of breath. Those last few feet had been damn slippery. Ronan, on the other hand, hadn't even broken a sweat. He reached to steady her, and although Brad's image intruded on her mind again, she was too busy gulping air to tell Ronan to remove his hand from her waist. She meant to tell him, but as soon as she recovered, he released her and led the way into one of the shallow caves. Moot issue. Never mind that she could still feel warmth where he'd touched her.

Okay, so she was attracted to the man; it didn't mean she was about to cheat on Brad. Maybe it was like Vegas—*what happens in*

Ireland, stays in Ireland. Right.

"Diarmuid and Gráinne lived in these caves while they hid from Finn Mac Cumhail," Ronan said.

Brenna looked down at the floor of the cave, muddy in places, spackled with sheep dung. Her lips quirked. "How romantic."

Ronan sighed. "Does nothing affect your modern cynicism?"

"Will you stop talking as though you just came through a time warp? Oh, wait, I get it. You're a Luddite, aren't you?" Brenna raised her eyebrows at him, but he shook his head.

"No."

"I see. Well, as long as we've cleared that up...." She turned around to look out from the cave mouth, and her own mouth dropped open in awe. "I think I get your point, anyway. This is even better than the view from Knocknarea."

Fields, farmhouses, hedgerows, blue sky with scattered clouds, all framed by the oval cave mouth—it was spectacular. No other word fit. Unwilling to take her eyes off the view for even a moment, she fumbled for her camera.

Ronan's growl of disapproval arrested her motion and turned her to face him. "This cave connects through the Otherworld to Oweynagat. Close your eyes for a moment, then tell me you can't feel it."

"Wha—?" Brenna had one startled instant to decide whether to back up—or not—before he loomed in front of her, put one hand at her waist to pull her closer and cupped the back of her head with the other. Then his lips descended onto hers and she forgot any retort she might have made.

What the hell is he doing? What the hell am I doing? Both questions went unanswered as she lifted her arms to twine around his neck. Her fingers wound through the silken smoothness of his pale gold hair, felt the warmth of the skin at his nape. She shivered. He nipped lightly at her lower lip, she inhaled a whiff of the tantalizing, wild scent that was uniquely Ronan, and then she was kissing him back as hungrily as if she'd gone centuries without a man's touch. Something screamed in the back of her mind for attention, some reason that she shouldn't allow this to happen, but she couldn't bring herself to care. Nothing remained in the world but the two of them. Here. Now. In this moment. He took the kiss further, and Brenna fell into a swirling blackness.

Ronan's arms supported her, but her body seemed heavy, as if she were rooted to the floor. She smelled the damp soil and limestone of the cave, the brackish smell of the trickling water, and let herself sink deeper into the earth, deeper into the man who held her. Some part of her was shocked when she hooked one of her legs around one of his to pull their bodies closer together, but at the same time another part of her sighed in recognition, in acceptance. Stillness enveloped her, like a blanket that blocked out sight and sound.

Then she heard it—the same slow *thrum* that she'd heard near the crossroads to Oweynagat, like a huge drum hidden deep below the ground. It vibrated through all her senses, pulling her into the water, soil and rock of the cave. Behind her closed eyelids, spiral shapes whirled into a vortex, down and down and down....

"No, stop! I can't!" It was her voice; at least, she thought it was. Something akin to panic crashed over her. Her eyes flew open. But she was back; she could see the cave and what lay outside it, as well as several darker clouds on the horizon that she hadn't noticed earlier. It looked like they were in for rain later. Normal, everyday world, with normal, everyday rain clouds. Normal.

Damn, why was she shaking? It hadn't been that good a kiss. Really.

"Forgive me. That was too much, too fast." Ronan pulled away from her, but her legs wouldn't move and she almost fell; she had to grab at his arms for balance.

"What did you do to me?" Brenna asked. Deep breaths. That should help.

"I grounded you. Helped you feel the lines of power—or at least that is what I intended. But you went deeper than I realized. When you sensed the trackway open between Keshcorran and Oweynagat, you panicked."

"Was that more *draíocht*? I may be planning to learn more, but I'm not so sure I need or want it used on me like that. I'll appreciate it if you don't do that again." Brenna let go of Ronan's arms; this time her legs held her weight—barely.

"Normally, I would not have. It's just that there is not much time left before...before you leave."

Brenna stared at him. The kiss had affected him, too; the evidence was there in the not-quite-steady tone of his voice, his quickened breath, the way he'd released her—gently but with obvious reluctance. She couldn't look at his lips; just the thought of them made her want to stumble back into his arms, which would be a serious mistake.

"Ronan, there's something you need to know. I have a boyfriend back home." There. It was out. Now he'd leave her alone.

"I'm not surprised. You're an attractive woman." He seemed unconcerned.

"Well, I've decided to break up with him, but since I haven't yet, I don't feel right about getting too involved with someone else. Call it an old-fashioned quirk, if you want. But I can't have you holding me or kissing me, or...grounding me."

He sighed. "I believe I already apologized for that."

"Yeah, for using magic on me, but not for...the rest."

He turned his back to her and stared out of the cave mouth. When he turned around again, she was relieved to see that he didn't look mad. The last thing she needed right now was to get a guy pissed off at her for leading him on—if that was what had happened. Right now, she wasn't clear on just who had done what to whom.

"I promise that I will not hold or kiss you again unless you wish me too. I apologize for doing so just now; I did not intend to make you uncomfortable." He spread his hands. "Will that suffice?"

"That'll do." She shot him an uncertain smile, but he didn't even blink. He just nodded as if the issue were settled and started off toward the cave mouth.

Feeling like the biggest putz on the face of the planet, she started after him. As she reached the opening, her hand brushed the rock. Vertigo hit her, hard. She scrabbled at the rock and tried to keep from tumbling out of the cave and down the slope. For one dreadful moment, the world spun around her and she couldn't see anything but the grey mist that filled her vision.

She shut her eyes, but she still saw mist. A moment later it parted, but then all she could see was a plain full of bodies. Some of them wore nothing but blue spirals like tattoos, while others sported varying degrees of armor. Huge, misshapen forms lay sprawled among palely handsome, humanlike bodies, but all bore hideous wounds. Gore bathed everything, and blackened gouges pocked the ground, as if some giant laser death ray had ripped through the battlefield at random.

Choking on the stench, Brenna scanned the battlefield, searching for...she wasn't sure whom. The fair-haired man from her dream, or the woman called Anand? So many of the corpses were mangled or burned beyond recognition that she had little hope of finding either one. Tears filled her eyes. When she began to sob, her knees buckled. One hit hard ground while the other sank into something damp and yielding; she didn't even want to know what it was.

Daireann! Brenna. See what is wrought when justice meets tyranny?

There is no gain without sacrifice. Look well, and remember.

Rain began to fall onto her face in stinging droplets, and a cloud loomed overhead, so black that Brenna stared at it in alarm. It hovered over the field of corpses for timeless moments before it broke apart into separate black forms, all croaking, cawing, descending on the slain. Skald crows, hundreds of them. The cleanup detail. Sickened, Brenna turned away. Something told her that the fair folk had triumphed over the monsters, but at what cost? At what cost?

"*Mór Ríoghain!*" she screamed into the wind. "Where are you? Why are you doing this to me?"

I have done nothing. Your pain is your own doing. Claim it, and remember.

"Brenna, are you well? Open your eyes. Look at me." A warm hand reached out to touch her face. She blinked, startled at both the touch and the dampness. Ronan was bending over her, his eyes shadowed with concern. The battlefield had disappeared, but the sky had gone grey and the wind was whipping raindrops down in harsh sheets.

CHAPTER EIGHT

Anger lanced through Brenna. How dare he? What game did he think he was playing? "Ronan, I thought you said you wouldn't use *draíocht* on me again!"

"I did no such thing. You just stopped and cried out. Then you fell. For a moment, I could not get you to respond." His concern and confusion seemed genuine.

Brenna's anger drained away as quickly as it had come. Of course, he hadn't done this—what had she been thinking? His dislike for Colm notwithstanding, Ronan was usually Mr. Chivalry, even when she disagreed with him. She had the feeling that if he made a promise, he'd keep it. Besides, she'd seen that battlefield before, in the nightmare.

She shivered. "I guess I had a vision, or a blackout. Or both. I don't know." Rain plastered her hair to her head and streamed down her face, and damn, it was cold.

"Do you feel strong enough to stand? The rain grows worse; we should get you somewhere dry."

Ronan put a hand under either of her elbows to pull her up.

That was when she realized that her knee was soaked from where she'd knelt in a patch of mud, but it didn't matter. If they didn't get back to the car right away, the rest of her would soon match the knee.

She took a step, then froze. She wasn't carrying anything, but she should have been. "My camera!"

"I have it. Hurry now, if you can."

She let Ronan steady her; in fact, at this point she wouldn't have made it back down the slope without him. On the way, the shower turned into a downpour. By the time they reached the car, Brenna was drenched and shivering. She fumbled the key into the ignition and cranked the heater, holding her hands up in front of the vents to warm them.

"You need some dry clothing. Do you have any with you?" Ronan asked.

"Um, I think I...yes, I do! I put an extra change of clothes in the duffel bag in the trunk—I mean boot. But in order to get it, I'd have to go back out there. I think I'm better off in here for the moment."

"What color is the bag?" Ronan reached for the door handle.

"It's black, but you don't have to—" Before she could finish the sentence, he was already out in the rain, headed for the back of the car. Belatedly, she remembered to hit the button to unlock the hatchback. Damn. Brad would never have volunteered to get out into a downpour like that. He'd have agreed that the heater was good enough and left it at that—not that she'd have blamed him.

In less than a minute Ronan was back. He slid into the passenger seat and handed her the duffel. She unzipped the bag, pulled out a pair of jeans and a sweatshirt, then realized that she had nowhere to change.

"Climb into the back. I promise not to watch."

Well, maybe he wouldn't, though for the promise of dry

clothes, she'd have stripped right in front of him if necessary. And even if he did peek, would that be such a bad thing?

With difficulty, she clambered into the backseat. Once there, she wriggled out of her soaked clothes in record time. She could make do without socks or bra, but the panties would just have to dry on her body; she wasn't about to wear jeans without them. Ronan faced front the whole time, but as she pulled on her dry things, her mind retuned to that kiss in the cave. His body had been so firm under her hands. His torso tapered to a trim waistline, but his shoulders were broad enough to suggest he worked out. What would he look like nude? What would it be like to kiss him with no barriers between them?

Brenna clamped her lips shut on a gasp of dismay. No. Oh, no; she *so* wasn't going there, and what the devil had brought up that thought, anyway? Back in the States, Brad must be going crazy wondering why she hadn't called him since the airport, and she owed him an in-person breakup before she did more than look at another guy. Anything else felt too much like cheating. The irony was that Ronan was being such a gentleman, while she was...well....

Brenna blushed as she tugged her sweatshirt into place. She wedged her feet into her damp shoes, then climbed back into the driver's seat. Guiltily, she glanced over at Ronan. If she had any luck at all, he wasn't telepathic in addition to being good at magic and too sexy for any woman's peace of mind.

"Better?" He arched an eyebrow at her.

She had to swallow before she could answer him. "Yeah." Then a different brand of guilt hit her. "Oh, no, you're still wet! I'm sorry; I wasn't thinking. Do you want me to drive back into Sligo so you can buy something at one of the clothing shops?"

He smiled. "That will not be necessary. These wool sweaters repel water, and I generate heat more easily than you do."

She eyed him, still dubious. He might be right; now that she looked more closely, he didn't seem to be as wet as she'd thought. In fact, even his jeans appeared only a little damp. How had he managed to stay so much drier than she had? Even as she puzzled over it, he pulled his dark grey Arran sweater over his head and tossed it into the backseat with his jacket. The blue flannel shirt he wore underneath seemed dry as well. Maybe he just happened to lead a charmed life.

Still acutely aware of Ronan, Brenna checked her map, put the car in gear and headed back toward Roscommon. She'd had enough tour for one day. Maybe typing up the middle section of the first article would serve to remind her of what she was here for.

It was harder to find convenient fast-food shops in Ireland than in the States, though they did exist. In Sligo, she stopped long enough to buy some sandwiches, then got back on the road to Strokestown. Ronan seemed horrified that she meant to eat while she drove, but after a brief protest, he subsided into his seat to stare at the road ahead. She offered him a sandwich, but he declined, so she had to eat both of them.

"Thank...I mean, I'm glad you went with me today. I learned a lot," she offered when the silence had begun to get on her nerves. The rain made for problematic visibility, but she needed to draw him out again, reclaim something of that carefree feeling she'd had earlier, before the cave experience.

"I enjoyed your company as well," he said. "But I am sorry that your experience at Keshcorran dampened your spirits."

"Well, it...what did you say?" Her gaze flew to his face. His mouth wasn't smiling, but his eyes were. Had he just made a joke?

"I do have a sense of humor, Brenna, despite what you might think." He did smile then, and she could have sworn the sun came out, though the rain hadn't stopped.

Wait a moment. The sun *had* come out, as though the day wanted to assert itself one last time before evening. It shone through the raindrops, casting rainbows at random.

"Oh, that's beautiful."

Ronan nodded. Yes, it is—careful!"

A horn sounded from behind them. In the rearview mirror, Brenna saw a green car pull out, ready to pass. But there was no passing lane, and a pickup barreled toward them in the other. By instinct, Brenna veered as far left as she could get without running off the road, while the pickup did the same on the other side. The green car shot through the space between them, gaining speed as it accelerated.

Brenna released her held breath, then filled her lungs again. Unbelievable. They were still alive, and the incident had taken less than ten seconds. Other than the way her heart pounded, there was no evidence that anything had happened.

"That was an experience I would rather not repeat," Ronan commented.

"Me, either," Brenna said. She took another measured breath. They were alive. No use freaking out about what might have happened.

The rain, which had slackened for a while, picked up again until it became a downpour. The car's steering changed, so Brenna firmed her grip on the wheel. They were close to home now—or what passed for home these days. All they had to do was make it just a few more miles, then they could wait out the worst of the storm in a warm pub. Something hot to drink sounded like bliss right about now.

The car drifted in the lane. When Brenna turned the steering wheel, the tires slipped. She eased off the gas, but it didn't help.

"What is wrong?" Ronan asked sharply.

"We're hydroplaning. Don't worry, we should be—oh, shit!" A horn blared. From the opposite lane, a truck blasted toward them. Brenna eased off the gas still more and tried to steer away, but the car might as well have been a metal box on pontoons. The truck didn't even try to give way. Its horn blared again, as useless as the Fiesta's steering.

There wasn't time to scream. Her body tingled, she felt a push from the right side, the car lurched sideways and the truck roared past, so close it almost brushed the car's side mirror. Feeling the tires connect with pavement, Brenna pumped the brakes. The Fiesta hit a puddle, then jolted to a stop in the ditch beside the roadway.

"Are you okay?" Eyes wide, Brenna looked at Ronan.

He nodded. "Yes. What about yourself? You look pale."

"Well, anybody would be, after a near-miss like that! I hate to be cliché, but...did anybody get the license number of that truck?" Brenna realized that her hands were shaking where they gripped the steering wheel. She forced herself to let go.

"License number? No," Ronan said.

"Well, that's okay. I didn't really expect you would have. We should have stopped in the last town, when I knew the road conditions were getting worse. Seems to be a habit of mine—driving when I shouldn't. Hang on; let's just pull to a flatter spot for a minute before we get back on the road."

She put on the gas, but the wheels on her side spun in the mud. Wonderful. Now they'd have to call for a tow truck. Again. At least this time she'd had the sense to get a cell phone before she got herself stranded.

Ronan was quiet, but he might need a moment of contemplation after the near-accident. Brenna peered at him, still not quite convinced they were both intact. Great. She'd almost killed him! She wouldn't blame him if he refused to ride with her again.

It took her a few minutes to call for a tow, but by the time she'd reported the accident and the towing company assured her they were on the way, her heart rate was back to normal—or what passed for normal under the circumstances.

Neither she nor Ronan said much while they waited. Once, he reached over and patted her hand, but most of the time he seemed preoccupied. Just when Brenna was about to break the silence, he grabbed his jacket from the backseat, opened his door and got out, undeterred by the rain or the failing light. As she watched, he began to walk around the car.

Brenna couldn't take it anymore. She got out and followed him as he paced. "What are you looking for? Do you think maybe if you pushed on the back and I gunned the motor, we could plow ourselves out of the ditch?"

"Perhaps, but that is not why I am out here. I have been thinking about the sequence of events since we left Keshcorran. I think we have a saboteur."

She frowned. "What do you mean?"

He glanced at her. "Just what I said. I think someone sabotaged the car. I should have thought to check for traces of *draíocht* before you began to drive."

"But it's been raining all day. We hit some water on the road and hydroplaned, that's all. It's just happenstance." *Please, let it be happenstance.*

"Is it? I'm not so certain of that. The storm came up suddenly while we were in the caves of Keshcorran, then not long after we returned to the road we had not one mishap, but two in succession. I could believe that one of those events was happenstance brought on by the weather, but both? The first near-accident was not related to the rain."

"Well, that's true." Brenna thought about it. Had the circumstances been normal, she might be able to chalk all of today's problems up to coincidence, but after the past several days.... The implications gave her chills. "I hate to admit it, but you may be right. But how?"

Ronan held his hands palm-outward toward the car as he continued to pace around it. He stopped in the front and squatted to look underneath. His shoes sank into the mud, but he didn't seem to notice.

Brenna found a spot of firmer ground to stand on and peered over Ronan's shoulder. "What is it?"

"Another sigil. A bind-rune and something else I don't recognize. From Annie's description of the one on your door, I would say this is similar, but more powerful."

"Great! Just freaking great! And wouldn't you know it; I don't happen to carry a bundle of herbs, a lighter, and a black feather in the glove box." She knew she sounded bitchy, but after all this, she ought to be entitled. Except that she was taking it out on Ronan again. Chagrin flooded her. "I'm sorry. I'm just stressed right now. How do we get rid of it?"

Ronan didn't answer her. Hands outstretched toward the car, he traced something in the air close to where he'd said the sigil was. Golden light flashed near the axle, and something in the air gave with a pop, like a burst balloon. After a few moments, Ronan straightened, dusting his hands together as if he'd soiled them somehow. To Brenna's eyes, his hands appeared to glow, but when she blinked, the light was gone.

"Finished," Ronan said. He started back toward the passenger seat.

"Wow. Didn't need a magic feather, huh? I'm impressed," Brenna said, happy to get back into the warmth of the car. She was damp but not soaked, thank goodness. One bright spot in a black hole. "How did you do that?" she asked when they'd shut themselves in again.

"It is difficult to explain. Think of it as if someone had tangled a ball of string, and then you found it and untangled it. Where once there was a pattern there is now a reversal of that pattern. It is...an unmaking, for lack of a better term."

Brenna frowned. "I think I get it. You just did it all in your mind?"

Ronan nodded. "Yes. I drew the energy through the Otherworld into this one, much as your enemies did when they made the sigil. That is an overly simple explanation, however. There is more to it, but we cannot speak of it now. Help has arrived."

Brenna twisted around to look over her shoulder. Help had indeed arrived—perhaps more help than she'd bargained for. There was a tow truck, whose driver was already moving his vehicle into position. But there was also a squad car. Now, where had they come from? Brenna's heart sank as two gardaí approached her door. When she rolled down the window, one of the officers leaned down to look at her. His short-cropped brown hair and grey eyes looked all too familiar; she recognized him as one of the two who'd responded to her call about the symbol on the cottage door. Garda O'Shea, he'd said his name was. Wonderful.

"Ah. It's you again," he said. "While you get out your license and papers, why don't you tell me what happened?" A smirk played around his lips—or maybe it was a grimace.

Brenna fumbled for the documents he wanted. "We had trouble with a lake in the middle of the highway, right about the time we met a truck. We slipped off the road. I think the car's okay, just stuck. The trucker didn't stop, and I didn't get his license plate number." *Someone sabotaged my car with another of those magical symbols you can't see. Can we just call it a day, already?*

"You were on the correct side of the road?" O'Shea asked.

"Yes, sir." She handed him the documents. He gave them a cursory scan and handed them back to her.

"And you—is that the way it happened, or were the Little

People to blame again?" he asked Ronan, who met O'Shea's sharp gaze with a level one of his own.

"It happened as she described it," he said, holding the garda's gaze for several long moments. The backs of Brenna's arms tingled, and she rubbed them absently, her eyes on Ronan. What was he doing?

O'Shea blinked, then nodded. "Right. Ma'am, I advise you to drive more carefully, then. And be sure to stay on the left side of the road. Have a safe evening."

He straightened up and left, stopping to speak to the tow truck driver before he drove off. Brenna fumed in silence. Left side of the road! He thought she'd had an accident because she'd pulled into the wrong lane! But that wasn't the only thing that bothered her.

As soon as the gardaí were gone, Brenna turned back to Ronan. "Did you do something to O'Shea? He looked like he was going to ask another question, then forgot. And for him to ask if I was on the wrong side of the road...why would he automatically assume that? Was it just because I'm American, or was there something more to that also?"

Ronan's tight smile confirmed her suspicions. "I did not wish him to continue his line of questioning, so I used a little—hypnosis, I suppose you would call it. I suggested different questions to him, and he made his own assumptions from there."

Brenna drew in a slow breath and let it out before she dared speak. "Do you often find that you need to control other people like that?"

He frowned. "Normally I do not. However, in this instance, would you have preferred me to have to explain to him that this happened because someone is empowering curse sigils and bindrunes against you?"

Brenna sighed. "No. He'd just think I was being the crazy

American again. I suppose it's better if he thinks I made a mistake—as long as he doesn't cite me for it. That was quick thinking." It was. But the idea that Ronan was that powerful was also a little disconcerting.

He shrugged. "I understand how difficult these last days have been for you, and I'd prefer to avoid any further problems. If you are ready, I suggest we get you safely back to your cottage now."

Relief flooded her. The cottage, and Annie's wards. If she was safe anywhere, she should be safe there, and it would give her time to think about today's events without worrying about stepping onto the wrong foot with Ronan.

"Now there's a good idea. I have a lot of work to do, and I'm a wreck."

As they retreated down the shoulder to watch while the tow truck pulled the Fiesta back onto solid ground, he gave her a look she was starting to recognize—concern, combined with something deeper that shook her to the core.

"Perhaps you should consider staying with Annie tonight," he said finally.

"Oh, I don't think that's necessary, do you?" Brenna asked. "After all, the freaks who did this don't have any reason to think their plan didn't succeed, right? I mean, they don't know I'm not bleeding on the road somewhere, and it'll take a while before they could find out for sure. Both you and Annie warded my house, so I should be fine for the night, at least. I'll talk to her about this when I see her tomorrow." She was babbling, but the words just tumbled out, arising as much from worry over her reaction to him as from his concern for her safety.

"I am not sure it is wise to wait," he said. "Today's events made it clear that your enemies have become more dangerous. They have begun to take more risks."

"Why do you say that?" Brenna asked, frowning.

"Because whoever cursed your car did it while we were in the caves. That is the only time we parked anywhere where there were not other people around. It is the only time the car was not in sight."

"Oh. Great. You're saying that they're following me around, now."

"Yes, I think it likely."

The chill was getting to her, but just as she started to shiver, he took off his jacket and wrapped it around her shoulders. She darted a look at him, but his expression hadn't changed.

"So I have at least one Sidhe enemy. And now I have another enemy who leaves nasty little magical calling cards. Do you think the two are related?"

Ronan shook his head. "If they are, I am not aware of it. The sigil on the car was a very human sort of spell. You can tell the difference by the way the *draíocht* was formed and directed. The clues are usually there in the energy left behind by the working—if you catch it before it dissipates."

"Could the human be working for the Sidhe you believe is after me?" Brenna asked. There had to be a connection.

Ronan looked surprised. "Possibly, but I doubt it. Direct human-Sidhe contact is rare these days. The situation would have to be extraordinary."

"Okay," Brenna said slowly, pulling his jacket closer around herself. "That's helpful to know, but now I'm not sure whether to be relieved or even more worried. What could these people want with me, if they aren't connected to the Sidhe or the Morrigan?"

"I do not know," Ronan said, and he sounded as worried and frustrated as she felt.

The man had no apparent reason to be so worried about her. Intense chemistry wasn't a reason, nor was the fact that he'd rescued her once before. It was even a little unnerving. Okay, a lot unnerving. Nevertheless, Brenna felt a sudden, irrational need to reassure him.

"Don't worry. Tonight I'm going to lock my doors, hole up with my laptop and try to do some of the work I actually came here for. I still doubt they'll do anything more right away, and after a little work with Annie, I'll know what to do to defend myself."

He gave her an exasperated look, but she stared him down. "I would offer to stay with you to help ensure your safety, but tonight I cannot. Just promise to be cautious regardless of the wards. No ward is unbreachable."

"I'm not taking anything for granted, Ronan," Brenna began huffily, but the look in his eyes stopped her from launching into a tirade. There was heat in that gaze, and it touched off a spark of awareness that zinged along her nerve pathways and threatened to bring on a replay of the careless moment in the cave, when she'd surrendered to instinct and an attraction she had no right to acknowledge.

He didn't touch her; he kept his promise and didn't even reach for her hand. But what his hands didn't touch, his gaze caressed, seduced, claimed. They stared at each other until the tow truck driver walked up to them with the paperwork, and Brenna realized she'd forgotten to breathe for some unknown amount of time.

Within minutes they were back on the road. Although the rain kept up a drizzle all the way to Strokestown, they had no further problems. Brenna dropped Ronan off near a bus stop as he requested, and after an awkward farewell, drove to her cottage.

Once alone, she could admit to herself that she'd have appreciated the security of his presence, had he been able to stay. But another part of her was relieved that he couldn't. That part of her was still trying to decide whether she could fully trust him. After all, he had hypnotized the gardaí so easily, and from what she'd seen, he seemed to have a lot of magical ability. Then there was the fact that along with misdirecting the garda's questions about the magic, he'd also managed to avoid giving them information about himself. He must have a reason for it.

For that matter, he still hadn't told her his last name, and with the...effect...he had on her, she kept forgetting to ask. That alone was frightening—or it should be, if she had any sense.

Hard as it might be to believe that magic was more than just a bunch of children's stories, she'd seen the flare of power when he'd removed the sigil. If magic was real and Ronan had that kind of power, mightn't it be possible that he'd been the one to put the thing on the car in the first place? If they'd collided with the truck, her side would have taken the brunt of the impact, while his magic might have protected him. The thought chilled her; she pushed it away. "Trust me," he'd asked her once. She wanted to, but he was holding something back from her; she could feel it.

Tomorrow, she would talk to Annie, but not just about psychic defense lessons. Whether or not Ronan was being honest with her, she was inclined to trust her assessment of the Irishwoman. Based on what Annie had to say, maybe she could put her doubts about Ronan to rest—or confirm that he was playing her. One way or the other, she needed more information before she did anything further.

The next morning Brenna phoned Annie, but got no answer. Biting her lip, she considered her options. She could wait and try calling again in a couple of hours; chances were good that Annie had gone into town or was outside and would soon be back. But what if she waited the two hours and then Annie still wasn't home? Magical stalkers or no, she still had a job to do, and she couldn't do it cooped up in the cottage.

If she went out today, she could keep an eye out for anyone suspicious. She could make sure she didn't leave and return to

Strokestown by the same road, and she had her cell phone in case it looked as though anyone was following her. Mace was illegal here, but with the house and car warded, basic precautions should suffice to keep her safe until she could figure out who was after her, and why.

She'd have to risk it. She wasn't about to wreck her career over some cultist weirdos—and that had to be what they were. Nothing else made sense; she didn't know enough people in Ireland to have made any personal enemies here, and the type of terrorists who hated Americans didn't tend to dabble in magic. A cautious excursion today should yield enough information to complete the first travel article. She'd call Annie again this evening and start magical defense lessons tomorrow—even though it would be Sunday, it was a safe bet that Annie wouldn't mind. Everything would be okay. The important thing was not to overreact; that was no doubt what the bastards wanted, and she wasn't about to give them that.

With that resolution in mind, she grabbed her camera and drove to Cong, close to the border between County Mayo and County Galway. As she'd hoped, the ruined abbey was picturesque enough to add to the article, but once there, she was drawn to the older sites nearby.

At the southeast end of the village she photographed a lichen-covered stone with five depressions carved into it. Her guidebook hinted that the prehistoric people who had made the nearby cairns might have created the stone for ritual purposes, which seemed likely. Even without Ronan or Colm there to give her details that weren't in the guides, she felt the pull of mystery. Who had lived in this place, centuries before? What were the standing stones for, and whose bodies lay in the cairns?

Something about the graves and circles in this area gave her a strange feeling, but she pushed on anyway. Once she got these pictures and notes home she'd have to organize the skeleton of the next piece. She wasn't about to tell Jay that she'd skipped any intriguing faery haunts just because they gave her the jitters. Too much caffeine made her jittery too, but she didn't plan to stop drinking it.

There were so many possibilities on her list that by the time she'd seen Cregotia, Ballymacgibbon, and Eochy's cairns, there was just time to shop in Castlebar for an Arran sweater like the one Ronan had worn yesterday and head back toward Roscommon. With luck, she'd have time to stop by Annie's on the way home. The good news was that she'd still managed a full day's work despite the erratic itinerary and constant looking over her shoulder for potential attackers.

By the time she pulled into Strokestown, late afternoon sun slanted through her car window. Her stomach lodged the complaint that she'd skipped lunch, so she headed for the café she'd earmarked as her favorite. She couldn't go see Annie on an empty stomach and trespass on her hospitality again, no matter how willing the woman might be to give it.

At the door to the café, Brenna heard someone come up behind her, though she hadn't noticed anyone that close to her on the sidewalk. A man's hand reached past her to close around the door handle.

"Allow me."

Stifling a shriek, she jerked around to face him. "Colm. We just keep running into each other."

He grinned. "And is that a bad thing?"

"No. Not in the slightest." Once she'd said it, she wasn't sure that was accurate. A part of her was glad to see him—he was the one with the I.D. and a verifiable job, after all. But another part of her—the part that was becoming increasingly gun-shy—was beginning to wonder just why Ronan had been so sure Colm was one of the Sidhe.

Colm smiled—the same movie-star smile she remembered from their afternoon at Rath Cruachan. "Since fate seems to keep throwing us together, why don't you let me buy you dinner? There's an informal *seisiún* near here tonight that we could go to afterward."

"A session? What's that?" Brenna asked. A polite cough alerted them to the fact that they were blocking the door. Colm turned his smile to the people behind them. With his free hand, he drew Brenna over beside him so he could hold the door open wider. The three women returned Colm's smile, but the man with them just gave a stiff nod as he passed into the café. Brenna couldn't tell whether he'd been mollified by Colm's manners or further miffed by the women's reaction.

At least the interlude gave her a chance to consider his invitation. She did need food, and no one was likely to attack her in a crowd. She'd led any potential murderers a merry chase today, since she'd been all over the place, never in one spot for long. They probably had no clue where she was. Besides, after the time she'd spent with Ronan, she wanted a chance to talk with Colm—make sure her initial assessment of him was correct. Since she wouldn't be alone with him, this was the perfect opportunity. With someone trying to kill her, and all the other weird things going on, she needed to decide whom she could trust. If Annie was right and she did have intuitive abilities, now was the time to use them.

Decided, she turned to her would-be companion, who still held the door for her. "I would like to have dinner with you, as it happens. I'd like to ask you questions about the sites I visited today."

"Good. That much is settled, then. I'm glad I caught sight of you." He followed her into the café, a guiding hand at her back. He even took her coat for her once they were inside. So far, so good.

After they were seated and the server had taken their orders, Colm continued with his previous topic. "A *seisiún* is a sort of musical gathering, true to the old forms and instruments. But after the traditionalists play, the younger set often starts in with the karaoke machine. It's a good way to loosen up after a day's work. It would also give you some local color for your article. What do you say?"

Brenna hesitated. She'd be pushing the safety envelope, but it *would* be fun to go out on the town. Maybe after she'd spent time at a party with nice, normal people who had nice, normal credentials, she'd be able to put all this past week's craziness into perspective.

"Yes, I'd like to," she told him.

"Perfect," he said, returning her smile. "I think you'll enjoy it."

Colm was legit on paper; he had a last name and a driver's license. He wouldn't have avoided giving the gardaí his information if he'd been in a car accident with her, and if he wanted anything from her, it was what any ordinary guy would want from a woman. Thank goodness for ordinary guys. In the time she'd known him, he'd given her no indication that he was anything but, which meant she was probably right and Ronan was probably wrong. The more she thought about it, the more sure she became.

He's just as good-looking as Ronan, and if I wanted to date him, I wouldn't have to wonder who he really is. The thought startled her so that she almost choked on a sip of water. Where had that come from? Yesterday, she'd fantasized about Ronan naked, and now she couldn't seem to take her eyes off Colm. She still needed to break up with Brad officially, before her libido kicked into a higher gear than it had already. And for that matter, as long as someone was stalking her, it was safer if she didn't fantasize about any guy.

The server arrived with their meals, which spared her from further conversation for a while. A couple of well-placed questions kept Colm in lecture mode, which left Brenna free to wrestle with the question of who her enemies might be and why they'd targeted her. She needed to be able to work without looking over her shoulder every minute, but if the gardaí couldn't help her, then how could she figure out what was happening?

"Brenna? Did you hear what I said?" Colm asked.

Brenna blinked. "I'm sorry; that was rude. I got distracted—too many ideas for the article in my head."

"Ah, you're a workaholic. I think I can forgive you for that, if you promise not to let your job keep you from enjoying the *seisiún*. Are you finished? We should go; it'll start soon." He checked his watch, then reached for the check.

"I'm ready." She couldn't back out of the party now, when he'd just bought her dinner. To tell the truth, she didn't want to go back to the cottage yet. Even stuffed-shirt Jay would think it strange if she didn't so much as comment about Irish nightlife. It was legit, and it might give her a chance to observe Colm with his guard down. How a person behaved with a few beers on board said a lot about his personality. She should find out, just to be absolutely certain she'd judged him correctly.

When Colm offered her his arm on the way out of the café, she hesitated. It was a common gesture here in Europe; she shouldn't read too much into it. But she'd waffled too long; or so she gathered from his slight frown. Had she offended him? Just as she started to reach for his arm, a hissing noise made both of them look down. A straggly-looking cat crouched against the wall near the alley, giving them the kind of evil glare that only cats do well. Colm glanced from the cat to Brenna, shrugged, grinned, and offered his arm again.

The cat began to wail, its back arched and tail fluffed out like a bottle brush. "Nasty little bugger, isn't he? Probably a stray," Colm said. "Someone ought to call animal control to pick him up."

"Yeah. He has got an attitude, doesn't he? Poor thing." Brenna took the opportunity to slip her arm through Colm's. He smiled at her and started them walking up the street, the awkward moment gone as if it hadn't happened.

When they entered the pub where the *seisiún* was to be, the place was full of laughing people, most of whom were watching a musician playing a *bodhrán* on a small wooden stage. As Colm found seats and ordered Guinness, Brenna allowed him to lead her. The bar atmosphere was familiar, but the talent and dedication of the performers was something else again. In the States, she'd have expected to pay a lot for a performance like this. Fiddle, drum, flute, voice...all were impressive, and Brenna began to feel as though she'd sneaked backstage without a VIP pass.

When the performance had begun to wind down, Colm smiled at Brenna and laid a hand on her arm. "I'll be right back."

Instead of heading for the bar as she'd assumed, he walked toward the stage. On the way, he stopped to confer with a man who'd played a flute solo earlier. The man grinned, nodded and handed Colm his instrument. Colm got up on the stage and began to play, a haunting melody that made people's eyes go round with astonishment. Before long, he had the attention of everyone in the pub. He coaxed sounds from the flute that Brenna hadn't known were possible, every note blended in a seamless melody that alternately made her want to tap her feet or burst out crying at the beauty of it.

She had no idea how long he played, but when he stopped, she jerked and blinked as though waking from sleep. Other people did, too, she noticed; he seemed quite gifted even by native standards. As far as Brenna knew, the U.S. had no flautist to compare with him. Why had he chosen to waste that talent on archeology? She'd have to ask him about his other hobbies. Bemused, she took another swig of her drink.

For several moments after he'd handed the flute back to its owner, the audience sat still, so quiet that Brenna could hear their collective breath. Then one man began to clap. Another followed his example, and soon the room rang with the smack of hand against hand and more than a few whistles. *Look out, folks! Elvis lives.*

"Wow," was her scintillating comment when Colm returned to their table.

"I'm glad you liked it, though *wow* might be a bit of an exaggeration. I've heard better." He was pleased with everyone's reaction, though. She could hear it in his voice.

"Nah! *Wow* doesn't even begin to cover it," Brenna said. "You should quit your day job, record an album. I swear that last jam made me dizzy. Or maybe that's just the Guinness talking." She could have sworn he glowed in the dim light from the hanging stained-glass lamps. He looked like a god with a cherub's smile and a body made for sin. Oh, yeah.

Oh, *no!* No, no, no! It was time to lay off the Guinness, if she intended to drive home. But she'd only had one or two, hadn't she? That shouldn't have been a problem. Wait. Hadn't she read somewhere that European brews were stronger than those back home? Or had she lost count? Shapes appeared hazy, and the room seemed to echo. She glanced at Colm and saw him watching her. A tinge of alarm sizzled through her veins along with the alcohol. Had he spiked her drink when she wasn't looking? She excused herself to go to the ladies' room, ignoring Colm's sharp look as she moved past him.

At the sink, she splashed water on her face and stared at the stranger she saw in the mirror. Her features were the same, but at this moment, she could swear she didn't have a clue just whom she was looking at. The Brenna Callahan she thought she knew would never drink more than she could handle. Who was this woman who lusted after guys she'd known for less than a week and couldn't remember how much stout she'd drunk in the past half-hour?

It would be easy to blame this on Colm, to believe he'd slipped something into her Guinness. But if he'd done that, wouldn't she have passed out by now? She wasn't unconscious; she could still think, even if it was a little too fuzzy for comfort. *Get a grip, Brenna,* she cautioned herself. *Get a grip, fast!*

As she made her way back to their table, she stopped at the bar to order a cup of strong coffee, even though she hated the stuff. It was time to wind things down, but she still needed time to process the last of the alcohol before she left the pub. If she was already to the stage of admiring the way Colm's ass looked in the trousers he wore, then no way could she let him drive her home.

CHAPTER NINE

Ring. Ring.

What a damned annoyance! Brenna groaned and turned over. *Ring.* The noise pulled her closer to consciousness. A cold, wet *something* nudged her cheek. When she flipped over again, her bare legs tangled in the bedcovers.

Bedcovers. Why was she in bed? Where were her clothes? The last thing she remembered was talking with Colm in the pub while she drank her coffee. The *seisiún* had degenerated into a karaoke jam, and the guys on stage could not have been much over the drinking age. What had they been singing? Her fuzzy memory insisted that it had been Santa Claus Is Coming to Town, but...the rest was just a haze.

Why couldn't she remember the drive home? People only lost their memories when they'd been very, very drunk, didn't they, and—oh, no! She *was* home, wasn't she? Please, please let this not be Colm's bed! She bolted upright, dragging the sheet with her, but the sudden movement made her head pound. She felt vaguely nauseous.

Ring. The black dog on the end of the bed whined and nosed at her hand. Oh, wait. If the dog was here, then it meant she was at her cottage, not at Colm's, thank goodness! So the ringing noise would be....

The doorbell. Someone—an impatient someone—was at the door. Brenna wrapped the sheet around herself, then stumbled down the hall. She had to struggle with the deadbolt and security chain, but after a moment she got the door open and tried to focus on her visitor.

"Ms. Brenna Callahan?" asked the freckled youth on the step. Brenna blinked at him, though she could barely see him behind the huge bouquet of roses he held.

"Yes, I am," Brenna said. Why did the sun have to be so bright? The glare behind the boy made it hard to focus.

"Delivery for you, Ms. Callahan. Have a good day." When he handed her the roses, she saw his gaze take in all that she wasn't wearing. A grin played about his lips for just a moment, but then he touched an imaginary cap to her and hurried back up the walk to his car.

Delivery, on Sunday? Brenna shut the door, then carried the roses to the kitchen. It was hard to concentrate over the dull throb of her head, and the scent of the roses made an odd contrast to the sour taste in her mouth. Vase. She'd need a vase to put them in. Who would send her roses?

She laid the roses on the table long enough to retrieve her bathrobe from the bedroom; the sheet just didn't cut it as a garment. Then she searched the kitchen cupboards and came up with a quart jar that could serve as a vase. She filled it with water and put the roses into it, unable to look away from the bright red blooms. For a moment, she wasn't sure whether the fluttery feeling in her stomach was from excitement or from the hangover. Had Brad made an international call to a florist to remind her to call him? That was more likely to be his motive than a romantic gesture, but with him, if a gesture could serve two purposes, then so much the better. He was all about efficiency.

She reached for the card attached to the roses. At the same time, the dog came up next to her, stuck his nose against her leg through a gap in her robe, and made a sound halfway between a growl and a whine. She jumped.

"Quiet. It's just roses, probably from my lawyer soon-to-be ex-boyfriend. When did I let you in, anyway? Did you just invite yourself inside last night when I staggered through the doorway? At least I assume I staggered in, since we're the only ones here today and no one seems to have left a note to the contrary."

She was babbling—to a dog, no less. Thoughts still whirling, she reached down to pet him. Her fingers stilled in his fur. It felt...odd. For the first time since the doorbell had awakened her, she looked at him fully. He looked scruffier than usual, and dried blood matted his coat in places.

"Oh, you poor boy. What happened to you? Have you been in a fight? Are you a warrior like Cuchulain? By the looks of you, it's a good name for you."

The dog whined, brown eyes fixed on her face. He didn't fight her as she wet a washcloth at the kitchen sink and used it to make sure none of his wounds were serious enough to need a vet's attention. By the time she'd finished, the dog looked better but she felt worse.

Brenna tossed the stained washcloth into the sink, and her gaze fell on the vase of roses. She was shaky and ill, but she couldn't go back to bed without first finding out who'd sent them. Her hand trembled as she removed the florist's card from its holder and opened the little envelope. The card read: *Wow! C.*

Shit! They weren't from Brad, they were from Colm. That card could only mean one thing. She'd done just what she'd been determined not to do. She'd gotten plastered, and she'd slept with the guy. It didn't *feel* as though she'd had sex, but she must have. Now he'd sent her two dozen long-stemmed red roses. Red, for passion. Oh, no.

Her stomach lurched and she ran for the bathroom.

She was still on her knees in front of the toilet when someone laid a hand on the back of her neck. She jerked around, too terrified to scream, until she realized that it was Ronan. She hadn't heard the front door open, but then, she'd been busy. Why did he always seem to pop up at random? She'd thought she was alone, but now here he was in her bathroom, no less, seeing her...like this. If this wasn't humiliating, she didn't know what was. The only way it could be worse was if she'd puked on his shoes.

"Don't you knock?" she asked, too drained to do more than flip the toilet seat closed.

"Your door was open," Ronan said quietly. He wet a clean washcloth at the sink, wrung it out and used it to sponge her forehead as if she was a child. Except that a child wouldn't be in this situation, one hoped.

"I'm so embarrassed. I don't know what to say."

"You do not have to say anything. If you want me to go, I will go. Or you could let me help you. It is what friends do for each other."

"Is that what we are? Friends?" She dared to meet his gaze, but all she saw there was concern, not ridicule. "Okay. Stay, then, but don't speak too loudly. I've only been drunk maybe twice before in my life, but now I remember why I decided never to do that again." She went back to the bedroom and sat down on the edge of the bed. Just now, it was all she had the energy to do.

Without a word, Ronan headed toward the kitchen. After a few moments, Brenna heard him bustling about, opening cabinets. Then she remembered the dog.

"Ronan, could you let Cuchulain out? I think he's been in a fight. I tried to clean him up and I think he'll be okay, but—"

"Cuchulain? You mean the dog? He is fine. He left when I came in," Ronan called from the kitchen. "Just lie back and relax."

She did. She wasn't in a position to do anything else. Her body ached, and no wonder. She'd poisoned herself. That, or she'd had some wild sex last night. Maybe both. Obviously, Colm had brought her here and dropped her off last night, after...whatever she'd done with him that prompted an assessment of *wow*. She wouldn't have been in any shape to drive, if she couldn't even remember getting plastered and then getting naked.

Why couldn't she remember? Fear coiled itself into an icy lump in her middle, which didn't help the nausea. Several hours of her life were lost in a black hole and she couldn't do a thing about it. She dragged the covers up farther and huddled under them in misery until she heard footsteps coming back from the kitchen.

Ronan came into the room with a glass of tomato juice and some unbuttered toast on a plate. He set them on the bedside table, then rearranged Brenna's pillows behind her so she could lean against them. It was sweet, thoughtful. Humiliating.

"Thanks." Oops. The word was out before she remembered, but she wasn't firing on all cylinders just now.

Ronan frowned. "Have you thought about what safety measures you plan to take?" It wasn't the reaction she'd expected, but in some ways, it was worse.

"I don't know. I'm already on the pill, and it's a bit late for a condom. Not that it's any of your business."

He looked blank, and she realized what he must have meant. Her cheeks heated. "Oh. Safety measures against whoever is after me. Well, I meant to, but Annie wasn't home yesterday when I called her, so I decided to try to get some work done while I still had a window of opportunity."

"And this was before you met Colm in town?" Ronan asked.

"Well, yes. I didn't know I'd run into him and he'd ask me out to a *seisiún* and—wait a minute! How did you know I met Colm last night? Are you stalking me?" She couldn't help it; the fear she'd experienced earlier got its icy talons into her again and squeezed tight.

Some emotion flashed behind Ronan's eyes, but she couldn't have said what it was. "Do I seem like a stalker to you?"

"Ah—I guess not. I mean, no." *Yes, sort of. But it's confusing. You're confusing.*

"I have told you that Colm is dangerous to you, yet you still disbelieve me." There was a wealth of concern and disapproval in his quiet tone.

"Listen, I know that you don't like him, but he's always been a gentleman to me." *Well, except for last night, maybe. Damn, I hope he used a condom.*

"The man is no gentleman, Brenna. What must I do to convince you that you should stay away from him altogether?"

He could be right. The ghost of a memory nagged at the back of her mind. Ah, yes. She'd gone to dinner and the *seisiún* last night to try to determine for certain whether Colm was what and whom he appeared to be, or whether Ronan was right about him. Unfortunately, she'd gotten nowhere in her assessment. As things stood, Colm was still the one with the credentials, the verifiable public presence. Ronan had given her nothing of the sort to go on.

She crossed her arms over her chest and gave him as level a look as she could manage. "This, from the guy who barges into my house whenever he feels like it and thinks he can tell me what to do," she began, but one look at Ronan's face told her that this wasn't a direction she wanted the conversation to take. Something in his eyes made her catch her breath, and suddenly she felt ashamed of her earlier doubts.

"Look, I'm sorry. You've been very kind to me, and I've repaid you by being a bitch. Let's start over. I don't want to discuss Colm right now, so let's just drop that subject. I had intended to go to Annie yesterday and ask for magical defense lessons, but things didn't go as I planned. I can't go over there now, with a hangover. But I promise I'll go tomorrow, right after I retrieve my car from town. Is that good enough?"

"It will have to do," Ronan said. He made to leave, but he paused in the bedroom door to give her a sardonic look. "In case you were wondering, you did not have sex with Colm last night."

"What?" Shock drove her upright, despite the throbbing in her head. "How would you know something like that?"

"What if I told you that I am...how would you put it? Psychic?"

"No good. Try again."

Ronan's expression changed to one of exasperation. "Very well. How about the fact that you take all your relationships seriously? Given that trait, I would guess that you do not give yourself in a casual manner. And then there is your lack of memory. From what little I do know of Colm, he would prefer that his bedmate remember the experience afterward. Either way, I assure you that I am certain you did nothing irreparable with him." He held her gaze until she blushed again and had to look away.

"I hope you're right, Ronan. I sincerely hope you're right." He might be. His logic made sense, and despite her initial reaction, she had to admit it was just possible that he really was psychic. Maybe he actually did know what she had or hadn't done. She opened her mouth to concede the point, but he'd already turned away.

"Be well, Brenna Callahan." He left the bedroom without a glance back. A moment later, she heard the front door open, then shut.

If he wasn't a stalker, then what was he? He always seemed to be there, whenever she...well...whenever she needed him. He treated her with more respect than her own friends and family did. He took care of her when she was hurt, ill, or soaking wet. Yeah, he really fit the criminal M.O.: Sir Galahad, the stalker. And yet, the fact remained that he seemed to have no I.D., no job or last name—at least, none that he'd mentioned. Even if she did remember to ask him to produce proof of identity the next time they were together, he'd no doubt find some way to avoid it, like he had with the gardaí.

He was an enigma, and yet she always had the overwhelming urge to trust him. Colm, on the other hand, had all the evidence of legitimacy, but every time she was with him, something felt wrong.

Staring at the opposite wall of her room, Brenna nibbled on the toast, sipped the juice, and tried to make sense of the situation. She had the feeling that she could think about this for hours, but the logic would still be tied in knots. She'd have to come back to it later, after the hangover wore off.

If I had to have a hangover, yesterday was the best day to do it, Brenna decided the next morning as she walked into town to retrieve her car. She'd spent the rest of Sunday lounging around the cottage in pajamas, recovering. She hadn't gotten much done on her article, but she'd finished reading the faery encyclopedia and was partway through a book on Irish mythology.

That one was hard going. For some reason, she couldn't seem to read more than a few pages at a time. It wasn't as though the tales were gorier or harder to believe than any other myths, but they gave her a strange feeling, almost like déja-vu.

Or maybe it was just that the hangover had persisted longer than she'd expected it to. The headache and nausea hadn't subsided until late yesterday afternoon; night had fallen before she felt well enough to go out. By then it was too dark, which was why she was now trudging into town on Monday morning, swathed in coat and rain poncho, trying to ignore the gusts of wind that kept blowing her umbrella wrong-side-out. With any luck, no one had towed the car.

She found it just where she'd left it—on a side street near the café. It didn't look as though it had been disturbed, but she had to be cautious. Brenna walked around it as Ronan had done, but she saw no obvious signs of tampering. After giving it the once-over, she bent to examine the undercarriage. If her enemies had planted another of those whammy symbols, could she detect it? She'd seen the magical energy of the previous two, but both sigils had required either Annie or Ronan to work *draíocht* to get rid of them. Brenna frowned. What could she do if she did detect one—walk home again and call in the cavalry?

She glanced around to make sure she hadn't already picked up any curious observers, then hunched down near the front bumper and extended a hand toward it, looking for...exactly what, she wasn't sure. A red glow? Ectoplasm? Black psychic ooze?

She glared at the spot where the sigil had been last time, but didn't see anything other than mud. Would mud cover up a magical symbol? She unlocked the car and rummaged for a tissue, then bent down again to wipe the area in question.

Still nothing, and now she had mud on her sleeve. She glared at the car, crumpling the tissue in her now-grimy hand. What had she expected? If there was another sigil on the car, she couldn't see it. With luck, this meant that Ronan's ward was intact, though she hadn't seen it, either. Maybe wards were harder to detect and dismantle than harmful symbols were. With magic, who knew? A little of the right sort of mumbo-jumbo, and all bets could be off.

As she started to get up, knife-sharp pain erupted between her eyes. The world tilted and she crumpled onto the pavement in front of the car, unable to do more than groan. Shreds of grey obscured her sight. Her hearing receded. The pain dulled, but it left Brenna adrift in blackness.

She could still feel her body, dimly, but it wouldn't move, no matter how hard she tried. Had she just had a stroke at the age of thirty? And if she had, why could she still think? Was this what dying was like? That particular pleasure could have waited a few decades, at least.

A loud *pop* startled her, and then she could see again. She looked down and gasped. Her body still lay on the pavement. The conscious part of her hovered above. Even as she thought about it, Brenna rose until she floated in the air, above the street, above the buildings. A long, silvery cord connected her to her body, far below.

She rose higher, looking down at Ireland. Now she could see more than one city, green and brown fields like squares on a quilt, the tiny forms of sheep and cattle. She was flying, just as she often did in dreams, only now she could feel the breeze on her face, albeit muted. The sensation was strange, yet familiar. She ought to worry now, but this floating was so peaceful, she didn't feel the need.

What bothered her was how it had happened. Out-of-body experiences were common enough among the psychic crowd—or so she'd once heard on TV—but she'd never heard of anyone just involuntarily popping out of body while awake and going about her business. So what had just happened? Maybe she *had* suffered a stroke.

Two shapes appeared in her peripheral vision. They resolved into men—neither of whom Brenna recognized, but both of whom looked determined. Whoever they were, they didn't look like angels or guiding spirits. Trying to ignore the wash of fear, Brenna backed away from them, but they followed. They moved faster than she knew how to, and they closed in on her, reaching for her even when she tried to bat their hands away.

"Who are you? Leave me alone!"

Neither man answered her. They floated up close to her and grabbed an arm each, dragging her with them, outward from where she'd been. Their fingers dug into her arms. She fought but couldn't pull loose.

Brenna felt a sensation like that of passing through a veil of cobwebs, and then the scenery changed. Where before it had been a misty daylight, the light in this new place dimmed like clouds gathering before a storm. She'd arrived in a shadowy thicket, and she no longer hovered. None of them did. The ground beneath Brenna's feet seemed as real as if she were physically standing on it. Twigs crunched when she stepped on them, and blackened, thorny trees loomed at the edges of her vision. The air bore the scent of lichen and damp soil.

"What do you want from me? Where is this place?" Brenna asked the two men, but again they didn't answer. The one with bad teeth loosed his grip on her arm. The bald man held her while Bad Teeth drew back his fist. She let her knees buckle at the last instant, so that his blow landed on her chest instead of her stomach. It hurt like hell—she could have sworn she heard ribs crack. For a moment, she hung gasping in Baldy's grip. Then he wrenched both her arms around behind her back and jerked her up to ready her for another punch.

Brenna forced herself to straighten, put all her weight on Baldy, kicked out at Bad Teeth's groin with both feet, and...yes! He dropped with a groan, clutching his balls. Physical self-defense, astral self-defense—maybe there wasn't much difference.

"That's it. Gloves come off now," Baldy said. She could tell by his tone that if he'd been determined before, he was furious now. He let go her arms but grabbed her around the neck with both hands, squeezing until her sight darkened. She couldn't drag enough air into her lungs. She clawed at his hands and managed to elbow him in the gut. He only grunted and pulled her up close against him so she couldn't get in another swing.

Fight them! The voice sounded in her mind. At least, she thought it was in her mind; neither of the men seemed to have heard it. As her vision faded, Brenna looked up. A large crow perched on a branch just above Bad Teeth's head. It looked at her, and she could hear its voice clearly—the same voice she'd heard several times since she'd come to Ireland. Anand. The Morrigan.

If you would save your life, you must fight them, for whatever happens to your energy body in this realm happens to your mortal body in the Earth realm. Remember who you are. Fight!

Fight how? Even as she thought it, Brenna released her grip on the hands around her neck. She let her astral body go limp, pretending to lose consciousness. It wasn't hard to fake. Far away, along the silver cord, she could feel her physical body choking as it fought for air. Baldy kept his grip, but his stance relaxed just a fraction. He thought he'd won.

Spear!

Brenna struggled to concentrate on the image the Morrigan thrust into her mind. The bronze-tipped spear she visualized came into her hands and fit as though grafted there.

"What the—?" Baldy swore. In that instant, Brenna threw her weight to one side and caught him off balance. He stumbled, his grip loosened; she brought the spear up as hard as she could. Her vision had gone so dark that she could barely see him, but she felt the shock of wood against skull. Then, just like that, he was gone. She didn't see where he went, but for now, it didn't matter. The spear dissolved in her grip, and without it to lean on, she fell to her knees. Somewhere above her, she heard the crow launch itself into the air with a triumphant shriek.

Blackness engulfed her, and her lungs didn't want to work.

With the last of her consciousness, Brenna obeyed the instinct to fling herself downward along the silver cord. She wasn't even sure how she did it; she just thought it, and it happened. Like a falling star, she hurtled out of the almost-physical dimension back into the astral and slammed into her body.

When she came to, she ached all over. Her vision was blurred, but she could feel the resistance as she dragged air into her lungs through a tortured throat. Her body was so heavy. Odd; she'd never thought of it being so solid and sluggish. For several moments, she couldn't get it to move at all. Finally she managed to move a finger, a hand, an arm. She had no idea how long she'd been out-of-body, but she had the feeling that the whole episode had taken only minutes.

"Miss! Miss, are you all right?" someone was asking as her hearing returned. Hands touched her, felt her head, neck and back for injury. When she'd managed to move enough to convince them that she had no spinal trauma, they helped her upright. A fit of coughing seized her then; she had to lean against her would-be rescuers while they helped her to sit on the curb. Through the dimness of her returning vision, she saw vague shapes to either side. Hands patted her and voices conferred with each other nearby.

Eyes tearing, she straightened, then blinked at the concerned faces. "I'm all right," she croaked through the pain in her throat. "Really. I'm okay."

"Swallowed something down the wrong pipe, did you?" an older man asked. A woman of similar age whom Brenna presumed must be his wife peered at her face.

"We'll drive you to hospital if you need us to," the woman said, her tone indicating that she strongly suggested Brenna take her up on the offer.

"No, I'm all right, thanks. I'm just a little shaky. I'll sit here until I get my breath back, then I'll go home. It's okay. Thank you for your concern."

The couple withdrew, their expressions still worried. The man took his wife's arm and started off down the sidewalk, both of them stopping to speak to some people gathered nearby. Every few moments, someone turned to look in Brenna's direction. Maybe they thought she'd had an epileptic fit.

She sat on the curb for a few minutes, breathing. When she was steady enough, she heaved herself to her feet, got into the car and started it, easing it onto the street. As she headed out of town toward her cottage, she glanced in the rearview mirror often to make sure no other cars were following her. Paranoia, maybe. But then, someone really was out to get her; their methods were just harder to trace than those of most attackers.

She glanced in the rearview again, then blinked as she caught a glimpse of her reflection. The Morrigan hadn't been kidding about the physical effects of her astral battle. She looked as though she'd seen a ghost, and her skin was pale. Trauma, no doubt—maybe even shock—and those things weren't the only evidence of how close she'd come to dying.

Her eyes were bloodshot from lack of oxygen, but that wasn't the worst of it. On both sides of her neck were several livid finger-shaped bruises.

CHAPTER TEN

Inhaling the calming scent of herbal tea, Brenna looked across the room at Annie, whose expression held a mixture of exasperation and concern. Brenna hadn't even been back to her cottage yet; she'd gone straight to Annie's after finding the bruises on her neck. Minutes ago, she'd found another bruise on her chest where Bad Teeth had punched her.

"I have no idea who these guys are or why they're after me, let alone how they managed to drag me out of my body in daylight, in the middle of the street."

"What you've described doesn't happen very often, dear," Annie said. "In fact, it's almost unheard of. With or without otherworldly help, they'd have had to use a powerful psychic punch to knock you out first and then drag you through the astral plane to the realm where they attacked you. That is why we need to get your shields up right away; if you'd been properly protected, they might not have been able to do it."

"Properly protected? Annie, my house is warded, my car is warded, and I've somehow picked up a stray dog who guards my doorstep every night. Short of a police-assigned bodyguard, how much more protected could I be?"

"You'd be surprised," Annie said. For a moment, something hard and dangerous flashed through her voice and eyes.

Brenna swallowed, then winced. "Okay, but first I'd just like to know why all this is happening to me. It's not as if I'm a pop star or anything. How could I have picked up any stalker, let alone two who seem to belong to some kind of dangerous magical cult?"

A dangerous magical cult. Cults could be involved in violence and all sorts of grotesque murders. Some of their rumored activities could be chalked up to urban legend, but still.... "Annie, could these guys have targeted me for ritual sacrifice? I mean, Halloween isn't far from now."

"Sacrifice?" Annie shook her head. "That's far-fetched, isn't it? Not outside the realm of possible, but unlikely. I think it more probable that you've made an enemy somewhere in the past. In a past life, I'd guess."

"And I flubbed the regression that might have told me who that was. Fantastic." Brenna searched Annie's face, looking for...what? Answers? Reassurance? "Other than digging back through ancient memories, how else can I go about finding out who's doing this to me and why?"

Annie put her hands on her hips. "If you're going to ask that question, then make sure you're doing so for the right reasons. Don't ask it because your rational mind still wants to explain it all away. Ask it because you're ready to accept that what you're up against is real, and because you're ready to do whatever's necessary to solve the problem. There are times when everything changes, and no amount of hidebound reasoning is going to put things back the way they were."

"I guess I knew that intuitively, even before this." Brenna said, running her finger around the rim of her cup. "At this point I can accept it intellectually, too. The thing is, even when my articles are finished and I leave here, there's no guarantee that the trouble won't just follow me home. Bottom line—I want to find out what these guys are after and show them they can't mess with me and get away with it."

Watching her, Annie nodded. "Good. We'll start now."

An hour later, Brenna knelt with her eyes closed on top of a small mound in Annie's backyard, trying to sense energy through an upright stone on its top.

"This is a bit like a game of Pin the Tail on the Donkey," she said lightly as she held her hand out toward the stone, not quite touching it. Annie said that everything had an aura, or energy field—even objects. When she held out her hand toward Annie, the cat, or a plant, she felt a vague sense of pressure in the air between herself and whatever or whomever she was trying to sense. It was the same when she brought her two hands toward each other. However, this stone and the earth beneath it were another matter—that, or she was doing it wrong.

"Not everyone senses earth energy right away," Annie said, "but I think you'll manage."

"Well, I..." Brenna trailed off. Now that she'd stopped trying so hard, she did feel something similar to what she'd experienced at Keshcorran. For a moment, she even heard that steady heartbeat deep underground. Experimentally, she imagined herself pulling at a flow of energy, sucking it into herself.

At first, she felt resistance, but the more she relaxed, the more easily the energy seemed to flow, rising through her body like water in a well. All the hairs on her arms lifted, and the energy tingled up her spine and through the top of her head, filling her until it felt as through her skin might burst. Her eyes flew open, and she glanced at Annie, who was watching her.

Even though she'd stopped trying to pull the energy, her body still vibrated with it. When she touched the ground to steady herself, the tingle subsided. "That was...different," she said as she got to her feet and brushed at the dirt on her pants. Annie was grinning.

"Got more than you bargained for, did you? This is the junction of several streams of energy," Annie told her. "I think of them as trackways, but some call them ley lines."

"Oh, I've heard of them. Don't they usually run between ancient sacred sites?"

Annie nodded. "Yes, that's often true, but not always. These are minor ones that I redirected for my purposes. I often tap into them so I don't use up all my personal energy for magical work."

"Can all witches feel them?" Brenna asked. "Are they the only outside source of power?"

"No to both questions. Some people are more sensitive than others to trackway energy, but a *bandraoí* can also draw energy up from the earth, down from the sky, or inward from the sea. You need to get familiar with all of them."

"I'll try. But how will this keep me from being dragged out of my body by psychic thugs?" Brenna asked. "And for that matter, how will it help me give as good as I get?" She came down off the mound to join Annie on the pathway that led to the back door.

Annie shot Brenna another of her exasperated schoolteacher looks. Instantly, Brenna felt as if she were twelve years old and caught without her homework.

"Do you think knowing what a weapon is made of might help a military scientist find a counter to that weapon or even duplicate it?" Annie asked.

"I...well, yes, I suppose it would."

"Then practice these exercises until you feel you could do them in your sleep. We'll have to move through many concepts much faster than I'd normally consider wise or safe, but we don't have a choice. You know by now that what happens to you in that particular astral realm also happens to you on a physical level." Annie grinned—more a baring of teeth than a show of real amusement. "Somewhere right now, one of those men will be lying around with an ice bag on his privates, and the other will be nursing a headache. It should take them some time to work up to another attack on the scale of today's."

"Well, that's a relief, I guess. But it would be more of a relief if I didn't have a huge bruise on my chest and more on my neck. It still hurts when I swallow." Brenna fingered her neck. The pain was a constant reminder that she'd nearly died, but it also firmed her resolve.

"It's just as well. They taught you caution in a way I couldn't have done," Annie said. "Now that you can sense the energy, it's time I taught you about shields. They shouldn't be able to take you by surprise again, but I think we both know that they'll try to find another way as soon as they regroup."

"That's what I'm afraid of. I can't predict what they'll do, or when they'll do it."

Brenna glanced at the carved stone on top of the mound—the king stone, Annie called it. Power centers, trackways, energy fields—it was almost too much to take in all at once, let alone the idea of another psychic battle against people who were obviously much better trained than she was.

"While we're getting your defenses in order, you might ask Ronan to teach you a few things," Annie said. The name sent an electric jolt through Brenna. Her gaze snapped back to Annie, but the older woman was already walking into the house; there was nothing to do but follow her.

"Annie, I know you like Ronan and you seem to trust him. For that matter, I'm tempted to do the same. But there's still too much

I don't know about him. For all I know, he could be one of the people who are after me." Even as she said them, the words felt wrong.

"Does he seem like a stalker to you?" Annie paused in the kitchen doorway.

"That's just what he asked me when I...oh, never mind. And no, odd though it seems, I don't get the sense that he's a stalker. But I'm just not sure *what* he is. That's what bothers me. I'd feel better if you could tell me what he does for a living, or what his last name is, or even where he lives."

Annie shook her head. "These are things you'd do better to discuss with Ronan. If he hasn't told you, he must have a good reason."

"Yes, but Annie, do *you* know any of those things about him?"

"Well...no. Not for certain," Annie admitted, sounding testy.

"See? That's what I'm talking about. And what about Colm Lachlann? He has a driver's license, a phone number, an address and a verifiable job...everything a decent guy should have."

Annie shrugged and led the way back into the kitchen. "I don't know Colm Lachlann, though I've heard his name before, of course."

"So from what you know of him, you'd say he's legit."

"Probably."

"Probably, but not definitely. This is the problem I'm having. I feel strange around both of these men—like I've met them somewhere before, but I can't put a finger on where and when. And then there's the fact that I'm extremely attracted to both of them. I always feel like I want to trust Ronan, but something about Colm makes me nervous, and those reactions are the opposite of what they should be. But Ronan and Colm weren't the men who attacked me on the astral, unless you can change how you look when you're out-of-body."

Annie frowned. "Well, as a matter of fact...."

"Oh, fabulous. So, for all we know, either or both of these guys could be the ones stalking me." Brenna dropped onto a chair at Annie's kitchen table, frowning at the grain in the wood. Maybe if she focused on her anger over the situation, she wouldn't feel so scared.

Looking unperturbed, Annie refilled the kettle and set it to heat on the stove. "Well, I don't know the answers to this dilemma, but I think you'd do well to listen to your intuition. Trust it. You have it for a reason, and if you continue to doubt it, you'll be easy prey for anyone who might want to hurt you in the future."

"Great. So my homework is to practice sensing the energy of everything around me, which might get me labeled a lunatic; figure out what I really feel about Ronan and Colm, which might drive me nuts in the process; and learn to trust my intuition, which may or may not steer me wrong."

"That's it, yes," Annie said, grinning.

"Well, okay, then. I'll get right on it." Brenna grinned back, but it felt more like a grimace. Ronan, Colm, Baldy and Bad Teeth. Were the four connected, and if so, how? Who wanted her dead, and who simply wanted her? If she'd hoped for easy answers, it was clear the universe wasn't just going to hand them to her. But at least she was learning to protect herself, and any guy who thought she'd be easy prey would just have to think again.

After her lesson with Annie, the prospect of spending the rest of the afternoon in front of the laptop held no appeal whatsoever. When it came time to turn off the main road toward the cottage, Brenna found herself driving on past. Almost before she realized it, she'd reached Roscommon city limits.

She glanced at the signposts and gave a mental shrug. Since she'd come this far, she might as well make an afternoon of it. On impulse, she turned onto the N63 and kept going until, after just enough of a drive to placate the gypsy in her soul, she found an access road that approached Lough Ree. It might not be a complete escape from the trouble she was in, but it would do for now.

Brenna pulled the car into a parking lot near the lake, turned off the engine and sat for a while, staring at the water. Legend had it that an entire settlement existed deep in the lake. It was one of many supposed underwater faery palaces in various places, but as with alleged lake monsters like Scotland's Nessie, no one had proof. Then again, no one had proven such things didn't exist, either, so who was Brenna Callahan to say they didn't? Besides, after this last week, she'd traded in her skeptic's hat for good.

She jotted some notes, then took her digital camera down to the lakeside. She wasn't close enough to any of Lough Ree's three islands to get good shots of them, so she'd need to come back later, but this much would do for now. It was enough effort that she could at least pretend she was working. She snapped several pictures of the shoreline and took time to get a good sense of the atmosphere before heading back to the car.

A caw from overhead broke her reverie. She looked up and noticed a crow perched on a bare branch above her head. Maybe it was her imagination, but the bird seemed to fix its bright gaze on her.

Soon two more crows landed on an adjacent branch. A series of raucous calls announced the arrival of three more. Another two or three followed them, while some of the earlier arrivals rose by turns to circle in the air before returning to alight on a branch again. Over the next several minutes, more and more crows showed up, until with all their wheeling and cawing, Brenna couldn't keep an accurate count. There must have been more than fifty of them, all engaged in an amazing aerial display right above her car. By turns, they wheeled, stooped and circled in an intricate dance around the leafless treetop. All the while, their cries and the sigh of their wings filled the air with a strange music.

Some time later, a feather floated downward to land at Brenna's feet. As if that were a signal, the crows began to leave the way they'd arrived, breaking off in groups of two or three at a time to disappear across the lake until only one remained.

Brenna bent to pick up the feather, and her camera swung out from where it hung from her shoulder. She blinked at it. Of course, she had a camera. But she'd stood there with the thing during the entire crow show and hadn't once thought to capture any of the experience via digital image. She'd been caught in the moment. Ronan would be proud of her.

Slowly, she got back into the car and started the drive back to her cottage. The sense of awed quiet she'd experienced under the tree stayed with her all the way, the image of those black wings in the sky imprinted on her memory.

As she drove she noticed a crow flying above and to the left of her car. It must have had a similar destination, because whenever she looked for it, there it was. Sometimes two others joined it. Sometimes it flew alone. But always the crow paced her, until she turned onto the road that led to her cottage.

When she got out of the car to go inside, the crow landed in one of the hawthorn trees and sat, its head turned toward her. Brenna blinked at it, unnerved. Had it followed her home? A quick glance around showed others perched atop the roof and in the branches. Crows. Crows everywhere. Her heartbeat kicked into high gear.

As she locked the car and hurried toward the house, a sharp image of the red-haired woman from her nightmare rose in her mind, watching her as intently as the crow that now perched on the roof of her car. It made the breath catch in her throat and clenched all the muscles from her shoulders upward. It was a classic fight or flight response, but all that adrenaline wouldn't do the least bit of good—not here. Not now. She knew that, and yet the urge to run was fierce.

Brenna spread her arms. "All right, Morrigan. *Mór Ríoghain.* I hear you. I see you. What do you want from me?"

I want you to remember. Is that so hard? I want you to reclaim what you once were, and finally become what you are supposed to be.

"I can't. I tried to remember, but I saw only pain, and blood, and myself as a traitor and a murderer. Is that what you want me to be? Do you want to see more blood on my hands? Is that why those men keep trying to kill me? You're a goddess of war. How could you understand that I just want to live my life in peace?"

You have forgotten me. Worse, you have forgotten yourself.

The crows all launched upward at the same time, making Brenna jump. Adrenaline rushed through her as she watched them sweep away toward Strokestown, wings pumping in unison. They reminded her of a fighter squadron, moving fast enough that soon they were dark specks on the horizon.

The phone was ringing as Brenna let herself into her cottage. Still zinging with adrenaline, she kicked the door shut behind her, threw her purse on the kitchen table and grabbed the receiver out of its cradle.

"Hello?" Her voice was a tad breathless, but not bad.

"Brenna? It's about time. I've tried this number at least three times, but you never seem to be there when I call." The male voice on the other end sounded peeved.

"Hi, Brad. It's good to hear your voice, too," Brenna said. Fantastic. He'd already left several messages on the answering machine, but she'd put off calling him for days, and he wasn't going to like what she had to say now. Could this day get any better? The crowning touch would be to have her mom call next.

She heard Brad's sigh on the other end of the line. "Ah, come on, Bren, I didn't mean it like that. It's just that you didn't call when you said you would, and I was worried. I tried your work, and Jay Marston said he'd gotten a couple of emails from you around the middle of last week, but hadn't heard anything since. He assumed you were making the most of your time there and were just too busy to check in."

"He's right, pretty much," Brenna said. "I meant to call a couple of days ago, but...things have been crazy here."

His voice softened. "I guess they would be. Your schedule is probably off kilter too, with the time difference. But I've missed you, sweetheart. The bed's pretty empty at night."

Brenna glanced at the clock on the wall; it read 2:30 p.m. That would make it 8:30 a.m. in Oregon. "I've been running around a lot. My rental car broke down, so I had to use public transportation for a while. But it's...you know...it's work as usual." She touched the bruises on her neck; the herbal salve and energy treatment Annie had given her just before she left had helped, but her throat was still sore.

"Ireland's that boring, huh? I thought you couldn't wait to get over there." Now Brad sounded amused, tolerant. He often called her his little gypsy and complained that he couldn't pin her down. She knew it was an unspoken metaphor for her lack of commitment, but he usually never pushed further than that.

"You're right—I couldn't wait," she said. "It's just different than I thought it would be. It is beautiful, though. And it's anything but boring." *You have no idea how* not *boring it is.*

She told him about some of the places she'd been, editing out the paranormal occurrences, which he wouldn't believe anyway. He filled her in on what he'd been up to since she'd been gone, nothing of interest. Just a conversation with no surprises, typical Brenna and Brad.

She should tell him about what had happened with Colm, but if she did that, she might as well tell him what she'd decided about their relationship. An in-person breakup was better, wasn't it? Classier. Still, bluffing her way through this conversation was proving harder than she'd thought. She was getting desperate; she had to be, or she'd never have asked for the boring, non-confidential details about his last court case.

"Why do you care about this, anyway?" he asked. "We're paying international rates right now, and you never want to hear about my cases when you're at home. What's up?"

"Nothing. Nothing's up." She swallowed. Now her throat was dry as well as sore. She pulled the phone cord over as far as it would stretch while she fished in the fridge for a bottle of water.

"Yes, there is. I can hear it in your voice. You've been distant the whole time we've been talking. If something's bothering you, just tell me." He'd used his lawyer tone, which meant he was calling her bluff and wouldn't let her weasel out of this.

Brenna uncapped the water, took a careful sip, then set down the bottle. She hadn't thought she'd be so nervous when it came down to it.

"Listen, there's something I need to tell you, but I'd rather talk about it in person."

"I think you should tell me now."

Brenna hesitated. "Okay, but Brad...you aren't going to like it."

"Go on." Brad's tone had chilled a little. Now it was Grim Lawyer Steels Himself for Bad News. Well, he'd asked for it.

"I've been thinking about us while I've been here, and I realized that I haven't been fair to you in this relationship."

"Uh-oh. You're right. I don't like it."

Brenna sighed. "There's just no good way to say this. Brad, I know you want to make things permanent between us, but being here and getting a little distance has helped me see that it isn't a good idea. I've finally had a chance to think this through, and I realized that I just can't be the partner you want."

"Brenna, you only think it's not working because you're over there and I'm over here. Let's table this until you get back. Then we'll discuss it at length and come to a reasonable decision."

"I've already come to a reasonable decision. As I said, coming here has helped me realize that I can't maintain this relationship, long distance or not. Your life is in Portland. You want a girlfriend or wife on hand to attend your parties and office get-togethers, or help you entertain clients. But I'm a travel writer. You hate it when I'm gone on assignment, and now that I've gotten to the international stage.... It hasn't been working for a while now; we've both been trying not to see that. I'm sorry."

Brad was quiet for so long that Brenna started to wonder whether the line had gone dead. "Brad? Are you still there?"

"You've met someone else, haven't you? One week in Europe and you've already found another guy." Anger clipped his words now. Brenna estimated she had about thirty more seconds before he lost it.

"Thanks a hell of a lot, Brad. Why would you jump to that conclusion?"

"Okay, if it isn't like that, then how is it? Tell me. Why break up with me like this, if it isn't some other guy?"

"It's...it's complicated, is what it is. Bottom line, I'm not the right person for you. If I was, I wouldn't have stalled our relationship this long. Even before I came over here, it wasn't right. I knew it, but I didn't want to admit it. You must have felt it, too. That, or you have the patience of a saint."

"Is this where you say, 'It's not you, Brad, it's me'?" He was royally pissed now; his anger came through the receiver in almost palpable waves.

"Well, it *is* me. I guess coming here just let me know that I haven't found myself yet. If I'm not sure of myself, then you can't be, either. I need to figure this out, and I don't want you to put your life on hold while I do it." She'd twisted the phone cord around her finger so tightly she had to unwind it to get the circulation back.

"You're thirty years old, Bren. If this is your idea of a not-quite-midlife crisis, it's pathetic."

"I know, but there it is. Look, I didn't even want to do this over the phone. I wanted to wait until I could speak to you in person, but you forced the issue. At least I can pay for your phone charges. Just send me the bill, or email me the amount and I'll get you a check as soon as possible." Her voice came out small, thin. Just the way she felt.

"Keep your damned money. What kind of jerk do you take me for? I can afford a damned international phone break-up, damn it!"

Brenna blinked back tears. "I'm sorry. Take care, Brad. I'll...I'll have one of my friends stop by later this week to pick up the stuff I left at your apartment."

"Yes, please do that." Brad's voice had gone from hot anger back to the stiff, cold lawyer tone again. "Goodbye, Brenna. I hope you find whatever it is you're looking for." Brenna heard a click, then a dial tone.

She stayed in for the rest of the day, huddled in front of the peat fire. Dinner was a frozen pizza that tasted like cardboard. When the black dog arrived that night, she let him inside with her, glad for the company. She soon found herself telling him all about Brad and her klutzy breakup—she never had gotten the knack of doing those well.

"What am I, stupid?" she asked the dog as he gazed up at her. "He was a sensible, stable guy. We could have had a comfortable life together, raised some kids, a dog like you, maybe.... But then I had to become a psychic apprentice witch with a bunch of crazies after her. And it seems I also had to go out with a guy I don't know well, get drunk, and have *wow* sex that I don't even remember."

The dog made a sound somewhere between a growl and a whine. Brenna smiled and scratched him behind his silky ears. Talking to him was a comfort even if he couldn't understand a word she said. At least he was a great listener.

"I made the right decision. Every word I said to Brad about us not being right for each other was true. It shouldn't have taken a night with Colm to tell me that much. I just wish I'd done the breakup much sooner, in person, before I had to break someone's heart from several thousand miles away."

The dog whined, then pushed his nose under her hand and flipped it up onto his head again. She petted him for a while, then used him to practice the energy sensing homework Annie had given her. He had a strong energy, which made him almost as good as having a human partner, and she needed all the practice she could get. This last encounter with her enemies had undoubtedly made them angry. Annie was right; she had no time to waste, even to grieve. Her relationship was dead. Now she had to make sure she didn't follow it into the grave.

CHAPTER ELEVEN

The next morning, Brenna was writing the first travel article when the doorbell rang. She got up and peered through the window, but the van parked outside bore a delivery service logo, and the woman holding the package looked bored. It was probably safe to assume that she had nothing to do with the stalkers. Probably.

"Delivery for Ms. Brenna Callahan," the woman said when Brenna opened the door.

"Thanks." She signed for the package, then closed and locked the door behind her as the woman headed back up the walkway.

Biting her lip, Brenna stared at the package for a moment before carrying it into the kitchen and setting it on the table. The delivery service might have been legitimate, but was the package? She hadn't ordered anything. Should she try to check for traces of magic? Would she be able to tell if there were? Gingerly, she reached out a hand to try Annie's energy sensing exercises on the box. Then she noticed the Brown Thomas store logo on the side. A closer look at the return address label showed that the sender was

Colm Lachlann. Brenna's stomach clenched. She still hadn't talked to him after the roses, and she'd hoped her silence would give him a hint that she wasn't comfortable with what had happened after the *seisiún*. What was he up to now?

Brenna's lip curled as she looked at the package. It might be a gift prompted by friendship and generosity. It might even be an attempt to rectify the humiliating "wow" roses scenario. But if she took all that had happened since she'd arrived in Ireland as a guide, then she might as well prepare for the worst.

She reinforced her personal shields and opened the package slowly—just in case someone else had sent it under Colm's name. It was nerve-wracking, this business of having to second-guess everything. By the time she'd slit the tape and opened the box, her hands were shaking. She folded back the tissue paper and reached inside to pull out something made of soft blue-green cloth. As it unfolded, she gaped at it.

It wasn't a booby trap from the psychos, but in many ways, it was worse.

It was a negligee. A *silk* negligee, like some of the expensive ones Brad had bought her in the past. She hadn't minded Brad buying her stuff like that—after all, they'd been sleeping together for a few months before he'd bought her the first one—but this.... She didn't even remember what she'd done with Colm that had been *wow* enough to rate morning-after roses, let alone lingerie. Brenna felt the hair rise on the back of her neck as she looked at the gift.

She dropped the garment back into its wrapping, retrieved Colm's business card from the bottom of her purse, and picked up the phone. It was time to settle this thing right now, before he developed any more fantasies about a relationship that didn't exist. Surely even the hottest teenage rock star didn't have this many stalkers at one time, sexual or otherwise.

Colm didn't answer the phone right away. Brenna was about to hang up when he finally picked up.

"What is it now?" he asked in a rougher tone than Brenna had ever heard from him.

"Colm? It's Brenna."

"Oh! I'm sorry, love. I thought you were the chap from the historical society. What can I do for you? Did you get my package?"

"Well, I...." She hesitated. How best to handle this? "Yes, as a matter of fact, I did. It's...lovely, Colm, and so were the roses, but I think we have a little misunderstanding." Make that a *big* misunderstanding.

"Oh? How so?" His tone was mild, but Brenna sensed something darker underneath.

"I believe I've mentioned before that I have to leave right after Halloween."

"Yes, I remember."

"Well, I don't know how things are here in Europe, but in the U.S., lingerie as a gift is...pretty intimate." She swallowed and hoped he didn't hear it.

"Ah, I see. Americans are odd about sex. Well, don't give it another thought, love. I just thought you might like it. It matches your eyes."

"Um, well, I appreciate that, but I can't accept it. I hope you understand. I enjoyed our outings, but I'm starting to feel really uncomfortable."

"Why? There's no need to feel that way at all, given the already intimate nature of our relationship."

"What do you mean, intimate?" she asked. Dread curled itself into a tight ball and lodged in her middle.

"My dear girl, I should think it obvious. After what you did to me in the car on the way back to your cottage after the *seisiún*, you ought to be able to figure it out."

"That depends. What did I do?"

Colm laughed, a rich, masculine laugh that made Brenna's toes curl inside her shoes. Shivers chased themselves down all her nerve endings. As soon as he stopped laughing, the feeling lessened.

"Ah, Brenna. You are such a delight. Perhaps I should have bought you a black dress with a white collar, apron and cap instead. Without pantaloons, of course. No sense in putting much on underneath, even for a Puritan."

"What?" She said it more sharply than she'd intended, but her temper had started to fray at the edges. Who did this jerk think he was? Who did he think *she* was? Even if he was the freaking King of the Faeries in disguise, he had no right to treat her this way.

"Colm, I'm telling you now that I do not remember having sex that night. I don't remember anything at all after the coffee at the pub. So tell me, damn it, *what did I do?*"

He laughed again and told her. A hot flush crept up Brenna's neck to her cheeks as he described it in detail. Moments passed before she could speak.

"Well, even if I did, the fact remains that I was blackout drunk—which has never happened to me before—and it doesn't imply that I wanted an intimate relationship," she sputtered at last. "And it does mean that I can't see you anymore."

"You're quite decided on this?" he asked stiffly.

Oh, great; now he was pissed off. Maybe she should just swear off men altogether. "Yes, I've decided," she said. "Thank you for all that you've done, but please leave me alone."

"You know, in some circles, thanks imply obligation. You've thanked me several times over the course of our relationship, and you've just said it again. I must conclude that you don't really mean to break things off, though I have no idea why you choose to play the tease. You already have my undivided attention. There is no need to play games."

Uh, oh. "Colm, where I come from, thanks is a word of appreciation for services already rendered. A sort of payment, if you will. It doesn't constitute further obligation on the part of the person who says it. I'm not playing games here. Haven't you heard anything I've said?"

"I hear you very well, Brenna, but I have work to do. Meet me for lunch tomorrow at your usual café, and we'll reason this out like adults. Until then, enjoy my gift and think of me. You've gone to such lengths to entice me; I promise I'll make it all worth your while." He hung up before she could say another word.

A stream of curse words crowded into Brenna's mind, but every one was inadequate. Mute, she carefully re-folded the negligee and returned it to its box, taped the cardboard closed again and slapped on the return label that had come with the packing slip.

As soon as it was ready, she called the delivery service to come pick it up. Returning it might irritate Colm further, but she didn't want it in the house a minute longer than necessary. At least the action of rejecting the gift and all it implied gave her the illusion of control, when the facts gave her anything but. No matter how or why it had happened, she now had not two enemies, but three.

A piercing yelp and a thump against the side of the cottage jolted Brenna awake. She sat up in bed, every nerve ending on edge. The *wrongness* she'd felt on her first night in Ireland was back—that much registered even before she noticed that the display on her alarm clock read 3:23 A.M.

Something screeched, raising the hairs on Brenna's arms and the back of her neck. There followed a series of thumps and the cries of a fighting dog. Cuchulain, the hounds of the Wild Hunt, or one against the other? Brenna's breath caught.

Cuchulain. It had to be him, fighting something off. She couldn't just hide in here, hope the wards held, and leave him out there to battle whatever it was alone. But what could she do? So far, all she knew was how to make psychic shields and gather energy. That didn't seem as though it would be much help, especially to a dog. Still, she had to try something.

Trying to ignore the feeling of gathering doom outside, Brenna sat cross-legged in the middle of the bed and tried to sense Cuchulain. Surprisingly, as soon as she was able to calm her mind enough to focus, she did sense something that she thought was his energy. She pictured him as clearly as she could and concentrated on forming a shield around his aura, but as she began, she encountered resistance. Something snapped, and her energy bounced back off him, as though he were already shielded. It was a strange feeling, like touching an electric fence.

Did animals know enough to shield themselves? She'd detected the edge of Annie's aura during their energy-sensing practice, but that was different, wasn't it?

Cautiously, she reached out to Cu again. This time she didn't try to shield him or alter anything about his aura. Instead, she pulled energy up from the earth, as Annie had taught her, and sent it out to him in a thin but steady trickle of green force, like an offering.

The dog's aura jerked as if she'd startled him somehow, but then she sensed an acceptance of—or perhaps only a decrease in resistance to—the energy she offered. At the same instant, the other presence turned toward her, as if without meaning to, she'd drawn its attention.

Still huddled in the middle of the bed, Brenna had a sudden image of talons reaching for the energy she was sending to the dog. She felt those talons close around the tendril and suck at it. A backwash of foul, greasy energy rushed in on her, and she dropped the connection to the dog, shuddering and gagging. Her shield wavered. She fought to steady it before it failed altogether.

Struggling, Brenna managed to reinforce and clear her shield, but the thought of what had almost happened left her cold. In trying to help the dog, she'd helped the Whatever-It-Was by accident. It was out there, attacking an innocent animal who for some reason thought he needed to defend her.

Stillness settled over Brenna, and she imagined the edges of her shield turning to points. She started to pull earth energy from the ground below the cottage, then remembered Annie's ley lines. She groped for them in the dark. For an instant, the world swam around her, as it had at Keshcorran. Then it righted, and a stream of energy flowed into Brenna, filling her until her skin felt tight and stretched. Gripping handfuls of the blanket as if it could anchor her somehow, she imagined another ball of energy like the ones she and Annie had practiced with, but hard and spiked. She poured all her fear and rage into it until she thought it might choke her.

When she could feel it fully formed inside her, she sent it down her right arm and into her hand. Her fingers tingled so sharply that she almost dropped the energy ball. Outside, Cuchulain yelped in pain. *Draíocht* surged inside Brenna and she lobbed the energy ball outward, toward those seeking talons. It hurtled through Annie's and Ronan's wards and struck something hard. Brenna heard another cry from the dog, followed by a human-sounding shout of pain, and then...nothing.

The silence went on for what seemed like years before Brenna dared get up, pull on a robe and go to the front door to investigate. A peek through the kitchen and living room windows didn't show her much. She'd have to depend on her non-physical senses to determine whether it was safe to open the door and look for Cuchulain—and right now those non-physical senses were inclined toward paranoia.

She waited for perhaps five minutes more, during which she prayed to whatever gods might be listening that the dog hadn't paid the ultimate price for protecting her. Then she unlocked the door and crept out onto the doorstep, scanning the yard for a body...or bodies. Someone had let out a bellow of pain there toward the end. If she had any luck, it had been one of the magic-wielding psychopaths, but luck hadn't graced her with its presence lately. The idea that it might have been Ronan lodged itself in the pit of her stomach and clenched as she searched the lawn by the light of the porch lamp.

After a minute, her gaze fell on a shape darker than the surrounding shadows, lying partway across the lawn. As Brenna watched, she thought she saw it twitch.

Steeling herself, Brenna left the doorstep and tiptoed across the lawn to the fallen...dog. Ah, shit. Swallowing hard, she knelt and murmured to him. The black tail twitched again at the sound of her voice, but when she touched his fur, her fingers came away sticky with blood.

"Oh, poor boy. Who did this to you? The Wild Hunt? The sick bastards who are after me? Someone else? I'm so, so sorry."

He needed a vet. But he was a huge dog; how was she going to get him to her car? And even if she managed that, where would she find a vet at this hour?

"Hang on, boy. I'll be right back."

Pulse pounding in her ears, Brenna got up, ready to run back into the cottage for the phone book and a blanket. As she turned, her eye caught a gleam of light bobbing over the field behind the cottage. It looked like one of the faery lights she'd read about in the encyclopedia—a Will O' the Wisp. On the other hand, she'd heard a man's voice earlier. It could just as easily be one of her enemies, coming back to finish the job.

Brenna ran toward the cottage and ducked into the shadows at the side. Her muscles started to cramp from holding herself poised to run or fight, but she'd be damned if she was going to hide under the covers again while whatever or whoever-it-was finished off her lone defender.

"Brenna! Brenna? Are you all right?" Annie's voice cut through the stillness, and when Brenna peeked around the side of the house, she saw that what had looked like a ball of light was in fact the blue-white glow of an LED flashlight.

She came out into view, knees weak from relief. "Annie! You scared me—when I saw your light I wasn't sure who or what was coming for me."

"Sorry. I felt a pull on the trackways—took me a while to realize you must have been the one who'd tapped into them. Any sensitive in the area could have tracked the disturbance here. What happened?"

Brenna hurried over to Annie and led the way to where Cuchulain lay in the yard. "He was guarding my doorstep like he does every night, and something attacked. It felt a lot like the presence I encountered that first night, when you say I got between the Wild Hunt and its prey. He fought it and I tried to help him, but I don't think it was enough. I was about to try and find an all-night vet when I saw your light."

Annie knelt beside the dog. When she touched his side, he barely moved. "Oh, my dear, I'm afraid we'll never get him there in time. He's in bad shape."

Brenna's cold fingers curled into Cu's fur. "Annie, I can't let him die because of me. He doesn't deserve this."

Annie sighed. "All right. Help me carry him into the cottage."

Together they got the dog onto a blanket and half lifted, half dragged him into the living room. Brenna couldn't help wincing the whole time they were moving him. She worried about possible internal injuries from lugging him around, but it was painfully clear that Annie was right about his condition regardless of anything they did. He didn't look like he'd make it through the night.

Tears threatened as Brenna followed Annie into the kitchen to find some clean rags. Poor, poor Cuchulain. Of all the humans he could have befriended, she was probably the worst choice possible.

"Annie, how do we—" She broke off as she saw that Annie had sat down in one of the chairs and closed her eyes.

"Hush, girl," Annie said in a gruff—though not unkind—tone, without opening her eyes. "I only know one person who may be able to help us with this, and I'll have to look for him on the astral plane. Look to your shields until I get back."

Biting back the urge to ask what a vet would be doing on the astral plane, Brenna spent the next several minutes trying to clean Cuchulain's wounds, alarmed by the raggedness of his breathing. He looked as though he'd been mauled by a bear, or—well—something with talons. In the light, he looked even worse than he had outside.

Just when Brenna was about to try the phone book anyway, Annie walked into the living room. At the same time, someone knocked on the door. Brenna started and lunged for the poker near the fireplace.

"That should be Ronan," Annie said soothingly.

"Ronan?" The mention of his name kicked Brenna's heart into overdrive. A boatload of questions crowded into her mind, but all she could do was stare like an idiot at the entryway while Annie went to open the door. The older woman didn't even seem worried that it might be someone else outside.

Of course, she'd been right; it was Ronan, right there, in the flesh. And somehow, Annie had used astral projection to call him here? A sense of unreality swamped Brenna, and she sat down heavily on one of the armchairs.

Ronan touched her shoulder as he passed, and something hard and cold unclenched and dissolved in her middle, though her heart seemed determined to keep thundering on as she watched him. He took off his jacket and tossed it onto a chair back, then went to Cuchulain, speaking softly to him as he placed a hand on his muzzle and the other on his chest. Brenna blinked as sparkling green-white motes began to flow from Ronan's chest down his arms, into his hands, and into the dog, who sighed and seemed to lapse into a normal sleep. A little at a time, his wounds began to close, the effect so gradual that Brenna had to blink several times to be sure she was really seeing it. Finally Ronan lifted his hands off the dog and the flow of light stopped.

Brenna got up and stared at Cuchulain, almost afraid to touch him. He seemed sacked out, and didn't even wake as Ronan rose and came to stand beside Brenna. She looked up at him, all her tangled thoughts trying to crowd each other out before she could give them voice.

"Okay, Ronan, you seem to have an amazing command of *draíocht*, and Cu looks so much better, but...will this affect you, somehow?"

He gave her a level look. "There is certainly a cost, but I think this is justified. I will manage."

That answer wasn't very reassuring, but it was obvious he wasn't going to elaborate further. She tried a different tack.

"I didn't know Annie could contact you on the astral plane, and I have no idea how you got here so fast after she did. That healing was the most amazing thing I've ever seen. I didn't think any of those things were possible. Every time I start to think I'm getting a sense of how *draíocht* works, something else happens."

You were right about Colm being dangerous, at the very least—and we really, really need to talk. I feel like I'm standing on the edge of a cliff with you, wondering if I should jump. She couldn't say the last part out loud, but the look in his eyes gave her the startling sensation that he knew what she was thinking anyway.

Taking a shaky breath, Brenna looked from Ronan to Annie. Her neighbor was watching him with obvious respect.

"Cuchulain is only partly healed; some of it he will have to do on his own. As to the rest...." Ronan spread his hands and gave Brenna a sympathetic smile. "I know you want answers, but I cannot stay long tonight." His gaze lingered on her face for a moment, and when he reached out to touch her, something deep inside her quickened in response. Hormones, nerves, or something else?

Something else.

The voice in her mind startled her so much that when Ronan stroked her cheek, she nearly jumped out of her skin.

"I will return tomorrow, and we will discuss matters." Ronan's hand dropped to Brenna's shoulder, then trailed down her arm to her hand.

Brenna stared at her hand in his, feeling a flush creep up her cheeks. He'd let her go if she pulled her hand free, but that simple touch was so comforting, she didn't want to. She let it stay for a moment more, then reluctantly pulled away. There were more important issues at stake right now, and she needed to focus on them.

She glanced across at Annie. "Will you teach me how to do astral projection? After tonight, I don't think I can afford not to learn it. I don't know who attacked Cuchulain, but at the end of the fight, I thought I heard a man's voice outside. Whether it was my stalkers attacking from the astral or the Wild Hunt itself, I need to be able to function in more than one dimension so I can find out what or whom I'm up against."

"Yes, that much is clear. Ronan, would you teach Brenna what she needs to know?" Annie asked.

Ronan nodded, never taking his eyes off Brenna.

She opened her mouth to speak, but Annie held up a hand to forestall her. "I could teach you, dear, but I'm sure Ronan's skills surpass mine in this. If you could learn a few things from him, I'd feel much better about the situation. Regardless, it's your decision."

Brenna hesitated. The tension running through her body wasn't all from apprehension. Did she trust him, or not? He'd been at least partly right about Colm. Cuchulain would likely be dead now if it weren't for him. He consistently went out of his way to help her, to protect her. He'd never gotten her drunk or made her feel like a slut. In the end, it wasn't so much whether she trusted Ronan's intentions, but whether she trusted her own instincts. With Colm, she'd used logic rather than instinct, and look where that had gotten her.

"I'd like to learn from you, Ronan, if you'll put up with me," she said after several moments.

Ronan and Annie developed identical expressions of relief, though there was something else in Annie's eyes that Brenna couldn't identify.

"I will return tomorrow night, Brenna," Ronan said. "Until then, be cautious. We are not yet certain what or whom tried to breach our wards tonight."

"I'll be careful. And Ronan, about Cuchulain...." She indicated the dog, who remained peaceful and oblivious to everything going on around him. "I don't understand how you did it, but th—"

He cut off her words with a finger against her lips, which made her breath catch. She stared into those blue eyes, lost, until Annie cleared her throat somewhere behind them. Brenna jumped; in those few seconds, she'd forgotten all about Annie and even about Cuchulain, who still lay on his side by the fire, snoring. She took a breath, acutely aware of Ronan's gaze; no doubt he was well aware of the effect he had on her, which only made it worse.

"Now that things have settled down, I'm off home. I'll ring you tomorrow, Brenna. *Slán agat.*" Annie preceded Ronan to the door. He opened it for her, and both of them went back out into the night, leaving Brenna with the slumbering dog and her tangled thoughts.

CHAPTER TWELVE

By the time the sun went down the next evening, Brenna had polished and emailed the first article to Jay and nearly finished the second. All afternoon she'd been ignoring the telephone, and now the answering machine tape held several increasingly insistent messages from Colm, conveying his concern and then anger over her having missed the lunch date she hadn't agreed to. If he didn't stop this, she'd have to get a restraining order, unbelievable as that sounded after less than two weeks' acquaintance. Maybe she'd set a record.

In between phone messages, she'd finished reading the book on Irish Mythology. The section on the Morrigan intrigued her, but even as she read it she had the feeling that some important details were missing from the account; the description seemed unbalanced. One passage read:

The Morrigan, sometimes called the triple Morrigan, is referred to by several names including Morrigan, Macha, and Badbh. Alternately, some texts refer to her as the Morrigu, that is Morrigan, Badbh and Nemhain. While some scholars conjecture that Macha, Badbh and/or Nemhain may be sisters to the Morrigan, others suggest that they are all one and the same being.

Reading over her notes, Brenna frowned. Almost all of the more recent stories, particularly the ones that dealt with the Irish hero Cuchulain, assumed that every appearance of "the Badbh" indicated an appearance of the Morrigan. That assumption wasn't quite right, though she couldn't say how she knew.

Darkness fell while she was still puzzling over the mythology. Brenna found herself checking the windows often, expecting to see Ronan striding up the walkway. When he hadn't arrived by eleven, she gave up and went to bed. Once there, she tossed and turned, torn between anger and worry.

She'd never asked him for anything before last night. It didn't seem like him to stand her up, especially if he was as concerned for her safety as he claimed to be. Now that she thought about it, it wasn't just that he showed up whenever she needed him; he came *whenever he thought she needed him.* If that wasn't a stalker move, she didn't know what was, and yet....

If she had any sense, she'd be running for the nearest airport, but for some reason, whenever logic said she should be afraid of Ronan, her body insisted otherwise. Now, that was frightening.

Where was he now? Why hadn't he kept his promise to come here tonight? Why were psychotic freaks intent on killing her? Why had Colm turned out to be a psycho as well, and for heaven's sake, how did her long-ago betrayal of the Morrigan fit into this already tangled mess? Questions chased themselves around in her mind like hamsters on a wheel until stress-induced exhaustion lured her into oblivion.

"Brenna. Wake now, love. It is time for us to begin our work."

The voice, soothing but magnetic, pulled Brenna out of a light doze. Right away, she noticed that something seemed odd. The room was still dark, though the darkness had changed to the deep blue-purple that precedes dawn. Nothing wrong with that. No, the strangeness lay in the fact that she seemed to be hovering near the ceiling of the room, while below, she could see herself lying on the bed.

A presence hovered near her, also looking downward. Brenna startled when she recognized Ronan. It *was* him, but at the same time, it wasn't. This being had Ronan's face, but he was so beautiful and shining that the sight brought tears to her eyes. It was as though his body was formed of opalescent light limned with gold. Even his hair reminded her of flame, but despite his altered appearance, she knew without doubt that it was he.

"I thought you weren't coming," she managed. "Or is this just a dream?"

Ronan didn't smile, but Brenna felt the warmth that emanated from him, like a fire meant to warm even the fiercest winter chill.

"You are out of your sleeping body, in the space between the physical world and the astral realm," he explained. "Annie mentioned that you had never consciously projected out of your body before, so I thought coming to you like this might help. Projection happens on its own when you sleep."

Without planning to, Brenna reached out to touch Ronan's face. He caught her hand and brought it to his lips, sending a deep shiver through her, body and soul. She had to look away—had to look anywhere but into those eyes that always wreaked such havoc.

Glancing at her hand in his, she noticed that she seemed to be just as luminous as he was. Astonished, she looked down at a taller version of herself that shimmered in the darkness like a being of light.

"We look like a pair of beacons," she said. "Anyone on the astral plane could see us from a mile away."

"Which brings me to the first lesson," he told her. "Watch."

She did as he asked, struck with wonder as he dropped her hand and began to change shape, his glow dimming to a shadowy grey. His face changed, jaw and ears elongating. His hair swept back into a mohawk which became a horse's mane. A moment later, the rest of him began to flow and shift, until the entire horse floated beside her. *He looks like a pooka,* she thought. Now where did that idea come from? Oh, yeah. The faery encyclopedia.

"Try it," he said, though no sound came from the horse's mouth; she heard the words in her mind. "It is called the *fith-fath*. Shapeshifting. In the astral plane and the Otherworld, you can take any form you wish."

Brenna thought of the crows circling in the sky above her head, perched atop the roof or in the hawthorn grove, flying alongside any vehicle in which she rode. They followed her even more closely than did the men who stalked her. But unlike men, crows had no fear; they were scavengers who fed off the dead on battlefields even before the battle had ended. They unnerved some people, but almost every culture in the world seemed to have stories of their magic. They inspired fear and dread, just as she meant to inspire fear in anyone who thought he could toy with her life or the lives of people she cared about. Unbidden, words flowed into her mind—words that carried a memory, an image, a voice.

I am the harbinger of fate. I am the scald crow of battle, the Badbh Catha. I am swift vengeance on black wings. What I seek I shall find, what I find I shall pursue, and what I pursue I shall destroy.

Brenna's back tingled as a shiver enveloped her body. Her astral self constricted, her feet curled into talons and her arms and shoulders fanned out into black-feathered wings. Her eyesight sharpened. Her mouth and nose lengthened, hardening into a beak designed to hook, rip and tear. Her scream became a crow's hoarse cry. She beat her powerful wings until she rose above Ronan's head to look down on the woman asleep in the bed below, faintly contemptuous of her pale, smooth body.

"I should have known you'd choose that form. It suits you," Ronan said from below her. In a breath, he shifted to the form of a hawk, which rose to hover beside her in a way no real bird could. "Fly with me," he said. His mental voice held a wildness—a hint of danger that attracted her every bit as much as his gentle, caring side. The look in his eyes said he knew it, too, damn him!

They flew through the roof of the house to dip and swirl above it. They rose and fell on astral eddies not unlike air currents in the physical world. The ground blurred below them as they flew over Strokestown, over Annie's house and a farm in the distance, then finally back to the rental cottage. Exhilarated and tingling, Brenna followed Ronan down to perch on the roof when he indicated he wished to speak with her.

"You must retain the sense of who you are at all times, or you can lose yourself in the moment and in the form you take," he said. "You can also spin off more than one astral double, but if any of them is harmed or cut loose in certain of the realms, your physical body may be harmed as well."

"I know," Brenna said, imagining she could feel the breeze ruffle her feathers. "When the two men attacked me and nearly choked my astral body to death, I had bruises on my neck when I woke up."

Ronan mantled, then let his feathers settle, as though he were a real bird. "When you journey into dangerous realms, you must go in a form other than your physical double so that you are not so easily recognized. And as you attempt to learn more about those who pursue you, you may wish to use another method of spying that might afford you more safety. For this we must borrow a physical creature. That one will do." He pointed toward the ground, where Annie's calico cat was stalking something near the hedge behind the cottage.

"What do you mean, borrow?" Brenna asked, but Ronan had already turned himself into a sparrow and fluttered to the ground near the cat. Brenna followed in crow form and landed a short distance away.

Ronan and Trixie stood eye to eye; the cat stared right at him, sniffing. Ronan's sparrow form dissolved into a golden mist. As Brenna watched, Trixie inhaled, then went rigid.

"Ronan!" Brenna shrieked. His astral body was gone. There was no other living creature near her but Trixie, who turned her head to stare at Brenna with intelligent green eyes.

The cat took a few steps toward her. Brenna had the urge to flee despite the fact that a physical cat shouldn't be able to hurt her astral form, but she stood her ground. She had to know what had happened to Ronan. Trixie met her stare for stare; then Brenna saw something stir behind those feline eyes.

"Ronan?" she asked.

I am here, and so is this furred one. She has allowed me to borrow her body for a time.

Ronan's disembodied voice in her mind startled Brenna, but not nearly as much as seeing a non-feline presence behind Annie's cat's eyes. Was it Ronan's soul?

We will jump onto the fence, so that you will allow yourself to believe what you have just seen.

Brenna watched, stunned, as Trixie turned and broke into a run. At the last moment, she launched herself into the air with a powerful thrust of hind legs, to land atop the stone fence. She pranced several paces toward Brenna before she jumped down again like a performing tiger at a circus. Trixie returned to Brenna's side and sat down in front of her, gazing up into her face. The cat opened her mouth and golden mist poured out, becoming Ronan's shimmering man-shape. Trixie watched him for a moment, then tried to twine herself around his astral ankles. After a moment she trotted away, apparently no worse for wear.

"Possession?" Brenna asked. Somewhere below her, she could feel her heart hammering. She changed back to human form and faced Ronan, hands on her hips, trying not to show how freaked she was.

Ronan came to her and took her hands, meeting her gaze. "Possession is not the correct term for this. Some call it *riding*, but you must first ask to share the creature's body before you attempt to ride behind its eyes, and you must never stay too long." That shocking pronouncement had Brenna shaking her head as she tried to take it in, not at all sure she wanted to.

"Can you possess a person just as easily?" She swallowed. Did she want to hear the answer?

Ronan looked worried. "Possess a human? On occasion, a non-corporeal entity might ride or lend his energy if the human gives permission, but that is not true possession. Forcible possession can result in insanity, or even displacement of the host body's spirit. Only a fool or a monster would do such a thing!" He sounded so horrified at the idea that Brenna relaxed.

"No. You're right; I don't think you would possess another person. I'm sorry I considered it even for a moment."

Ronan dropped her hand and floated near her, his expression grave. "If you cannot trust me, then this has all been for nothing."

Brenna stared at him. Once again, it was down to intuition or logic.

"I do trust you, Ronan," she whispered, and released the shield Annie had taught her to form with her aura. If she showed him she was willing to be vulnerable in his presence, he'd understand that she meant what she said. Tentatively, she let the softened edge of her energy field flow toward his.

The shimmering glows touched and began to merge. Desire, sharp and sudden, flooded her at the contact, and she heard

Ronan's gasp echo hers. She trembled, gripping his arms to keep herself from falling, which was silly, given where they were. But that was how he made her feel—as though she were falling.

Maybe she was. But even if that were true, it was too late to catch herself. Far, far too late.

"Brenna, I thought you didn't want—" Ronan's mental tone sounded a little strangled.

"I was wrong," Brenna said, and lifted her face toward his. She could no more have stopped the motion than she could have held back the tide. It was a silent acknowledgement, a surrender and a claim, all at once.

His lips came down on hers so softly that she melted into him. Suffused with warmth, wrapped in his aura, she gave herself over to the sensation. It wasn't a mating of bodies, but it was a mating of souls, and it shook her to the core.

Time seemed to slow and then stop altogether. Nevertheless, when Ronan pulled away—slowly as though it pained him to do so—it seemed too soon.

"I cannot stay longer, Brenna, *mo grá*. I am needed elsewhere now," he said. She could hear the regret that colored his tone.

"But Ronan, I...." She trailed off, still shaken at the abrupt separation.

"I would not leave you for the world, but I have no choice. I will return as soon as I am able," he told her. "There are...things of which we must speak."

He seemed as though he might kiss her again, but stopped just short of touching her aura. The heat in his eyes made her shiver, and without meaning to, she reached for him again. Her astral hand touched empty space; he'd already faded away, gone back to his physical body, wherever that was.

"Damn." For a moment, she wondered if he was just a figment of her imagination. A dream lover.

Bereft, Brenna re-formed her shields and followed the silver cord back to her body.

She woke, but didn't open her eyes. Moments later, she turned over, suppressing a groan of frustration. Her body tingled with desire; even the brush of the sheets against her skin teased her sensitive flesh so much that she wanted to scream. Wonderful. Just freaking wonderful. All revved up with nowhere to go. Apparently, she'd surrendered to her instincts a little too well.

She solved the problem as best she could alone, then hit the shower and turned the water down to lukewarm. Cold was just masochistic, which she wasn't. Usually.

When she emerged, she was still as grumpy as a wet cat, but she'd get through the day regardless. Once Ronan returned, she and he could sort out whatever was happening between them. In the meantime, with all this pent-up energy, she'd be able to tend to all the everyday issues that demanded her attention—the second travel article, a magic lesson with Annie, Cuchulain's wounds.... Nothing too ambitious. Just an average Thursday for a seasoned travel writer.

Yeah, and cats had wings.

Halfway through the morning, Brenna glanced up from her laptop as Cuchulain rose stiffly, padded to the living room window, and nosed aside the curtain to look out into the yard. He'd done a lot of healing in the past twenty-four hours. If Ronan hadn't arrived to heal him and Cu had made it to the vet's, he'd still be in intensive care. As it was, he was already to the grumpy, impatient stage.

Brenna's lips curved into a smile as she watched him. She'd let him out only briefly since his near-fatal battle, but if he was already pining at the window it wouldn't be long before she'd need to turn him loose so he could go back to wherever he stayed when he wasn't with her. She'd gotten so used to him being around that she sometimes forgot he wasn't hers. It would be hard to leave him when she went back to the States.

A rumbling growl drew Brenna's gaze back to the window. Cuchulain's hackles were raised and the rumble kept coming even when Brenna set the laptop aside and crossed the room to join him. She had to push him aside so she could peek out to see what had upset him; even then only his head moved, his huge body planted, straining toward the window. For a moment, Brenna was afraid he'd go right through it.

When she managed to see past her furry bodyguard, an icy jolt shot through her middle. Colm stood in the yard, arms crossed over his chest, staring at the cottage. He must have noticed movement at the window, because he turned to look at Brenna. Their gazes locked through the glass.

"Brenna!" he yelled. "Come out, darlin'. We have things to discuss."

Even at a distance of several yards, his gaze was compelling. His voice pulled at Brenna despite the way her brain yammered for her to ignore him. Maybe she'd overreacted about what had happened between them Saturday after the *seisiún*. The roses had been beautiful and the negligee *had* matched her eyes. Maybe she'd been a fool to dismiss Colm so hastily.

Brenna sighed. Just look at him. He was so...beautiful. She had to go to him; they could talk this out.

Brenna dropped the curtain and took a step toward the door, but Cuchulain was suddenly there, blocking her exit. All at once her lovable teddy bear of a dog friend bared his teeth at her and growled—that same low threat of violence that he'd just been leveling at Colm. That was...messed up, though in just what way, Brenna wasn't sure. It felt as though dust bunnies had taken up residence in her brain.

She heard Colm call, "Brenna, I know you're in there,

sweetheart. You weren't at the café yesterday like you promised. I'm worried about you, and I think we need to talk. Come out so we can discuss this in a reasonable manner."

Brenna took a step toward the door, reaching for the handle just as Cu lunged. With all the force of his greater weight, he hit her broadside and knocked her on her ass. The wind went out of her in a *whuff*. As Brenna's lungs struggled to regain her lost breath, the haziness started to clear from her mind. Logic returned with a rush, causing her to gasp anew.

Colm was using *draíocht* on her! And if that was true, then it also explained what had happened after the *seisiún*.

Damn. Did everyone on this island except the gardaí play around with magic as a hobby, or was it just her bad luck that she'd landed herself in a *draíocht*-user's hot spot? The idea that Colm was somehow connected to her other stalkers didn't help things either, but she had to consider it. The other explanation—that Ronan was right and Colm was one of the Sidhe—also came to mind. The thought made her shiver.

With her return to sanity, Cu had backed down and was now licking her face, as if making an apology he didn't owe. Somehow, he'd known what was happening to her and he'd just saved her from running out there and throwing herself into Colm's arms like a bewitched idiot. Brenna patted Cuchulain and got back to her feet, surprised at how shaky she was. This time, when she headed toward the door, the dog didn't try to stop her, though his gaze kept tracking between her and the window.

Brenna checked to be sure the deadbolt was engaged, then took a few moments to shore up every psychic shield she had and add a few more for good measure. Then she ducked into the kitchen to peek through its window. Colm was still staring toward the living room. When he shifted his weight and then began to pace, Brenna noticed that he limped. That was new. Her lips tightened, and she glanced at Cuchulain. She'd heard a man's voice outside right after Cu's nearly fatal battle. Watching the way Cu reacted every time Colm called out to her, she was willing to lay odds on whose voice that had been.

"Brenna! Open the feckin' door!"

No feckin' way, asshole.

He *dared* to think he could force her? Well, whether he used magic or not, he wasn't above the law. She could and would nail his ass to the floor with it. Involving the gardaí was a risk, but Colm had an identity and a reputation to maintain. He probably wouldn't be stupid enough to throw it all away. If he did decide to attack them with magic, then maybe they would finally believe her about what had been going on in their jurisdiction.

Brenna picked up the telephone receiver and dialed, keeping one eye on his whereabouts while making sure to stay out of his line of sight. As soon as the emergency operator picked up, she reported his presence and behavior and gave the address, then hung up despite an injunction to stay on the line. After a moment's consideration, she moved back behind the door, the only area in the front of the house that had no windows. The kitchen made her feel too much like a fish in a fishbowl with a cat sitting nearby.

"Don't think your wards will keep me out forever," Colm was yelling. "Someone besides me has been at them. Sooner or later, I'll find a crack to slip through, and then you'll have to listen to me. You'll have to remember what we've shared, what we've meant to each other. It's our destiny to be together." During his tirade, Colm's voice had shifted from furious to wheedling. "I know you're confused right now, Daireann, but I'll make you remember, and then everything will be all right."

Even through her anger, his words ran a finger of ice from Brenna's scalp to her tailbone.

Daireann—that had been her name during the ancient

lifetime she'd refused to finish remembering. A laugh forced its way out of Brenna's dry throat. If things got any stranger, she'd write this up as a script and send it off to Jay along with the second travel article. That way if she didn't make it home, Jay could sell the story to Hollywood and make a mint.

The only problem was that she didn't know how this story was going to end.

Colm's verbal abuse stopped so suddenly that adrenaline surged through Brenna's veins. What was he up to now? Had he found some way to get in? The fact that Cu had stopped growling made the silence worse, because there was no way she was going to open the door to see what Colm was up to.

Someone knocked on the door, and Brenna jumped.

"It's the gardaí, Ms. Callahan. You can open the door now."

Brenna hesitated. For all she knew, Colm might also be a ventriloquist as well as a...whatever he was.

"Ms. Callahan? It's all right."

She glanced at Cu. He was wagging his tail; that was a good sign if she'd ever seen one. By the way he'd been growling before, it seemed that whatever Colm had done to bewitch her didn't work on dogs.

She went to the living room window and twitched the curtain aside. Sure enough, a garda stood on her doorstep. Another stood beside the squad car by the road, watching Colm, who now sat in the backseat. Brenna hurried to open the door.

"Officer, thank you so much for coming."

"Right. I'll need a statement of complaint, and then we'll take him in to the station." This garda was all business, and brusque with it. But at least he wasn't one of the ones Brenna had already dealt with. She felt enough like an idiot already without having to tell Garda O'Shea about the morning-after roses and the negligee.

Briefly, Brenna detailed the situation for this garda's report, and when at last he headed back to the squad car, she was sagging with relief. She hadn't known how tense she'd been until the immediate source of stress had been removed. As soon as the car drove away, she headed straight for the kitchen to brew a pot of tea.

As she waited for the water to boil, she tried to make sense of her situation, but the answers she needed seemed to be floating behind a veil just out of reach. Brenna sighed, resigned. She needed to call Annie. Like it or not, she had to go through that regression again and see the rest of the memory. Annie had obviously been right; what was happening to her now was somehow connected to that past life. But how, and why? And even if she found out, what could she do to resolve matters before one of the magical attacks proved fatal? Brenna turned off the burner and headed for the phone.

CHAPTER THIRTEEN

As she reached for the phone, Brenna glanced through the kitchen window toward the stand of hawthorn trees near the road. A flash of black caught her eye and she paused, hand on the receiver. At least thirty crows perched in the highest branches, silent and unnerving. A drizzle had begun just after the gardaí had taken Colm away. Brenna had read on the internet that crows tended to congregate in tall trees during storms—nothing too unusual there. But hers wasn't the tallest grove in the area, and she'd rarely seen crows perched in the neighbors' trees, storm or no storm.

Fear tingled through her, coupled with an odd sense of excitement. Less than two weeks left in Ireland, and even less time in which to connect all the pieces of this puzzle. She had the feeling that if she solved it, she'd emerge stronger than she'd ever been. If not, she wouldn't emerge at all. Was that the message the Morrigan was trying to send her?

Cuchulain gave a happy little bark and ran to the door. Brenna looked toward the walk, and blinked. While she'd been staring at the crows, Ronan had appeared and was now coming toward the house. For all the drizzle, he didn't look any more soaked than he had when the rainstorm had caught them at Keshcorran. Her heart gave a lurch as she hurried to open the door for him.

"Brenna, are you well?" His smile as he came in made the breath catch in her throat. She fumbled the door closed and turned to face him, then wished she hadn't as her gaze fell on his chest. Damn, why did he have to have a body like that? Under that shirt, he probably had sculpted abs. She drew in a lungful of his rain-kissed scent and sighed, feeling the morning's tension begin to fade. At the same time a different tension started to build.

"Brenna?" Ronan asked again. She blinked. He was looking down at her in concern. Why? Oh, right. Because she hadn't spoken.

"I...I'm fine. I had a run-in with Colm this morning."

He started to speak, but she held up a hand. "It's okay. I had him arrested. You were right about him. He's trouble, and magical trouble at that."

Ronan seemed to relax. "I am glad you are safe. And I am relieved that you have changed your views about Colm." She was short enough that he had to bend his head to look down at her. He was so close that she could feel his warmth when he took off his jacket, which he tossed onto the back of an armchair.

She fidgeted for a moment, then asked the question that had been bothering her since Colm's arrest. "Ronan, at the heritage center, you told me that you believed Colm was one of the Sidhe. I thought you were wrong because he had human credentials, but then this morning, he tried to use *draíocht* against me—I'm sure of it. In fact, he almost had me for a moment. If Cu hadn't interfered, I'd have gone outside into his arms. So I need to know—why do you think Colm is Sidhe?"

Ronan's expression didn't change. "I believe that because the moment I saw him, I recognized his life energy as Sidhe. His energy field is subtly different from a human's, if you know what to look for."

Brenna sucked in a breath, then let it out over a five-count. "Okay. Let's say I believe you. If Colm is Sidhe, then what are you? You've told me very little about yourself and produced no I.D.—not even a last name. You use *draíocht* in ways I'd never have begun to imagine until recently, like when you healed Cuchulain. Then there was also the way you looked on the astral plane—nothing at all like the two men who attacked me. At first, I just assumed you'd amped up your appearance as a demonstration for me, as part of the lesson, but the more I think about it, the more I believe that was your true form. *You* are one of the Sidhe, aren't you?"

"Yes," Ronan said.

For a moment, all she could do was stare at him. Right now, he looked just the same as he always had, but...he was Sidhe. And...he was real. A flesh-and-blood faery. Right here, right now. And she'd been fantasizing about his abs.

Ronan looked amused. "Should it matter that I am Sidhe? Does that affect your willingness to trust me?"

"On principal, no," she said slowly. "But I know Colm's been using...I guess it's glamour, isn't it? Is that what you've been doing, too? If you have, you should know that using magic to make someone want you is just wrong." Her heart was pounding. Could he hear it?

"Truth between us, Brenna Callahan," he said, holding up a placatory hand. "I swear to you by whatever you find holy that I have never used glamour on you, and never will, unless you ask it. Whatever you feel for me is real—as is what I feel for you."

"And that is...?" She gazed up at him, waiting, almost afraid to breathe. From the first day, he'd been so protective of her, so conscious of what she needed, even when she didn't know herself.

If he was willing to swear he wasn't using glamour on her, she was willing to believe him. Beyond that, she wanted—needed—this connection she'd been feeling between them. Except for him and Annie, she was alone here in Ireland, surrounded by things that really did go bump in the night. Inexplicably, in the middle of all the chaos and fear, Ronan felt like home.

Without conscious thought, she moved closer to him. She had an overwhelming need to touch him, and it was no use denying it any longer. If she was lost, if there was no turning back, so be it.

He hesitated, though his hand settled on her shoulder. "What of your boyfriend?"

Again, there was that familiar lurch in her chest. "Um…I no longer have a boyfriend. I broke up with him earlier this week."

"If I were inclined to lie, I would tell you that I am sorry to hear that."

"But you're not sorry." Some imp must have taken control of her body, because she leaned farther into him as she asked the question. It seemed so natural that for a moment, she had a startled feeling that this wasn't the first time she'd done it.

"No, I am not sorry," he said. He lowered his head until his lips hovered just an inch above hers, and her body began to tremble. No alcohol on board. No lack of memory. No excuses.

Maybe it was time to get to the bottom of this foolishness. To be honest, she had been attracted to Ronan since the moment he'd picked her up off the muddy ground in the dark. He appealed to her on so many levels she couldn't begin to sort them out. She was tired of overthinking everything. Right now, she didn't want to think. She only wanted to feel.

She lifted her chin and brushed her lips against his, just a tentative touch, nothing she couldn't back away from if it got too intense. For a moment, he made no move to kiss her back, just let her explore his lips. He was so still he might have been a statue, but a statue didn't radiate heat. A statue didn't have a heartbeat that sped up beneath her fingers as she traced them across his chest.

She gave in to the urge to nibble at his lower lip, ignoring the little voice in her head that warned she was moving too fast, taking too many chances. He parted his lips for her, and she slid a hand up around the back of his neck, her thumb caressing the pulse at the side of his throat. Memories of their moment in the cave crashed over her, superimposed by images of things they definitely hadn't done. It was madness, but what wasn't, lately?

Before she could think better of it, she put a hand against his chest and gave him a push toward the couch. He pulled her with him so that she landed on top of him, their legs tangling together as the couch cushioned their mock-fall. In that moment, Brenna knew that she couldn't lie to herself anymore. She wanted him; that was all, and...oh, yeah, he wanted her, too. She hadn't been wrong about that. She positioned herself more comfortably on top of him, length for length. The contact made her shiver, stirred so many other sensations that she had to make an effort to steady herself. She barely knew him. Yet, she did know him. Every part of her being insisted that she did.

Past lives. Maybe he'd been behind one of those other doors. She might never know for sure, but maybe it didn't matter. Maybe nothing mattered right now except this. Ronan rolled her over beside him, their bodies practically fused together. His hand around her back kept her from rolling off the couch; she could feel its heat through her shirt as though he were touching skin. Her breath caught again at the thought. In a minute, they'd get to that.

"*Mo grá*, we need to talk." His voice came out harsh, his breathing unsteady. The fact that she'd done that to him without the aid of Sidhe glamour sent a thrill of power through her.

"In a minute. Please, Ronan," she said, her voice no steadier than his, "I need this. I need you. I'm only human."

"But, Bren—" Whatever he'd been about to say was cut off as she stopped his mouth with her own.

His lips burned hers, and she couldn't hold back a moan as his tongue stroked into her mouth, slow, erotic, as if they had all the time in the world, though the hardness that pressed against her belly said otherwise. One of his hands pulled up her shirt; in another moment, that heat would be on her skin, setting it on fire. Her breasts tingled and her nipples hardened, though he hadn't touched them yet. Damn sexy man...Sidhe...whatever. Definitely too sexy for his shirt. That and a few other things would have to come off, so she could make him moan, too. And she *would* make him moan. It was inevitable, like the rain outside. She started to undo his buttons, then froze at the sound of the doorbell.

"Damn! Who could that be?" She wrenched herself up off him with a groan and hastily tried to straighten her clothes.

The doorbell chimed again, but for a moment, Brenna couldn't take her eyes off Ronan. She could still feel the places where he'd touched her, and her body was silently shrieking in protest at the separation. He sat up and straightened his clothes too, but his blue eyes burned into hers and it was all she could do not to fall back onto him, strip off every inch of fabric and have what she'd almost gotten before someone rang the *damned* doorbell.

Brenna hurried into the tiny foyer between the kitchen and living room. She glanced through the peephole to the front step and jerked backward, heart pounding. No. This could not be happening! What were the odds, a thousand to one? If this was the luck of the Irish, they could have it back.

She glanced over her shoulder at Ronan, who stood in the living room doorway. What was she supposed to do now? As if in answer, the doorbell chimed again. Trying to ignore the clenching of dread in her midsection, Brenna undid the locks. She opened the door and held it open, staring helplessly at Brad, who stood on her doorstep soaked from head to foot, holding a suitcase. His dark hair was even darker from the water, and a silk suit she recognized as his second-best...wasn't, anymore. His overcoat hung over his arm; it seemed he'd neglected to bring an umbrella. Bad signs, all of them.

"Brenna. Thank God, I'm in the right place. Those signposts...." he trailed off as he looked past her to Ronan, who stood in the doorway of the living room, as composed as if he hadn't been about to make love to her on the couch just moments before. Brad paled, and Brenna saw his hand tighten on the suitcase handle. Just to forestall any other bad ideas he might have, she took it from him, set it inside the door to the kitchen, then returned to where the two men were staring each other down.

Well, Brad was trying to stare Ronan down. That intimidating lawyer glare usually cowed anyone—in the courtroom or out—but it wasn't working on Ronan, which no doubt pissed Brad off as much as finding another guy here in the first place.

"Brad, this is Ronan. Ronan, Brad. Ronan's been helping me with my article research." *Oh, what an understatement.*

"Hello," Brad said, sounding as though he'd forced the word out against his better judgment. Ronan nodded, but his face gave nothing away.

Brad studied her so closely that Brenna knew he must be noting every facet of her appearance—taking evidence. Her lips were probably swollen, her face flushed, and...had she fastened that top button right? She glanced down at it. No, of course she hadn't.

"Brenna, could I speak with you for a moment in private?" Brad asked. He had his lawyer face on now, playing calm for all he was worth.

"Ronan, please excuse us," Brenna said. Damn, this was awkward, like a bad chick flick.

"Of course." Ronan went into the living room, where he picked up a book from the end table and sat in one of the armchairs as though he intended to read. There, he knew his part, too. Brenna had the urge to laugh, though none of this was funny. It was raining men; hallelujah.

She followed Brad into the kitchen and checked the teakettle on the stove to see whether it had enough water left in it. The least she could do was offer Brad a hot drink after his trek through the rain to...well, what had he come here for?

"Why are you here, Bradley?" she asked aloud, proud that her voice didn't betray the tension she felt.

"After that phone call, where else would I be? You didn't sound like yourself. I started to worry that you'd gotten into trouble, so of course I came after you. But now I see I was wrong." His tone remained quiet, though some of the anger came through.

"Bullshit. You weren't worried about me. You just didn't like the way I broke up with you, so you wanted to prove to yourself that I cheated on you. You came to argue your case and try to convince me I made a mistake. The lawyer in you doesn't like to lose." The words were harsh; it hurt to say them. But they were true.

"Got me all figured out, have you?" He was losing the lawyer cool now, and she couldn't do a thing about it.

"No, but I've got *me* all figured out, at least about us. I'm not right for you, and you're not right for me. You're a wonderful man—" The look on his face stopped her.

"*Don't.* Just...don't. I get it. I saw the guy in there, okay? Damn it, Brenna! We've been together for two years. Two years! When you got back, I was going to ask you to marry me. I had the prenup already drafted. I'd bought a ring. I had dinner reservations. You were going to come home to a house full of flowers. Hell, I might even have rented a limo to pick you up at the airport. I know how much you love romantic gestures."

"A pre-nup. Yeah, that's really romantic." She popped a teabag into a mug and poured hot water in, then held it out to him. He ignored it, so she set it on the counter. Apparently, one person's comfort measure was another's annoyance.

"Don't you see?" she said after a moment. "All the things you've said—they're just examples of what I mean! You've always got to be the one in control. You plan everything, you adjust everything and everyone to suit you. You're the hotshot lawyer. You want your life to be just so, like your china and your paintings and the ties on your tie rack. But sometimes things aren't just so, Brad. Sometimes things get out of hand whether you like it or not. I'm one of those. I get out of hand, and that won't ever change."

"You mean this, don't you? You're willing to give up on us, just like that, to go after a man you've known for less than a month. Or have you known him longer?" A look of horror crossed his face, and he actually backed up a step. "This isn't one of those internet dating things, is it?"

"No! And no matter what it is, it's none of your business. I already told you, I didn't break up with you for some other guy. I broke up with you because once I got away from Portland, I realized that we just don't work as a couple. It was okay, but it was never...right. Do you know what I mean?" She was trembling with tension now; hopefully, he couldn't see it.

Brad was staring at her as if he'd never seen her before. "No, I don't. And if I don't, then maybe you're right. You aren't making any more sense than you did on the phone, but now that I see you face to face, I can see that you believe this nonsense you're feeding me. You ran off to Ireland to find yourself; then you found yourself another guy. Ergo, I'm not right for you, and you're not right for me. That about sum it up?"

"No! Well, sort of, but...no. I told you before; it's complicated."

"Complicated. Yeah, I can see that. But it's also pretty simple.

You moved on; I wasted my time. Open and shut. The defense rests. I'm finished here." He grabbed his suitcase and overcoat and headed for the door.

Sudden dread came over Brenna. She hurried after him. "Brad, what are you going to do now?"

He laughed. "Hell, I don't know, Bren. Maybe I'll go to Disneyland. But in the meantime, I'm going to get in my car and drive back to my hotel, before things get any worse."

"Don't leave angry," she pleaded. A part of her ached in sympathy; he didn't deserve this kind of pain. Knowing she couldn't help him only made it worse.

"We're long past the time when you could tell me how to feel," he said quietly. "If you feel guilty, that's your problem."

On his way out, he took extra care when closing the door. With Brad, that was worse than a slam.

Brenna leaned her forehead against the door and groaned. Suddenly she felt tired, all the way down to her toes. This whole trip had been a disaster. Oh, the writing had gone well, but that was about the only thing that hadn't gone up in flames. Her assessment of the other night had been right; she was hell on men.

A warm hand touched her shoulder, and she jumped. Ronan. She'd forgotten he was here. How much of the debacle had he heard? It was a small house; he must have heard it all.

"It is all right. You need not say a word. Do you wish me to leave?" His hand rubbed the back of her neck, fingers pressing here and there, releasing the knots that had formed during her fight with Brad. That was Ronan: always the gallant knight.

She leaned back against his chest and tilted her head to look up at him. "Stay with me, please. I don't think I can get back in the mood for making love, but I'd like your company."

"Of course. Whatever you need. But there are some things of which we must speak, before—"

Outside, a car engine roared. Someone yelled. There was a *thump*, and the sound of the car speeding down the gravel road away from town. Adrenaline crashed through her. Brad.

She wrenched the door open and ran outside, Ronan right behind her. A white Jag was parked on the verge beside her fence, a dark form crumpled on the ground in front of it.

"Brad!" Brenna screamed. She ran to where Brad lay, knelt beside him and reached out to touch his neck. Her hand shook, but she finally located the carotid artery. The pulse was weak, but it was there. His breath fogged against her hand, but he didn't wake or move. Brenna chewed her bottom lip. If they left him out in the cold, he'd never make it. But if anything inside him was broken and they moved him, he could die from that.

"Get some blankets and call for help," Ronan said, his gaze steady on hers.

"Can't you heal him like you did Cu?" she asked, desperate.

Ronan shook his head, his expression kind but grave. "I cannot pull enough *draíocht* to undo all the damage, but I can at least keep him warm until the healers arrive."

"Healers? You mean EMT's? Never mind, I'm going." Swallowing down her fear, Brenna dashed back down the path toward the house.

When she returned, cell phone in hand, she found Ronan frowning. Her fear resurfaced. "What is it? Is he...?"

"No. He's not dead." Ronan's voice lowered, and Brenna covered the cell's microphone so that the person on the other end of the emergency call couldn't hear him. "I feel the taint of magic on the road. All of the tire tracks are gone, along with any other possible traces of the accident."

Rage boiled up inside Brenna. She stared at Ronan. "You mean it wasn't just any hit-and-run driver," she said quietly, keeping the phone's mouthpiece covered. "You think they waited for him to come out, then they ran him down before he could get into his car. They figured he was with me, so they went after him, just like that."

"Perhaps," Ronan said. "That, or they mistook him for Colm, which could mean they are also hunting Sidhe." His usually warm eyes had gone so cold that Brenna shivered.

All at once, she remembered the cell phone, and put it back to her ear. "Yes. Yes, I'm here. Sorry. I'm trying to wrap him up, but it's hard to do that without moving him. Yes, he's still breathing on his own." In between talking with the emergency dispatch, she helped tuck blankets around and under Brad as well as she could. At least when she placed her hand on his forehead, he wasn't too cold to the touch. Ronan's spell must have worked.

After what seemed like a long time, the wail of a siren announced the ambulance's imminent arrival and perhaps the gardaí as well. Maybe now they would believe that someone was after her, not that they'd be of much help if they did.

"Yes, that's the ambulance. Thank you so much," Brenna said into the cell phone. As soon as she could, she hung up.

"Well, that's it. Those bastards have just gone too far," she muttered.

"What are you thinking?" Ronan asked.

Brenna grimaced. "I'm going to stalk the stalkers, Ronan. I refuse to just sit around and wait for them to attack me or anyone else I care about. I'm going to track them down—on the astral plane or this one, I don't care which. Before, it was just scary. Now it's personal."

Ronan studied her for a long moment. Then his body began to fade, until soon she could no longer see or touch him. Another Sidhe ability, no doubt. Even though he'd admitted to being Sidhe and she'd accepted it intellectually, seeing him phase out like that was startling. At least it explained why he always seemed to arrive and leave so quickly. At least she understood now why he wouldn't want to answer questions from the gardaí about his nonexistent I.D.

A few moments later, Brenna could see both gardaí and ambulance coming around the bend. She thought Ronan had gone, but then his warm breath against the side of her face made her jump.

His disembodied voice whispered against her ear. "Brenna, in regards to what you have just resolved to do...."

She tensed. Now he would tell her not to take foolish chances with her safety, or hit her with other cautionary advice, and she wasn't going to give an inch. If he tried to stop her, she'd...she'd....

"I will help you," he said.

CHAPTER FOURTEEN

B renna spent the rest of Thursday and most of Friday wearing a track between Brad's Galway hospital room, the gift shop and the cafeteria. Friday night he woke briefly, but he was still so groggy she didn't get to speak to him. Saturday, he woke up on three occasions, all of which she somehow managed to miss. Saturday night she called Annie, who called her a "right eejit" and said she'd take a bus into Galway the next day.

Sunday morning, the lobby doors opened to admit Annie, who took one look at Brenna and opened her arms. Brenna went into them, a little embarrassed at how relieved she was at seeing the older woman. Annie's warm affection nearly undid her careful façade of calm.

She was like a child who wanted comfort. For a couple of hours, there, she'd even contemplated calling her mother. Her *mother!* Brenna shuddered at the thought of Wendy Callahan flying over here, clucking around Brad, berating her daughter for what she'd consider a senseless breakup. Mom had always liked Brad—so nice, so successful, so *normal.* He hit all the points on the checklist. Mom would be devastated enough at the breakup, let alone Brad's accident. Her next phone call was sure to be an unmitigated delight.

"Are you all right?" Annie asked. She stepped back from Brenna and studied her face again.

"I'm fine," Brenna said, trying to meet that kind gaze without tears. "Just a little shocked, is all. I...Brad...we...."

"You don't have to explain a thing to me, dear," Annie said. "But I'm glad you rang me, so I could be here for you."

"I appreciate that, Annie. But it seems like all I've done since I arrived is cause trouble. I never intended to." She realized she was hanging on to Annie as though she were a lifeline, and tried to relax her grip.

"Well, of course you didn't," Annie soothed, patting Brenna's shoulder. "Now, why don't we get you some non-hospital food and then get you home so you can sleep? You've been here over forty-eight hours. I'm sure Ronan is concerned about you."

"Where is he, anyway?" Brenna asked. "I thought he might come with you."

"Oh, no, dear. Somehow I doubt he'd set foot inside a hospital unless he had no choice. I'm sure he'll come see you once you're back at the cottage."

"Can't say I blame him for staying away from this place," Brenna said. The longer she stayed here, the tighter her skin felt. All the typical hospital noises seemed to echo through her skull. Worst of all was the oppressive sense of other people's pain. It surrounded her, bearing down on her like a crushing weight. She put up a hand to rub her temples and caught Annie's sharp gaze on her.

"Shall we go now?" Annie asked. "You look exhausted."

"I think I'll just go look in on Brad once more. Then I'll be ready," Brenna said. She wanted nothing more than to follow

Annie through those doors right away, but she couldn't. She had to say goodbye, because she had no idea whether she'd be back.

"I'll be here," Annie said. She sat in one of the chairs and picked up a magazine, which Brenna was sure she didn't intend to read—unless she had a jones for rock stars. Thank goodness for Annie; if she wasn't around, things would be a hell of a lot harder to handle right now.

In the doorway of Brad's room once more, she hesitated. They'd drawn a curtain around his bed; she could see someone in a white coat there. A nurse bustled past, carrying a syringe.

"Please, what's happened? Is Brad all right?" Brenna asked.

The nurse looked at Brenna and her expression softened. "You came in the ambulance with him when they transferred him from Roscommon, didn't you? If you've been here all this time, you need some rest. I'm sure Mr. Carlson wouldn't want you to pass out from exhaustion."

"But you haven't answered my question. What's going on in there? Is he worse, better, what?"

The nurse looked surprised. "Oh, didn't you know? He's awake again. He's doing very well, with all he's been through."

"Oh! Oh, that's...that's good news. Maybe I'd better just go, then." Brenna started to back out of the room, but a familiar voice stopped her.

"Wait, Brenna, is that you?" The voice sounded scratchy and weak, but it was Brad's.

"Yes, it's me." Brenna followed the nurse into the room as the doctor drew the curtain aside and headed for the door.

"Come here, Bren," Brad said. "Please."

She went to his bedside, watched as the nurse uncapped the syringe, inserted the needle into a port in the I.V. tube, and slowly injected the medication.

"I don't know what to say," Brenna told him. "I'm just glad

you're alive."

Brad huffed what he must have intended as a laugh, but which ended in a pained cough instead. "What are the odds, huh? That car just came out of nowhere. I didn't even get a make on it."

"Well, how could you? I heard a yell and a thump, and when I got outside, you were already lying on the road unconscious."

Brad closed his eyes for a moment, then opened them and looked at the nurse. "Would you mind if I spoke to my...friend...alone, please? I promise I won't go anywhere."

"Very funny, Mr. Carlson," the nurse said, but she smiled a little at the tired joke. "I'll be back in a few minutes. I've clipped the call button to the sheet beside your good hand, in case you need me sooner."

When she'd gone, Brenna stood beside Brad's bed, at a loss as to what to say to him. She began by telling him all the things she'd told him while he was unconscious—that she'd called his partners at the law firm, that his partners were hiring him a personal assistant, and that his sister Patrice had flown out soon upon hearing the news and should arrive at any moment. He listened, impassive as he searched her face. When she'd finished, he managed a half-smile.

"That's fine, Bren, thanks. I just have one question."

"What's that?" she asked over the lump in her throat.

"Why are you still here? Don't stay with me out of guilt."

Brenna swallowed. "What makes you think I feel guilty?"

"Because I know you—better than you think. Don't beat yourself up anymore, okay? I'll get over this. I'll even get over *you*. But I can't do it with you hovering at my bedside."

She gazed at him for a moment, at his dark good looks marred by bandages, tubes, and traction equipment. Even now, the world was all very black and white to him. It had rules; it worked in a logical manner. Brenna envied him that. Nothing for her would ever be that certain again, but she'd just have to live with it. At least Brad was still in the world, even if he wasn't in hers.

"Brad, I...you're right, I have to go. But I don't know how to walk out of this room and leave you lying here."

"You just do it, Bren. Look me in the eyes, tell me goodbye, then turn around and walk out the door. We'll both get through this. People do, you know." He looked pale and exhausted, but his gaze remained steady on her face.

"I know," Brenna said softly. "Goodbye, Brad. I...wish you all the best."

"Me, too. Be careful out there, okay?" His gaze held regret, but it also held the steely resolve that had won him so many cases over the years. She looked into those familiar eyes for a moment more, then turned and walked out the door.

When the cab from Strokestown pulled up in front of Brenna's rental, rain was drizzling, and the afternoon light had already faded to dusk. A light shone from her kitchen window; she couldn't remember whether she'd left it on before the accident or not. She'd already had the cab drop Annie off, and she'd let Cuchulain loose just before leaving for the hospital, so she'd expected to come home to an empty cottage. Cautiously, she extended her senses, but as far as she could tell, her wards were intact.

Brad's rented Jag was still parked beside the road; she'd have to leave word for his personal assistant to come pick it up after he or she arrived. Colm's Range Rover was gone, though. Maybe the gardaí had come after it. Brenna paid the cab driver, got out and hurried down the walkway.

By the time she'd gone the short distance from the cab to the cottage door, she was already wet. She started to dig in her pocket for the keys, but the door opened before she could get them out. Her heart leaped as she saw Ronan, and her tilted world seemed to right itself. Ronan held the door, helped her peel off her coat, took her purse from her and set it on a chair. It seemed the White Knight had moved into her house while she'd been gone. It even looked cleaner than when she'd left it, other than the fact that he'd left his jacket hanging over the back of the sofa. Brenna bit back the giddy urge to ask him if he did windows, too.

"Are you all right?" he asked. "Never mind. I can see you are exhausted. Go and wash while I get you something to drink." He gave her a gentle push toward the bathroom. Somehow she made it through the motions of stripping, showering and pulling on fresh clothes while he puttered around in the kitchen as if he owned it. She was too tired, too grateful to question why he happened to be in her cottage, and of course he wouldn't have needed a key to get in. If Ronan had been here at least some of the time while she was gone, the people who'd run over Brad might be confused as to her whereabouts. Did they know she'd returned, or did they think she was still at the hospital?

"Ronan, did anything else happen while you were here without me?" Brenna asked as she came into the kitchen.

"No," he said in a grim tone. "I thought something might, which is why I returned, but it has been quiet. Trouble is coming, though. I can feel it in the air."

All through the police reports, the ambulance rides, the tense wait during Brad's surgery and the two days afterward, she'd held it together—probably because she was numb with shock. But now the fury Brenna had repressed battled with the desire to curl up in a corner and wait for the nightmare to end. It must have shown on her face, because Ronan caught her gaze and held it as if he could steady her by force of will.

Well, maybe he could. He opened his arms to her, someone offering her comfort for the second time in as many days. With Annie the gesture had been motherly, but with Ronan it was something far different. For some reason, all the emotions Brenna had struggled with since she'd arrived in Ireland burst in on her at once. Wracked with tears, she collapsed into his arms.

He picked her up and carried her into the living room, then sat in an armchair with her on his lap and held her while she cried. At first, she barely made out the sound of his soft brogue over her sobs, but then the English language seemed to desert him and he began murmuring to her in Irish, or maybe something older. After a while she quieted, her forehead cradled in the hollow of his neck and shoulder. His steady heartbeat beneath her ear lulled her, as did his scent, his voice. Reminded of that first night, she pulled away just enough to look up at his face.

"How is it that you always come to my rescue, while I've never done anything to return the favor?" she asked him.

"But you have rescued me, Brenna Callahan. Or you will, one day soon. You owe me nothing. Just having you here in my arms is favor enough for now." His warm breath feathered across her ear. She shivered.

"If you keep talking like that, I may fall head over heels for you and all your blarney," she said. Then she yawned. The long, anxious hours followed by her subsequent storm of emotion had left her drained.

"You need sleep," Ronan said.

Brenna sat up and twisted around so she could look at him. "No, I can't sleep now. I have to find out why those other men want me dead so badly they're willing to kill people around me as well. I need to do a little astral reconnaissance mission, and I need you to help me get out of body, like you did before."

Ronan's lips thinned. "Brenna, this is not...isn't...a good idea. It isn't wise to make such an attempt when you are exhausted."

Brenna shrugged. "I'm sure that's true. But Annie said I'd have to go through a learning curve she wouldn't normally consider wise or safe. I've already lost two days waiting for Brad to pull through. I need to do this now, tonight, before those guys take another shot at me—or at someone else. Besides, if you put me to sleep and then pull me into the astral plane, my body will be sleeping anyway."

"Yes, but in this case, you will not be resting. There is a difference."

"Still, I need to do this. Will you help me, or not?"

They stared at each other for a long moment, gazes locked. Finally, Ronan sighed. "If I do not, you will attempt it anyway. I seem to have no choice. I will help you, as I promised."

"Smart man." Brenna gave Ronan as confident a smile as she could muster and pushed herself off his lap and onto her feet. "Now, how do I find my enemies once I get onto the astral?" She'd avoided stewing over these particular details all during the bus ride into Strokestown and then the cab ride to the cottage; now she felt like the victim of a feral butterfly attack.

"You are the only one who *can* find them, Brenna, the same way they keep finding you," Ronan said. "They have attacked you and tried to tether your energy to theirs. You have broken most of these tethers in your defense lessons with Annie, but your enemies' attempts to re-form them will have left traces nonetheless. You will feel the connection like a pull on your energy body. As it is a malign one, it will cause you discomfort; you must be ready for it."

"So I find these traces and we follow them to their source? Then we find out who and where these guys are and get the hell out? Sounds simple enough. Let's get this over with."

"Come, then." Ronan got up and turned toward the bedroom, holding out a hand to Brenna. Something lurched in her chest again, but she tamped down on that reaction fast. She couldn't get distracted now, in either a good or a bad way.

Brenna turned off all but one small lamp in the living room, leaving the bedroom door open to admit the muted light. Then she kicked off her shoes and stretched out on the bed with her clothes still on. Ronan lay down behind her, pulled her against him and wrapped one arm securely around her. Brenna closed her eyes with a sigh, loving the way they fit together. It fell far short of what she wanted, but it would have to do for now.

"Try to open your mind to me and let my words draw you in. It will make this easier," he advised.

She let her body go limp while she searched for the meditative state that Annie had tried to teach her in their sessions together. As Ronan murmured in her ear, Brenna concentrated her attention on the cadence rather than trying to make out individual words. Spoken Irish had a lyrical ebb and flow that reminded her of the ocean. She soon found herself drifting with it, carried along on the warm tide of Ronan's voice. Whether it was a spell or just a long story, it was working. She'd have been happy to stay where she was indefinitely, just so she could listen to his voice.

Almost too soon, she felt a gentle tug upward. She opened her astral eyes to see Ronan hovering beside her, golden and luminous as before. His expression was grave.

"Are you ready?"

She nodded. "I am."

He gave her a look so intense that she shivered. "We must not take long at this. And when we return, we will have a serious conversation." She started to move away, but he took her by the shoulders and leaned toward her. She thought he meant to kiss her, but instead he touched his forehead to hers and closed his eyes. A wave of sensation swept Brenna from head to toes until she quivered with the force of it. For an instant it seemed as though she'd entered the heart of a bonfire and become part of it, blazing, glorious and filled with the most incredible music she'd ever heard. Too soon Ronan drew away and it all faded back to whatever passed for normal in this dimension.

Once more she was herself, just plain Brenna Callahan, in a copy of her physical body, all of her senses alert. Bereft but strangely calm, she centered her awareness, visualized herself in crow form as she had before, and let the tingling shift take hold of her energy body. On the astral she didn't need to flap her wings to fly, but she did so anyway. If she didn't, her stalkers might realize she wasn't a real crow. With a powerful downsweep, she launched herself up through the roof, then settled into a wide circle over the nearby countryside—a search pattern, or so she hoped. Ronan duplicated her crow form and followed her; she could feel him close behind, and his presence bolstered her confidence. She could do this.

Ronan had said there would be strands connecting her to the men who wanted her dead—strands, or remnants of strands. Unsure what to look for, Brenna cast all her senses outward. As if from a great distance, she heard what she now recognized as the Morrigan's voice in her mind.

In order to track something, you must first establish a connection between yourself and that which you seek.

Establish a connection? How? Brenna wheeled in a slow circle. When she stopped trying so hard to focus on details of the physical world, the astral flared to life before her, a riot of images and echoes.

"How do I even recognize my own energy?" Brenna asked Ronan mentally.

He smiled. "Look into my eyes, and see yourself as I see you."

Their gazes locked, and suddenly she could see herself reflected in his eyes as a shining coalescence of color, motion and sensation that expressed itself as the being called Brenna Callahan. And yet, it was a Brenna Callahan she'd never seen in a mirror, with none of the human limitations she was used to living with every day. This being was taller, stronger, larger than she expected, its energy more powerful and yet more controlled than she had ever imagined.

Learning that he saw her this way humbled her and took her breath away all in the same startled moment. Learning to see herself the same way might just take the rest of this lifetime. At the very least, it certainly provided a high bar for which to aim.

She couldn't speak, couldn't find an appropriate response to the gift he'd just given her. So instead she took a shaky breath and tried to scan the area for energy of the same colors and sensations that he'd shown her—as if she were tracking someone else entirely, and not stolen fragments of herself. It wasn't easy.

After a while she sensed a vague pulling sensation. She followed it until she glimpsed a ragged tendril of pale blue and gold light. Cautious, she brushed it with a wing. The broken-off bits were so warped and tainted with a slimy greyish *something* that just the one touch made her feel ill.

"You must reabsorb and cleanse it," Ronan told her mentally. "Draw it back into yourself, bathed in white light, transmuting the energy as you go. Only leave a little by which to follow them, so they will not notice its absence right away."

He was right. Disgusting as it was, some of that energy was hers; she needed it back. The rest, however foul, would lead her to her quarry.

On a fly-by, she snagged a waving blue tendril in her beak and imagined herself sucking it up like a spaghetti noodle. It resisted at first, but after a while the tainted strand drifted toward her. What had begun as a tug-o-war ended in a flood of her own altered energy. Brenna concentrated on pulling it into herself. She visualized the energy changing, suffusing with white light as she reabsorbed it through the energy center in the middle of her chest, but the energy seemed to fight the cleansing. Her concentration broke several times, and the dim sense of her physical body breaking into a sweat nearly pulled her off the astral. It took all of her will to stay with it, but she held on until the only bit left was a strand of brownish-grey that reached off into the distance, connected to her at the throat level.

Of course, it *would* be the throat level. Brenna could almost feel the faded bruises on her throat. She shuddered and had to fight not to gag, but she forced herself to continue following the slimy cord of energy to its source.

Tracking the connection was harder than she'd expected. Brenna had to change directions so often that she feared she'd end up with the cord as tangled as a cat's ball of yarn. After several minutes she stopped. She was getting nowhere, and the longer she remained connected to the soiled energy, the sicker she became.

Ronan hovered near her, and somehow she could sense his concern. It warmed her, steadied her.

"Relax and focus," he said. "They chose to retain a connection to your energy. That means you can find them. See them in your mind's eye, just the way they appeared when they attacked you. Then be prepared for the worst. I recommend some further means of camouflage before we move on."

Camouflage, she could do. She concentrated for several long moments while she imagined herself dividing into a murder of crows. A series of tickly sensations swept her as pieces of her energy pulled away from her core and began to take the shapes she envisioned. Soon seven copies of her crow-self wheeled and banked beside her, following her movements like a school of black fish. Ronan joined them so smoothly that she blinked and almost lost track of which of the dark shapes he was.

"Now, Brenna. Find them."

Taking a deep breath, she conjured up her attackers' faces in her mind, trying to remember as much detail as she could. It didn't help that she'd been fighting for her life when she'd seen them in that other almost-physical realm. Hmm. One had bad teeth; the other was mostly bald....

All at once, Brenna could picture Baldy and Bad Teeth as clearly as if she stood in front of them. The grayish energy line quivered. There was a jolt, a sensation of hurtling through space, then...stillness. One moment, she'd been hovering over Strokestown; now she sat on the windowsill of a small house somewhere out in the country—she couldn't tell where. But she'd returned to the invisible space between the physical world and the astral plane; she could see a rusty blue car parked in the driveway, a few trees and a half-collapsed stone fence through the half-light of dusk.

Still in crow form, she peered through the streaky glass into a cramped main room with a couple of chairs, a desk, and a woodstove in one corner. She could almost smell the peat. A man with his back to the window had the firebox open and was poking at the fire with an iron rod. When he finished his task and turned around, Brenna recognized Baldy. He was shaking his head as he turned toward someone else in the room.

Brenna's pulse sped up. They'd warded the place; when she tried to slip through the window, something gave her a painful jolt, as if she'd touched an electric wire. But so far Annie had taught her defensive magic, not offensive.

"Ronan, can we dismantle this ward the same way you did the sigil on my car?" she thought to him. "Oh, but that wouldn't work, would it? They'd notice it was gone."

His answering thought came through as clearly as if he'd spoken aloud. "Correct. But there may be another way to get in without unmaking the ward. Reach out to it; see whether you can get a sense of how it is formed."

Standing on the windowsill with the rest of her spun-off flock perched on the roof above her, Brenna tried to do as Ronan directed. In this dimension, the ward appeared as a bluish rune-type symbol full of complicated loops similar to those she'd seen on the cottage and car.

Something Colm had said came back to her as she stared at it. *Sooner or later, I'll find a crack to slip through.* And he'd been talking about her wards....

She tried to assess the ward in front of her, to feel its boundaries and weak spots—if it had any. After some time, she sensed an emptiness toward one side of the pattern.

"Ronan!"

"I sense it also," he said. "Working together, we will try to widen it. Do as I do."

She opened her mind to him as fully as she knew how. Fortunately, her lessons with Annie had taught her some of what to expect when working with a partner, and she managed to follow the flow of his energy as he extended it to probe at the pattern of the ward. As he did, she centered her awareness on it and imagined the space enlarging as they pushed steadily against the energy.

It hurt—a lot more than she'd bargained for.

Pain burned through her astral body, but she didn't let go. Jolts of pain kept hitting her until she could barely see, could barely tell whether her efforts caused any change in the ward at all. When she couldn't stand it anymore, she let go and backed off, breathing in short gasps. She could almost feel her body doing the same, all that distance away. She felt raw, burned. Ronan's face hinted that he hadn't fared much better. But a close inspection of the ward revealed a gap much wider than it had been at first. It might be enough. If it wasn't, she wasn't sure they had the strength to enlarge it further.

She looked at Ronan. As she watched, his astral form altered again, elongating until he was little more than a thread of vapor—or smoke. She felt his brief touch in her mind, and then he headed for the breach they'd made in the ward. For a moment, he shimmered and almost disappeared, then he steadied.

Anxiety tightened her muscles—or at least, it felt that way. Taking a deep breath, Brenna imagined herself as a tendril of smoke, long and reedy. As smoke, she absorbed the pain she'd just experienced in widening the ward, even though it singed every part of her being. As the thinnest line of smoke she could imagine, she drifted through the breach she'd made. Needle-sharp agony shot through her whenever she happened to touch any part of the ward.

Back in her physical body, her heart was probably pounding, but the part of her that was in this dimension just vibrated faster until she flickered like a strobe in her distress. Would the men notice what was happening? Here she and Ronan were, *inside* the warded space! What if it closed behind them and they couldn't work it back open?

"Steady," Ronan said in her mind.

One worry at a time. Focus on the task at hand. Right. She tamped down on the fear as hard as she could, and the flickering calmed somewhat. Still in the form of smoke, she drifted upward toward the ceiling above the fireplace. Then she oriented her vision downward and had a good look at all the men in the room.

Great. She'd expected Baldy and Bad Teeth, but there were two other men here as well. None of them seemed to notice her, but all of them were frowning—well, glaring at each other was more like it. She'd drifted into the middle of what sounded like an argument.

"This thing hasn't gone right from the start, Lars," Baldy was saying.

"Well, whose fault d'you think that is?" asked a man seated in a faded armchair nearby. His legs were so long that he had to stretch them out in front of him; if Baldy hadn't called him Lars, Brenna would have dubbed him Beanpole. "If you'd just shot the bitch the first chance you got, you'd be home now. The Sidhe wouldn't have managed to shut down your last few attempts, and you wouldn't have had to call me in to clean up your mess."

Brenna stared at Lars. Shot the bitch? She flickered again in the area where her diaphragm would be. They probably weren't talking about a stray female dog. And...had they said the Sidhe had foiled some attempts? Maybe that was why these jerks hadn't attacked her since that day in Strokestown. So when they hadn't been able to get at her with magic, they'd decided to run her ex down on the road, and now they planned to shoot her? Fantastic.

"Look, I don't know about you, but I have a family to support; I can't have murder charges. Remember your oath as a Sentry, you said. Work a few baneful spells, you said. Send the woman running home, you said. You never said anything about murder." That had come from the fourth man, who sat on a kitchen chair, drinking something from an unlabeled brown bottle.

While Lars had the Nordic looks that fit his name, this last man looked part Asian. His speech, however, indicated he'd been raised in an English-speaking country. Baldy and Bad Teeth had such generic complexions they could have come from anywhere, though by their accents, they must be from the States and England. Her would-be murderers seemed quite the mixed bag, but what that meant in terms of their organization, she didn't know. Were there more "Sentries" out there somewhere, or was this it?

"Oh, come on, Chang, what did you think would happen when you planted the sigil on her car? It was always gonna be murder, traceable or not," Baldy said.

Brenna tensed. They couldn't be talking about another woman. They'd been trying to kill her with magic since she'd arrived, but she'd survived two weeks despite their efforts. They were right; if something didn't change soon, they'd get desperate enough to shoot her. She hadn't been at this stuff long, but as far as she knew, even the best ward wasn't proof against a bullet.

"Look, I know at first we said we'd just scare her off," Bad Teeth said. "Problem is, I've done some research and I've concluded that's not going to work. Even if we get her to leave Ireland before Samhain, there are other portals, other times when the veil is thin."

Chang looked confused. "You mean the Sidhe can use her to open more than one *cómhla breac?*"

Brenna's gaze shot to Ronan, but with his smoke tendril form, she couldn't tell whether he was looking at her or not. From what she could sense from him, his focus seemed intent on the men.

Lars shrugged, then tilted his chair back and propped his feet up on the desk. "Maybe. I don't see why not, as long as she can channel the Sovereignty. All she needs to open a speckled gate is a liminal place or time. If the Sidhe miss this window, they can try again on a different Sabbat in a different place, until they get what they want from her. And they will; then they'll pour into the earth plane like a plague. We can't let that happen. We have to kill her."

Sovereignty? Speckled gate? A chill swept through Brenna, and this time she could sense Ronan's attention focused on her. Was this what he'd meant when he'd said they needed to have a serious conversation? Just what *did* he want from her?

"Now you tell us. That's just great, Lars," Chang said. He sounded angry. "I'm supposed to look into my kids' eyes after I help kill a woman who doesn't know why she's a target?"

"You've already helped. You took the oath. You don't go back. Besides, it's war. Them or us. Think of it like that. In war, there's casualties." Lars's eyes narrowed as he looked at Chang. His gaze swept the room, fixing on the other men in turn. Then he stiffened. His legs came down off the desk and he leaned forward, brows drawn together. "Wait a minute. Something's not right."

"Well of course it isn't," Chang said. "We're trying to kill somebody."

"No. That isn't what I mean. Something feels off. Have you checked the wards lately?"

"Brenna, get out!" came Ronan's mental warning, but she was already moving.

She thinned her energy out as much as possible and streaked through the room toward the breached ward. As she passed over Baldy's head, he brushed the air above him as though bothered by a fly. His arm passed right through Brenna, but she didn't stop.

She dove through the hole in the ward, crying out as parts of her astral self brushed the ward. Being in this dimension seemed to magnify every sense she had. Even when she'd forced her way outside, the odor of burned flesh mixed with the scents of peat and rain. Despite the pain that crackled through her, she morphed into crow form again. The door to the house burst open and two of the men ran out, looking around in every direction, trying to see what had invaded their space.

Brenna pulled hard at her other bits of spun-off energy, which brought the illusory flock of crows back toward her. Somewhere in the chaos she'd lost track of Ronan. Had he gotten out, or was he trapped? Whatever he or the rest of the Sidhe wanted from her, he'd been so protective all along that it was impossible to doubt he cared for her. If he was in danger now, it was because of her. She hesitated. A Sidhe should be able to hold his own against any human magical attacks, shouldn't he? But he'd said Brad had likely been run over because he looked like Colm, who he believed was Sidhe, and these men considered the Sidhe to be their enemies. Who knew of what the Sentries were capable?

A presence grew within the house and began to press outward—she could feel it as it expanded. With a sickening jolt, Brenna realized that one of these men, these Sentries, was about to project into the astral to give chase.

"Did you see that? Did you see the damn flock of crows? There!" Baldy stood in the light that spilled through the door, his finger pointed at Brenna.

Invisible. I'm invisible, Brenna thought. *You don't see me.* She imagined herself blending into the dark, rain and tree branches.

Baldy squinted. "Shit. They were right there. Now they're gone. We got the damn Morrigan on our tail, Lars!"

Brenna didn't wait to let them prove themselves wrong. Her flock hit her en mass; she shook with the force of the returned energy, though it wasn't anywhere near the amount of energy she'd expended in making it. In moments, she was the only crow left.

The instant she could move, Brenna beat wings for the road, doing a quick fly-by of the mailbox on the way so she'd have the address. Now, if she could just double back and find Ronan....

She heard a sound from behind and sneaked a peek over her shoulder. Lars was on her tail, close enough that she could make out his features with ease. Either he didn't know how to change form or hadn't bothered, but he was adept at astral travel and he was damned fast.

She felt like a tired runner facing a steep hill, and knowing he was almost breathing down her neck didn't help matters. And *how* had he seen her? She was supposed to be invisible! Brenna glanced down at herself and saw that her astral form had begun to flicker between her crow form and her body's double. For a moment, it was like some of the nightmares she'd had as a child—the ones in which she tried to run from whatever pursued her, but could barely creep forward.

She gagged, choking on something that twined around her neck and dragged her backward. She looked down and saw that it was the soiled tentacle she'd used to locate the Sentries. She'd forgotten to break it when she left their house, and now Lars had attached it to himself and was choking her with it.

She was growing weaker. Lars' cord pulsed as he drew on it, sucking down her power and drawing it into himself. The thought of Ronan came to her, and she clung to it even as her movements slowed. What was happening? Energy flowed out of her through the greyish cord, until she couldn't think, couldn't struggle, couldn't move.

"Brenna!" Suddenly Ronan was in front of her in his astral hawk form. Putting himself between her and Lars, he struck at the grey cord with beak and talons, ripping and tearing. Lars let loose a bolt of greyish-yellow light that struck Ronan broadside; he grunted but didn't stop tearing at Brenna's tether.

"Ronan, what...?" she began, struggling to fight off the lethargy that had kept her immobile.

"Break it!" he yelled. "Break it and get back to your body now!"

She tried. Fighting to hold to her crow form, she tried to attack the cord as Ronan was doing, but she had minimal success. Another blast hit Ronan, throwing him into her. Ronan turned and lunged at her, the top of his head hitting her in the chest. She gasped as power roared into her from him, her light brightening as his dimmed. His astral body shielded her from the energy bolt Lars aimed at her.

"No, don't!" she cried, but Ronan ignored her, intent on what he was doing.

The energy filling her was like a torrent, wild, savage, and sweet. It was all the elements in one, intoxicating like strong wine. But it was also thin, and its flow was uneven. Instinctively she knew it was failing. With effort, she stopped its flow and reversed it, throwing it back toward Ronan.

"Stop it! I'm okay!" To convince him, she ripped at the grey cord with her beak, shredding it until it came loose and fell from her, drifting back toward Lars, whose attack had ceased.

Ronan's hawk form shimmered and faded.

Ronan! Brenna's mental shriek echoed in her ears. Lars was drifting away from her now, and it seemed he wasn't about to renew his attack. She didn't know whether he was hurt, just gathering his strength, or trying to assimilate all he'd stolen from her. If the latter, she hoped he choked on it.

CHAPTER FIFTEEN

Brenna shrieked again, looking all around her in case he was still there. "Ronan!"

"Go back, beloved. I will guard your retreat."

"No way! Come back with me."

"I cannot—not now. Please, just trust me, and go."

Stubborn didn't begin to describe him, and his insistence on staying in the danger zone terrified her. But his mind-voice sounded so desperate that she did as he asked. As she had done before, she thought about her body and experienced the sudden pull on her silver cord. Seconds later, she slammed through the roof of her cottage down into her body, which awoke with a gasp.

"Are you all right?" Annie asked as Brenna's eyes flew open.

Brenna blinked at the other woman, who was sitting at her bedside, fully clothed though a little disheveled, as if she'd dressed in a hurry. "Annie, what are you doing here? Did Ronan call you?" Ronan. Where was he? Her brain felt fogged, and she was having trouble focusing.

"Yes, in a manner of speaking." Annie was all business. "Now, answer my question, girl. Are you all right?"

Was she? Brenna didn't answer for a moment, taking stock. Her skin hurt wherever anything touched it—including her clothes and the bedcovers—as if she'd been out in the sun for too long. Wincing, she sat up. Even the roots of her hair hurt.

"I'm okay, I think, but I feel like I've been crispy-fried," she said at last. A memory surfaced. "I had a hard time getting through a ward, I think."

Annie reached out until her hand hovered an inch above Brenna's body, and began to trace the outline of her aura. Brenna shivered at the sensation. It was like balm on her burned flesh, and if she let her eyes unfocus, she could see a pale green sparkle of energy pour from Annie's hands to merge with her aura. Her gaze shot to the other woman's face, but Annie's eyes were closed in concentration.

After several moments, the flow of energy stopped. In that brief time, Brenna's skin had gone from feeling as though she'd been pan-seared to lightly toasted.

"Better?" Annie asked her.

"Much, thanks." she murmured. There was something she needed to tell Annie right away, but exhaustion pulled her down and she couldn't summon the energy to roll over, much less sit up and have a conversation. Despite her mind's feeble struggle to stay awake, her eyes drifted closed, and she slept.

When Brenna awoke again, she was still lying on top of her bed, and sunlight was creeping through the window to slant across her pillow. She sighed and stretched as the haze of sleep receded. Vaguely she remembered a dream of herself flying—as a crow. No, many crows. But then....

Memory flooded back, and she bolted upright. It hadn't been a dream. She'd used astral projection to spy on her stalkers, and when she'd had trouble getting away from them, Ronan had come after her and helped her get loose.

"Ronan!" she yelled, staring around the room. He didn't reply and he didn't appear, which touched off another surge of anxiety. Then she remembered. He hadn't come back with her; he'd sent her back alone; he'd asked her to trust him. And Annie had been in the room with her when she'd returned to her body.

"Ah, there you are," Annie said, coming into the room as if on cue. She looked tired but unperturbed. "I was just about to make breakfast."

Brenna got up at once and followed Annie into the kitchen.

"How long have I been out?"

"If you mean how long have you been sleeping, it's been six hours since you returned from the astral plane," Annie said. "You were exhausted. If I'd known you intended to go on your little spy mission right after getting back from Galway, I'd have taken you over my knee."

Despite her anxiety, Brenna grinned. "It's a good thing I didn't tell you, then."

"Cheeky Yank," Annie grumbled, but she smiled. "It's lucky you are that Ronan went after you. Next time, be more cautious."

"Ronan went with me. He helped me get onto the astral in the first place."

"Did he?" Annie looked thoughtful. "Then I guess he thought it was important."

"Well, I told him that I didn't dare wait for the psychos to regroup after they ran over Brad. I had to find out why they wanted me dead, before they hurt anyone else close to me."

"And did you find out?" Annie asked, watching Brenna closely.

"Yes, but while we were inside their wards, they detected us and we had to escape. They almost had me, and then Ronan got between us and took the brunt of their attack. He looked like...well...like he was running out of energy, or something. He sent me back here. I wanted to stay and help him, but he didn't want me to. He asked me to trust him." Pain in her shoulders and jaw told her how tense she was, but she couldn't help it. Where *was* he?

"Well, he ought to know what he's about," Annie said calmly.

"I hope so. But he was trying to tell me something before Brad came and got run over, and we never got the chance to finish talking." She blushed at the memory of why they'd never completed that conversation. Annie gave her a sharp look but didn't comment. Brenna went on. "Based on what I found out from the Sentries—that's what they call themselves—I think this mess is even more tangled than we thought."

Annie nodded. "Right. Well, tell me everything while I make breakfast. Maybe we'll have a clearer picture afterward."

Annie took charge, bustling around the kitchen making tea and slicing bread, just as if she hadn't been rousted out of her bed in the middle of the night. Brenna told her all that had happened since just before Brad had been run over, including Ronan's admission that he and Colm were Sidhe. Annie's eyebrows raised at that, but she listened patiently until Brenna finished, ending with Ronan sending her back to her body after their battle with Lars.

"It sounds as though you learned a lot," Annie said. "Now, what are we going to do about it?"

Brenna narrowed her gaze at Annie. "What do you mean, 'we'? From here on out, things are bound to get even more dangerous, especially for anyone the Sentries think is close to me. We've already seen what happened to Brad, and we don't even know what happened to Ronan. Maybe you shouldn't get any further involved."

Annie sat up straighter. "I'm already involved, my girl, and there's an end to it. Now we need to put some of these pieces of information together if we're to get anywhere at all."

Brenna frowned at the tabletop. "Problem is, everything I learned just brings up more questions. I don't know why the Sentries think I can open this speckled gate, whatever that is. And I have no idea why the Sidhe would want me to do it, nor why the Sentries would kill me to prevent it from happening. Can you tell me anything about it?"

"Speckled gate. The *cómhla breac*," Annie said.

"Yes! That's just what Lars called it. What is it? Why's it speckled?"

"In Irish, *breac* normally means trout, but it also means speckled. In ancient lore, the term *speckled* refers to something of a magical nature, so a speckled gate is a portal to the Otherworld. These Sentries must think you can open it and allow the Sidhe to come through. As to why that would even be necessary, I'm not certain. Although now that I think on it....Sidhe used to pass between the worlds all the time, but they're rarely seen any more." Annie drummed her fingers on the table. "Hmm. I was afraid something big was brewing. I could feel it along the trackways the morning after you arrived."

"But why me, Annie? What's so special about me? If the Sidhe need a human to open this portal, why not get someone local? Someone already sympathetic and respectful. Like you, for instance."

Annie shook her head. "I doubt it's that simple, dear. But I don't know the answer. There must be a reason why they need you specifically. You should speak to Ronan about this when he returns."

"I intend to—assuming he does return." She swallowed. The idea that he might not was making her insides twist themselves into knots. "Since he didn't come back last night, he never got to tell me whatever it was that he wanted to tell me. But the fact that he's Sidhe changes the meaning of every conversation we've ever had. It explains a lot of things I thought odd at the time they came up."

"Such as?"

"Such as why you advised me not to thank him, how he has such a deep knowledge of magic, how he managed to heal Cuchulain and keep Brad from dying on the road, why he uses such archaic language, why he knows things that aren't mentioned in the Irish mythology books, how he sometimes just seems to disappear...should I go on?"

"No need," Annie said in a quiet voice.

Brenna traced a finger over a knot in the wooden tabletop. "Annie, why didn't you tell me about him? It would have been helpful for me to know whom—or what—I was dealing with."

Annie sighed. "I didn't know for certain until now, dear; I just had a strong suspicion. In any case, it wasn't my secret to tell. If you've read the books I gave you, you'll know what tends to happen to humans who expose the Gentry's secrets. The fae don't like having their confidence betrayed, and who could blame them?"

"But you must have had some idea why he was here or what he wanted with me. You knew about the Wild Hunt. You knew I had no clue what was going on, but you told me you trusted Ronan. And he brought me to you that first night. That has to mean something!"

Annie looked down at her hands. "I haven't known Ronan long," she said after a moment. "I encountered him about six months ago on the astral plane. He was polite and formal, though he did mention that the smaller fae remember me fondly for my leaving out the milk and bread. That is all. He never said he was Sidhe, and I didn't ask. Most people hereabouts who still believe will tell you that it's always best to leave Themselves to Themselves.

But my intuition tells me that Ronan is a good man, whether he's Sidhe or human. I've learned to trust my intuition—it's never led me wrong."

"Do you believe what some of the stories say—that the Sidhe are damned, that they have no souls?" Brenna realized that she'd clenched her hands in her lap, but she couldn't seem to loosen them.

"I don't." Annie didn't even hesitate, and Brenna let out a breath she hadn't realized she'd been holding. "I don't believe it for a minute. They feel pain, they suffer, they don't disparage anyone else's religion even if they don't follow it themselves...they are capable of great kindness and charity. And great love. Oh, yes, there has often been great love between Sidhe and human. Anything capable of love has a soul, I say. It's what an individual chooses to do with that soul that makes the difference."

"Thank you," Brenna said, blinking back the tears that had sprung to her eyes. "That's...that's what I needed to know."

Annie studied her closely. "Oh, I see. You've fallen in love with him, haven't you?"

"What...what makes you say that?" Brenna asked. How had Annie learned to read her so well in such a short time?

Annie was shaking her head, but her eyes were kind. "I'm not an eejit, and my eyes and ears work just fine."

"It's just so complicated," Brenna said. "There's no map for a journey like this."

"There never is, dear," Annie said with feeling. "But we can try to determine the lay of the land. Let's start with what you know."

Brenna groaned. She needed answers. Real answers, not speculation and puzzles.

"Okay; first, Colm called me Daireann—the name I had in the past life when I was a murderer. So I know there's a connection there, even if the thought of it makes me ill. I've always had the feeling that I knew Ronan. There's been something between us from the start, and it's been getting harder and harder to ignore, which is probably part of why I feel the way I do about him. Given that Ronan and Colm happen to be Sidhe and the Sentries seem determined to keep me from helping the Sidhe, I think it's safe to assume that both Ronan and Colm have plenty to do with this *cómhla breac*."

"Sound reasoning," Annie agreed.

"But there's another player in this drama. What about the Morrigan?" Brenna shivered. Did speaking the name aloud somehow draw the owner's attention?

"What about her?" Annie asked. "She's Sidhe as well; one of the Tuatha De Danann."

"Annie, everywhere I go, crows turn up. I've heard what I think is her voice in my head, telling me I've forgotten her and that I have to choose. But choose what? Human or Sidhe? War or neutrality? Good or evil?"

Annie snorted. "Things are never just black or white. At the age of thirty—plus a few lifetimes—you should know that."

Brenna shifted uncomfortably. "Fair enough. Now, if I've pieced the evidence together right, I somehow betrayed the Morrigan once—possibly by murdering that woman, Clothra. She might want vengeance for that. Or she might want me to open this *cómhla breac* so that she can go after the Sentries. Or both. Do you think that's why the Sentries want to keep me from doing it? To keep the Morrigan from killing them and then running amok in the human world, starting wars?"

Annie gave her a hard look. "We humans are quite capable of starting wars without help from the Morrigan. She isn't just a battle goddess. She has several titles, several functions among the Danann. It's just that most books don't stress her other duties. They get sidetracked on the battle aspect and ignore the rest."

"What other duties? In my dreams and visions, I only saw her on the battlefield."

"Then you haven't looked hard enough. For one thing, she is a great *bandraoí*, a sorceress and seer, bearer of the Foreknowing."

"Foreknowing—what's that?"

Annie shrugged. "She can see into the future."

"Oh."

"Her name also holds an important clue. *Mór Ríoghain* means Great Queen, she who is the Sovereignty of the land for her people. Once a year, she and the Dagda, her consort and King of the Danann, used to conduct a ritual mating meant to connect him to the essence of the land through her—in effect, to give him the sovereignty. There's a lot of power in that."

Brenna frowned. "She gave the Dagda the sovereignty? I suppose you don't mean they were just role-playing? They did actual sex magic once a year?"

"Of course."

"When? When did they do this? It wouldn't be on Samhain, would it?"

"Samhain, or close to it, yes," Annie said. "Why?"

"Because that's what the Sentries were talking about! They said I could open the gate if I was a channel for the Sovereignty. And they said the Sidhe meant me to do it on Samhain because that's when the veil was thin."

The two women stared at each other in shocked silence. Finally Annie said, "I suppose that is where Ronan and Colm come in. To play the part of the king in a sovereignty ritual."

"So...I'm supposed to recreate the Morrigan and Dagda's sex ritual with Ronan or Colm?" It was all Brenna could do to say the words in front of Annie. But Annie looked more intrigued than embarrassed.

"Why would they send two men to court you when all it would

take is one?" Annie wondered aloud.

"They want a threesome to make the magic more potent?" Brenna blurted before she thought. "Yech! But no, Ronan doesn't like Colm. Hates him, in fact, so it can't be that."

"I suppose it might be a form of sport for them, though it sounds far too important a thing for them to turn it into a game." Annie tapped a finger on the tabletop, frowning.

"Again, yech!" Brenna said. "I don't suppose they're so desperate for this sovereignty magic that they sent me a selection of lovers to make sure I'd choose one? How dare they? I hate users. It's bad enough feeling like I've been one, with this Brad business. I don't like the idea that I'm being used by a couple of Sidhe, much less an entire race. And I trusted Ronan! Damn it!"

"And Ronan's given you no reason not to," Annie soothed. "You said yourself that he'd been trying to tell you something earlier. But we still need to know why it must be you."

Annie looked deeply into Brenna's eyes, and Brenna saw the shadow of worry behind her gaze, as well as caring warmth that made her feel even closer to this woman who had already taught her so much. "If you have ties to the Sidhe, they must come from deep in your past," Annie said. "Perhaps you do owe them a debt, and they've come to collect."

All of which brought her back to the failed regression. Ronan's visit the other day followed by Brad's arrival and accident had stopped her from calling Annie to stage a do-over. But she was here now.

Brenna frowned, pushing her tea mug back and forth on the tabletop. The idea of going back to the odd dolmen-like entrance that lay askew from all the other doors in the hallway of memory filled her with dread. So, of course, that was where she had to go. In movies, whatever you feared the most was what you had to do in order to solve the mystery. What did not kill you made you stronger.

Fabulous.

Well, she was wasting time she couldn't afford. If there were answers behind that dolmen, she needed them now. This time there'd be no backing out, no running from truths she didn't want to own.

Brenna sat up straight and met Annie's calculating gaze across the table. "I need your help with something," she said.

Maybe Brenna's recent practice in visualization had helped—or maybe she just hadn't known true desperation before. Whatever the cause, she followed Annie's regression imagery with ease. While her body lay relaxed in the depths of an armchair by the fire, the rest of her slipped quickly into trance and headed straight for the entrance to her hall of memory.

Once inside, she hesitated. The dolmen lay at the far end, but what if she'd missed a more important door last time? What if the answers lay scattered throughout her lifetimes? She had to get this right the first time; she didn't have time to go back if her most ancient life didn't provide all the answers.

A *caw* sounded from behind her, and Brenna glanced over her shoulder to see a crow enter the hallway. It glided past the first door and perched on a candle sconce on the wall, watching her with beady eyes. As she stared at it, it cawed again and tipped its head at her as if trying to figure out what she would do next. *What, indeed?* came the voice in her mind.

All those closed doors stretched away down the hallway to a point she couldn't see. They might as well have been a jury of hundreds, silently accusing, chiding without words because she'd been a wimp last time and refused to acknowledge one obscure memory from an ancient past life. Maybe if she hadn't choked and bolted, she'd have learned enough to defeat the Sentries before they'd started trying to kill people she cared about. Maybe she would already know why the Sidhe needed her to open their *cómhla breac.*

Damn it; she was tired of being a victim, always on the defensive. Tired of being ignorant, tired of being stalked. Tired of feeling guilty for a crime she'd committed in another lifetime. And most of all, she was tired of letting others herd her toward an unknown fate. She'd always thought she was in control of her life and her choices. She wanted—no, needed—that belief to be true. She glanced back at the crow, which was still staring at her.

Sudden, black rage rose from deep within Brenna's soul. With it came a rush of power such as she'd never experienced before. Instinctively she drew it in until her body tingled and her pulse pounded, drowning out the fire, the wind, the rain and every other sound her physical ears had registered. Every vestige of sensation from the physical room around her disappeared; she couldn't even feel the cushion beneath her. The rage and power buoyed her until it was as though she were hovering in midair over the back of the armchair, though in a simple meditation she didn't leave her body.

No more secrets. No more hiding. Show me who I am! Show me now! Rage and *draíocht* pulsed through her body like black lightning. It was heady, dangerous, but she didn't care. With the cold rush of power in her veins, Brenna began to walk. Ahead of her, doors burst open all the way down the hallway. Some flapped on their hinges, others blew off altogether. Scattered memories poured into her mind like DVD images on double time fast-forward.

Brenna screamed as her mind struggled to accommodate the flash flood of recall that threatened to overwhelm her. It twisted, forced, seared its way through her brain. Behind her eyes, images flickered like strobes. And still she walked down the hallway, moving toward the dolmen in the farthest corner.

She was a housewife in New York in the early 1800's. A Native American before the first white colonists arrived. A toddler who died of smallpox in a tiny German village. A soldier in medieval France. A woman in Italy who gazed in wonder at her newborn child. A boy scribe taught by Eastern monks. A brown-skinned jungle-dweller. An Egyptian priestess stabbed to death by a soldier in Julius Caesar's army. In many lifetimes she was of Irish descent, though none of the lifetimes seemed to take place in Ireland itself. Still, they were full of deaths, births, accidents, moments of joy...and pain. So much pain. And through it all, a fierce longing for acceptance and a return to the one place her soul called home. The images flooded into Brenna's consciousness, flickering, stabbing, burning until her head felt as if it might explode.

She couldn't bear it. She was about to burn herself out, or give herself a stroke. But it didn't matter; she wouldn't pull herself out of trance now, nor would she allow Annie to pull her out. Not until she had what she'd come for.

As the other images began to ebb, she reached the dolmen that marked the entrance to her first lifetime. Gritting her teeth, she ducked under the capstone. Moments later, she pushed through the crack of light at the far end, as she'd done before.

This time she emerged in a silent courtyard surrounded by a stockade wall of sharpened wooden posts. The grass beneath her boots was stiff and frosted, and overhead, stars winked coldly at her. She wore the same black leather battle armor as before, padded underneath with wool and reinforced in spots with blackened bronze plating. A charcoal-colored woolen cloak topped everything else, pinned in front with a blackened bronze fibula. She stood atop the earthen rampart that circumnavigated the stockade wall on the inside. From that vantage she could see far across the field outside to the forest beyond. If trouble came, it would come from that dark mass of trees.

Or maybe she was wrong. A shadow just a touch darker than its surroundings detached itself from the nearby wall and paced toward Brenna. In the torchlight, Brenna could see the hard glint in the woman's eyes.

"Daireann." The woman almost spat the name. "I'm surprised that *an Mór Ríoghain* gave you watch duty. It almost seems as though she wants us to be attacked."

"Why do you say that, Clothra?" Brenna/Daireann asked, though she already knew what the other woman was implying. Let her say it, then, and expose the dispute under the open sky.

"Not hard," Clothra said. "You are worthless as a tracker, worthless on watch, worthless in the field. Your *draíocht* is weak, and your battle skills even more so. You will never be worthy to join the ranks of the *Badbha Catha*! I will not be surprised if you fail to complete the gauntlet tomorrow night."

The words hurt, though Daireann would rather have died than admit as much. "And you, of course, dragged yourself from bed and came all the way out here in the dark and cold just to tell me that? I name you a coward, then, Clothra. Why do you not say what you mean?"

"Very well. You are weak because of your Fomorian blood. You are not fit to fight beside the other *Badbha!* Our queen coddles you."

"The *Mór Ríoghain* coddles no one, myself least of all. I cannot help it if my father was forced into a treaty marriage with a Fomoire. He upheld his vows with honor, as did my mother. As I uphold mine." Daireann's hand tightened around her spear haft, and she hoped Clothra hadn't seen it in the dark. For all that she was the most hateful woman Daireann had ever known, she was still a superior in rank, and thus required respect—or the appearance thereof.

"You? Uphold a vow? Look at what Bres did to the Danann, betraying the trust we placed in him as king. Fomoire blood will out, every time."

"Lugh Lamfada is half-blood, and he is our greatest champion. No one fears he will turn against us, and no one questions his motives. I don't believe this is just about my parentage—is it, Clothra? This is about Ronan. You wanted him, but he chose me. Even when you offered him your favors as well, he declined."

Clothra's expression changed, becoming something lean and ugly. Hate glittered from her eyes. Inwardly, Daireann recoiled.

"Ronan will see how wrong he was when you betray us all. He will stand with the others when they cast you out, if the Hunt does not run you to ground tomorrow and save us the trouble." Clothra's voice held the weight of absolute conviction, and Daireann was shocked anew at the strength of the woman's anger.

The vision shifted then. It was early evening, and Daireann stood in front of a dark hole which she recognized as the unembellished entrance to Oweynagat, the Cave of Cruachan. Behind her in the fading sunlight stood two rows of female warriors, all dressed in the black armor of the *Badbha Catha*, the Morrigan's elite Crows of Battle. Named after Anand's sister, Badbh, all were skilled at spear, sword and bow, all excelled in the arts of tracking. Nearly all wielded the ancient forces of *draíocht*. Tonight, Daireann would fulfill a lifelong dream and become one of them. She had but one task left to prove herself worthy. After three hours alone in the depths of Oweynagat, she would emerge into the darkness to run a night-long race against the soul-eating Wild Hunt. If she survived and returned by dawn, she would become a full *Badbh Catha*.

Anand ni Ernmas, the *Mór Ríoghain*, Great Queen of the Tuatha De Danann, stood at the entrance to the cave. Daireann shuddered with awe at the woman's presence. Anand always seemed so much larger than life that it was hard to remember that she, too, had known joy and heartbreak, that she'd had lovers and borne children. She could inspire warriors to battle harder just by appearing within their sight, and her beauty didn't hurt, either. Her rank and power weren't merely inherited. Anand was one of the few Danann who could alter her physical form to that of a scald crow and still wield *draíocht* while she flew over the battlefield. The others who could do it, including her sisters Macha and Badbh, tried often to teach the younger warriors to manage the feat. Thus far, few had been able to, though many journeyed in crow form when their spirit bodies traversed the Otherworld realms.

Someday I'll master the art. I know I will, Daireann promised herself as she clasped arms with the *Mór Ríoghain*. Anand's deep blue eyes looked into Daireann's soul, and Daireann gasped at the intimate contact. She'd known to expect it, of course, but she hadn't quite grasped the reality until this moment. To become a *Badbh Catha* was to connect with the essence of what made Anand who she was. It was, in effect, to share a portion of the *Mór Ríoghain*'s power, a power derived from the depths of the land itself. Once a woman became one of Anand's warriors, she would never again be alone. She'd have friends, allies. Sisters.

Daireann craved that sense of belonging more than anything else. When others like Clothra reviled her because of her half-Fomorian parentage, Anand accepted her. She, of all people, understood Daireann best, knew her need for acceptance and welcomed her devotion. Anand judged her warriors by their deeds and their hearts, not their pedigrees.

When Daireann returned to her queen's side just before sunrise, the *Mór Ríoghain* would bestow upon her the fearsome warrior name that every *Badbh* used in battle. At last, she would truly belong.

"Prepare well, for I would not lose you this night," Anand said. "If you succeed, I believe you will rise far within the ranks of my *Badbha*."

"Thank you, my Queen," Daireann said as Anand released her.

A prickle at the back of her neck caused her to look over her shoulder, where she caught Clothra's eyes on her, hard and furious. The woman was close enough that she might have overheard that last exchange. She would not appreciate such a mark of favor bestowed on any half-breed, least of all Daireann, especially given the nature of their personal dispute. It was like adding fuel to a roaring fire. Trying to ignore the hate emanating from Clothra, Daireann slipped through the low entrance to Oweynagat.

The vision shifted again, so fast that Brenna reeled, dizzy.

A leaf-bladed knife whipped through the air toward her. She ducked just in time and the knife stuck fast in a tree trunk. Nearby, Clothra circled her, mixed fear and loathing apparent on her face even in the darkness. In fact, the dark seemed not to impede her vision much at all. Daireann matched the woman's steps, anticipated her next move. From the depths of her mind, a black rage surfaced.

"Why, Clothra? I thought you said I was weak and powerless. If I am, then why ambush me like this? If I am so weak, the Hunt will finish me off with no help from you. Then you can try to get Ronan for yourself—if he would have you."

Clothra moved in as if for a blow, then feinted to the left and lashed out with a splayed hand. The spell shredded Daireann's armor as though it were cardboard. Pain lanced through her side and she felt the rush of warm blood. It was bad, but not fatal if she ended the fight quickly. Hounds bayed somewhere in the distance; she had to hurry.

Another spell blasted her, and she fell to her knees. The already dark night seemed to darken further—or was it her vision that darkened? In a sudden burst of clarity, she realized why Clothra's spells were so potent.

"You are drawing power from someone else," she gasped. "Someone else aids your purpose, and they mean you to kill me."

"No, not kill you," Clothra said, her voice full of satisfaction. "One *Badbh* may not kill another—not even a half-blood like you—but if the Hunt kills you, no one will think anything amiss. This is just...a surety for a desirable outcome. You did not think everyone in the ranks was overjoyed at the prospect of your joining us, did you?"

Pain stabbed at Daireann, followed by anger. "This treachery is beneath any *Badbh*. When *an Mór Ríoghain* finds out—"

"She won't." Clothra sounded certain. "True sisters of the *Badbha Catha* take care of their own."

Pain and sharp despair swelled again within Daireann. When the Hunt arrived, she'd die without having known the triumph of becoming one of the *Badbha*, or the sweetness of true joining with Ronan. She'd thought to belong at last, but Clothra's sabotage made it clear that she never would.

By sheer force of will, Daireann dragged air into her lungs, but she could feel them filling with liquid. Beyond herself, beyond the pain, she could feel Ronan's presence, feel him sense what was happening. She also felt his anguish, but there was nothing she could do about it. They were close enough in spirit that they could link mind and magic if necessary, but it was forbidden for any *Badbh* to do so on the night of initiation. She was allowed her own abilities and magic only; any help would invalidate the initiation, and that would shame both of them.

On the other hand, this was no valid initiation—not when attack came from within her own ranks. What would he want her to do? What would Anand want her to do?

If she died, she could never redress the wrong, and that could undermine the *Badbha Catha* from within. If Clothra was capable of this kind of subterfuge, then she was capable of other treachery as well. Anand had to be told about this, which meant that Daireann must survive. By any means necessary.

In the end, it was no decision at all.

Tears streaming from her eyes, Daireann reached out to Ronan until she felt his energy clearly. Without finesse, without warning, she latched onto it and pulled—hard. It came in a rush, healing damage to her body, tingling through her spirit until she glowed in the night. She knew, too, that this would also bring the Hunt, but there was no help for it.

The patterns of a last, desperate spell whirled through her thoughts. She formed it, powered it with some of the life energy she'd stolen from Ronan, and hurled it at her opponent with all the force hate could muster. Like a ball of solid air, it struck Clothra in the face and snapped her head to the side. She crumpled, wheezing. Daireann was on her before she hit the ground. All she had to do now was get herself and Clothra out of here before the Hunt arrived, and she could resolve this before it turned into tragedy. Revulsion filled her as she looked down at her unconscious enemy, but tempted though she might be, she wouldn't lower herself to Clothra's level and take the woman's life. On the heels of that thought, a strange feeling gripped her.

Of its own volition, Daireann's knife hand whipped up and back. Horrified, she struggled against the bonds of air that forced her, but she wasn't strong enough. The power she'd taken from Ronan flowed backward through the link, leaving her weak. But her knife hand remained in the air, poised above Clothra, whose eyes snapped open as she drew a ragged breath.

"Please, Daireann, no!" Clothra rasped. Her eyes flashed with terror, but it was too late. Without her conscious direction, Daireann's knife plunged toward Clothra's unarmored neck.

Blood showered them both, and Daireann couldn't even give voice to the shriek of horror that welled up inside her. The spell that had controlled her movements released her, and she dropped the knife, scrabbling backward away from Clothra's now-motionless body.

"Excellent." The voice came from nearby, accompanied by applause.

Daireann looked up to see a tall, beautiful man walking toward her, smiling. With horror, she recognized Bres mac Elathan, former king of the Danann and the traitor who had incited the Fomoire to war against them. "Now, my dear, we must get you away from here, before the Hunt finds you. Even if they do not kill you outright, they will be none too pleased to see you, after what you have done."

"It...was you," she gasped, still struggling to move backward, away from the man moving inexorably toward her. "You stole the *draíocht* I used to fight Clothra, and then you used it—and me—to kill her! Why?"

He laughed. "Why not? She made me an offer I could not refuse. You, discredited before the *Badbha Catha*. She believed that if she pushed you hard enough, you would invalidate your initiation and pull *draíocht* from your lover to save yourself. If that power then passed into me, it would damn you in his eyes—and indeed, in the eyes of all the Danann. Stealing power from your lover, using it against one of your sisters, then giving it to Bres the traitor. Tsk, tsk." He shook his head at her, still smiling.

"Why kill her, if you planned this together?" Daireann stared at Bres as an icy cold crept in around her heart. She'd been set up, but apparently, so had Clothra.

Bres snorted. "She was a means to an end. If you killed her and gave me the stolen power, it would prove your guilt and incite suspicion against all the half-breeds in the Danann ranks, including their vaunted champion, Lugh. Clothra had friends who hate half-breeds as much as she, and with you and me both known as traitors, they will now cry out against Lugh, the only other half-breed of any importance in your camp. It will weaken the Danann and aid the Fomoire cause. My cause—and now yours."

"But I didn't give you the power. You took it. And I won't go with you. I won't turn traitor for you."

"Oh, yes, you will. If you do not, I will implicate your beloved Ronan. Many know of your close bond. It *was* his power you used to kill Clothra."

"*You* used," Daireann began furiously, but at that moment, the first of the hounds burst through the trees at the far end of the long clearing, followed by the Huntsman, Nemhain, Macha, Anand...and Ronan. For an instant, time seemed to slow.

Bres chose that moment to grab Daireann and plant a bruising kiss on her lips, making sure the distant watchers could see it. Then he pulled away from her, a cold mist already rising from the ground near his feet. "What is it to be, Daireann? Come with me and spare your lover, or allow him to die the death of a traitor with you?" Bres faded into the mist, leaving Daireann standing alone, frozen in indecision.

Even at this distance, though, she could feel Ronan's presence, even more so his shock and anger. Clothra had been right. Ronan believed she'd betrayed him. And Anand believed it, too. Daireann could sense a growing pressure in the air, a thunder without sound.

Again, it was no choice at all. Whatever Ronan believed about her, she could not allow him to die for her. Bres was powerful enough to make good his threats. If he said he could implicate Ronan in this travesty, he meant it.

Time seemed to restart itself, and the Hunt surged forward.

With a despairing cry, Daireann ran into the mist after Bres, summoning every ounce of *draíocht* she had left. If she was ever to master the *fith-fath*, now was the time.

Draíocht slammed into her from the trackways, but this time it wasn't the gentle, tingling energy she'd grown to recognize.

Tainted with her rage, it burned through her body, almost bending her double as the magic began to force parts of her into the Otherworld while other parts remained in the physical realm. Daireann shrank in on herself as feathers popped out from her bleeding skin. Her mouth gaped in a scream that became a crow's hoarse shriek. Intense pain slowed her as she ran, but she kept going. If she stopped, the Hunt would have her; she'd die before she ever got off the ground.

Ignoring the pain that told her she could not take one more step, she pushed off with her legs and pumped with her arms, which in that moment became black wings. Suddenly light, she caught a current of air and rose, wheeling toward the tops of the trees. Her body was wracked with agony, but she'd done it; she'd mastered the *fith-fath*. Anand had been right; she would have risen high in the ranks of the *Badbha Catha*. Higher than Clothra, perhaps higher than any but Badbh, Macha and Nemhain.

I could have flown with the *Mór Ríoghain* herself. Sorrow choked off Daireann's elated cry as she changed the angle of her flight toward the distant Fomoire stronghold on Tory Island. The irony tasted bitter in her mouth. In the midst of what should have been her greatest triumph, her greatest despair swallowed her whole.

CHAPTER SIXTEEN

Brenna came to herself huddled in the depths of the armchair, shaking. Scattered memories still flashed through her mind. When she opened her eyes, the room pitched and rolled around her until she thought she might be sick. Minutes passed before the world righted itself and she managed to uncoil from the tight, miserable ball she'd made of her body.

"Are you all right?" Annie asked her dryly, though Brenna noticed that the other woman's face seemed pale. "I hope you got what you wanted. You were screaming like the banshee herself, and I couldn't bring you out of it."

Brenna took a shuddering breath. Her throat was sore. "I got something, all right, but it wasn't what I wanted," she said. Briefly, she told Annie what she'd seen. By the end, she was in tears, but somehow recounting it shored up her resolve. "At least I know what I have to do next," she said shakily, wiping her eyes with the tissue Annie handed her.

"I'll leave you to that, then," Annie said, pushing back her chair. She stopped to pat Brenna on the shoulder. "I need to go into town this afternoon; I've some business to see to. As to the sovereignty and the *cómhla breac*.... You're a brave girl with a good heart. You'll sort this out, but you won't have to do it alone. When I finish my business in town, I'll look through the books I have at home—see what turns up. I may go onto the astral, as well. It may be that if the smaller fae are fond of me, they'll be inclined to return a favor or two. I may be able to find out why these Sentries think the Sidhe want you to open a portal for them, and why they're so keen to prevent it."

"Oh, Annie, maybe you shouldn't do that! The Sentries do very strong projections. No offense to your magical ability, but I have the feeling that it's only been Ronan's wards on this cottage that have kept them out of here, and he and I had enough trouble with Lars alone on the astral. There are four Sentries, after all—at least, four that I know of for sure. I'd love to have your help, but I couldn't stand it if anyone else got hurt because of me."

Annie gave her a grim smile. "Don't take so much on yourself, girl! You don't think I live where I do and practice *draíocht* for no purpose, do you? For years, I've taken it upon myself to keep people from mucking about with the local trackways and the few fae who travel the astral in the area. It's an important duty, and I've no intention of neglecting it."

Brenna stood up and hugged her. "I'm sorry, but you must be careful. Those men had auras that made my skin crawl, even when I wasn't wearing any skin."

Annie smiled. "Don't worry; I'm always careful." She pushed her tea mug away, scooted her chair back from the table and headed for the door, fastening the buttons on her coat as she went.

Annie was right. She was an experienced practitioner; she'd be fine. Nevertheless, Brenna trailed her out of the house and watched until she'd crossed the adjoining field and gone out of sight.

The Internet was an amazing resource. Where else could a desperate woman access almost every ancient Irish manuscript in its entirety, already translated into English, with just the click of a button? The language mightn't sound as lyrical, but at least translated, Brenna could read it reliably. After all, even if she had known Irish in a past life—heck, even if she'd been one of the monks who'd scribed the originals—she couldn't count on past-life memories to get her through the manuscript in *Gaeilge*.

After she'd read the complete text of *Cath Maige Tuired*, she leaned back and stared at the screen, one finger tapping against her bottom lip. It seemed that the Morrigan did indeed mate with the Dagda on Samhain, and other references online had information about the concept of the sovereignty of Ireland—the magical means by which a queen or goddess endowed a king with the right to rule.

Some of those references also said that Samhain was a traditional time for otherworldly creatures to mate with mortals, which brought up a host of ideas that Brenna didn't want to examine in the light of day. But no matter how much the idea of being some kind of Sidhe bedroom prize made her guts turn to ice, she had to consider it.

If the Sentries were right about the Sidhe wanting to gain the sovereignty through her—however that was supposed to work, since she wasn't technically Irish, much less royalty—then she had to assume that Ronan meant to seduce her into doing the necessary sex magic on Halloween...er, Samhain. That was only six days from now.

Well, she had thrown a wrench into everyone's plans, however inadvertently. Ronan was now missing because of her, and she had no idea when he might be able to return, while Colm was either behind bars or released under a restraining order. The latter might not stop him from trying to use *draíocht* on her, but now that she understood what he was, she might be able to guard herself against him. What an idiot she'd been! With excruciating clarity, she remembered the night Ronan had visited her and tried to warn her.

"I suppose now you'll tell me that whatever the hounds were after is horribly evil and depraved, and that—he, did you say?—turns into a monster during certain phases of the moon."

"Yes to the first part, no to the second. Wrong mythology. We're talking about the Gentry, here. The Sidhe—not werewolves."

"You can't be serious. The...Gentry...are just legends. Superstitions. They don't exist."

Brenna shivered. Oh, what a difference two weeks made. Now that she thought about it, she *had* noticed odd things about Colm, even if he was more conversant with modern language and customs than Ronan was. Aside from his extensive knowledge of ancient Irish history—one which seemed to go beyond the norm even for an archeologist—Colm shared Ronan's habit of turning up at unexpected times and places. He could play the flute better than the Pied Piper. And she had seen him using glamour that night at the pub; she'd just assumed that his seeming to glow was a trick of the light and too much alcohol. Now she had to wonder whether those lost hours were caused by a glamour or something nastier. What had made that particular night so different?

Vaguely, she recalled an element of horror, of resistance, right before the part of the night she couldn't remember. She'd been ready to pour coffee down her throat to help her sober up. She even remembered buying the coffee. Everything after that was a haze.

At least now she could safely assume that Ronan must have known what he was talking about when he said she hadn't had sex with Colm. But if Ronan was supposed to seduce her by Samhain, then why was Colm here? Her regression didn't include him and offered no clues as to what relationship they'd had—if any.

Ronan claimed he had never used glamour on her to make her want him. Now she knew why. Unlike the missing memories of Colm, every time she thought of Ronan, memories swamped her until she was awash in a flood of longing and regret. He'd tried to talk to her the other day—perhaps to explain how it was between them—and she'd been so distracted by the physical attraction that she'd put him off. Perhaps it was poetic justice that now, just when she'd found him again and begun to reach for the happiness they should have had so long ago, she found it was all part of another elaborate set-up.

It seemed the Sidhe weren't above playing with people's emotions if it served their purpose. They meant to use her—her and Ronan, both. Had they chosen him for this task because they hoped she wouldn't be able to resist him, or had he volunteered? Had he loved her and missed her all this time? Or, when she'd returned to Ireland, had he jumped at the chance to sweep her off her feet so he could get some long-overdue revenge for her betrayal?

"Ronan," she said aloud, just in case he was lurking somewhere in a nearby dimension and could hear her. "Where are you? You were right. We really, really need to talk."

When he didn't answer in her mind, come down the walkway, or materialize in the kitchen, Brenna glanced at the phone. He hadn't left any means of contact; it wasn't as though she could just dial 1-800-S-I-D-H-E or surf the web for an Otherworldly-R-Us contact form.

The important thing was that she'd agreed to trust him, and Annie had also advised her to trust her intuition, which amounted to the same thing. She'd have to take a leap of faith—faith that he could forgive what she'd done to him all those years ago. Faith that they could make things right.

Ronan wasn't the only one she needed to talk to, either.

Whether she'd intended to or not, she'd betrayed the Morrigan as well, and now after millennia of silence, it was time for a reckoning. No wonder she'd been hearing voices.

Brenna shut off the computer, got up and took a step toward the kitchen door. All at once, the bottom seemed to fall out of the floor, leaving her staring into a vortex of black space. She grabbed the countertop for support as images flooded her mind, so fast that she couldn't follow them at first. As seconds passed, one sequence began to separate itself from the others: Baldy and Lars grabbed Annie outside her house, forced a gag into her mouth, bound her arms and legs and dumped her into the boot of a big blue car with a dented front fender.

The images stopped as abruptly as they'd begun. Brenna stood still, clutching at the countertop. What had just happened? It had looked so real; but it couldn't be, of course. That would be ridiculous. She wasn't psychic. That she'd had memories and visions of the mythic past didn't mean she could also see the remote present or the future. But what were the odds she'd have a vision like that just when she'd been about to face another hurdle on her karmic obstacle course?

She grabbed the phone and dialed Annie's number. By the ninth ring, she had broken into a cold sweat. Annie had intended to go into town this afternoon. She might be there still. Nevertheless....

Brenna put on her rain shell over her coat, grabbed her cell phone and keys, and slipped out the door, taking precious seconds to lock it behind her. Instead of heading for the road, she went along the side of the house to the back, where she could cut across the fields behind and follow the now-familiar track to Annie's house. Better to show up unannounced and feel like a fool than assume that magical coincidences didn't happen when she already knew too well that they did.

The rain kept up a steady drizzle the whole way. By the time she reached the stile where Annie left out milk and bread for the fae, the hems of Brenna's pant legs were wet, her socks were damp and her sensible shoes didn't seem quite so sensible anymore. She started around to the front door, but thought better of it and headed for the back yard first.

The grove and small mound where Annie had set the junction of the leys seemed off somehow; Brenna didn't even have to focus on the energy to sense its agitation. It felt...violated. Brenna reached out to it for an instant but had to pull back; just touching it made her skin crawl.

While all her senses screamed caution, Brenna crept along the side of the house toward the front. *Please, please let Annie be here with a good explanation for the vision and that mess of draíocht out back. Please, if any benevolent forces are listening....*

Shrinking against the wall, Brenna reached the front of the house and peered around it. Nothing looked out of place, but she'd learned the hard way that first appearances weren't always accurate. The Sentries had managed a spell to erase their tire tracks when they'd hit Brad, so presumably they could have done the same thing here.

Brenna bit her lip. She didn't have any backup. Only the gods or the Sidhe knew where Ronan had gone, and the gardaí were no help where magic was involved.

Okay. On the one hand, she could just go knock on the door. Maybe nothing was wrong, and she was paranoid. On the other hand, that might be just what the Sentries hoped she'd assume. She could walk right into a trap. What, if anything, had they covered up?

As well as she could while crouching beside the house, Brenna grounded, centered, and spread out her senses much as she had while on the astral plane. The patter of rain on the hood of her vinyl rain shell, not to mention her hands going numb from cold, made it hard to concentrate. Nevertheless, she managed to connect with the energies of the place again, through those angry, thrashing leys and the earth, rain and air.

When she stopped trying so hard to focus, her inner sight cleared until she could sense the motes and flows of *draíocht* hanging in the air above the lawn and along the front of the house. They had a rhythm she could almost hear as music—a sly, subtle music that said, much as she had done on the astral, *you don't see me. I am not here.*

Only in this case, it wasn't a person who was trying not to be seen. It was more that a person had left behind that no-see-me energy to conceal something else. Ronan might have called it a glamour. What had he said about the sigil on the car? He had...*unmade* it. Maybe she could unmake this glamour of invisibility.

She imagined herself looking through a puddle of murky water that gradually began to clear until she could see objects reflected in it. When she opened her eyes to look at the front lawn, it seemed blanketed with a similar murky energy, which she imagined clearing while she pulled energy through the leys.

It was a struggle. The leys were sluggish, so she closed her eyes and bypassed them, pulling energy through the earth below her feet. With a ponderous slowness, the muddled sensation began to dissipate, but she had to keep as steady a flow of *draíocht* as possible or it tried to close in again. Clear. Reveal. Expose. Clear....

By the time Brenna opened her eyes, sweat beaded her forehead. But the energy from the front yard seemed different. Cleaner. She peered around the side of the house to see if things looked any different.

As soon as she saw the front door, adrenaline surged through her chest. She'd done it! The door hung open, and a scarf she recognized as Annie's lay trampled near the walkway. Without moving, Brenna could see footprints in the mud nearby. It was something. Damn. Why couldn't she have been wrong?

She had to call the gardaí, for all the good they could do. Maybe they could make something of all those prints in the front, or maybe there'd be some other evidence in the house. Just in case the Sentries had left someone in the house to wait for her, Brenna sneaked back to the stile and crouched down behind the wall before she took out her cell phone and punched the gardaí's emergency number.

They arrived quickly, but she was still shivering with cold before she heard the squad cars pull up. Even then she waited, to give them time to find out whether any kidnappers had holed up inside Annie's house. It was no good coming out too soon and making herself a hostage as well.

When she deemed she'd given them sufficient time to check things out, Brenna rose from her cramped position and started to trudge back across the section of side yard to the front of Annie's house, careful to avoid the footprints the Sentries had left, which two gardaí were examining and photographing.

"Officers?" she called, and several heads snapped toward her. It was probably a good thing the gardaí didn't carry guns. Probably.

Brenna recognized the garda who approached her—of course, it would be O'Shea—but this time she was too concerned about Annie to care what he might make of this.

"Here we are again," he said, shaking his head at her. "Every time I see you, you're in some kind of trouble, and that's a right shame. Can you tell me why I'm looking at you now?"

"Um, because I'm standing in front of you?" Brenna asked. She could have bitten her tongue when O'Shea scowled at her. He was right; this was no time to be flippant. But she was pissed, too. It wasn't as if she wanted to stay in his radar. If she saw any more of him on this trip, they'd have to start dating just to make things convenient.

"You know what I mean, Ms. Callahan. How do you know Annie Murilly, and why were you the one to find her missing?"

Brenna looked him in the eyes. "I'm sorry, Garda O'Shea; my sarcasm isn't called for. And you may as well call me Brenna. I met Annie the night I arrived; she gave me a place to stay when my car broke down. She also happens to be the caretaker for the house I'm renting, and recently, she's been teaching me about...meditation techniques. We've gotten to know each other pretty well.

"Anyway, I came over here to see her, and found...this. When I saw all the prints on the ground and the door hanging open, I called you for help. Heaven knows I don't need any more trouble while I'm here, and it seemed like the right thing to do. The rest you know."

Ronan had been right to lie after they'd run off the road. The gardaí would never believe her if she told them all the truth about magical stalkers and the sovereignty; all she'd achieve would be to establish without doubt that she was a lunatic, and possibly a dangerous one at that.

O'Shea wrote in his notebook for a few minutes, then looked up, studying her as if trying to make sure she was telling the truth. Finally, he nodded. "All right, Brenda. Stay here while I talk to the others."

"It's *Brenna*," she said to his back; he was already moving off toward the other gardaí, who'd just come out of Annie's house.

"Inside's been ransacked, but we didn't find any other evidence," she heard one of them say. "No blood. No note."

O'Shea shook his head. "It's a bad business altogether. Take the evidence you have, then call it in."

Brenna took a step closer to him before she remembered he'd

told her to stay put. He turned back to her.

"There's not much more we can do here, Ms. Callahan. I'll need you to sign a statement. I'd also recommend that you don't leave town until we can see this thing through."

Brenna blinked at him. "Are you saying...I'm a suspect?"

O'Shea gave her a grim smile. "Not necessarily, no. But you're the only witness we have to this either before or after the fact. And you have to admit we've seen more of you than we ever want to see of any tourist. First you call us out over invisible vandalism on your door. Then you run off the road. Then your American boyfriend is run over in front of your cottage, but there are no tire tracks on the road. And now a respected member of our community appears to have been abducted, and you're the one to call it in. I can see men's boot prints here in the yard, but that doesn't rule out involvement on your part."

"You forgot that I also had another respected member of your community arrested for stalking me," Brenna said tartly.

O'Shea looked confused. "What?"

"Colm Lachlann, the archeologist. He came over to my cottage the other day and started shouting threats at me from my yard. I called the gardaí in and they arrested him. I suppose he made bail already?"

"I'm sorry, Ms. Callahan, but I haven't heard anything about this. When did you say this happened?"

"Last Thursday."

O'Shea gave her a strange look. "Could you give us a moment?"

At her nod, he walked away to speak to the other officers in turn. After a few minutes, he returned.

"I'm starting to wonder what we're dealing with, Ms. Callahan. No one here remembers any such disturbance. Are you sure this happened Thursday?"

Brenna gawked at him. "Yes, I'm sure! Brad was run over the

same day. Garda O'Shea, are you saying that Colm Lachlann is running around without even a restraining order because no one remembers me calling in a complaint against him?"

"It's possible, but I can't be certain until I do a follow-up. Could be you've just gotten your days mixed up, and I'll find the report when I get back to the station. I'll check into it. In the meantime, I suggest you keep yourself to yourself and leave these other matters to the gardaí."

"But—!"

"Now, I don't want trouble here. I'm sure either there's a logical explanation for all this, or you're the unluckiest tourist I've ever met. We'll straighten this out right enough. Just you be careful, stay in the area, and be available in case we need to talk to you. Is there a number where I can reach you?"

"Ah, my cell...I mean my mobile." Brenna wrote the number down for him, read and signed the statement he showed her, then waited miserably in the drizzle while he and the other gardaí finished searching Annie's property.

"Go home, Ms. Callahan," O'Shea said when they'd finished. "By home I mean to your hired house. Dry yourself off, have some tea, read a book.... I'll be in touch as soon as I can. You have my word on that."

"Thanks. I'm sure you have everything under control. I won't get in the way." Sure, she wouldn't. Not on purpose, anyway. The last thing Brenna wanted was to get in the gardaí's way. But it was past noon, and unless they could find the Sentries today with a few footprints and Annie's mud-encrusted scarf, they'd never get them in time to save anyone. Brenna started back across the fields to her cottage, but she couldn't get the vision of the abduction out of her mind. To the gardaí, she might seem like a crazy woman, but unless she missed her guess, the Sentries wouldn't allow either her or Annie to survive the night.

When Brenna got back to the cottage, she found a folded sheet of paper in a plastic bag on her doorstep. Taking a deep breath to combat the adrenaline shock, she picked it up. It didn't look like a flyer or a newspaper. Could it be the ransom note the gardaí had expected to find at Annie's house?

Inside, she locked the door, tossed her coat and rain shell onto the floor and slipped the paper out of the plastic.

Rath Cruachan, tonight at midnight. Come alone—no gardaí, no Sidhe. Bottom line: you die tonight and the old woman goes free, or she dies tonight and you die later.

Brenna's lips curled into a sneer. The implication was clear. Even if she were the type of person who could live with the idea of letting Annie die tonight so she could escape, the Sentries would just kill or hurt anyone who got close to her, one by one, until either she gave in or they managed to kill her. If she went to them tonight, she could end it all right here. She could trade her life for Annie's and those of her family, friends, and anyone else who might get in the way.

Or maybe not.

If she gave herself up, would the Sentries let Annie go? Odds were, they'd get Brenna within their sights, shoot her, then shoot Annie later for being able to identify them—unless they hadn't let Annie see their faces and hadn't encountered her on the astral plane. If they'd been careful, Annie wouldn't be able to identify them; if that were the case, they *might* be able to let her go. But judging by the fact that they always seemed to use their own forms on the astral, the odds of that happening couldn't be good. In which case, trading her life for Annie's was a useless act anyway.

She could call the gardaí, but then Annie would die for sure. She'd tried calling out to Ronan, but either he couldn't answer, or he wouldn't. Either way, she couldn't wait for him to come to the rescue again. Someone needed to save the day—or the night, as the case might be. By default, the job fell to Brenna Callahan. But just how did an ordinary person manage such a feat?

She glanced at the clock. Nine PM. Just three hours left in which to figure out a battle plan, for battle it would be. She wouldn't let Annie go without a fight, but she damn well wasn't just going to stroll in and let Lars or Baldy pick her off from forty paces.

If only she'd been able to learn more about why they wanted her dead before Lars had sensed her presence at their house! Why was it so important that she not complete the sovereignty ritual on Samhain? Why were the Sentries so intent on keeping her from helping the Sidhe with their *cómhla breac*?

Assuming it really was a portal between dimensions, what would be the detriment of opening it? Maybe this portal was somehow dangerous to the human world. Maybe it had to be kept closed or it would rip a hole in the space-time continuum.

Nah, too sci-fi.

Brenna tossed the note from the Sentries onto her table and plopped into a chair beside it. Groaning, she rubbed her temples as if that would help her concentrate. Where was the key to all this? There had to be one.

If someone wanted a door opened, they obviously intended to use that door, which could mean the Sidhe wanted to come through the *cómhla breac* into the human world and for some reason couldn't do it without help. But if that were true, how had Colm and Ronan gotten here?

Even assuming most of the Sidhe had somehow lost access to the human world over the millennia, why did they want it back now? And why did Brenna Callahan seem to be the one person who could give it to them? There had to be plenty of younger but more experienced witchy types who would be happy to cooperate. What was it about her lifetime among the Tuatha De Danann that made her so special?

The Sentries had demanded she come to Rath Cruachan with no gardaí or Sidhe. Yet however incredible it might seem, she'd once *been* Sidhe—half Fomoire, half Danann, according to her regression. If that was how she'd first come into existence, then by rights, her soul should retain a mixture of those energies. But ever since she'd messed up that first lifetime so badly, she'd had nothing but human lifetimes. Some dim, long-buried memory insisted that this had been deliberate on her part, and that it wasn't normal. Somehow, she'd slipped into a different level of incarnation, removed from her base origin. Did that make a difference? Did souls change depending on where and how they'd been incarnating? Was any part of her still Sidhe, or was she just human now? Confusion swirled in her mind. Regaining her memories should have shown her who she really was, but now she was even less certain than before.

At least she knew why the Morrigan had called her *fealltóir*, betrayer. Regardless of her reasons, the fact remained that she'd left the Danann and gone with Bres to the Fomoire all those lifetimes ago. And then she'd left the Sidhe to go and live as a human, and never in all of that time had she made amends. Whatever the Sentries' reasons for not wanting her to help the Sidhe reemerge into the physical world, Brenna had older scores to settle.

That was where she had to begin the night's work—face the Morrigan and try to set things straight. She had no idea how her former queen and captain would react, but she had to take the chance, or she and Annie would both soon be dead.

Morrigan, I'm ready to hear you now, she breathed into the darkness. She thought she heard an answering thrum from deep within the earth, as she had at Oweynagat after her visit to Rath Cruachan.

Then come to me. Come to me at once, while you still can.

Come to her? If Brenna had to go anywhere, only one place seemed appropriate. Still trembling with tension, she ran through the house gathering her things—trying to gather her wits while she was at it. On a sort of mental auto-pilot, she put on a turtleneck, her Arran sweater, coat and rain shell, stomped her feet into the pair of boots she hadn't bothered with earlier, grabbed her purse and keys and headed for the door. She stopped there, hand on the knob. Would the Sentries have someone watching the house? She would, if she were in their position.

"You don't see me. I am not here," she whispered, imagining the fog that had made her first trip down this road so difficult. The rain had stopped earlier, she realized, and a hint of whiteness hovered near the hedgerows.

"*Mór Ríoghain*, if you want me to get to you in one piece, please help me now. Don't let the Sentries see me on my way to you." Even as she said it, she shivered under her layers of clothing. The Morrigan could kill her for that long-ago betrayal. But if that were her intention, wouldn't it be far easier to allow the Sentries to do it for her?

Tense, she peered out through the window near the door. A whiff of something cold and wet reached her nose, though as far as she knew, the cottage didn't have a draft. The whiteness seemed to intensify; she could see it in the light she'd left on in the kitchen.

"Yes. Fog to hide me." Brenna visualized the clinging whiteness, breathed it, called to it, tried to pull its essence through the distant leys. It was as much a wrestling match as dispelling the Sentries' cloaking magic at Annie's house had been. Apparently, her human body limited her use of the bits and pieces of Sidhe magic she now remembered.

She sensed something like a presence near her. It watched and weighed her, as if it were making a judgment. *Please, oh, please!*

No—something wasn't right. She was trying too hard, not connecting with the essence of fog. It wasn't something she could force; she had to coax it into being.

She stared into the blackness of the hawthorn grove and let her eyes unfocus. Fog was greyish-white; it clung, it swirled, trailed its chill dampness along skin, tried to wend its way into a body with every indrawn breath. Formless, it could take a million shapes. It knew few boundaries, rose up from standing water, water become vapor, vapor borne on the air…. Brenna took a breath and relaxed into the sensation of what it would be like to be that vapor. A fatalistic calm settled over her. At peace, she allowed her eyes to focus once more.

And the fog rolled in. It filled the roadway and the path from the cottage to where she'd parked the car. The lights from the cottage barely cut through it. She opened the door, moved out onto the step and then onto the walkway, into fog's embrace. She couldn't see more than two feet ahead of herself, but she walked unerringly to the car, unlocked it and got in.

She'd have to drive without the lights, or the fog's cover would be useless. But how could she drive without them? Brenna relaxed again into the sense of fog, visualized a thinning that extended a few feet in front of her on the roadway itself.

She started the car and let it roll forward until she'd gone far enough that anyone watching the cottage would not be able to see the Fiesta. It was slow going, and damned hard to drive the car in the dark and influence the fog at the same time.

Perhaps two kilometers out the fog thinned, not at her request. If the Morrigan had helped her just now, that help only extended so far. The rest, Brenna would have to do on her own. How typical of the Universe; of course things couldn't be easy or even particularly convenient for long where she was concerned.

Her lips tightened into a resigned smile. Given her checkered past life, it couldn't be any other way.

CHAPTER SEVENTEEN

She parked the car some distance from Oweynagat so the Sentries wouldn't see it and guess her location. About two-and-a-half hours remained before they'd expect her to arrive at the rendezvous they'd planned. If things went well in the cave, she might never have to show up at Rath Cruachan. If things went badly, the next person to enter the cave would have a horrible shock when they found her body.

The walk to Oweynagat was chilly and wet. Even without the torches Brenna remembered from when she'd come here so many centuries ago, déjà vu lent the situation a marked sense of unreality. Part of her expected to wake at any moment, safe in her bed back in Portland after one hell of a nightmare. But of course, this one was real; she'd have no safe warm bed tonight. Facing the Morrigan was just the beginning of her agenda, if she survived that much.

Flashlight in hand, she crouched at the manmade entrance to Oweynagat and slipped under the capstone, feet first. There was mud beneath her boots, but she ignored it and half crawled, half slid down to where the passage formed a junction. To the right was a small hollowed space which either had never extended farther or had been blocked off at some point in the past—her memory download hadn't included that detail.

To the left was a longer passage. Brenna followed it, hunkered down at first until the passage heightened enough for her to stand nearly upright. However, at that point the downward slope increased so that she slid in the mud, bumping and scrambling over stones and boulders that had once been hewn steps.

It was dank, chill, and silent at first, except for the faint ringing in her ears. Then memory superimposed itself upon reality, and in her mind she heard the drums the *Badbha Catha* had used on the night of her attempted initiation. She'd reached the bottom of the descent; when she stood in the middle of the open space, she could almost hear those huge drums as clearly as if they were outside now, marking time, their rhythm leading her into a meditative trance.

The first time she'd descended into this cave, it was to examine her motives, to determine whether she was fit to race the Wild Hunt and join the *Badbha Catha*. Tonight, contemplation wouldn't help her. The Morrigan would either accept her apologies, or not.

In the thin glow from her flashlight, she moved farther across the main chamber, stopping before the floor began to slope upward toward the back of the cave. Other than the drums in her head, the drip of water was the only thing that interrupted the stillness of this place, this sacred chamber where two worlds...almost...met.

"Once, it was far more potent. But over time, the power has waned."

Brenna whirled at the sound. The dark steel in that tone was a warning, and a promise. But a promise of what? Trembling, she peered into the shadows at the back of the cave. They seemed to coalesce into a tall female shape with eyes that glowed much the way she'd seen Ronan's do.

"*Mór Ríoghain*," she said. It wasn't a question. The Morrigan's presence stirred every cell in her body and shuddered through the fiber of her soul; there was no mistaking it. "Are you actually here?"

The limestone cave walls began to give off an eerie, whitish glow. Blinking, Brenna switched off her flashlight and dropped it into a pocket of her rain shell. It was just an illusion of control, anyway.

"I am here, and I am not," the Morrigan chided, "A part of me has joined you here, while the rest of me remains in the Otherworld. Now, have you come to question me about astral dynamics, or have you come to beg forgiveness for your crime?"

"Both, I guess. I don't know. But please, before we talk about me—is Ronan safe? Did he escape the Sentries?"

The Morrigan looked at Brenna steadily for a moment, as if assessing her. Her gaze softened, but only a fraction. "He is safe. Now, will you account for yourself at last?"

Brenna swallowed down the relief and fear and tried to concentrate on her answer. She thought of several things to say, and discarded them all. Finally, she met the Morrigan's gaze and gave the only answer she had—the truth.

"I just want to make things right. Everything that's happened since I came back to Ireland has led me to this, but now that I'm here, I haven't a clue what to say to you. I've only just forced myself to remember what happened between us during my Sidhe lifetime, and even now there are still holes in the story."

"Then I will fill in some of them for you," the Morrigan said, blue eyes flashing in the phosphorescent light. "The *Badbha Catha* were divided in their opinions of whether you were guilty. After the initial shock, Ronan soon realized what must have happened that night. He revealed the source of your rivalry with Clothra, and urged me to look into the matter further, deeper into the ranks of the *Badbha*. After some...persuasion...Clothra's two companions disclosed the bargain she had struck to discredit you. But by then, reports said you had become Bres's lover in truth. Then you disappeared and no one heard from you again—until now. To this day, when our people refer to a traitor, they say he or she has gone the way of Bres."

"Gone the way of Bres." Brenna shuddered. "What a way to be remembered."

Unwelcome memories of the man from her vision surfaced and lay on Brenna's mind like a skim of spilled oil on a lake. Like Daireann, Bres mac Elathan had been half Fomorian, half Tuatha De Danann. Unlike some Fomoire, he was extremely attractive, and he milked that for all it was worth. When the Danann King Nuada lost an arm in battle and couldn't rule, Bres assumed the throne. He'd overtaxed and starved the people, and when they'd forced him to step down from what was supposed to have been a temporary kingship, he'd sold them out and persuaded Fomorian chieftain Balor to wage war against them.

Those had been horrible days, but it was the personal memories that made Brenna cringe. After Bres had manipulated her into defecting to the Fomoire, he'd taken her in, played on her sympathy by emphasizing their similar heritages, and used every art he knew to seduce her. Heartsick over what had happened with Ronan, she'd been lonely and vulnerable enough to let Bres comfort her for a time—a short but nauseatingly memorable time. No wonder she'd blocked it out.

"Bres told me that if I didn't go with him, he'd implicate Ronan in killing Clothra and helping discredit Lugh. To my shame, I believed him," Brenna said though a throat tight with grief.

The Morrigan's lips curled in distaste. "You were not the first to believe Bres's threats—nor were you the last. Fortunately,

Clothra's companions' loyalty to the Danann went deeper than their distrust of half-breeds, and his scheme against Lugh failed. Had it succeeded, Danann history would have been vastly different, as would human history."

"I should have found a way to stop Bres. I should have found a way to murder him in his sleep." Even as Brenna said the words, cold calm spread through her, giving her words the weight of absolute conviction. She'd been weak, back then. She could never afford to be that weak again. The Danann had won that war, but at great cost. How might history have been different if Daireann had been stronger?

"None among the Tuatha De Danann will ever forget the atrocities Bres visited upon us," the Morrigan said quietly. "What you have forgotten in your current form is that Sidhe memory does not fade over time. When humans die, they forget; it is their gift and their curse. Isn't that why you became one of them? To forget that you were once both betrayed and betrayer?"

"Yes," Brenna said in a near-whisper. "But *how* did I do it? How did I manage to get into the human incarnation stream?"

"None of us has been able to fathom that," the Morrigan said. "In all our history, those few who managed the trick have never returned to share the knowledge with the rest of us. Not many Sidhe would choose such a fate in any case. Such short, heavy lives, living and dying over and over again...." The Morrigan shrugged. "Even when we were mortal, we lived many more years than humankind does now with their modern medicine and advances of technology."

"Humans call you...us...the Shining Ones," Brenna said, the breath catching in her throat. "The Ever-Living Ones. The People of Peace. I never knew that life. All I knew was war."

"Even so, you should know peace better than most," the Morrigan said. "Who better to understand what peace is, and how dearly bought, than one who has known war?" Her low, husky voice was tinged with a mixture of pain and utter calm, a black lake with a deep, still center. That tone took Brenna aback and caused her to look more closely at Anand ni Ernmas, the woman who had once been her queen and battle commander.

Every line of Anand's strong, almost nude body spoke of one who'd made war her business. Her abdomen was muscled like a woman who hit the gym every day of her life. But she hadn't bothered to use glamour to hide the faint stretch marks, and what little clothing she had on was white, which made a sharp contrast to the blue-black color of the woad spirals that decorated her body.

Her red hair was plaited into the traditional nine braids to symbolize wholeness, but...had she actually allowed someone to dye her fingernails with the woad? That seemed such a feminine conceit for a warrior goddess, yet those same fingernails were cut short so as not to spoil her grip on spear or sword. The message was clear: any attempt to pigeonhole her would fail. Each of her attributes represented a different truth—facets of the Morrigan that were all equally valid.

Brenna stared at her. "Annie tried to tell me there was more to you than what I'd read, that you weren't just a goddess of war, but I guess a part of me didn't listen."

The Morrigan smiled a little. "Another human gift, this *not listening*? I told you that you had forgotten me."

"I remember now." Emotion tried to squeeze Brenna's throat shut, but she forged on anyway. "But the truth remains: I did betray you. Ronan told me that in the Sidhe, time can move either forward or backward. If that's so, then send me back. Let me make amends."

"No. What's done is done. You could not change your past without changing whom and what you are now. Besides, we were mortal then. Our experiences and choices in those times molded us. When we gained the mantle of immortality, we Sidhe lost our ability to change. We are now what we have been all these millennia. It is you who hold the power of change."

"Another human gift and curse?" Brenna asked.

"Something like that."

Brenna sank to her knees. "Then if I can't go back, what can I do? How can I atone for my actions? Why do you need me to open the *cómhla breac*? And why can't you do it yourself? You are the Sovereignty."

The Morrigan smiled—not a comforting smile, but genuine. "So many questions. In that respect, you remain the same. I will answer because there is great need for honesty between us. Listen well, then, and remember."

Brenna scrambled back to her feet—the cave floor was muddy, and her legs were now soaked. Again. She found a larger rock among the rubble and, at the Morrigan's nod, sat on it, like a child preparing for a story. But she knew before another word was spoken that this tale wouldn't be a pretty one—no bedtime story. A ghost story, then, full of shades from the past. A Halloween tale meant to teach and frighten, from the ultimate of terrifying narrators.

"To begin, you will call me Anand. It is not my soul's true name, but it is close enough for what must pass between us."

Brenna blinked. She'd once called the Morrigan Anand on occasion, but never to her face. That familiarity was for close friends or associates, not the lowest rank of subordinates. Morrigan did mean Great Queen, after all. She wasn't the only queen among the Tuatha De Danann, but she was among the most powerful of them, and she embodied the Sovereignty. To deny her the deference due her rank was just...well, it just wasn't done. But she had just put them on a first-name basis—not the expected treatment for a former traitor. It had to come with a price.

It does, Anand's voice said in Brenna's mind. Aloud, she said, "Do not worry that I will always lurk in your thoughts or sort through your most private affairs. But tonight, time is short."

"Morrigan—Anand," Brenna said. "I have a petition for you. If you grant it, I may be able to save a woman's life tonight."

"Annie Murilly. I know," Anand said. "First, you will listen to me. Then I will listen to you in return." Her tone held rebuke—mild for that of which Brenna knew her to be capable.

"As you suspected in your musings earlier, we Sidhe have lost our ability to come fully into this world," Anand continued. "Over time, much of the old *draíocht* has leached away to other dimensions. With our loss of connection to the human realm, the veils between the Otherworld and the physical world have thickened and shifted. In order to effect lasting change in the Sidhe, we require some kind of anchor in the Earth realm to bridge the gap and allow *draíocht* to flow through the veil. But since we can no longer come here in true physical form to set those anchors, we are effectively trapped within the Otherworld and our influence on this realm is limited."

Brenna frowned. "But...you're here. You're standing here talking to me now. I could reach out and touch you. You're solid."

Anand shook her head. "Not that solid. As I told you, I am only partially here in the Earth realm. The core part of me is still in the Otherworld. I am...how would you understand it...? I project myself here the way you project yourself into what you call the astral plane, albeit in a more substantial form. I cannot maintain it for long. It takes nearly all of the Tuatha De Danann's combined *draíocht* for one of us to manifest this way. Soon enough, I will have to return to the Otherworld."

"But then how is Ronan able to be here? He didn't feel like a...projection." Brenna's cheeks flushed—a silly reaction, given that Anand was sure to know what had passed between her and Ronan.

"Ronan's projections have been the strongest we Danann can manage, with many of us working in concert. We manifest him almost fully in this realm, but we can only do so for a few hours at a time. He must leave you at intervals, so as not to deplete our waning *draíocht* and life force. It is why he has not been able to return to you since your last foray onto the astral plane. If the *draíocht* is ever depleted, we Danann will fade into the next realm, wherever that may be."

"I knew something was wrong that night," Brenna muttered. "Why—"

Anand held up a hand. "Since you began to incarnate as a human, the Fomoire have gained in ferocity, hatred, and numbers. We banished them to the nether realms, but the enmity between our tribes never ended. Those Fomoire who escaped have multiplied and gained allies from other dimensions as well. Constantly they press at the borders between our realm and theirs, and we often battle on Otherworld playing fields. Neither side has gained advantage—until recently.

"We Danann left the physical world to prevent further bloodshed between Sidhe and human, but the Fomoire are not content to stay in exile. We have learned that they mean to retake the lands we forced them to vacate in the human realm. If they manage to open a *cómhla breac* and return in force, your fears of terrorist attacks or world wars will be as nothing compared to what will follow."

The thought made Brenna shudder. She'd seen Fomoire atrocities firsthand. Anand was right; the human world would be a hellish place under Fomorian control—and that was if they didn't execute most of the humans outright. "But how do I figure in all of this? Why do you all seem to think I can part the veil and open the speckled gate?" Brenna's mind reeled, trying to make sense of the Morrigan's words.

"Not hard. Your soul first took form as one of the Sidhe, and you were half Danann, half Fomoire," Anand said.

Realization hit Brenna all at once. "*I'm* the anchor. I'm the only female Sidhe incarnated here in a physical form, even if it's a human one. That's why both the Tuatha De Danann and the Fomoire want me. I could serve as the anchor for either race, couldn't I? But how would that work?"

Anand's gaze was steady on Brenna's face. "You know that through the ancient sovereignty magic, we once tied the king of the tribe to the land? This connection also forms the basis of the *cómhla breac*. Both the Fomoire and the Danann have managed to send one agent through in a solid enough form to enact the rite with you on Samhain. On that night, the veil is the thinnest it will be until we reestablish connection to this realm and reawaken the old *draíocht* through the trackways. Your ritual mating with one of the men will tie the *cómhla* breac to that man's tuath and close it off to the other."

"Then if Ronan's the Danann you sent to seduce me, the Fomoire must have sent...Colm. Fantastic. Now things are starting to make sense. The Sentries must have learned what the Fomoire are planning, and that's why they want to—"

"Kill you so that you cannot open the Cruachan gate. Yes; now you begin to understand. But what the Sentries do not realize is that whether you die or not, the Fomoire will continue to search for another way to come into the human world. Eventually they will find one. When they do, the Danann will be all that stands between the Fomoire and their dominion over this realm and many others. Danann power springs from the Earth regardless of which dimension we inhabit, but it is not so for the Fomoire, who also leach power from other beings. We cannot allow them free rein, or the cost will be high for human and Sidhe alike."

Brenna swallowed. "So it's all on me, then. The betrayer.

Fealltóir. You sure I couldn't just clap my hands and say I believe in faeries?"

Anand gave Brenna a severe look, though her lips twitched a little.

"Sorry. If I do this sovereignty magic with Ronan, then the Tuatha De Danann will have access to this realm again, you'll regain your lost *draíocht,* and should you choose to do so, you may be able to help humanity hold the line against the Fomoire. But I happen to know that even the Danann aren't all noble and perfect. Take Clothra, for example, and Dian Cecht, and plenty of others I remember. You'll be a mixed bag, not all of it good. A lot like humans, but with better firepower.

"When trouble inevitably ensues, I doubt my fellow humans will thank me if they ever find out I let Thing One and Thing Two out of the box—as I'm sure the Sentries would attest. But if I work the sovereignty magic with Colm or don't do it at all, the Fomorians overrun the world, the Danann are lost forever, and the human race is toast anyway."

"Yes," the Morrigan said.

"Great. Just feckin' great."

The Morrigan studied her as if trying to judge how much she could take. "There is more."

Brenna threw her hands in the air. "Why am I not surprised?"

"You were not a queen among the Tuatha De Danann, and you have no knowledge of the sovereignty rite. In order to do this, you will have to allow yourself to be a vessel."

"For Ronan, representing the Danann." Brenna shrugged, though her heart leaped into a gallop at the thought of what that might mean for them. "I understand."

Anand sighed. "No, you do not. Traditionally, Eochaidh Ollathair—the Dagda—and I enacted the rite. He embodied the Kingship of the Tuatha De Danann, while I became the Sovereignty."

"So this time, Ronan's king to my queen. I get it."

"No, you do not. You cannot embody the sovereignty unless you descend from Danu directly, which you do not. Nor is Ronan king of the Danann. You and he cannot succeed in the rite unless an actual King and Sovereignty funnel their *draíocht* through you. In order to do that, we would have to ride you."

"You'd have to...oh. Oh!" Brenna clapped a hand over her mouth. "You can't mean what I think you mean," she mumbled.

Anand nodded. "I can, yes. But it is important that you agree to this. I would not make it a foursome if I had any other choice." A faint smile played over her lips as if in some way she found the situation amusing, but her eyes held sympathy.

Brenna cleared her throat. "So, uh...if you and the Dagda have to...uh, *ride* Ronan and me in order to make the magic work right, then why don't you just possess us outright on Samhain and leave our consciousness out of the equation? Wouldn't we just wake up later after everything was done?"

Anand shook her head, frowning. "Ronan spoke to you of possession, did he not? It can have serious consequences for both beings. If I take you by force, the *draíocht* may go awry or fail altogether, and your mind might not survive it. Do not forget that this will be intimate for me as well. If we are to do this at all, we must settle our outstanding issues or it could be disastrous for both of us."

Brenna sat on the rock, lost in thought. The request was disturbing on so many levels. And yet, wouldn't she do the same if she were in Anand's position? It couldn't be often that the Morrigan had to ask for help from anyone, especially this kind of help. But she was secure enough to do so if the situation warranted it, even if it meant she had to be on intimate terms with a traitor. How did she know that Brenna wouldn't run screaming back to the United States right now, leaving Annie and the Tuatha

De Danann to their respective fates?

I don't, Anand's voice said in Brenna's mind again. *But that is the nature of trust, and if we do not have trust, we have nothing.*

"That's just what Ronan said." Brenna looked up at Anand. "But all the time he was with me prior to my getting my memories back, he neglected to remind me of who he was and what we were to each other."

"Your relationship with Ronan is as ancient as your relationship with me," Anand said. "Each must be dealt with in its own time. Here, tonight, you and I must reach an agreement, if it is possible to do so. You should know that if you do not agree, the Sentries will take your life, after which you will be reborn into a world ruled by the Fomoire."

"And you should know that even if I do agree, the Sentries are likely to kill me anyway. If I'm doomed to die regardless of my choices, I'd rather you killed me yourself," Brenna said. "Better for you to stop my heart than for the Sentries or the Fomoire to do it."

"So I am the least in your choice of evils?" Anand didn't sound happy about that. Not surprising, from a woman who'd once showered her enemies in blood and called fire down out of a clear sky. She wasn't a fluffy-bunny type of person...er, Sidhe...er, goddess.

"Not the least of evils, no," Brenna said carefully. "It's more like you're the greatest good I can see in any of this. Surely you admit that the whole situation sucks."

Anand smiled. "Rather crass term, that. But yes, it does. Now you must choose. Then you may make your petition."

Brenna glanced at her watch. It had stopped. Fear shot through her. Was she late meeting the Sentries? Had they decided she wasn't coming and already killed Annie?

"You still have two hours left," Anand said. "I, however, do not. Will you choose?"

Brenna closed her eyes and tried to match that calm. Instinctively, she grounded, but the instant she did, she sensed the push of *draíocht* from deep in the earth beneath her. She opened her eyes to find Anand watching her, patient but wary. Brenna took a breath and let it out; the sound seemed loud in the hollow chamber.

"Fine. If I survive the night, I'll do it. I'll work the sovereignty magic with you, Ronan and the Dagda, and however many other Danann you might need to make it work. We'll party like rock stars. But first, I need a favor from you. I don't suppose you can pull enough *draíocht* to just go 'poof' and save Annie from the Sentries?"

"Deus ex Machina?" Anand smiled. "I would gladly put your enemies in their place, but I am already fading." She was. Her form seemed to be losing cohesion, as though she were about to merge back into shadow.

Brenna frowned. "So soon? But why? Ronan's stayed with me for much longer at a time."

"We fought a battle earlier. It took most of our reserves. If you want a less costly boon from me, ask now, or I will again be little more than a voice in your head."

"This one costs me more than you. I want you to let me re-run the gauntlet against the Wild Hunt. Let me finish my initiation as a *Badbh Catha*. Now, tonight, in the near-physical Otherworld."

Anand looked at her sharply. "You do realize what you are asking? Your body is mortal, and your use of *draíocht* is limited in that form. The Wild Hunt is neither mortal nor limited. It is a law unto itself. If you die in that part of the Otherworld, you also die in the Earth realm. You're no good to me without a physical form."

"I know. But if I leave this cave and meet the Sentries at Rath Cruachan, I'm dead anyway. Please, *Mór Ríoghain*. Let me do this. Give me the chance to make things right for all of us."

Anand's temporary physical form was fading rapidly now; she'd become a transparent glimmer of light that almost blended with the dimming glow from the cave walls. Brenna fumbled for her flashlight, then switched it back on.

"Very well, Brenna Callahan, do as you will. If you are victorious, I will name you one of my *Badbha Catha*, and you will help me open the *cómhla breac* for the Tuatha De Danann. If you fail, I will track you down in Tír na nÓg after your death, and then you will battle Fomoire until all our *draíocht* is spent. Either way, you fight for me. Never again will you fight against me. Those are my terms."

Brenna swallowed, then nodded. "Done."

The Morrigan smiled, sending shivers down Brenna's spine. Those cobalt eyes flashed once more from the shadows, and then she was gone, back to the other side of the veil.

CHAPTER EIGHTEEN

Alone in the cold darkness of Oweynagat, Brenna found it hard to relax. It wasn't as though the Morrigan had brought warmth or even much light with her; it was just that when she was near, nothing else seemed significant. Now that she'd gone, the rough ground was all the more evident. Brenna's pants were wet and getting wetter and the feeble light her flashlight gave off didn't offer much relief from the complete blackness.

She couldn't do anything about the first problem, but she could respond to the others. Brenna got up, took off her rain shell—which wasn't adding a great deal of warmth anyway—and spread it on the least-damp patch of earth she could find. Sitting back down on top of the shell, she switched the flashlight off to save the battery and stowed it in a pocket again. She'd either need it to find her way out later, or she'd be dead, in which case the lack of light wouldn't matter.

Now that was a comforting thought.

She crossed her legs and closed her eyes, trying not to think about the dark, the chill, or her fear. In this moment, they were all one. She grounded, reaching her senses to touch the trackways deep in the earth beneath her. The heart of Oweynagat's power responded, ancient, powerful, and more insistent than it had been the first time she'd sensed it, aboveground that day with Colm. The power called to her, and the magic in her soul answered.

The vague idea of visualizing a protective circle entered her mind. One of Annie's witchcraft books had said that witches used circles to protect themselves psychically while they did rituals. If her body wasn't safe here in the Morrigan's cave, it wasn't safe anywhere; where her spirit was going tonight, all the circles she could summon might not be enough. Still, she visualized a ring of white light around her, just in case.

"Earth, watch with me, hold me in your embrace, guard me with your silence," she said, using the first words that came into her head. She felt a little foolish, yet somehow it seemed important to alert the Earth to her intent.

"Sky, look down upon me, enter me as breath, air that sees all but is seen by none. Water..." Blindly, she reached out and touched the dampness of the cave wall, then brought the moisture to her lips. Somewhere nearby, water dripped, a counterpoint to the drums that still beat in her head and thrummed beneath her along the leys. "Water, flow with me, sustain me, carry my spirit home."

She drew a breath, listening. Was there magic here, or had it all been gibberish? The elements she'd called were the three she'd read about in an ancient Celtic triad poem, but how that fit into the context of modern-day magical ritual, she hadn't a clue. Not all of the memories she needed had come back. She'd have to make things up as she went along and hope for the best, just like any magic practitioner who wasn't one part human, two parts Sidhe, and several parts fool. She took another breath, relaxed, and let her senses drift.

It was time to make the jump onto the astral, but she'd never yet managed to get out-of-body without help. If she couldn't project under her own steam, she'd fail this test before she began it; then both she and Annie would die tonight.

No. If one of them had to die, it would be Brenna Callahan, alone. No way was Annie dying because she'd gotten sucked into an ancient war without realizing it.

You won't take Annie, she thought at the Sentries. *You can't have her. It's me you want, and it's me you'll get.*

Rage came easily, but instead of the molten fury she'd experienced in the hall of memory, this time it ran cold, the deep cold of an underground river. Brenna acknowledged it, relaxed into it and pulled *draíocht* through its energy, melding the two, letting them buoy her. *Draíocht* surged up through the cave floor and flooded through her bones. She heard a pop, and then she could no longer feel the rocks under her butt and legs. The chill in the air receded, and the faint music in her head grew louder along with the drums.

The roar in her ears sounded like crows' screeches, which resolved into women's voices. They were aboveground, waiting for her. In her mind Brenna clawed her way up through the darkness, out the mouth of Oweynagat into the night air to face a double row of ululating, chanting *Badbha Catha* in black battle armor.

They all wore black feathered masks, so Brenna could not see their faces. Nevertheless, the shock of recognition hit her hard as she met their eyes, and tears started to form in her own. She blinked the moisture away. Though familiar, this was no scene conjured from memory. This was real; she'd projected into the Otherworld. These women were the *Badbha Catha*, the Crows of Battle, past and present blended into one seamless reality. Anand would be somewhere in one of the lines, as would Macha, Nemhain, and Badbh.

Other war names crowded into Brenna's mind. Fea, Scaoll, Be

Chuille. Were they all here as well? Some of these women had probably died in the second Battle of Moytura, then rejoined the group when the Danann transitioned out of the physical world into the spirit realms. Some might have been born in the Otherworld. Others, like Anand herself, had been with the Tuatha De Danann all along and had lived in both worlds. Newer recruits or old, these women carried their battle names with pride, never cringing from who and what they were. Under the weight of their stares, Brenna took a deep breath and lifted her chin. She could do this.

"What would you have of us, *bean Sidhe*, formerly of the Tuatha De Danann?" a voice asked from somewhere in the ranks.

"Not hard," she began. That was the ritual response to questioning. The rest, she'd have to ad lib. "I, Brenna Callahan, ask that you summon the Wild Hunt to test my mettle. If I win through to dawn, I desire to take my place among you. Whether I live or die, I desire that you regard me as traitor no longer. I have faced my past and reclaimed my soul. I ask that you reclaim me as well. If I live, I will open the *cómhla breac* so that you may pass through into the human world."

Silence. It lasted for so many heartbeats that Brenna lost count. Even with the promise of the cómhla breac, would they say no? If their distrust of her was still too strong, they might, and then it would come down to whether Anand wanted her here badly enough to fight them for it. That would be a huge risk—one Anand might not be willing to take. If the Badbha divided, if they turned on each other, then how many would be left to help fight the Fomoire? Sidhe didn't reproduce as fast as humans did, and some of these women were already wearing bandages, no doubt from the battle Anand had mentioned earlier.

Finally, the woman closest to her nodded. "It is meet, if you keep your promise. May the strength of Danu sustain you. Of your own will, walk this dark corridor and face your death." She gestured down the aisle that had opened between the two rows of *Badbha*.

If only it were that simple. Death was, after all, just a soul's transition between one world and another. But if the Wild Hunt took her, it would absorb her soul. She'd become part of it—trapped and ravenous, preying on other souls whenever the Huntsman released the Hounds. Other than serving as a test of mettle for would-be members of elite groups like the *Badbha Catha*, the Wild Hunt's main function was to run down enemies or traitors. Brenna gave a short laugh under her breath. How apt. Tonight, they'd do both.

She didn't have to outrun them altogether. She just had to avoid them until dawn. That wasn't so hard, was it? Just like the games of Ghost in the Graveyard she'd played with her friends as a child, outside at night in someone's backyard. Yeah.

Brenna squared her shoulders and started walking between the *Badbha*, her gaze trained ahead. She wouldn't let them see her fear. All warriors knew fear, but a *Badbh Catha* never let it show.

As she walked between the rows of armed women, they reached out to thump her with their fists or smack her across the shoulders and backside with their leather gauntlets. It was traditional, but damn, it hurt! By the time Brenna reached the last two women in the line, she could already feel the bruises starting to form. Had it hurt this much last time? She couldn't remember it being this bad, but then, last time she'd been Sidhe, not human, and last time...oh. Last time, she'd been wearing armor.

She looked down at herself and let the breath she'd been holding out in a frustrated huff. She'd forgotten that on the astral as well as many other non-physical realms, you had to visualize what you needed. If you didn't keep it steady in your mind, it tended to fade away. Just now, she wasn't wearing the armor she should have had on. Instead, she wore athletic shoes, blue jeans and a T-shirt—a black one with a logo that said "Wicked."

Great. Maybe she should be glad she wasn't naked.

With that thought, her jeans and T-shirt started to fade away. No! No bare skin and woad spirals—not tonight. A blue streak started to wind itself up her arm, indulging the last careless image in her mind, and Brenna thought she heard a muffled snicker from the ranks behind her.

Cheeks burning, she thought of black armor, the same armor that the *Badbha Catha* wore. A bit of concentration brought up the memory of what hers had once looked like, how it had fit, and the places where it had chafed or needed alteration. It formed around her in moments, just as she remembered it, but with minor adjustments. It was light but tough, and it wasn't solid black—more like charcoal, covered with spirals in different shades of dark grey, a nighttime camouflage. Hopefully it functioned the way she'd envisioned.

"Finn Mac Cumhaill, open your gates; release your hounds! Swift of justice, sharp of tooth, unrelenting, the Wild Hunt preys tonight."

The low voice right behind Brenna made her jump. She'd never forget that voice again in any time or any plane of existence. Every nerve ending in Brenna's body prickled as the Morrigan called down the Wild Hunt like a missile strike on her position.

Brenna peered into the blackness at the inner landscape of Old Erin. This was one of the shadow worlds that bordered the Earth plane, but its form was that of Ireland in ancient days, not modern Ireland. She'd have to call up every speck of memory of the old terrain and hope that would be enough.

"Run!" Anand said in her ear.

Oh, shit. Were they coming already? Brenna broke into a full-out sprint away from Oweynagat toward the tree line she could see some distance ahead. Connacht had once been wooded, she remembered now; the chase would be all the harder if she had to twist her way through trees and undergrowth. On the other hand, she wouldn't last long without cover. She couldn't outrun the Wild Hunt—no one could. But she might manage to outmaneuver it.

When she reached the forest edge, she began to circle and zigzag, to muddle the trail as much as possible. When she had to stop for a breather, she crouched behind a limestone outcropping, trying not to pant too loudly, ears straining for the sound of the Hunt behind her. This realm seemed as solid as the physical world. At the least, it was real enough to make sweat trickle down her body, where it lay back in the Oweynagat of the Earth plane. She could feel pine needles under her fingers when she touched the ground, and when she inhaled, she caught the scent of lichen and wet forest.

Earthly hounds tracked by scent and sound, but the Wild Hunt was a strange admixture of form and spirit, which no doubt gave it an advantage. By what other means might it track its prey? She lifted one hand to brush back a stray lock of hair and saw the pale shine of her own skin, a reminder of how she'd appeared while on the astral with Ronan. Right now, her soul's light wasn't as evident as it had been that night, but she had the sense that if she drew on the *draíocht* here to work any type of spell, she could light up like Vegas. Realization made her gasp.

Auras. It had to be. The mass of energy that formed an aura was just like—what had she said to Ronan that night?—a flaming beacon. On this plane, the Wild Hunt didn't need to track her by scent or sound; they'd follow her soul's light or seek out the glowing thread of her lifeline the same way she'd done to the Sentries on her near-fatal reconnaissance mission.

Brenna could hear the Hunt now—too close. She had to move, or the hounds would bring her to bay so fast that she wouldn't even last the Otherworld equivalent of an hour. No doubt some of the

Badbha didn't think she could do it. At that thought, her chin came up. Clothra and some of the others had thought her tracking skills weak, hadn't they? They'd thought her *draíocht* was weak, too. No doubt even Anand had doubts about whether she could do it, especially now that her physical form was so much weaker as a human than it had been as a Sidhe. She'd seen it in their eyes as she passed between them earlier. They were thinking that she wouldn't make it, that she wasn't worthy, that all she'd forgotten and all she'd become had made her so much less than they.

We'll see about that.

Brenna took off again, angling her course toward the forest edge. She burst from the trees and bore south with all the speed she could muster. A glance over her shoulder revealed a writhing dark mass behind her, low to the ground, coming fast. A foul wind gusted against her back.

The belling of hounds rose and crested to an eerie pitch that made all the hairs stand up on her neck and arms. They sounded like the screams of men in terror, and...maybe they were. Who knew exactly what accompanied the Hounds of the Fianna or any other branch of the Hunt? Every European country seemed to have its own version. Who could say what really happened to the souls swept up in that dark horde?

All the muscles in her legs burned, and her lungs ached. In a non-physical realm, she shouldn't have these symptoms. It was true, then; whatever happened to her in this realm would also happen to her physical body. If she died here, she'd die there. Popping back into her body would not save her.

She forced herself to ignore the excited noises from the starved souls behind her. She would think only of Anand, of that sleek, black shape looming over the battlefield. She'd think of the crow, the spirit essence of the *Badbha Catha*. Power in motion, inspirer of strength and fear, retribution on dark wings.

She reached for the *draíocht* in the ground beneath her, pulled it through her physical body back in the cave, up into the body she wore on this plane. At the same time, she summoned the essence of the crow. The two energies crashed into each other within her spirit body.

Pain erupted between her shoulder blades, so intense that she stumbled and nearly collapsed. If this were the astral plane, the *fith-fath* would have been effortless, but here in the near-physical plane, it...ah! It hurt like hell.

She hit the ground, rolled and came to her feet running. The hounds were so close now that she could imagine their hot breath on her neck. She risked another glance backward, saw the gleam of yellow light in the leader's eyes and got a jumbled sense of bristling black fur, fangs, and a body like a Newfoundland/wolf cross on steroids.

Eyes streaming, she tore her gaze away and glanced up toward the sliver of moon, into the sky where she so desperately needed to go. She pulled at *draíocht*, which shot a jolt of pain through her again, but still her form did not alter. Her vision, however, did.

All at once it seemed as if she were somewhere outside herself, watching two different scenes unfold like a TV screen on a multi-channel function. In the one scene, she lay on a cave floor in the Earth realm, twisting and writhing in such agony that it looked as though her body were trying to fold inward on itself. That body was screaming—screaming until its throat was raw, clawing at its back, legs and abdomen. Was it dying? She peered at it with clinical interest.

In the second scene, her projected double ran through the Otherworld, stumbling, hunched over in agony twin to what the physical body experienced, about to be overrun by a horde of doglike monsters and misshapen soul-forms. This body, too, screamed. The third part of her drifted like vapor, able to touch both worlds at the same time, in a state of calm, just an observer of her own story. This part was unwilling to give itself wholly to either experience, and it seemed to be the only part unaffected by the pain her two other selves were experiencing. Clinical, disengaged, safe. Ah, there was the problem.

There is no separation between me and thee. We are all one, and we are Badbh!

She couldn't tell which part of her thought it, but in that moment, it was true. In an instant of pure focus, the three streams of power and three sets of consciousness united in the middle form, the one in the Otherworld. Wings erupted from her back, and with one last convulsive wrench, her Otherworld form changed to that of the scald crow, a *badbh* in truth.

With a shriek she sprang into the air, black wings powering her upward. She dimmed her spirit's glow, fine-tuned it until it matched that of any other corvid, and indeed she soon found several real crows as their spirits soared over the tops of the trees in a group called a murder. How ironic. She had a wild hunt, and a murder. Now all she needed was Garda O'Shea to come on the scene and the mystery plot would be all set up.

For a time Brenna joined the murder in their flight, wheeling along with them until they'd migrated far enough from the vicinity of the Wild Hunt that the hounds could not tell which winged being was true crow spirit, and which the Sidhe spirit they sought.

She could just stay with the rest, or perch in a tall tree and wait for dawn. As long as she remained hidden in plain sight, she now stood a chance of avoiding the Hunt. She'd have nothing more to prove; she'd be full-fledged *Badbh Catha* in this world and any other. Now that she'd made it this far and gone through this much, it was tempting. So tempting. But that wasn't the reason she'd come.

She concentrated on the astral plane, pulled so much *draíocht* that it tingled along her feathers, and wheeled away from the crows to arrow downward toward her body in the Earth plane. Just short of Oweynagat, she pulled out of her dive to hover over Rath Cruachan. The dim streetlights in nearby Tulsk told her that she'd returned to the real-time zone just below the astral level—just where her hunting ground must be tonight.

She had no timepiece, but it had to be near midnight, the time when the Sentries had told her to meet them at Rath Cruachan. Sure enough, as she scanned the roadway she soon caught sight of a battered Chrysler speeding along toward the rendezvous point.

She let them pull over and park, just in case they had Annie with them. As far as she could tell, they didn't, unless Annie lay tied up in the trunk. All four Sentries she'd seen before were there: Baldy, Lars, Bad Teeth and Chang. Lars had the gun; he got it out from beneath the driver's seat and stuck it in his waistband. She didn't see any firearms on the others, but even if they were clean at the moment, it didn't change a thing. They'd tried to kill her more than once, they'd nearly killed Brad, and they'd taken Annie. The gardaí couldn't protect anyone against their magic; they were too dangerous to leave at large.

Still in crow form, she let her aura fill with the *draíocht* that flowed upward to her from beneath Rath Cruachan and the surrounding area. She formed it into a ball of hardened energy, aimed, and let fly at the side of Lars' head. On his way across the field, he stumbled and clutched his head. A moment later he toppled, unconscious. Brenna grinned mentally; so that *was* how they'd knocked her out the other day! She hadn't been sure it would work.

She formed another energy ball and hurled it at Baldy, who hadn't yet recovered from his surprise at seeing his leader felled. He went down much the same way, which left Bad Teeth and Chang.

Or not. Lars' unconscious self had already spun off an astral double, and Baldy looked as though he were about to do the same. Quickly, Brenna hurled a third energy ball at Bad Teeth, who shuddered and fought a lot more before he passed out. She wouldn't have pegged him for the hardest to knock unconscious, but you just never knew about some people.

Lars had seen her by now. Rage and disbelief warred on his face; she saw him start toward her, then hesitate. She knew what he must be thinking. Was she the Morrigan, come after him, or was she the human woman he sought? Without the energy tether as a giveaway, he had no way to know for sure. Did he dare call her bluff? She didn't wait for him to decide. She gathered a last energy ball and lobbed it at Chang, but it didn't knock him out as she'd hoped. He staggered, dazed, but didn't fall.

Damn. She needed them all on the astral in order for this gambit to work. She swooped down past Lars, shrieking. When his astral self ducked and covered his head, she dove at the half-conscious Chang, latched her talons into his aura, and yanked as hard as she could.

His body sagged to the ground with an audible groan. A moment later, Brenna floated face to face with an astral double of him; he looked surprised and gratifyingly scared shitless. The shock only lasted for a moment, though. All four of them were recovering, staring from her to each other and back again.

A snarl crossed Baldy's face as he drifted closer. He took a swipe at her, but she backwinged out of his reach, then paused to hover. She shifted back to her Sidhe form then, dropping all the glamour she'd used to dim her aura. It rose and filled with a blue-gold shine that eclipsed the muddyish hues of the men. She was a Shining One, damn it—or she should have been. Let them see her as she truly was. Let the Wild Hunt see her.

Please, Mother Danu, let the Wild Hunt see her!

"You want me? You'll have to kill me here," she yelled at them. "No guns. You're so good at this kind of stuff, come get me. Or can't you handle one little Yank with an attitude? And I do have one, because you've really pissed me off!"

"That's it. You die now," Lars grated. Apparently when he got angry enough, it reduced him to caveman speech. Nice.

Brenna pulled *draíocht* and headed for the middle of the field, all four men close on her astral heels. When she glanced over her shoulder, she thought she saw Lars pulling energy strands from the others. Great. Whatever he was up to, it wasn't good. A twisted mass of energy began to form in his hands, knotted together. A rope? No. A web? A net! They meant to snare her with their combined energy and then kill her.

Damn it, where was the Hunt?

They were on the wrong plane; that had to be the problem. Brenna rose as high into the upper astral as she could and wolf-whistled at the men below her. She'd never been able to whistle in the physical world; her lips just wouldn't make it happen. But here...well, here, anything could happen, which could be either very good or very, very bad.

"Come and get it, boys!" she yelled. She shot upward toward the dimension where the Sentries had attacked her before, and where she'd begun her run against the Hunt. At first she thought the Sentries had opted not to follow her, but after a few tense moments all four men popped into the middle of the open field she'd left not long ago.

"You can die in this place, you know," Bad Teeth said, smiling at her from ten feet away.

"I know," Brenna said calmly. "I'm counting on it."

She started to run, knowing they'd reach her in a matter of moments. Lars had visualized a long-bladed knife, Chang had called up a baseball bat, and the other men now had weapons in hand as well. Brenna swallowed. They were physically stronger than she, and this realm was the almost-physical. No matter how much battle knowledge she might be able to dredge from memory, she couldn't last against the lot of them for long. She upped the energy in her aura as far as she could so that it sang through every cell of her almost-body. Then she opened her mouth and let loose a crow's raucous shriek, letting it carry on the night air.

A gust of chill wind blasted into her just as Lars did. She hit the ground, him on top of her. She felt a blow against her side. Lars started swearing at her—at least, she figured they were curse words, but they were all in Swedish or whatever his native language was. She got the gist of it, though. Her Otherworldly armor had turned his blade, which bounced away into the grass. He had to scrabble for it while he kept her pinned down.

She could have worked with that, but if he stayed on top of her, things would go horribly wrong. A chorus of howls rang out; the Hounds had found her.

One way or the other, she was out of time.

She visualized Lars' knife, in her hand. It appeared and she clenched her fist around it, but Baldy stepped on her wrist, holding her hand down. Chang stepped over her, his baseball bat gripped in his hands. The hands shook, but his face was set in a mask of determination and regret. For a moment, Brenna saw herself standing over Clothra, just before she'd killed her. She almost pitied Chang. Almost.

Lars wrenched his knife from her trapped hand and leaned over her, his foul breath in her face. He looked half-crazed. Make that completely crazed. He looked her in the eyes and positioned the knife at her throat. "Time's up," he said.

"Yes it is." Savage joy coursed through her body as she pulled *draíocht* through the trackways in both worlds. She directed all of it into a single point of focus and saw the world enlarge around her.

One moment, she was looking up at Lars. The next, his blade slashed across empty air as she zoomed upward in the form of a bluebottle fly, far above his head. Behind the Sentries, a chorus of shrieks and savage growls rose as the Wild Hunt closed in.

CHAPTER NINETEEN

As a fly, Brenna stayed long enough to make sure the Hunt had done its job on the Sentries. The sight made her spirit cringe. Seeing someone's soul ripped apart was far worse than her most vivid nightmares. The Sentries shrieked, cried, pleaded. Brenna knew their screams would haunt her nightmares for years to come. They hadn't joined the Hunt; they'd been consumed by it. She wanted to gag, cry, scream along with the men she'd trapped, but she couldn't give away her position.

As soon as she was sure it was over, she sped away to hide among the leaves in the forest until dawn. She'd much rather have changed back into crow form and hung out with the murder for the duration, but she couldn't risk having the Wild Hunt detect her presence again. Their task was to seek her until dawn's first light. The chase would end no sooner, no later. The moment the Otherworld sky had begun to lighten in the east, she beat wings back to the astral plane. The *Badbha Catha* probably expected her to claim her due for succeeding in the challenge, but she had other priorities right now.

Her astral self popped into the real-time zone right above the Sentries' car, but a quick search proved that Annie wasn't in it. Brenna rushed to the little house in the country where the Sentries had had their headquarters, and then she had to look through every room before she finally found Annie on the floor in the root cellar, so battered that she was barely recognizable. The Sentries hadn't even bothered to tie her up; they'd obviously left her for dead.

"Oh, Annie," Brenna groaned.

Annie's eyelids fluttered, opened. She looked up, straight at Brenna. There was something in those eyes—a different level of calmness, a resignation—that gave Brenna a jolt of alarm.

"Quite a pair, aren't we?" Annie said with no little irony. Her lips didn't move, and it took a moment for Brenna to realize that she was hearing Annie's thoughts, rather than her voice. "I should have listened to you and stayed away from the Sentries, but I was never one to back down when I ought. Are you all right? You look...pale...even for a spirit."

Brenna looked down at herself and winced. The glow that normally lit her skin on the astral plane had grown so dim that she did look like a ghost version of herself. She didn't feel right, either. Her energy was at a low ebb, and when she tried to pull *draíocht*, it brought on a wave of dizziness.

"Well, I'm not dead—or at least, I don't think so. The Sentries are, though; I led them into the path of the Wild Hunt while I was...settling accounts with the Morrigan."

Despite her obvious pain, Annie's eyes gleamed. "Ah. Well, I'm glad you found the courage you needed. You must never be afraid to be who you are."

"I won't. Not ever again, I promise." Brenna felt her energy waver, though she wasn't sure whether it was from worry or from her physical body's distress. "How badly are you hurt? Can you get to a phone to call for an ambulance?"

"I'll try. But I think this old body's had enough. Maybe it's my turn to see what's on the other side of the veil."

"No! Annie, I worked too hard to save you. Just hang on!" Brenna blinked away the tears that threatened. She could not have succeeded in getting rid of the Sentries just to lose Annie. No freaking way.

Could she get back to her body in time? Her cell phone was in her purse, in the car. But the car was some distance from Oweynagat, and the dim sense Brenna had of her body was that even if she got back to it quickly, it might not be inclined to function properly.

"You don't look in all that great a shape yourself, my girl," Annie said, as if she'd heard Brenna's thoughts. "Once you make it back to your body, I doubt you'll be going far with it. You've stayed out so long that you've half killed yourself as it is. Just get back there now; don't worry about me. There's no sense in both of us dying, and from what I heard from those Sentries, you still have a lot of work to do."

"No. Not until I know help is on its way to you. How did you contact Ronan on the astral plane that night?"

For a moment, Annie looked stubborn. Then she coughed, and Brenna saw that her lips were flecked with blood. "Go...to the upper astral level...focus on him, and call him. He should hear you. It's...not difficult. Time and distance work differently where you are."

"Hold on!" Concentrating, Brenna rose above the Sentries' house and into the upper part of the astral plane. Senses reeling, she tried to find her bearings. She thought of Ronan's face, of the look in his eyes whenever she caught him watching her, of the ties that, even now, connected them across time and space.

She felt a sudden sense of warmth, a rush of energy and a tug somewhere in the region of her heart. Distant voices reached her ears, with one voice gradually separating itself from the others.

Hurry. Their time grows short.

Hurry, or all is lost.

Hurry.

"Beloved, I am here."

Brenna hadn't realized she'd shut her eyes until she opened them, and Ronan was beside her, his arms gathering her close. She didn't have time to give in to the relief, though. As she tried to move away to get back to Annie, another wave of weakness hit her. She shuddered, and Ronan's arms tightened around her.

"Annie," she gasped, gesturing downward. "In the cellar."

Almost on Ronan's astral heels, the Morrigan appeared, and the two exchanged a look.

"What?" Brenna demanded, dread rising.

Ronan sighed and met her gaze. "I sense her there, and I also sense that her injuries are severe. If I pull heavily on the *draíocht*, I might be able to save her life. But the other recent healings and uses of power have taken their toll. The Danann have so little *draíocht* left that if I try to heal Annie, I will not be able to manifest in physical form on Samhain to complete the rite of sovereignty with you. We must hoard what power we have until Samhain, or all our efforts here will fail."

Brenna swiped at the tears with the back of her hand and blinked at Ronan, still trying to comprehend. "So...we're going to sacrifice Annie so the Tuatha De Danann can return to this world to fight the Fomoire? Annie is the price of your *cómhla breac?*" She couldn't help the anger that swept through her. She glared at Ronan, and when the kindness in his eyes was too much, she turned to glare at the Morrigan instead.

"Come with me," Anand said firmly. "There is something you should see."

She wrapped an arm around Brenna, and in the next moment,

Brenna found herself swept downward though the roof of the cottage, back to where Annie lay on the floor. Annie's breath came in rasps and more blood stained the floor and the front of her blouse, but she was crawling slowly toward the short flight of stairs that led to the root cellar's trapdoor. Brenna's chest felt tight, and unshed tears blurred her vision.

"Annie." The Morrigan's voice came softly. Leaving Brenna to float, she drifted downward, gradually taking on substance until she appeared as an almost solid apparition in front of Annie. Annie blinked and reached out a hand, which the Morrigan caught and held fast.

"My Lady," Annie rasped. "Is it time, then?"

"Nearly," the Morrigan said, her voice soothing, calm. "But I have one task for you yet. Our Brenna will need your testimony to the human police, implicating the Sentries and exonerating her of any suspicion in this affair. Lean on me and we will get you to the telephone."

"Of course," Annie said. Then she winced. "I think we'd better hurry." With the Morrigan's help, she half-crawled, half-dragged herself up the stairs, one excruciating step at a time. Helpless, Brenna drifted behind, heart lurching every time Annie bit back a cry of pain or stopped to cough more blood from her lungs.

When they finally reached the top, Annie lay still for a moment, gasping, unable to raise the trapdoor. She glanced at the Morrigan, and then her gaze fastened on Brenna, still hovering nearby. Brenna was shaking, astral arms wrapped tightly around herself, but she tried to appear calm. It was hard, when Annie's gentle face kept blurring in front of Brenna's eyes and she had to blink hard to maintain focus.

"Oh, it's not so bad, girl," Annie said aloud, with so much asperity that Brenna couldn't help but smile through the tears. "I have no regrets. Neither should you."

Perhaps out of sheer stubborn will, she heaved herself upward against the trapdoor just as the Morrigan exerted a short burst of *draíocht*, and the door swung upward, teetered for a moment, then fell open. Face set, Annie resumed her slow, painful crawl until she reached the kitchen. Lips pressed tightly together and with considerable help from the Morrigan and a wooden chair, she managed to lever herself up enough to reach the phone. Brenna could see her fingers shake as she dialed a number.

Brenna's pain numbed to a kind of shock as she listened to Annie speak to the emergency personnel. When the time came to confirm the address, Annie looked blank for a moment, and worry crept into her eyes.

"Brenna," Ronan said from behind her.

Confused, she glanced from him to Annie. Then she gasped. Of course. The hope in Annie's expression nearly crushing her, Brenna relayed the address she'd gleaned on her ill-fated astral recon mission so that Annie could tell it to the person on the other end of the phone line.

After a few minutes, Annie sank onto the floor, still clutching the receiver. She seemed to be having trouble catching her breath, and her face, which had been pale before, went paler still.

The Morrigan touched Annie's shoulder gently, which seemed to ease her breathing, but gradually her eyes drifted closed.

"Hold on, Annie," Brenna pleaded. "The EMT's should be here any minute. It can't take them long."

Annie's laugh turned into a cough. When she recovered, she grimaced, but her eyes were open and her gaze was steady. "I'll hold until they come, my girl, but not so they can save me. Part of being a guardian of the ancient sacred sites is the need to recognize the greater good—for both Sidhe and human. It's never about just one person."

"I know," Brenna whispered. "But sometimes that one person

makes a bigger difference than they ever realize." She laid her hand on top of Annie's, even though she knew Annie wouldn't be able to feel it.

The sound of sirens came from outside, and the Morrigan straightened, her semi-solid form dissipating until she was fully on the astral plane with Brenna again. "I will wait for you," she told Annie, who smiled at her, a look of worship in her eyes that made Brenna's throat feel tight and raw.

"There is no gain without sacrifice," Annie told Brenna, her mental tone gentle but firm. "Just remember that it's one I was happy to make."

The latch rattled, and then the door burst open as though someone had kicked it. Garda O'Shea and his partner rushed in, followed by the emergency personnel. No one saw Brenna or the two Danann hovering nearby. The E.M.T.'s surrounded Annie, assessing her injuries, trying to start an I.V., hooking up oxygen. Annie pushed the oxygen mask away and grabbed O'Shea's arm.

"I may not have long, so you'll be taking my statement now," she said clearly. Brenna saw O'Shea's eyes widen, and his face actually paled as he met Annie's gaze.

"Yes, ma'am," he said, and got out a digital voice recorder. Brenna noticed that his hand shook just a little as he turned it on. She felt a flash of pity for him. Annie's situation had struck a nerve somewhere, but he showed her the calm professional she needed to see. Brenna's estimation of him rose several notches in that moment.

As O'Shea took Annie's statement, Brenna's astral form flickered again, violently. Head-splitting pain and vertigo made the world seem to tilt. She felt Ronan's arms wrap around her again, supporting her, but everything was trying to dissolve into a chaos of flashing color and light and sound. Too bright, too loud.

Beneath it all, she heard Annie's voice, calmly telling O'Shea everything that had happened, naming the Sentries, describing each of them. Brenna heard her own name, delivered in love and pride as Annie assured O'Shea that Brenna Callahan was the Sentries' main target, that they'd kidnapped Annie to try to trap Brenna, and that Annie wanted O'Shea's promise that he would do everything in his power to make sure her American friend wasn't harmed.

Ronan's grip helped steady her, but Brenna could feel herself growing weaker. He was saying something to her, but she was having trouble concentrating on what it was. Then cries of dismay from below drew her attention, and with an effort of will, she managed to focus on what was happening in the house. O'Shea had backed off, and the emergency people were working on Annie. They had a defibrillator and paddles, and Brenna could only watch in terror as they shocked Annie's chest again and again.

The lines on their instruments went flat and stayed that way. For a long moment, Brenna gripped Ronan's arms hard as if he could keep her from falling, as if he could save her from the pain of what she was seeing.

Then to Brenna's eyes, a glow began to coalesce and rise like mist from Annie's motionless body. Slowly, Annie's glowing spirit separated itself from her body and rose to join the Morrigan, who held out a hand to her, smiling. "Well met, friend of the Sidhe," Anand said softly.

Annie, looking more like a woman of Brenna's age than the age she'd actually been, sighed and stretched, her eyes closing momentarily in apparent relief. When she opened them, her gaze fell on Brenna, and she frowned—the same stern frown she'd used so often over the past couple of weeks.

"Why are you still here?" she asked. "You get back to your body this instant, or I promise whether you're Sidhe or not, I'll track you down and whip your disembodied arse—unless my Lady beats me to it!"

Brenna caught the brief look of amusement that passed between Ronan and the Morrigan, but their concern was evident as well. Another wave of weakness and nausea broke over Brenna, and her astral body wavered. Annie was right; she'd overtaxed herself. If she didn't return to the physical immediately, going back would no longer be an option. She'd be an oathbreaker all over again.

"Care for her, then return," Anand instructed Ronan. "Annie will be fine now." Brenna had the feeling that last was directed more to her than to Annie, who seemed completely unperturbed by the fact that the men below were disconnecting their instruments from her motionless corpse, unfolding a body bag, and conferring with one another in hushed tones.

"Brenna," Ronan warned.

Brenna reached out to Annie's serene spirit-form, squeezed her hand once, then re-visualized her silver cord and hurtled back toward her body, still lying in the depths of Oweynagat.

Re-integration was difficult, since she'd been out for so long. Her body was chilled and stiff. She sank into it, appalled at how sluggish her heartbeat was and how sick she felt. She could hardly move, but she had to.

With a supreme effort of will, Brenna opened her eyes and groaned. Every cell in her body hurt, and the blackness was so complete that for a moment she wondered whether she'd gone blind. Then the drip of water nearby and the feel of her wet pant legs penetrated the grogginess. Yeah, she was alive, but that didn't say much.

Something moved nearby and she felt a hand touch her wrist. A faint glow rose until she could just see the outline of a head and shoulders above her.

"Ronan?" Brenna croaked. Her heart pounded, and the pain in her head pulsed in time with it.

"Shh; just lie there," he soothed, and gave her hand a brief squeeze. Then he began to briskly rub her arms and legs until the circulation returned. With it came a bout of shivering, as though her body had ceased to do that for a time, and now the ability returned in force. Ronan pulled her into his lap and held her until she could move again, but even once she'd regained a semblance of control over her limbs, she felt less steady than a newborn colt.

As soon as she sat upright, she wished she hadn't. If Ronan had told her the cave had turned upside down, she'd have believed him. Shaking, swallowing bile, Brenna crawled across the floor until she reached the upward slope to the entrance. Even with his encouragement and support, it seemed to take an eternity to emerge from the dark womb of Oweynagat.

When she finally reached the outside world, the purplish-grey sky that preceded sunrise seemed like an extreme amount of light after the blackness. Eyes streaming, she lay on the wet grass for several moments, trying to re-learn how to operate her body.

As Ronan emerged from the cave and bent over her, Brenna's gaze went to his face as if drawn there by a lodestone. He represented everything she'd lost. After Bres, Ronan had had ample reason to refuse to do the ritual with her, to send another of the Danann men instead. Yet here he was, taking care of her as though none of the terrible things had happened. Of course, he was trying to save his people. But the look in his eyes said he had other more personal reasons.

Conscious of what was at stake for Ronan and for the Danann if they ran out of *draíocht*, Brenna levered herself up and tried to stand, but her knees buckled even with his support. He swung her up into his strong arms and carried her rapidly toward where she'd parked her car. Maybe she was in shock, but the potential humor of the situation struck her as she clung to him. What if he dematerialized and dropped her? That was funny, but not. Oh, wait. What if on Samhain, he dematerialized right in the middle of—?

Very humorous. The thought sounded like his voice even though it was in her head, and for an instant she fancied she caught a feeling of sarcasm from him. Just as quickly, the feeling was gone, leaving her to wonder whether she'd imagined the exchange.

For the moment, she could do nothing but lean her head against his shoulder and let him carry her, as he'd done that first night. Part of her rebelled at the weakness, but another part recognized that she wouldn't have made it to the car without him. Any warrior worth her salt knew when to accept help with grace. Or as much grace as she could muster with a pounding head, trembling muscles, and a dull ache in every part of her body.

"Ronan," she began tentatively, but he shook his head.

"Wait. I must see that you are well, and then we will have the conversation we should have had the day you arrived." The words were businesslike, but his gentle smile warmed her more than any blanket could do. Brenna felt the odd lurch in her chest again, but he was right; this wasn't the time to speak of what it meant.

"Annie—"

"Is fine now, as the Morrigan said. Annie will pass onward to the next phase of her journey, and when the time comes, she will have the choice of whether to return to a human body or choose another destination. She has earned that right." Ronan paused in the act of buckling Brenna into the passenger seat. "Just now all my concern is for you."

For a moment, Brenna stared at Ronan, drawing strength from his calmness. He was right, of course. Hadn't she and Annie mused earlier that death wasn't exactly what people feared? Unless you'd gotten yourself into a huge mess like the Sentries, death was just a means for the spirit to change location, to step through the veil to another dimension. Annie would find it an adventure, and unless Brenna missed her guess, she was no stranger to the reincarnation process. She'd be all right—much better than the people she left behind.

Though she couldn't hold back all the tears that threatened, Brenna took a shaky breath and lifted her chin. She was a *Badbh Catha* now, or would be as soon as the *Mór Ríoghain* could make it official. If Annie was strong enough to put her convictions first and do what had to be done, then the least among the *Badbha* could do no less. Anand would expect no less.

"I'll miss her," Brenna said with quiet sorrow.

"I am sorry, *mo grá*," he said, and she could tell he meant it.

He seemed about to say more, but instead he just finished what he was doing, got into the driver's seat and cranked the ignition. A moment later, he pulled the car smoothly onto the road as though he'd been doing it for years.

"I thought you didn't drive," Brenna said, keeping her gaze fixed on the road ahead to combat the dizziness. She tried to take deep, slow breaths, but the motion still made everything within her visual range seem to dip and sway around her.

"I do not have a license, and this is my first time, but...I watched you enough to know what is involved," Ronan said. "This is an emergency; we could not leave your car parked in the area. The sun has begun to rise, and it will not be long before someone finds the bodies in the fields of Cruachan."

Oh, yeah. The bodies. Closing her eyes against the too-fresh memory, Brenna said, "The Gardaí will find it hard to explain why the Sentries are lying out there in the field, looking like they've been mauled by wild animals."

"Yes, but it will tend to exonerate any humans as suspects, and most of the local people will be on the lookout for a wild dog pack for some time to come." Ronan's voice was grim.

"Just the way I planned it. Yech," Brenna said, surprised at her own satisfaction, tinged with nausea and regret that it had to be that way in the first place. It was so...vigilante. But the Sentries hadn't left her any choice, and perhaps that was part of what it meant to be a *Badbh*.

By the time a hot shower had driven the last of the cold from Brenna's body and she was propped up in bed under the comforters, she was exhausted all over again. She still had one final reckoning left, though—the one she dreaded most but longed for so much that she ached.

Ronan sat on the edge of the bed, watching her. Mute, they gazed at each other, letting the silence grow until it felt as though it had weight. Conflicting emotions rose until Brenna could hardly breathe past them. Finally, she couldn't stand it any more.

"Just so you know; I promised the *Badbha Catha* that if they let me run against the Wild Hunt to complete my initiation as one of them, I'd open the *cómhla breac* and let the Tuatha De Danann through to this world."

"I know. The Danann were much relieved at the news."

"And you? Were you relieved?" She realized that she was trembling, and this time it wasn't from her ordeal.

He looked surprised. "How can you ask me that question? Have I not made my feelings plain to you from the start?"

"Well...." She wasn't sure how to answer. "I'd like to think so. But now I remember what happened the night I left for the Fomoire with Bres, and you have every right to be angry with me. You might have just been courting me this past couple of weeks so that I would choose you over Colm, for the sake of the Danann. Or you might have been courting me as a form of revenge for how I hurt you...for the way that I left you, and what I allowed you to believe."

He shook his head. "If I were motivated by revenge, I would have used glamour on you as Colm did, and you would have had no choice in the matter at all. I wanted to see what you truly felt, not what I wanted you to feel. At first, you seemed to want nothing to do with the Sidhe or anything that might remind you of your origins. And you seemed to feel that I might be deceiving you, even if only by omission. You were overly concerned with my lack of...plastic. I believe that you have come to trust me to keep you safe, but you still do not trust me to love you."

His words hit her like a kick in the stomach, and for a moment, all she could do was stare at him. He was right. She'd been so cautious, so afraid of deception that she'd fought her instincts every step of the way.

"I am so very sorry," she managed at last. She drew a shaky breath. "I see that I lied to myself more than you ever held back the truth. Until I got those memories back, I didn't really know who I was. I guess I didn't want to know, and that denial nearly got me killed. And where it concerns you, I've been an idiot."

"You've been the woman I love," he said, his gaze locking with hers as soul spoke silently to soul. *"Tá mé riamh mise, mo chroí."*

I am ever yours, my heart. Her spirit leaped and for a moment, she forgot to breathe as his words confirmed what she'd seen in his eyes. She must have swayed toward him, because the next thing she knew, she was back in his arms, breathing that intoxicating scent, feeling his warmth through every layer of fabric between them. Long-denied emotions swept through her like a storm, but in its wake, there remained only peace and a profound sense of rightness.

"Ronan," she said when she dared speak. "I may not say it as beautifully as you do, but I love you, too. I'll be here on Samhain, and no matter what I give the Danann, my heart belongs to you. It always has."

He sighed as though she'd just lifted a great weight from off his shoulders. When he met her gaze, his eyes were filled with the warmth she'd been craving for so long.

"Thank you."

She blinked at him. "What...hey, you just said—"

"Yes."

"But doesn't that mean you—"

"Yes."

"Then I promise never to abuse the trust you've shown me." She leaned in to him and touched her lips to his, lightly.

"As I also promise, *mo grá.*" He put one hand behind her head and kissed her until they were both breathless.

After a few minutes, he pulled away from her and stood, stroking a finger along her face, from her temple to her jawline. She shivered in reaction. "Damn. Do you have to leave now? Something always interrupts us just when things start to get interesting."

"I must leave, or I will not be able to return to you. The Danann must horde our power for the next several days, until the eve of Samhain. But I assure you that when I return, things will get...much better than interesting."

"Promises, promises," she joked, but despite her exhaustion and all the trauma, her body and soul still reacted to him, still longed to renew that connection they'd shared so briefly on the astral plane. When he removed his hand from her face, she felt the loss like a physical blow.

"One last warning," he said, his expression serious. "As you may already know, Colm has disappeared. I have searched for him, but I cannot find him on the astral, nor can I find him anywhere in Strokestown or its environs. I fear he is still at large, and he still intends to claim you for the Fomoire."

"I've been worried about that myself," Brenna said. "Apparently he hoodwinked the gardaí into letting him go and then forgetting they'd arrested him."

A thought struck her. "Ronan, how is it that you can only project to this realm for a few hours at a time, while Colm seems to live here? I mean, he has a car and a house and everything. He has I.D., for goodness' sake."

"That is because he is fully here in the earth realm. His form is true corporeal matter."

"But I thought you said none of the Sidhe could manifest here fully—not even Anand."

"That is true. But Colm did not project himself here as I did. Do you recall what I said to you about possession?" Ronan's tone was hesitant.

"Yeah, but...oh, no! Do you mean that Colm Lachlann isn't really, ah, himself? A Fomorian managed to possess some poor archeologist?" Her mouth went dry at the horror of the thought. "What happened to the real Colm, then? Where's his soul? Buried beneath the Fomorian's?"

Ronan shook his head. "I do not know. All I know is that the real Colm Lachlann, the human soul who should own that body, does not seem to be present. When he looks at you, a Fomorian soul looks out of his eyes—one that should be familiar to you. I believe he is—"

"Bres," Brenna said, with a shudder of revulsion. It was true. There had been clues there, too, if only she'd let herself see them. One of Annie's books said that all the deepest secrets of a soul could be found within the eyes, as she'd just experienced with Ronan. But she'd never looked deeply enough into Colm's.

"I'll be careful," she told Ronan, trying to ease the worry on his face. "I'll be on the watch for him, and at the first sign of trouble, I'll call the gardaí. He shouldn't be able to get through the wards on this cottage, and...well, I'm a Battle Crow now. That ought to count for something, though in the physical world, I'm not sure what."

He leaned over and kissed her on the forehead. "It's a pity you can't have your watchdog here with you while I'm gone."

Brenna sat up straighter, frowning. "My watchdog? Wait a minute. I haven't seen Cu since the night Brad was run over. He's been gone as long as you have." Her eyes widened. "My *watchdog*. Oh. Oh! Ronan, you promised we'd have truth between us, but you're still holding out on me! All this time I've been telling my deepest secrets to what I thought was a sweet, innocent dog, and here you were, listening to everything, eating dog kibble I bought, sleeping on my bed...." She stopped her tirade to glare at Ronan, who was laughing softly.

"It's true that I did persuade the dog to visit you at night. I did ride behind his eyes so that I could make sure you were safe when I could not be with you. But I assure you that I did not harm the dog in any way."

Brenna sighed. "I guess I'd have done the same thing if I were in your shoes. I'm just not used to being such a valuable commodity."

"You are no mere commodity to me, love. I value your life much more highly than my own."

"Spoken like a true non-corporeal being. Never mind; I understand. But sometimes a girl likes to gab to a friend who won't reveal her secrets. From now on, a dog is just a dog, all right?"

"Agreed," Ronan said. "That was the last of my secrets. I cannot ride behind your furry friend's eyes over the next several days in any case. I cannot use any more *draíocht* whatsoever, if we are to be successful on Samhain. And now I must go. Be watchful."

"Back atcha," she said, trying for a casual tone, and failing.

He gave her one last toe-curling smile and then faded where he stood, until she could see through him, and finally could not see him at all.

Garda O'Shea stopped by later that day. He told Brenna all that had happened from his perspective, including the details she already knew about Annie's death. His eyes were kind, especially when he said that Annie had asked him to tell Brenna goodbye and make sure she was safe.

"You've had a run of hard luck since you've been here, Ms. Callahan. I hope you don't go away with a bad opinion of Ireland, after everything those sickos put you through. And I'm sorry about Ms. Murrilly."

"Thank you, officer," Brenna said, fresh grief and weariness making her voice ragged.

O'Shea's speculative glance took in her pajamas and robe, her tousled hair and no doubt haggard appearance. "I should leave you to your rest. You look wrecked."

Brenna managed a smile. "I *feel* wrecked. Good luck with your investigation. I hope there aren't any more of those—what did you call them?—sickos. The way you say they died gives me the creeps, but I can't say I'm sorry they're dead. I sure don't need any more kooks after me for God-knows-what reasons."

O'Shea shook his head. "These cultists can be an odd lot—not the full shilling, in my opinion. If there are any more out there, we'll get them, Ms. Callahan. Don't worry about that."

"It's Brenna. And I won't. I didn't sleep very well these last couple of nights, so I think I'm exhausted enough to take the edge off any more worrying. I just...I wish Annie were here." Every word was truth, even if she couldn't tell him all of it.

"There's one more thing," O'Shea said. "I checked into your claim that you'd called in a complaint on Colm Lachlann. The two gardaí who responded to your call didn't remember a thing. But when I checked the telephone logs and the files, there it was, staring back at me."

Brenna opened her mouth to speak, but O'Shea held up a hand.

"Ms. Callahan, I don't know what forces are at work here. But in reference to that first day when I made the comment about the Little People...."

Brenna kept silent, letting him stew. He cleared his throat.

"Right, well, I don't claim to know much about such things. I'm not even sure I believe in them. But when the records of an arrest and a garda's account of it don't agree, something isn't right. We'll be watching for Mr. Lachlann, and we'll find out what actually happened. In the meantime, I apologize for not taking your problems more seriously."

"I appreciate that, Officer," Brenna said. "Oh! Wait a minute!" She could feel his curious gaze on her back as she went into the kitchen, grabbed the tape out of the answering machine—thank goodness it was the old cassette style, and not digital—and brought it to him.

"This is the tape from my answering machine. There's at least a dozen messages from Colm on it; it's full of stalker-talk. Maybe you'd better take it; it should help support the paperwork you found, even if no one remembers the arrest but me."

He nodded and took the tape from her, putting it into a jacket pocket. Then he reached into the opposite pocket and handed her a business card printed with his name and a phone number. He pulled out a pen from his notebook and wrote an additional number on the back of the card.

"Right. Take this; the second number's my personal mobile phone. Ring if you need anything, or even if you just want to talk. Good afternoon, Ms. Callahan."

After she watched him stride back up the walk, she closed and locked the door, then stowed his card in her purse. O'Shea wasn't a bad guy at all, once you got to know him.

She was about to go back to bed when the doorbell rang again.

Now what? A quick glance through the peephole made her scowl, but she unlocked the door and opened it anyway. Garda O'Shea was back, holding a small wrapped box. He'd changed his jacket for a heavier one, though the rain was beginning to die down.

"Can I help you?" Brenna asked, fighting annoyance. Couldn't he just leave her to her misery?

"I'm sorry to disturb you again. I nearly forgot. We found this in Ms. Murrilly's house. Since your name was on the card and the box wasn't in one of the ransacked areas, I didn't admit it to evidence. Just do me a favor and don't mention it in the future."

"I...won't. Thank you," Brenna said, taken aback by the gesture.

He gave her a nod and left. Brenna locked the door behind him again, carried the box to the couch and opened it, blinking at the contents through fresh tears.

There was no note, just the card with her name on it. Inside the box was a small stone, carved with a spiral design much like the one on the much larger La Téne stone at Castlestrange. There were Ogham lines on the back, but she hadn't had enough time yet to learn what letters they stood for.

When she opened her senses to it, she caught a faint tingle of magic that felt similar to the energy of the wards on her house. Annie must have meant it as a protective talisman, and hadn't had time to give it to her before...before....

Blinking back tears, Brenna took the stone and set it on top of the mantle. Its bottom was flat enough to allow it to stand upright. Although it looked out of place amongst the china plates and other knick-knacks already on the mantel, it was comforting to think that she had something nearby that Annie had touched and empowered with magic on her behalf. No matter what happened on Samhain and beyond, she'd always miss the other woman's dry humor and straightforward common sense even in the most negative of situations.

Even her joy in finding Ronan again couldn't offset the injustice of Annie's death. It seemed as though the world should be falling down around her ears right now, but it just kept going on as usual, as oblivious to the growing struggle between Tuatha De Danann and Fomoire as it was to the passing of a woman who'd given her life to a probably doomed Save the Humans campaign.

CHAPTER TWENTY

The morning of Samhain, Brenna woke with a start, all her nerves humming with tension. She'd spent the time since Annie's death in a sort of shocked daze, but the knowledge of what today would bring shook her out of her lethargy.

Oh, she'd come out of it enough to function—enough to deal with all the things the Sentries had forced her to put off—but it had taken effort. She'd finished the third travel article and sent it to Jay, checked her bank and credit accounts, and even called her mother to tell her about Brad and the breakup. As predicted, Wendy came unglued, and by the time she hung up, they were both in tears.

No one asked her to attend Annie's wake—not that she expected an invitation when no one in the community knew her. Still, it hurt not to be included. Trixie must have run away or been taken in by some unknown friend of Annie's; in any case, the cat wasn't at Annie's house. Without Ronan's interference, Cuchulain hadn't returned to see her either. In some ways, Brenna was more alone than she'd ever been in her life.

When the silence grew too loud, she ventured out to a few more destinations, playing tourist while keeping a watchful eye out for the missing Colm...er...Bres. It was a considerable risk and she'd no doubt catch hell from Ronan for doing it, but she couldn't hole up for a week without going stir crazy.

Bres hadn't appeared or otherwise shown his hand—a relief and a concern both at once. Brenna called Garda O'Shea, who informed her that although "Mr. Lachlann" was still at large, they had put a detective on the case. It was only a matter of time before they found him, O'Shea assured her. Lachlann couldn't hide forever.

Which, of course, was the real problem. If he wanted the sovereignty for the Fomoire, Bres would have to make his move on her soon. She could accept that the attack was inevitable, even logical. Waiting for him to try it was going to drive her right around the bend.

As Samhain approached, a different worry intensified. She had no way to prepare, no way to know what to expect at this ritual for which Annie had sacrificed everything, and yet the lives of the Danann and countless humans depended on it. By the time darkness fell on Halloween night, Brenna was a nervous wreck.

It wasn't that sex with Ronan would be so bad—she'd have jumped his bones long ago if things hadn't kept interrupting—but the idea of sex with Ronan, the Dagda, and the Morrigan all in one go was more than Brenna's human brain wanted to process. Nevertheless, she'd made a promise and she'd keep it.

She imagined that Ronan would arrive sometime around eleven; midnight was the liminal hour, the between time when they needed to do the sovereignty magic. At nine, she took a long bath, adding a little salt for purification. She soaked for a while and tried to relax, but the human part of her was too keyed up for that.

Before she morphed into a prune, she got out and pulled on the most attractive nightgown she'd brought with her—an extra-large black T-shirt. The T-shirt bore no resemblance to the red silk negligee that she now wished she'd brought with her from Portland, but it looked better than the boxy plaid pajamas she'd lived in for the past several days. For an instant, she almost wished she hadn't returned the negligee that Colm...Bres...had sent her. Lingerie would be sexy, and she wanted to feel sexy. But he'd clearly intended it for tonight, and that idea was too creepy to contemplate. The T-shirt would do fine.

When the clock neared ten-thirty, she brushed her hair, curled it into nine long spirals with a curling iron, and put on makeup. Staring into the mirror, she considered adding spirals to her skin, but decided against it. She didn't have enough blue or black eye shadow to do her whole body, and she wasn't about to go at it with a permanent marker.

None of this preparation was for Ronan's benefit, anyway, or even Anand's. Sure, she wanted to look good for Ronan, but he'd already seen her at her worst and not been turned off by it—or if he had, he'd had the grace not to say so. Anand probably wouldn't care whether she woad-spiraled her body or not. The person she was most worried about was the Dagda. Whatever Ronan saw or felt, Eochaidh Ollathair would see and feel. She should consider herself lucky that the Dagda didn't intend to manifest in solid form and leave Ronan out of it altogether. Even when she'd been with the Danann, she hadn't known Eochaidh well, and the idea of a bout of ritual sex with him was just very...nerve-wracking.

She pushed the thought aside as best she could and busied herself with getting out every candle she had in the cottage and lighting them. Soon they stood on windowsills—well back from the curtains, of course—on tables and countertops, on the bathroom sink, on the mantle.... She turned off all the lights in the house and let the candles' soft glow illuminate everything. It made the place look like...well, like Faeryland. Or rather, it looked like what she'd have called Faeryland until recently.

Shaking her head at her own foolishness, she tried to settle down with a bargain bin medieval romance novel, but suddenly all the intimate scenes seemed to lack realism, the heroine protested too much, and the lack of historical accuracy tempted her to throw the book against the wall. Instead, she gave up on reading and packed her suitcase for tomorrow's trip to the airport, then set it beside the kitchen door.

That done, she looked around the kitchen, considering. Wine. Wine might be good here. She climbed up on a chair to retrieve two glasses from the topmost cabinet and put them on the counter near the sink. After a moment, she shrugged and climbed back up to get two more, just in case. Then she got her last bottle of wine out of the cabinet, set it inside a ceramic pitcher and dumped crushed ice around its sides to chill it.

Unnecessary fussing, maybe, but it passed the time. It just didn't take quite long enough. By eleven-thirty, she was pacing between the living room and the kitchen.

If Bres were to attack, how would he do it? The day she'd had him arrested, his ploy to lure her outside failed, so he might not be so quick to try that again. The night he'd hurt Cuchulain, Bres had tried to launch some kind of an attack from outside, but he hadn't been able to destroy the wards.

The wards. How long had it been since she'd checked them? Since before Annie died? A sick feeling gripping her, Brenna reached out to the energy around the house. Instead of steady warmth, all she felt was the cold, tattered remnants of energy. What little *draíocht* remained seemed to be seeping away, as if it were being pulled somewhere else.

On impulse, she glanced at the mantle, where Annie's stone talisman stood. The Ogham lines on its side seemed to stand out, and when she extended her senses to it, she could feel the *draíocht* that it emitted in steady pulses. Each pulse lashed outward, then pulled inward; when Brenna followed the ripples of power, it was like being on a boat in the middle of a choppy ocean storm.

She was three times an eejit.

It wasn't a gift from Annie at all. And Garda O'Shea's second appearance probably hadn't been made by O'Shea himself, but by Bres under glamour.   He'd staged the arrival of Annie's posthumous "gift" so Brenna would bring his poisonous magic inside the cottage, like Snow White's apple.

It must have been subtle at first, so she wouldn't sense its true purpose. But now that she concentrated on it, she could feel the spell chugging away at maximum speed, pulling power from the wards, and...oh, great. From her, too. No wonder she'd been so tired over the past several days. She'd put it down to her ordeal in the Otherworld and depression over Annie's death, but it was more than that.

Gritting her teeth, she grabbed the Ogham stone off the mantel and hurled it to the floor. It hit the concrete hearth and shattered. Before she could sweep up the pieces, someone knocked on the door.

Brenna tensed. Was it Bres? She peeked out the window by pulling the curtain aside just a crack, and breathed a sigh of relief when she saw Ronan on the step. Quickly, she unlocked the door to let him in, scanning the darkness behind him for any sign that he'd been followed. As soon as he stepped inside, she locked the door.

"Ronan," she began, her voice sounding breathless even to her. "I'm so glad to see you. I just checked the wards. After you left, Garda O'Shea...I mean Bres under glamour...brought me something he said was from Annie. But I just found out that it's been eating away at the wards for the past few days, and—"

Calmly, he took off his jacket and hung it on the coat rack. "Don't worry. We'll reinforce the wards. But first, come here and let me look at you."

Brenna's heart sped up as he took in her T-shirt ensemble, his gaze lingering on the hem of the shirt that skimmed her thighs not so far below her crotch. She hadn't bothered with underwear, as he was just going to be taking it off anyway.

"Not as seductive as lingerie, but I like it," he said. With a wicked grin, he advanced on her, swung her up into his arms and carried her into the living room. She gave a startled squeak as he tossed her onto the couch and followed her down, his weight pushing her into the cushions.

"Brenna, Brenna, Brenna. It's been too long, and I have no patience left. Kiss me, now." His lips came down onto hers with so much force that she bit her tongue.

On reflex, she opened her mouth to his kiss, shocked when he forced his tongue far deeper than he ever had before, pushing, demanding. She could feel his body hard against hers; he hadn't been kidding about his impatience. After all those times they'd been together and had to break things off before either of them was satisfied, he must have been very frustrated—and he remembered waiting centuries. But even so....

She pushed at his shoulders and he drew back, panting. "What is it?" he asked. "Why did you stop me?"

Brenna wriggled partway out from under him, staring up at the lines and features of that face she now remembered so well. As she looked over his shoulder, her gaze fell on the coat rack and the jacket hanging on it. Ronan never hung up his jacket. Why had he chosen to do so now?

"What's the matter?" he asked. "Don't you want me? Or is it Bres you really care for?"

A chill wound through her as she unfocused enough to see his energy field, and the vague halo that surrounded the normal limits of his aura. Was he using glamour? Ronan had promised her that he'd never used glamour on her, and never would.

Ever since Ronan had admitted to being Sidhe, he'd materialized directly into or out of the Otherworld, but when he'd returned just now, he'd come up the walkway. He was more forceful than he'd ever been with her before. He'd commented on her lack of sexy attire. Realization sent ice skittering through her veins.

She'd just let the wolf in the door.

She swallowed and carefully began to ease herself farther out from under his body. If she could just delay him for long enough....

He stopped her with a hand on her shoulder. "Are you trying to make me believe that you didn't care for Bres, even once he'd had you?" he asked. "I thought it was him you wanted. He's the one you ran to after you killed Clothra. He's the one who held you, comforted you...." His voice trailed off, and he seemed caught in the grip of some strong emotion.

"No," she said slowly, watching his reaction. "Bres was seductive, yes. I can't say that he never got my rocks off. But he's cruel, and he's hard—and not in a good way. I never loved him even when I'd convinced myself he was the only future I had. That's part of why I ran. Why I found a way to become human and forget. I needed to forget him and all the sick things he made me do."

"You little bitch," he hissed, rage breaking over his features as he sat up, straddling her lower body, his weight keeping her trapped on the couch. His furious gaze bored into hers.

Brenna reared up and grabbed the sides of his face, staring into his angry blue eyes. All of the secrets of a soul lay behind the eyes. She locked gazes with him and bent her will against his to keep him from looking away.

"You might as well drop the glamour, Bres. It's wasted on me."

At that, his features changed. Colm—or rather, Bres in Colm's body—pushed her down, his lower body still pinning hers to the couch.

"Daireann. How nice to be recognized at last. Took you long enough, Darlin'." With the last words, he gave a vicious little push with his hips. She could feel his erection, stiff and large beneath his trousers. He ground his hips against hers again, and she gasped partly in anger, partly in pain.

"You going to rape me now? That'd be your style, but I don't think it gets you the sovereignty," she said, making her voice hard and cold and hoping he didn't feel the quiver that swept through her. Remembered pain and humiliation played like video clips in her mind. She couldn't let it happen again. Never again. She'd die first, and somehow she'd take him with her.

"Oh, I won't need to rape you, little human-Sidhe," Bres said. "You've already done the preparations necessary to make this night a success."

She snorted. "Please. Don't delude yourself into thinking that I'll give you the sovereignty. You have way too much to answer for, though somehow I doubt you'll live long enough to be questioned."

Bres gave a short laugh with no humor. "I know you expect Momma Morrigan and the others to join you soon. You think they might save you and make up for your mistakes. But you didn't think I'd come without reinforcements of my own, did you? Balor! Ceithlenn!"

Something gleamed behind his eyes, and Brenna recoiled despite herself. The air became thick, almost too heavy to breathe. She sensed another presence outside her aura—two presences, in fact. When she let her eyes unfocus enough to see into the astral realm, they appeared as a pair of roiling energy bodies, both as twisted and misshapen as Ronan's and Anand's had been shining and beautiful.

One of the dark entities descended into Bres's aura. The moment he met her gaze again, she could see someone else behind his eyes as well—someone even older and far more powerful. Balor of the Evil Eye—the Fomoire chieftain Bres had allied with in his vendetta against the Tuatha De Danann. One thing interested Balor: power. He had it to spare, but he could never get enough of it and he didn't care how many lives or bodies he destroyed in pursuit of it.

Brenna wrenched her gaze away so that Balor wouldn't see her fear, but he laughed. Bres rocked forward again so that his erection and the seam in his trousers ground painfully against her skin, making her gasp in pain.

"Do that again, and I'll kill you," she said calmly, though whether it was actual calm or a kind of horrified numbness, she couldn't say.

"Oh, no," Balor said through Bres, smiling. "Before long, you will hear yourself beg for my touch."

Brenna couldn't have said how she knew which entity spoke, but she knew. Balor's thunderous presence pressed behind Bres's eyes, and Bres himself seemed to watch gleefully, content to let Balor control events while he provided the conduit with his stolen human body.

"What did you do with the real Colm, Bres?" she asked to distract them. "Did you just squash his soul down inside that body, or did you kick him out altogether?"

"Ah, now that would be telling." Bres answered. He and Balor seemed to be melding energies; as the lines between them started to blur, Bres's aura changed to a muddled greyish-brown fog that hung over his head and shoulders.

A presence thumped against Brenna's shield, and a sense

of gathering doom pressed against her mind. The other entity, Ceithlenn. *Balor's wife*, Brenna's hole-riddled memory banks supplied.

Brenna pushed her shield out against the still-hovering presence, but the pressure only intensified and she drew back, panting. Damn, Ceithlenn was strong.

It is you who have made me so, Ceithlenn thought at her. *'Twas you who accepted Bres's gift, you who opened the doorway to this house, and you who will open the cómhla breac to the Fomoire. Now, let me in!* The pressure increased until Brenna's head throbbed in time to her heartbeat.

"You...will...not...possess me!" Brenna grated. "Get out of my head!" On instinct, she reached out to the *draíocht* in the land beneath the cottage, but opening to the power seemed to give Ceithlenn some edge she'd been waiting for. With a snarl, the Fomorian struck against Brenna's shields again. Horror stabbed at her as they began to crumble.

"You can't possess me, Ceithlenn. If you take me over against my will, you can't channel the Sovereignty through me."

Ceithlenn laughed. *Did Anand tell you that? It is a limitation for the Danann, not the Fomoire. Our power does not depend upon such niceties of balance.*

Great. Just great. Another little detail that would've been good to know. Brenna reinforced her shields, but as fast as she built them up, Ceithlenn battered them down. The onslaught was so fierce that Brenna barely felt Bres's weight anymore. Or maybe her legs were just going numb. The pressure on her mind increased until she cried out.

You can't have her, said another voice in Brenna's mind, low and deadly calm. *She is pledged to me, and what is mine, I protect.*

The Morrigan. Her presence washed over Brenna like cool rain and boiling lava together. The ground thrummed beneath the floor like a metaphysical earthquake. Brenna started to open her shield to allow Anand in, but the channels were blocked. *Do not*, Anand warned. *We must defeat this one first.*

Still straddling Brenna's hips, Bres/Balor grabbed her T-shirt by the neck and ripped.

"Get off her!" The air to Brenna's left rippled as Ronan materialized beside her. He grabbed Bres by the shoulders and dragged him sideways. The two men rolled onto the floor, grappling like a couple of drunks in a brawl.

"Watch out, Ronan! He's already let Balor in!" Brenna yelled, and scrambled off the couch, out of the way of the fight.

Well, not altogether. Something concussed in the air above her, Anand's shimmering silver form now visible along with Ceithlenn's brownish-green. The two queens were locked in battle. Non-corporeal bronze swords flashed as they feinted and stabbed, blocked and parried. They met, then danced apart. Sparks flew in the ether between them as they battled each other with weapons and *draíocht*, quick as thought. They stepped right through an armchair like a pair of ghosts.

Brenna glanced at the solid-looking Ronan, still grappling with Bres/Balor on the floor. Consequently, she just happened to be looking in their direction when the air above them shimmered with another Sidhe's arrival.

A greenish-gold streak rippled through the air above the struggling men and arrowed down into Ronan's blue-gold aura. He lit up like a rainbow, bands of color layered one atop the other like a shield reinforcing a shield. *Draíocht* surged with the force of a thunderclap, and Brenna saw another image superimpose itself upon Ronan's features. For an instant, she saw a much heavier man, dark, with arms muscled like a blacksmith's. Eochaidh Ollathair, the Dagda.

His arrival should have improved the odds, shouldn't it? As

soon as he entered Ronan's aura, Ronan's blows seemed more effective—at first. Then they began to slow. Bres's nose streamed with blood, but Ronan looked as though the fight had taken some toll on his manifested body as well. Great. How much *draíocht* were the four of them using up in the course of this fight?

As if in answer, the candles flickered all at once.

We must end this quickly, the Morrigan said in Brenna's mind.

Balor/Bres landed a blow to Ronan/ Eochaidh's stomach, and the latter rolled to the floor, gasping. Seconds later an energy ball slammed into Brenna's shield. Blackness and shooting points of light filled her vision; for a moment, she thought she'd pass out. Somehow she stayed upright, though she had to grip the back of an armchair for balance.

Somewhere in that blackness, the pressure on her mind returned. Sharp pain at the base of her skull drove her to her knees. She screamed, fighting Ceithlenn's overpowering presence, which pressed in on her soul until she thought her skin would burst like rotten fruit.

Brenna could feel the *draíocht* in the earth beneath her, close enough to touch. If she could just get it without opening herself to Ceithlenn—if she could funnel the *draíocht* to Anand instead....

She waited for a moment when Ceithlenn reeled back from one of Anand's blows, grounded in an instant and reached for the *draíocht*. She could feel it, trying to flow up into her, through her. Just a moment more and she'd have a stream of power that Anand could use. She reached for it, struggling to touch it.

In the instant of connection, blackness descended as Ceithlenn's presence fell into her like a stooping hawk. There was a sharp pain, then an almost blessed numbness and a sense of distance. It was as though Brenna were observing events on TV rather than right in front of her. When her arm rose, she stared at it, shocked. She hadn't meant to move it. One foot lifted and came down to stamp the floor as if testing its firmness. She hadn't meant to do that, either. Her mouth stretched into a grin. Her body moved like a marionette and she fought to regain control of it, but when the heavy presence sitting on her laughed at her efforts, Brenna's spirit recoiled. Somehow she'd let her guard down even though she hadn't meant to, and like a swooper at an online auction, Ceithlenn had possessed her body.

She could still see Anand in spirit-form nearby. The molten rage that crossed those beautiful features made Brenna shiver. Or maybe it made Ceithlenn shiver, as well it should. But Ceithlenn now had access to the *draíocht* Brenna had drawn up through the earth. Brenna sensed that she was preparing to launch some nasty spell. Anand wouldn't be able to stop her, either, because if she killed Brenna's body, all was lost.

Or was it? The dregs of a very old memory tugged at Brenna's soul. Ceithlenn had blocked her from accessing her brain pathways, but the spirit always held a copy of whatever the brain knew, anyway. Damn. What did she need to remember?

Ceithlenn pulled most of the *draíocht* through Brenna's body into her hands and formed it into a barbed mix of electric current. Like a barb, it would penetrate anything she threw it at, and what she was about to throw it at was...Ronan. The human body made a wondrous conduit for a Fomorian spirit, or for energy. Such potential. No wonder Bres had just possessed one outright instead of making a corporeal body for himself as Ronan had done. Fantastic.

A prisoner in her own body, Brenna could only watch the scene from that muffled distance. Ceithlenn glanced at Anand, triumphant, and Anand's furious gaze met hers as she moved to counter Ceithlenn's spell. Formed of the *draíocht* of two worlds, the spell was what movie special effects wanted to be when they grew up. Its physical form was pure electricity that wouldn't dissipate until it found a target.

Since she wasn't fully in the corporeal plane with everyone else, Anand could only counter that spell in one way. She'd have to get in front of it and try to absorb its energy, which would shatter her astral body and might even kill the one she'd left back in the Otherworld—and that was if she was successful. If she failed to absorb it or if she let it go, it would kill Ronan/ Eochaidh, who was still grappling with Balor/Bres.

Trouble didn't even begin to cover it.

Another failure. Another notch on the cosmic damage meter. Well, I'll be damned if I let it happen again! Rage lanced through Brenna, and she sensed Ceithlenn's start of surprise. Evidently, it had been a long time since the Fomoire queen had been in a body on the earth plane, and she'd misjudged how potent emotions could be in this state. Brenna allowed all her pain, all her fury to flow from her spirit into Ceithlenn's, and she sensed again that start of amazement. Thinking fast, she summoned up all the tangled emotions she'd ever had, drawn from hundreds of lifetimes of memories, and poured those into Ceithlenn's spirit as well. Ceithlenn wasn't prepared for that; she stumbled and the arm with the barb lowered. Good.

With that flood of memories came the one Brenna needed—the scary, risky, ballsy one she'd been unable to recall until now. Now that she had it back, Brenna knew why she'd chosen to block it out. But it was the one memory-turned-weapon that just might turn the tide.

Kill me, Anand, Brenna sent desperately to the Morrigan. *Kill my body so she can't use it anymore!*

Ceithlenn didn't react, so it seemed she hadn't heard the exchange. After all, it had been her decision to block Brenna's spirit off from access to the brain, keeping Brenna and Cethlenn separate within the same body. Served her right. Brenna wasn't thinking to Anand with her physical brain, but with her spirit-mind. Ceithlenn wasn't privy to the direct exchange, which was her own damned fault.

Brenna sent what little *draíocht* she'd horded within her spirit body toward Anand. It was earth energy, part of the *draíocht* that Brenna had drawn minutes before—all that Ceithlenn hadn't already stolen from her. Passed through to Anand on the non-physical plane, it would make a potent weapon in either world. *Draíocht* was always most powerful when drawn through the veil, like a temporary bridge between the worlds, a mini *cómhla breac.*

Take it. Take it all, then come hang onto me so I don't get sucked back to the human incarnation stream when my body dies. Do it! Trust me, please!

A moment of hesitation—and in her entire lifetime with the Danann she'd never seen the Morrigan hesitate—then the channels opened between them and the *draíocht* Brenna offered poured into Anand. Anand's aura rose until she grew so bright she was blinding. A Shining One, fit to make mortals cry at her beauty or scream out in terror. Moments later, a huge energy ball slammed through Ceithlenn's shields. Brenna's body dropped like a puppet with cut strings.

Ceithlenn's shock was so great that she loosed her hold on Brenna. Free, Brenna rose up out of her body and hovered, watching it twitch on the floor as if it'd been struck by lightning. She counted. One. Two. Three.

Brenna's heart twitched. Stopped. Ceithlenn boiled up out of the body, enraged, but also white and frightened, still partially attached. Brenna couldn't feel the body anymore; the cord that bound her to it started to dissolve. A void opened over Ceithlenn, and a whirling vortex of white light reached toward her. It looked terrifying, but familiar. Brenna smiled grimly. It was a wonder so many Sidhe had missed such a simple concept. If you possessed a human body—even a comatose one—you went where the human spirits went when that body died, and unlike the original owner of the body, you didn't get time to settle any unfinished business.

Be careful what you wish for.

As Ceithlenn's spirit brushed past her, Brenna plucked the electric dart from the enemy's hand and held on, though it tingled and sparked, hurting. Feeling herself being sucked away, Ceithlenn clutched at Brenna's spirit.

"Anand!" Brenna shrieked. The Morrigan threw herself onto Brenna and wrapped her in that silvery glow, pulling her away from Ceithlenn. For an unbearably long moment, Anand crouched over Brenna's spirit body, shielding it while the vortex sucked Ceithlenn's spirit upward and funneled her, shrieking, into another incarnation stream—one she'd never known before. Unless she managed to escape somehow, she'd wake up as a human baby somewhere, with no memory of whom and what she'd been before. Brenna shivered. Some poor mother was about to get a real bundle of joy.

The transition between lives got easier after you did it the first time. A few centuries later, it was old hat, but Brenna was willing to bet true humans made the leaps with a lot less trauma.

As the seal closed behind the vortex, Anand unfolded her spirit-self from around Brenna. Still holding the crackling dart, Brenna straightened and peered down at her body on the floor below them.

"Here goes nothing," she said brightly, and hurled herself down the frayed remnant of her silver cord. Just before impact, Brenna lobbed the dart at the body's chest. It jolted. A second later, she hit the body hard. Flesh closed around her, and everything went black.

CHAPTER TWENTY-ONE

Brenna opened her eyes and coughed weakly. She dragged air into her lungs, then coughed again. Smoke hung in the air around her. Several tipped-over candles had set the draperies on fire.

She rolled over onto her stomach, pushed up from the floor, and looked for Anand. She finally caught sight of Anand's almost spectral form hovering behind Ronan and Eochaidh, but the Morrigan seemed frozen in place as she stared at Bres/Balor.

Anand! For Danu's sake, what's wrong?

It is the Evil Eye, Balor's curse. As long as Balor keeps us in his sight, he leaches draíocht from us. I...cannot move. He snared me just after you dove back to your body. If you'd hesitated, or if I hadn't blocked you from his view, he'd have you, too. Her mental voice held such rage that she should have erupted in flames.

Damn. I should have taken you with me right then! But...how can Balor keep his eye on you when he's busy fighting Ronan and the Dagda? Brenna asked, careful not to make any sudden moves that might draw Balor's attention.

Balor is not using physical eyes to see me; he watches while Bres fights. You cannot reach me without coming into his view. If the battle tires him before he takes too much energy from me, I may be able to break free, but—

That will be too late, Brenna finished for her. *Fantastic.* On her hands and knees, Brenna began to crawl toward the living room door, just beyond the men. If she could reach the kitchen, she might be able to find a weapon. Of course, once she found one, there was the minor issue of being strong enough to wield it.

As she inched forward, Brenna tried to reconnect with the Earth, tried to pull *draíocht* up into her body and perhaps heal some of the damage she'd suffered. She had to stop once when her vision blurred and she nearly passed out again, but the scent of smoke and the knowledge that her allies couldn't last much longer kept her struggling forward.

Bres/Balor kept raining blows into Ronan's ribs. Ronan still held the double aura that meant the Dagda was with him, but it dimmed even as she watched. Ronan was no weakling and his body wasn't human; merged with Eochaidh, he should have been an unstoppable force. But Ronan's body wasn't a fully physical one, and therein lay the problem.

Bres/Balor wore the human body Bres had heisted from Colm Lachlann. Being anchored in a corporeal form already gave them the advantage, while Ronan and Eochaidh had to use the Danann's fading supply of *draíocht* to hold Ronan's manifested body together. All the while, Balor's poisonous stare leached their power and life force.

With one look at Ronan's face, Brenna could see the strain taking its toll.

The Fomoire hadn't given Balor the appellation "Strong Smiter" for nothing. His fists were like bricks, and in Colm's body, he could pull at least some *draíocht* from the trackways. As he drew back his fist, Brenna saw a faint glow surround it. The fist smashed into Ronan's face, bouncing his head against the floor. His manifested form flickered and nearly winked out.

Brenna crawled, avoiding flame and debris as best she could. All the while, the smoke thickened. Ronan/ Eochaidh hurled a spell at Bres, but it seemed to bounce off him.

Brenna inched forward. Ronan/ Eochaidh's form flickered again. In a few moments, they could fade entirely, and if that happened, there might not be enough *draíocht* left to bring them back. They were all out of time. Her eyes stung; smoke and tears blinded her for a moment.

Blind. Tears. Of course!

Blinking to clear her vision, Brenna gathered what strength she had, took a lungful of the air nearest the floor, hauled herself up off her hands and knees and broke for the living room door. She dive-rolled across the tiny hallway into the kitchen, ninja-style. Bres looked up, startled, as she ducked out of sight around the corner near the sink.

Her hip throbbed from where she'd rolled into a kitchen chair, but Brenna scrambled to her feet, grabbed a can of cooking spray and ripped off its cap. The harsh male curse from the living room made her smile. She could appreciate Bres's position, really. If he moved and took Balor's gaze off her, "Momma Morrigan" might be able to blast him with *draíocht*. But the prize was getting away.

Sort of.

With her right hand, she reached toward the pitcher on the counter and hefted the wine bottle by the neck. With her left, she brought the canister of cooking spray up in front of her as if it were a firearm. She heard Bres's steps in the hall an instant before he lurched into the room.

"Brenna, what the feck—ahhh!"

Her thumb clamped down on the release button, and a cloud of cooking spray hit Bres in the face. Guttural Fomoire curses filled the room as he clawed at his eyes. He stumbled backward and tripped over Brenna's suitcase. Ducking around behind him, she let fly with the wine bottle at the back of his head.

"I've always wanted to do that," Brenna said, then coughed violently as she inhaled a mouthful of smoke.

Bres grunted, fell on his face and didn't get up. Brenna snagged her purse off the back of a chair with one hand and scrambled back through the kitchen doorway, trying not to inhale more smoke.

With her eyes squeezed nearly shut, she almost tripped over Ronan/Eochaidh in the entryway as Ronan lurched toward her, a look of grim determination on his face. As Anand's spirit body flashed past them toward the kitchen, her voice echoed in Brenna's head.

Get out! Hurry!

Brenna fumbled with the doorknob, unable to understand why it wouldn't open. Ronan reached past her with an almost transparent hand to undo the locks; a moment later, he hauled the door open and shoved Brenna through. Wracked with coughing, she stumbled out onto the lawn to collapse several feet from the house. From somewhere behind her came the sound of breaking glass.

"Ronan!" Brenna reached out blindly to grasp at empty air. Her throat felt raw, and she couldn't seem to get enough air into her lungs. "Ronan!"

"I'm here, love. *Mór Ríoghain?*" Hands—not as substantial as they should have been—steadied Brenna, and she sensed Ronan's presence at her back. He was cold to the touch, as though there were no longer enough *draíocht* left to generate a semblance of warmth. She shivered. They were too late. They'd won the battle, but lost the war. And there'd been casualties.

She thought of Colm Lachlann, whose body Bres had stolen.

Where was his spirit now? Had she ever met the real man, or had Bres been camped out in his body long before she'd come to Ireland? Now she might never know. Colm had been doomed the moment Bres possessed his body, which was dying now, trapped in the burning cottage. Brenna dragged in a pain-filled breath and her lungs rebelled.

Open to me, Anand said in her mind.

Brenna cracked her eyes open to find Anand's spirit-form hovering near her. It flickered, as did the remnants of Ronan/Eochaidh's manifested form. She was about to lose all three of them.

"What?"

Let me in, Anand said. *You asked me to trust you. I did. Now trust me in return.*

Ronan's eyes were full of love and pain. Behind them she saw the shadow of the Dagda. Ronan flickered again and began to fade.

Will you? Anand asked again, urgently.

"I will. I don't understand how this will help now, but I will," Brenna choked out.

Anand touched her face and looked deep into her eyes. Suddenly Brenna was drowning in blue fire as the Morrigan's spirit poured into her body. Brenna knew a moment of fear as their auras began to merge, but she forced herself to relax. She would keep her promise. She was the betrayer no longer.

A tingle began at the crown of her head and spread down her neck, to her arms and shoulders, to her fingertips. Down her spine through her torso, hips, thighs, calves. Through her feet and downward into the very earth itself.

The familiar thrum began under the soles of Brenna's feet, like the beat of an ancient heart. She registered Anand's presence as an electric thrill within her body—felt her reach, stretching downward until she touched one of the trackways, deep within the land itself. Anand connected with it, like a plug to a socket, and pulled.

Draíocht surged up from the Earth in a rush of heat through Brenna's body, healing damage as it came. For an instant, branches and vines of greenish-white light superimposed themselves upon her vision.

Anand pulled at the trackways again, and every cell of Brenna's body suffused with light. She lifted her hand—her still-human hand—and found it glowing with the iridescent, color-shifting light that only the Shining Ones possessed.

"Come to me, Eochaidh," Anand said with Brenna's voice. Brenna swallowed experimentally and found that her throat wasn't sore; the flow of air through her lungs wasn't painful.

Ronan/ Eochaidh drifted forward, wraithlike; they no longer had enough *draíocht* to make an indent of weight on the lawn. Brenna/Anand extended a hand toward Ronan's chest, which was now little more than a thick mist.

Draíocht pulsed through Brenna's hand into Ronan's chest. He took a breath like a sigh of relief, head tilted back, eyes closed. At first it seemed as though nothing happened, but then warmth began to grow beneath her hand. Brenna watched, awestruck as his misty form began to solidify before her eyes. He took on weight, feet coming to rest on the ground. As his flesh warmed, it also began to change hue, reminding Brenna of the difference between a black-and-white drawing and a full-color photograph.

But he was far more real than a photograph. When he opened his eyes to look at her, Brenna gasped. His skin gave off heat and light, shining almost as much as hers did. For a moment, she was afraid to touch him, afraid she'd just imagined him all too well. This might be nothing more than a dream—but a dream wherein she stood in the middle of the lawn in front of her burning rental cottage, barefoot, dressed in nothing but an oversized ripped T-shirt?

Nah. In a dream, she wouldn't have remembered to grab her purse.

Ronan smiled at her, and under his gaze, her heart sped up. So what if the Dagda was watching and in fact could see an exposed breast where Bres had ripped the T-shirt? He'd soon see a whole lot more than that. Despite the chill of the night, warmth flooded Brenna's body. Anand stirred behind her eyes.

Ronan took her hand in his and pulled her close while the Morrigan and the Dagda locked gazes in the Earth realm for the first time in millennia. In that moment, Brenna would have sworn that the weather in Ireland on Samhain was just like a heat wave in the tropics.

A soft rain began to fall, but Brenna barely noticed it. After that first jolt of contact with the Dagda, Anand drew back to some corner of Brenna's mind. When Brenna looked into Ronan's eyes, she saw that the Dagda had done the same. Anand and Eochaidh were still present, but it seemed that Brenna and Ronan were to be allowed a moment of relative privacy. Anand's energy was a low vibration deep within Brenna, waiting to come to the fore at the right time.

She was trembling, but not from the rain or the cold. Ronan pulled her in against the warmth of his body, which only made things worse. Brenna braced her hands against his chest. He seemed different—perhaps more solid than he'd ever been before, but now that she understood the mechanics, she realized that Anand had been correct. He was just a projection. A dream lover. One solid enough to give her real, physical pleasure—but still a projection.

"I love you," she said, her voice so low it was almost a whisper. "I missed you even when I didn't remember you existed, and no one else could ever measure up. After tonight, I'm not sure I can go back to living without you."

He smiled at her in a way that made her pulse start to race. "I am yours, *mo grá*, always. Though you live in this realm and I in another, there is no true separation between us. When we are finished tonight, I must return to the Sidhe, at least for a time; I am needed there. But with the *cómhla breac* open, I will be able to return to visit you." He smiled down at her. "As often as possible." His fingers rubbed little circles over the nape of her neck while his thumb rested on the quickening pulse at her throat.

"Then we'd better get this speckled gate open, hadn't we?" Feeling a little breathless, she ran her hands up his chest and twined them around his neck. A sense of exhilaration rose and tingled through her whole body.

Ronan swung her up into his arms, kissed her lightly and started walking toward the hawthorn grove. Brenna wrapped her arms around his neck and held on. It wouldn't have mattered where they went. He could take her anywhere; she'd even do it in the backseat of the Fiesta if that was what it took to get him inside her. A couple weeks of metaphysical foreplay on top of multiple lifetimes of separation could do that to a person.

The air rippled in front of them as Ronan carried Brenna right through a hawthorn tree into the center of the grove. Outside, it looked the way it always had. Inside, there seemed to be more room than she'd expected, as if the grove had morphed into a smallish clearing ringed by hawthorns.

Inside the circle, the air was warm and the grass was the high green of summer, soft and fragrant under Brenna's feet when Ronan set her down. She looked through the gaps between trees, where the cottage was still visible. How long did it take the authorities to respond to a fire, anyway? Maybe no one had seen or reported it yet.

"No one can see us here, and we have all the time we need." Ronan replied to her unspoken question. "In this place, we are between the worlds, touching both at once."

Outside the grove, rain continued to fall. Inside, the pale sliver of moon shone down upon Brenna and her lover as if in benediction. When a light, warm breeze blew a caress across her skin, Anand's awareness rose into her mind again.

Draíocht began to seep into her body, some from the trackways below the Earth realm, some from the Otherworld. The two streams of energy met at the junction of her thighs and began to coil together, coursing through all her nerve endings in a wash of white heat. Anand flowed to the front of her consciousness, and the pulse of energy in Brenna's body intensified. Suddenly she knew what to do; saw how it—they—all fit together.

She held out her arms to Ronan. "Come to me."

He knelt at her feet and began to kiss his way up her legs, stopping sometimes to bite gently. His hands followed his tongue and teeth, tracing patterns on her skin where the woad spirals would have been.

Every time he bit her, the *draíocht* responded with a pulse, and within Brenna's mind, Anand welcomed Eochaidh's touch. By the time Ronan reached her most sensitive area with that hot, seeking tongue, Brenna had to hold onto his shoulders for support.

Just before her knees could buckle, he rose and ran his hands up her body, drawing the ripped T-shirt up over her head. He tossed it aside, and in the next breath, all the clothing on his body disappeared.

That's convenient, Brenna thought.

Your convenience is my pleasure, came Ronan's reply in her mind. Behind it, she heard the Dagda's laughter.

Brenna had an urge to touch Ronan as he'd touched her. When she knelt at his feet, Anand used her hands and tongue to trace ritual symbols from his toes to his abdomen; all Brenna had to do was follow her lead. It didn't matter whether the low moan that burst from Ronan's lips originated with him or with Eochaidh—she was a woman with a mission. Every touch, every caress, brought an odd duality of sensation that mounted until their collective reactions reached a point somewhere between pleasure and pain.

The pulse of *draíocht* built within Brenna slowly; she'd expected it to erupt in instant heat, but its seduction was more subtle. It played like music in the back of her mind, responding to Anand's every whim.

Experimentally, Brenna pulled a little of the energy and sent it looping back into Anand—fair play and all that. In her mind she heard Anand's gasp of surprise. A sharp spike of pleasure bowed Brenna's spine and she echoed the gasp aloud.

And we thought you needed us, came Eochaidh's thought, laced with Ronan's amusement.

"I need you. Oh, dear gods!" Brenna groaned.

"Exactly," Ronan/Eochaidh said as one.

Brenna's knees did buckle then. Ronan caught her in his arms and lowered her to the ground. His double aura glowed, as did her own, a warm light like the roomful of candles she'd set up before the house became a fiery battleground.

Ronan pulled Brenna against him, his lips finding hers. As before at Keshcorran, the power pulled her down into a vortex of sensation, but this time such light pierced the darkness that Brenna's eyes streamed with tears.

Anand pulled on the *draíocht* again, reaching out to the Dagda and beyond, bridging the gap between the worlds. Stars winked in the sky above Brenna's head while the Earth pulsed softly beneath her. In the space between, a void began to open like a hole cut in cloth. Brenna realized then that she could feel the veil between worlds; the four of them were within it now, suspended in a fold of the fabric of the universe.

Anand pulled at both worlds as if she could make them meet in front of her. Ronan's tongue found Brenna's breast, and she arched toward him, shivering. No. She'd been half-right. The worlds wouldn't meet in front of her. They'd meet *within* her.

A flood of *draíocht* poured into the gap in the veil, boiling up from the depths of the earth and down from the heavens, but it wasn't enough—not yet. Brenna/Anand writhed under Ronan/Eochaidh's hands and lips, pleasure lancing through them, building as the gap between worlds opened, stretched, reached....

Now, Eochaidh! Anand moaned.

"Please, yes, Ronan. Now!" Brenna burst out.

Yes!

The assent burst from Ronan and Eochaidh both at once. Pulling Brenna beneath him, Ronan speared deeply into her in one smooth lunge. She gasped, her shoulders arching backward against the ground, legs locking around Ronan's waist to hold him closer as he began to move inside her.

Every thrust ratcheted the flow of *draíocht* higher and sent it surging through their bodies in an exquisite agony of pleasure. As her climax built, Brenna felt the press of vast power in the air around them. A low *boom* echoed through both worlds, while the portal Anand had formed in the veil began to shimmer like the surface of a midnight lake.

Ronan pounded into her, harder, faster. Brenna's hands curled into claws and she dug her nails into his shoulders. She and Anand both cried out as the orgasm hit, rocking them with wave upon wave of searing pleasure. Something locked into place in the veil just before Ronan joined her in the throes of a full-body climax that seemed to go on and on until Brenna thought she might fly apart altogether.

When the final pulses ebbed, he collapsed on top of her and then rolled over onto his back, his strong arms gathering her close as they both worked to regain their breath.

Thank you, Anand said in Brenna's mind, softly, and began to withdraw. Brenna's eyes snapped open in surprise. The crown of her head tingled as Anand's aura lifted away from hers. As Brenna watched, Ronan's double aura began to separate also. Two shimmering energies drifted upward to re-form a short distance away. Ronan pulled out of Brenna's body as well, leaving her bereft after such a surfeit of contact.

The Morrigan and the Dagda, nude and shining with power, materialized before them. Anand's head rested against Eochaidh's shoulder; one of her arms was around his waist. Tall, broad Eochaidh had one arm looped over Anand's shoulder and he was grinning, eyes sparkling in delight. Despite some self-consciousness, Brenna had to fight the urge to laugh; they looked for all the world like any couple who'd just had amazing sex, but it had been so much more than that.

Ronan gathered Brenna's tousled hair in one hand and pulled it over her shoulder. Then he leaned in to place a kiss on the shoulder he'd bared, which made her shiver all over again. Her hearing had returned, but her legs still trembled.

"We will leave you to your privacy now," the Dagda said, the edge of laughter in his voice. "You have done enough for one night." He smiled at Brenna, and she smiled back, feeling herself blush. He was a stranger to her, yet she now knew intimate things about him that no one would ever find in the mythology books.

"The Danann owe you a debt of gratitude, Brenna," Anand said. She pulled herself away from Eochaidh—reluctantly, Brenna thought—and became every inch the queen again, proud and inscrutable. As the Dagda phased out, Anand asked, "What would you have of me?"

"A name among the *Badbha Catha*," Brenna said without hesitation. "And your friendship."

"The latter, you have already," Anand said. "And my trust into the bargain. As to the former, I leave it to you to choose. Most of our warriors choose a name that represents something fearsome, to strike dread into the hearts of our enemies. Often it represents a particular *Badbh's* greatest fear or greatest challenge. By claiming the name of the darkest part of your psyche, you take its power back into yourself. But you need not use such. I understand human military handles are different from this. By what name would you be known among the Badbha?"

Brenna thought a moment. "*Feall*. Treachery. I became its victim, and I committed it, but I reclaimed the power it had over me."

Anand's lips twitched. "A fearsome name indeed. Done. But since you intend to claim status as a *Badbh*, I find I have further need of your services."

"Question me. I am a *Badbh Catha*," Brenna said formally. A thrill ran through her body reminiscent of the mind-blowing sex of just minutes ago. She had done everything they'd asked of her. No matter what body she wore, she was truly of the Tuatha De Danann now, truly *Badbh*.

"Will you stay in Eire and serve as keeper of the *cómhla breac?*" Anand asked. "It will be some time yet before things settle on both ends. The Fomoire will continue their attempts to find a new gateway to the human realm. With Annie Murrilly now beyond the veil, we need someone here who understands both worlds. A liason, and a guardian. What say you?"

Ronan's hand tightened against the back of Brenna's neck in a tacit caress, a silent message that he would go along with whatever she decided. He was, after all, Sidhe. With the *cómhla breac* open to the Danann, he could reach her in Portland, or here in Ireland, or wherever she decided to go.

She didn't need time to think about it. There were many places of beauty in the world, but only one home.

Brenna reached over her shoulder to grasp Ronan's hand. She leaned her cheek against the back of it, breathing in his warm, intoxicating scent. He smelled of earth and green things and male. Out in the physical world, the rain fell, a silent witness to promises made or broken.

"Of course I'll stay," she said.

With the agreement struck, Brenna could think about more immediate needs. After a search, Ronan retrieved the remnant of her T-shirt and slipped it over her head. The front gaped open, but most of the back still clung to the collar and sleeves. He'd conjured a damp cloth from somewhere, but until she could get to the purse she'd dropped in the yard, she'd have to do without a comb. After she'd made herself as presentable as she could under the circumstances, he pulled her back into his arms for a long, tender kiss.

"I will return as soon as I am able," he said when they came up for air. "Take every care."

"I will." Brenna leaned her head against his chest and wrapped her arms around his narrow waist, only drawing out of his embrace when Anand cleared her throat nearby.

"It would be best if I return some of the damage you suffered in the battle," Anand said. "Battered and suffering from anoxia and smoke inhalation, you will fare better with your human authorities when you tell them that Colm Lachlann forced his way into your cottage and assaulted you."

"Anoxia? Smoke inhalation?" Brenna's eyes widened as she stared at Anand. "How is it that you're so much more up on current human terminology than Ronan is?"

The Morrigan smiled. "I've always been good at eavesdropping when it seemed necessary."

"Then I'll watch what I say about you behind your back," Brenna said, grinning.

The distant wail of sirens on the Earthward side of the veil made her tense. "Well, gang, I guess it's time for me to go back. I can hardly wait for Garda O'Shea to find me half-naked in the mud." She met Ronan's gaze and smiled at his worried look. She put a hand on his cheek; he pulled it downward and pressed a kiss into her palm. "I'll be okay. After what I've been through since I came back to Ireland, this should be the easy part."

"It will be painful," Anand warned.

Brenna nodded, still looking into Ronan's eyes. "I'm ready. Hit me."

A blast of raw power surged into her. Time seemed to slow. She saw Anand at the edge of the trees, watching her. For a moment, she saw other figures within the veil, moving through the *cómhla breac* in both directions. Annie passed by her, smiling tenderly before she continued on her way to the next stage of her journey.

As the Morrigan's power spun her through the *cómhla breac* back to the Earth realm, Brenna closed her eyes and let herself drift. She might be an unhappy camper when she woke up, but for now she knew nothing but a sense of completion, of balance, for the first time in centuries.

It was, after all, Samhain. The time when the veil between the worlds was thinnest. The time when spirits walked the earth again and returned to visit the living. And maybe...just maybe...the time when a spirit in exile could find its way home.

www.ingramcontent.com/pod-product-compliance
Lightning Source LLC
Chambersburg PA
CBHW030659120726
47905CB00001B/282